Charles Dickens, Andrew Lang

Christmas Stories

Charles Dickens, Andrew Lang

Christmas Stories

ISBN/EAN: 9783337384296

Printed in Europe, USA, Canada, Australia, Japan

Cover: Foto ©Andreas Hilbeck / pixelio.de

More available books at **www.hansebooks.com**

CHRISTMAS STORIES

FROM

"HOUSEHOLD WORDS" AND "ALL THE
YEAR ROUND"

By CHARLES DICKENS

WITH INTRODUCTION AND NOTES

BY

ANDREW LANG

In Two Vols.—Vol. I.

WITH ILLUSTRATIONS BY A. JULES GOODMAN

LONDON: CHAPMAN & HALL, Ld.

NEW YORK: CHARLES SCRIBNER'S SONS

1898

INTRODUCTION.

The "Christmas Stories" of Dickens are entirely distinct
from his "Christmas Books." In these earlier fantasies he
worked single-handed. The sketches are merely his con-
tributions to the Christmas numbers of his two periodicals,
Household Words (1850–1859) and *All the Year Round*
(1859–1871). These journals fulfilled Dickens's old desire
to have a miscellany of his own, whose popularity should
be helped by that of his name, while the labour would be
shared by other writers. These were many and excellent.
Some, like Mr. Sala of genial memory, imitated the master;
some, like Mrs. Gaskell, worked on their own lines. Dickens
devoted to his editorial work much time, and all of his un-
sparing energy and capacity for business. The great public
probably never had better cheap literary papers; the taste for
interviews, and photographs of the Queen's dolls, if it existed,
was not then "catered for," as people say. The Christmas
numbers had a "framework," a very ancient device, and familiar
to the Hindoos of remote ages. That framework Dickens
himself devised and supplied, while his allies contributed
many of the stories which it enclosed. In the first, the old
Christmas sentiment prevails. "The Seven Poor Travellers"
were wound up and set a-going, in an environment very
appropriate. Wassail was introduced, and Dickens freely

confessed his own delight, familiar from his letters, in his skill as a brewer of punch. To him punch was rather a symbol than a beverage, and he regretted that Mr. Forster had no taste for this modern Graal-cup. It meant Christmas —meant the whole of "Carol philosophy." His only other contribution was the pleasing sentimental history of Richard Doubledick, with its fine admiration of true soldier-like qualities, and the character of "The Happy Warrior." This sympathy again finds expression in the "Perils of Certain English Prisoners." The events are of a kind which Dickens rarely handled. "The moving incident" *was* his "trade," though disclaimed by Wordsworth. But military incident, the fighting with pirates in a Treasure Island, was more congenial to Mr. Stevenson. The plot is cunningly laid, and Christian George King is a pleasant kind of villain, and an opportune invention. But Dickens left other hands to get his prisoners out of their quandary: in real life they would not so easily have escaped destruction. It is perhaps an error to show us so little of the tyranny of Sergeant Drooce. The same loyal sympathy, with seamen in place of soldiers, declares itself in the "Wreck of the Golden Mary."

The Holly-Tree Inn, not to dwell on the delightful fancy of the eloping children, connects itself with several of the other Christmas sketches in illustrating what we may call "the night-side" of Dickens—his strong interest in exceptional psychical experiences. Thus he alludes to his many repeated, indeed nightly, dreams of his wife's dead sister, Miss Mary Hogarth, to whom he was tenderly attached. He tells how the visions ceased, when he recorded them in a letter, and speaks of a dream of her in Italy, apparently uncertain whether it was a sleeping or a waking vision. It occurred in September, 1844, at Genoa, and is described as a vision of painful sleep, in a letter to Mr. Forster. Dickens, in that letter, enumerates the ordinary reminiscences out of which he thinks that the dream was built. In the sketch he speaks more mystically. We may refer to the first of his two "Ghost Stories" here (vol. ii. p. 106): "I have always noticed a prevalent want of courage, even among persons of superior intelligence and culture, as to imparting their own psychological experiences when those have been of a strange sort. . . . To this reticence I attribute much of the obscurity in which such subjects are involved."

This is a sagacious remark. We are in a world "not realised," and common sense has long bullied us out of any serious attempt to realise some of its phenomena. Dickens was always much interested in stories which seem to suggest the existence of supernormal human faculties, but he also lived in an age when "spiritualistic" quackeries were leading even distinguished men through a wilderness of nightmares' nests. He therefore very judiciously kept a stern watch over his own "mystical" tendencies, and we often observe the contest between his sentiments and his common sense. Even to Forster, after all, he expresses his doubt as to whether he should regard his experience at Genoa as "a dream, or an actual Vision."

He probably never made up his own mind. In "The Haunted House" he laughs naturally, nay inevitably, at the messages d'outre tombe revealed to the sect of "Rappers." These, certainly, do not suggest to any sane mind the idea of the presence of incarnate intelligences. But they are not always explicable as mere impostures, any more than was the hallucinatory presence of Dickens's father, then "alive and well," beside his bed. "Nothing ever came of it;" it might be an after-image of a forgotten dream, or perhaps a telepathic reflection of a dream then entertained by the prototype of Mr. Micawber. The anecdote does not occur, I think, in Mr. Forster's *Life* of Dickens, but it may have been among the "ghost-stories" which Dickens liked to tell.

Here it is told as a prelude to the story of the occupation of a haunted house of the usual noisy type. Having once taken part in a similar quest, I can recognise the accuracy of most of Dickens's remarks. "You can fill any house with noises, if you will," he says, "until you have a noise for every nerve in your nervous system." Doubtless Dickens could do this if he liked, but my humble experience was that *ne fuirt ce tour qui veult*, and that the noisy house was rather unusually quiet. On the other hand, the "real terror" of the Odd Girl, who, for all that, "made many of the noises we heard," is an authentic touch of nature. Indeed, even to persons not on the level of the Odd Girl in education, the temptation to produce "phenomena" for fun is all but overwhelming. That people communicate hallucinations to each other "in some diseased way without words," is a modern theory perhaps first formulated here by Dickens. But, having set his allied story-tellers in motion, he deserts his psychological researches, and, dropping into autobiography, tells us how, in Copperfield days, his bed was "thrown into a lot" with "a brass coal-scuttle, a roasting-jack, and a birdcage." Thus the certainly unprogressive study of haunted houses makes no advance in Dickens's hands. His two ghost-stories are based on such flashes of intuition, or second sight, or whatever we should call it, as are pretty well attested in most ages and countries. But his ghost in a court of justice is of an "outdacious" description, and worthy of his nurse, ill named Mercy, to whom he again refers in this volume, as in *The Uncommercial Traveller*. Decently well-attested spectres never reach the solidity and activity of the agent in the banker's narrative. It opens well, but the supernatural is distinctly overdone, and the terrible yields place to the absurd. The tale of the signal-man (vol. ii. p. 189) makes less overwhelming demands on the judicial faculties of the reader. It is probably based on some real story of the kind, some anecdote of premonitions. There are scores in the records of the Society for Psychical Research.

These interests, and this element in Dickens's character, connect him with many persons of genius, but, of course, are not preponderant factors in his intellect. Away from such dark corners are Mrs. Lirriper, that jewel of a landlady, and the waiter in "Somebody's Luggage," and Doctor Marigold. All these are the result of Dickens's intense powers of observation, and unwearied interest both in the commonplace and the odd aspects of humanity. Mrs. Lirriper, whose inclusive and Thucydidean style is a masterpiece, must be pronounced the most sympathetic, while only Dickens could have collected, as it were, such queer specimens as her Wandering Christians, and motley array of servant-girls. The waiter illustrates that vein of intellectual high spirits which had been almost worked out, as far as the long novels were concerned. Indeed, a critic might have something to say for himself who argued that there is more of the genuine, fresh, early Dickens in these papers, than in the more laboured novels of his closing years. He writes with more freedom and less responsibility: he "lets himself go" joyously, whereas joyousness is remote indeed from *Little Dorrit* and *Our Mutual Friend*, with their ambitious aims and social satire. Dickens is more at home with a plump Head Waiter at the Cock or elsewhere, with a sentimental Cheap Jack on a common, with a garrulous good landlady in the gritty calm of a June evening in Norfolk

Street. In " Doctor Marigold " he introduces one of the many
shrews whom he discriminated so finely. Mr. Gissing, in his
excellent work on Dickens, has noticed his variety of shrews—
Mrs. Snagsby, Mrs. Gargery, Mrs. Varden, Doctor Marigold's
wife, and many others. Not one of the women named is a
termagant by reason of drink; all are born to be so, and their
case defies diagnosis—defies any treatment save that which Old
Orlick applied with a hammer. There is a dipsomaniac
shrew in *Hard Times*, but she is an exception, and comparatively intelligible. What is the quarrel of these women, with
their husbands, their children, and the world? Dickens occasionally converts them. He converts Mrs. Gummidge and Mrs.
Varden; but they are really beyond hope, short of a miracle.
They are far from being unknown in any rank of life, but, in
the less comfortable ranks, where there is no escape from
them, they drive more men to drink than all the temperance
lecturers and Local Options in the world can reclaim. Their
husbands, in Dickens, do not adopt Petruchio's method; it
is they, not the shrews, who are tamed. The mind broods
hopelessly on this vast world-problem of the termagant, from
Sarah Marlborough to Mrs. Doctor Marigold. That philosopher married on the briefest possible acquaintance. Prevention is better than cure. By careful observation the
young might discover, not too late, whether attractive girls
"have a temper;" and, by scientific study of woman in the
kitten stage, man might leave the worse species of cats to
perpetual maidenhood. But love is blind, or, at least, nascent
passion is incapable of calm psychological study of the fair.
Probably Dolly Varden grew up, like the wife of Mr. Boswell
of Auchinleck, to be "a cat, and cross, like other wives."
But Mrs. Boswell had provocations, while Mrs. Gargery and
the rest had none.

In the young women described by "The Boy at Mugby," we observe characters in training for the career of termagant. They " come into the business mild," as the boy remarks; they come in like lambs, but go out, into married life, like lionesses. " Refreshmenting " is, indeed, "a constitutional check upon the public." The essence of the Circumlocution Office is thin and weak, compared to the scorn of the Railway barmaiden, "the eighth wonder of monarchical creation." Mrs. Sniff holds a lofty place among Dickens's amateur Queen Elizabeths of private life. Their empire has waned, to a certain extent, in the general *bouleversement* of our institutions. " An assorted cold lunch," in a basket, can be procured, on certain lines. Of the luncheons at York, for example, a Briton must think with fondness; and you can even dine, it is said, in some railway carriages. Dickens, so far, has really effected a reform, but our sandwiches and butterscotch are on the old feudal level. The present philosopher, like all who get their living out of the Public (as Dickens himself observes), has not the very loftiest opinion of that aggregate, "this great stupid Public," as Thackeray styles it. Coleridge was not more favourably disposed, and we know the opinion of Mr. Henry Fielding, with his " D——n, then, so they *have* found it out !" Thus many authors can partially understand Mrs. Sniff's and Miss Piff's relations to the Public with whom they are brought into such close and stereotyped relations, of a nature necessarily hurried and hostile. We understand, but *tout comprendre* is not always *tout pardonner*. On this topic one is reminded that, among all his waiters, Dickens never drew a German waiter in England. The topic is full of matter, not agreeable matter, and is respectfully suggested for the consideration of Mr. Anstey.

The purpose of "Tom Tiddler's Ground" seems to have

been that of discouraging a tendency to commence Hermit. This is not a very widespread inclination, but the topic allows Dickens to fire his broadside, as usual, at the good old times. He denounces eremites in general, without regard to religious and social conditions. It is scarcely worth while to defend the early Scottish and Irish hermits here, or to say a word in favour of the dwellers in the Thebaid, or the Forest sages of India. They did not at all resemble Dickens's dirty Mr. Mopes, who, in truth, is a mere peg whereon to hang Christmas stories. The actual hermit lived near Stevenage, and was visited by Dickens, Mr. Helps, and Lord Orford, in 1861.

In the melodramatic piece, " No Thoroughfare," Dickens's share, as far as composition goes, was slight. He wrote the Overture (in which the dialogue is decidedly of the stage) and the Third Act. The rest was by Mr. Wilkie Collins, who turned the whole into a play for Fechter, while Dickens was on his second visit to America. Mr. Collins was a friend of Dickens's for about twenty years, and his method in fiction had a good deal of influence upon the elaborate plots of the later novels.

" The Lazy Tour of Two Idle Apprentices " commemorates a real expedition made by Dickens (Goodchild) and Wilkie Collins (Idle) to the north of England, at the end of August, 1857. It was " a little tour in search of an article, and in avoidance of railroads." The "article" was found, fiction being freely intermingled with descriptions of real adventures, such as the ascent of Carrock Fell (1500 feet) in the rain and mist. Though Carrock Fell is only, in Dr. Johnson's words, " a considerable protuberance," mist makes all climbing dangerous, and the tourists might be thankful that they were not caught by the darkness a little further north, at

Loch Skene, with the Grey Mare's Tail in front of them. Collins actually sprained his ankle, the compass was really broken, and the descent was achieved (as is easiest in such cases) by finding a burn and following it. The little romance on the man who shared a double-bedded room with a corpse may be founded on a similar incident in the early life of Sir Walter Scott. But Scott slept nearly as soundly as the occupant of the other bed, who did not waken.

The incident of the "half-dozen noiseless old men" in the Lancaster Inn has this odd peculiarity, that precisely the same experience occurred to a lady, well known to the editor, on her arrival one night at the same hotel. Six men, like waiters, stood in a row before her, and, when she looked about for one of them to remove her luggage, they were not, nor could she find any trace of them. Next morning, on leaving, she was presented with a copy of Dickens's chapter, and read with amazement about his similar experience. Mr. Forster throws no light on any real vision, or dream, which Dickens may have had in the hotel, and philosophers may argue, either that his mind produced the effect on the lady's, by unconscious thought transference, or that six ghosts were about; or that the lady unconsciously read back into her memory what she had only gathered from Dickens's chapter. She is a person of meticulous veracity, and has herself no theory about the occurrence, now remote in time. The lady's old men did not speak; all that part of the tale is obvious embroidery. But did Dickens see the six old men?

The chapter on Doncaster and the Leger expresses Dickens's own theory of "that gigantic engine of national demoralisation," as Lord Beaconsfield called it, the Turf. He was haunted by memories of Palmer, the sporting poisoner. The man who "took the horrors" was said to have lost £1500 or £2000 at the races. Dickens thought that a boy with a turn for betting might be cured by "being brought to Doncaster races soon enough;" but this is a perilous homœopathy. The "Lazy Tour" is full of his old high spirits, and attests his extraordinary physical energy. Mr. Wilkie Collins can scarcely have enjoyed himself much on the expedition.

ANDREW LANG.

CONTENTS OF VOL. I.

LIST OF ILLUSTRATIONS.

VOL. I.

A CHRISTMAS TREE

[1850]

A CHRISTMAS TREE.

I HAVE been looking on, this evening, at a merry company
of children assembled round that pretty German toy, a
Christmas Tree. The tree was planted in the middle of a
great round table, and towered high above their heads. It
was brilliantly lighted by a multitude of little tapers; and
everywhere sparkled and glittered with bright objects. There
were rosy-cheeked dolls, hiding behind the green leaves; and
there were real watches (with movable hands, at least,
and an endless capacity of being wound up) dangling from
innumerable twigs; there were French-polished tables, chairs,
bedsteads, wardrobes, eight-day clocks, and various other
articles of domestic furniture (wonderfully made, in tin, at
Wolverhampton), perched among the boughs, as if in preparation for some fairy housekeeping; there were jolly, broad-
faced little men, much more agreeable in appearance than
many real men—and no wonder, for their heads took off,
and showed them to be full of sugar-plums; there were
fiddles and drums; there were tambourines, books, work-
boxes, paint-boxes, sweetmeat-boxes, peep-show boxes, and
all kinds of boxes; there were trinkets for the elder girls,
far brighter than any grown-up gold and jewels; there were
baskets and pincushions in all devices; there were guns,
swords, and banners; there were witches standing in enchanted
rings of pasteboard, to tell fortunes; there were teetotums,

humming-tops, needle-cases, pen-wipers, smelling-bottles, con-
versation-cards, bouquet-holders; real fruit, made artificially
dazzling with gold leaf; imitation apples, pears, and walnuts,
crammed with surprises; in short, as a pretty child, before
me, delightedly whispered to another pretty child, her bosom
friend, "There was everything, and more." This motley
collection of odd objects, clustering on the tree like magic
fruit, and flashing back the bright looks directed towards it
from every side—some of the diamond-eyes admiring it were
hardly on a level with the table, and a few were languishing
in timid wonder on the bosoms of pretty mothers, aunts, and
nurses—made a lively realisation of the fancies of childhood;
and set me thinking how all the trees that grow and all the
things that come into existence on the earth, have their wild
adornments at that well-remembered time.

Being now at home again, and alone, the only person in
the house awake, my thoughts are drawn back, by a fascination
which I do not care to resist, to my own childhood. I begin
to consider, what do we all remember best upon the branches
of the Christmas Tree of our own young Christmas days, by
which we climbed to real life.

Straight, in the middle of the room, cramped in the
freedom of its growth by no encircling walls or soon-reached
ceiling, a shadowy tree arises; and, looking up into the
dreamy brightness of its top—for I observe in this tree the
singular property that it appears to grow downward towards
the earth—I look into my youngest Christmas recollections!

All toys at first, I find. Up yonder, among the green holly
and red berries, is the Tumbler with his hands in his pockets,
who wouldn't lie down, but whenever he was put upon the
floor, persisted in rolling his fat body about, until he rolled
himself still, and brought those lobster eyes of his to bear
upon me—when I affected to laugh very much, but in my
heart of hearts was extremely doubtful of him. Close beside
him is that infernal snuff-box, out of which there sprang a
demoniacal Counsellor in a black gown, with an obnoxious

head of hair, and a red cloth mouth, wide open, who was
not to be endured on any terms, but could not be put away
either; for he used suddenly, in a highly magnified state, to
fly out of Mammoth Snuff-boxes in dreams, when least
expected. Nor is the frog with cobbler's wax on his tail,
far off; for there was no knowing where he wouldn't jump;
and when he flew over the candle, and came upon one's hand
with that spotted back—red on a green ground—he was
horrible. The cardboard lady in a blue-silk skirt, who was
stood up against the candlestick to dance, and whom I see
on the same branch, was milder, and was beautiful; but I
can't say as much for the larger cardboard man, who used
to be hung against the wall and pulled by a string; there
was a sinister expression in that nose of his; and when he
got his legs round his neck (which he very often did), he was
ghastly, and not a creature to be alone with.

When did that dreadful Mask first look at me? Who put
it on, and why was I so frightened that the sight of it is an
era in my life? It is not a hideous visage in itself; it is
even meant to be droll; why then were its stolid features so
intolerable? Surely not because it hid the wearer's face. An
apron would have done as much; and though I should have
preferred even the apron away, it would not have been
absolutely insupportable, like the mask. Was it the immovability of the mask? The doll's face was immovable,
but I was not afraid of *her*. Perhaps that fixed and set
change coming over a real face, infused into my quickened
heart some remote suggestion and dread of the universal
change that is to come on every face, and make it still?
Nothing reconciled me to it. No drummers, from whom
proceeded a melancholy chirping on the turning of a handle;
no regiment of soldiers, with a mute band, taken out of a
box, and fitted, one by one, upon a stiff and lazy little set
of lazy-tongs; no old woman, made of wires and a brown-
paper composition, cutting up a pie for two small children;
could give me a permanent comfort, for a long time. Nor

was it any satisfaction to be shown the Mask, and see that
it was made of paper, or to have it locked up and be assured
that no one wore it. The mere recollection of that fixed
face, the mere knowledge of its existence anywhere, was
sufficient to awake me in the night all perspiration and
horror, with, "O I know it's coming! O the mask!"

I never wondered what the dear old donkey with the
panniers—there he is! was made of, then! His hide was
real to the touch, I recollect. And the great black horse
with the round red spots all over him—the horse that I
could even get upon—I never wondered what had brought
him to that strange condition, or thought that such a horse
was not commonly seen at Newmarket. The four horses of
no colour, next to him, that went into the waggon of cheeses,
and could be taken out and stabled under the piano, appear
to have bits of fur-tippet for their tails, and other bits for
their manes, and to stand on pegs instead of legs, but it was
not so when they were brought home for a Christmas present.
They were all right, then; neither was their harness uncere-
moniously nailed into their chests, as appears to be the case
now. The tinkling works of the music-cart, I *did* find out,
to be made of quill tooth-picks and wire; and I always
thought that little tumbler in his shirt sleeves, perpetually
swarming up one side of a wooden frame, and coming down,
head foremost, on the other, rather a weak-minded person—
though good-natured; but the Jacob's Ladder, next him,
made of little squares of red wood, that went flapping and
clattering over one another, each developing a different
picture, and the whole enlivened by small bells, was a mighty
marvel and a great delight.

Ah! The Doll's house!—of which I was not proprietor,
but where I visited. I don't admire the Houses of Parliament half so much as that stone-fronted mansion with real
glass windows, and door-steps, and a real balcony—greener
than I ever see now, except at watering places; and even
they afford but a poor imitation. And though it *did* open

all at once, the entire house-front (which was a blow, I admit,
as cancelling the fiction of a staircase), it was but to shut it
up again, and I could believe. Even open, there were three
distinct rooms in it: a sitting-room and bed-room, elegantly
furnished, and best of all, a kitchen, with uncommonly soft
fire-irons, a plentiful assortment of diminutive utensils—oh,
the warming-pan!—and a tin man-cook in profile, who was
always going to fry two fish. What Barmecide justice have
I done to the noble feasts wherein the set of wooden platters
figured, each with its own peculiar delicacy, as a ham or
turkey, glued tight on to it, and garnished with something
green, which I recollect as moss! Could all the Temperance
Societies of these later days, united, give me such a tea-
drinking as I have had through the means of yonder little set
of blue crockery, which really would hold liquid (it ran out of
the small wooden cask, I recollect, and tasted of matches), and
which made tea, nectar. And if the two legs of the ineffectual
little sugar-tongs did tumble over one another, and want
purpose, like Punch's hands, what does it matter? And if I
did once shriek out, as a poisoned child, and strike the
fashionable company with consternation, by reason of having
drunk a little teaspoon, inadvertently dissolved in too hot
tea, I was never the worse for it, except by a powder!

Upon the next branches of the tree, lower down, hard by
the green roller and miniature gardening-tools, how thick the
books begin to hang. Thin books, in themselves, at first, but
many of them, and with deliciously smooth covers of bright
red or green. What fat black letters to begin with! "A
was an archer, and shot at a frog." Of course he was. He
was an apple-pie also, and there he is! He was a good many
things in his time, was A, and so were most of his friends,
except X, who had so little versatility, that I never knew him
to get beyond Xerxes or Xantippe—like Y, who was always
confined to a Yacht or a Yew Tree; and Z condemned for
ever to be a Zebra or a Zany. But, now, the very tree itself
changes, and becomes a bean-stalk—the marvellous bean-stalk

up which Jack climbed to the Giant's house! And now, those
dreadfully interesting, double-headed giants, with their clubs
over their shoulders, begin to stride along the boughs in a
perfect throng, dragging knights and ladies home for dinner
by the hair of their heads. And Jack—how noble, with his
sword of sharpness, and his shoes of swiftness! Again those
old meditations come upon me as I gaze up at him; and I
debate within myself whether there was more than one Jack
(which I am loth to believe possible), or only one genuine
original admirable Jack, who achieved all the recorded
exploits.

Good for Christmas-time is the ruddy colour of the cloak,
in which—the tree making a forest of itself for her to trip
through, with her basket—Little Red Riding-Hood comes to me
one Christmas Eve to give me information of the cruelty and
treachery of that dissembling Wolf who ate her grandmother,
without making any impression on his appetite, and then ate
her, after making that ferocious joke about his teeth. She
was my first love. I felt that if I could have married Little
Red Riding-Hood, I should have known perfect bliss. But, it
was not to be; and there was nothing for it but to look out
the Wolf in the Noah's Ark there, and put him late in the
procession on the table, as a monster who was to be degraded.
O the wonderful Noah's Ark! It was not found seaworthy
when put in a washing-tub, and the animals were crammed in
at the roof, and needed to have their legs well shaken down
before they could be got in, even there—and then, ten to one
but they began to tumble out at the door, which was but
imperfectly fastened with a wire latch—but what was *that*
against it! Consider the noble fly, a size or two smaller than
the elephant: the lady-bird, the butterfly—all triumphs of
art! Consider the goose, whose feet were so small, and whose
balance was so indifferent, that he usually tumbled forward,
and knocked down all the animal creation. Consider Noah
and his family, like idiotic tobacco-stoppers; and how the
leopard stuck to warm little fingers; and how the tails of the

larger animals used gradually to resolve themselves into frayed bits of string!

Hush! Again a forest, and somebody up in a tree—not Robin Hood, not Valentine, not the Yellow Dwarf (I have passed him and all Mother Bunch's wonders, without mention), but an Eastern King with a glittering scimitar and turban. By Allah! two Eastern Kings, for I see another, looking over his shoulder! Down upon the grass, at the tree's foot, lies the full length of a coal-black Giant, stretched asleep, with his head in a lady's lap; and near them is a glass box, fastened with four locks of shining steel, in which he keeps the lady prisoner when he is awake. I see the four keys at his girdle now. The lady makes signs to the two kings in the tree, who softly descend. It is the setting-in of the bright Arabian Nights.

Oh, now all common things become uncommon and enchanted to me. All lamps are wonderful; all rings are talismans. Common flower-pots are full of treasure, with a little earth scattered on the top; trees are for Ali Baba to hide in; beef-steaks are to throw down into the Valley of Diamonds, that the precious stones may stick to them, and be carried by the eagles to their nests, whence the traders, with loud cries, will scare them. Tarts are made, according to the recipe of the Vizier's son of Bussorah, who turned pastrycook after he was set down in his drawers at the gate of Damascus; cobblers are all Mustaphas, and in the habit of sewing up people cut into four pieces, to whom they are taken blindfold.

Any iron ring let into stone is the entrance to a cave which only waits for the magician, and the little fire, and the necromancy, that will make the earth shake. All the dates imported come from the same tree as that unlucky date, with whose shell the merchant knocked out the eye of the genie's invisible son. All olives are of the stock of that fresh fruit, concerning which the Commander of the Faithful overheard 'the boy conduct the fictitious trial of the fraudulent olive merchant; all apples are akin to the apple purchased (with two others) from the Sultan's gardener for three sequins, and which the tall black slave stole from the child. All dogs are associated with the dog, really a transformed man, who jumped upon the baker's counter, and put his paw on the piece of bad money. All rice recalls the rice which the awful lady, who was a ghoule, could only peck by grains, because of her nightly feasts in the burial-place. My very rocking-horse,—there he is, with his nostrils turned completely inside-out, indicative of Blood!—should have a peg in his neck, by virtue thereof to fly away with me, as the wooden horse did with the Prince of Persia, in the sight of all his father's Court.

Yes, on every object that I recognise among those upper branches of my Christmas Tree, I see this fairy light! When I wake in bed, at daybreak, on the cold dark winter mornings, the white snow dimly beheld, outside, through the frost on the window-pane, I hear Dinarzade. "Sister, sister, if you are yet awake, I pray you finish the history of the Young King of the Black Islands." Scheherazade replies, "If my lord the Sultan will suffer me to live another day, sister, I will not only finish that, but tell you a more wonderful story yet." Then, the gracious Sultan goes out, giving no orders for the execution, and we all three breathe again.

At this height of my tree I begin to see, cowering among the leaves—it may be born of turkey, or of pudding, or mince pie, or of these many fancies, jumbled with Robinson Crusoe on his desert island, Philip Quarll among the monkeys, Sandford and Merton with Mr. Barlow, Mother Bunch, and the Mask—or it may be the result of indigestion, assisted by imagination and over-doctoring—a prodigious nightmare. It is so exceedingly indistinct, that I don't know why it's frightful—but I know it is. I can only make out that it is an immense array of shapeless things, which appear to be planted on a vast exaggeration of the lazy-tongs that used to bear the toy soldiers, and to be slowly coming close to my eyes, and receding to an immeasurable distance. When it comes closest, it is worse. In connection with it I descry remembrances of winter nights incredibly long; of being sent early to bed, as a punishment for some small offence, and waking in two hours, with a sensation of having been asleep two nights; of the laden hopelessness of morning ever dawning; and the oppression of a weight of remorse.

And now, I see a wonderful row of little lights rise smoothly out of the ground, before a vast green curtain. Now, a bell rings—a magic bell, which still sounds in my ears unlike all other bells—and music plays, amidst a buzz of voices, and a fragrant smell of orange-peel and oil. Anon, the magic bell commands the music to cease, and the great green curtain rolls itself up majestically, and The Play begins! The devoted dog of Montargis avenges the death of his master, foully murdered in the Forest of Bondy; and a humorous Peasant with a red nose and a very little hat, whom I take from this hour forth to my bosom as a friend (I think he was a Waiter or an Hostler at a village Inn, but many years have passed since he and I have met), remarks that the sassigassity of that dog is indeed surprising; and evermore this jocular conceit will live in my remembrance fresh and unfading, overtopping all possible jokes, unto the end of time. Or now, I learn with bitter tears how poor Jane Shore, dressed all in white, and with her brown hair hanging down, went starving through the streets; or how George Barnwell killed the worthiest uncle that ever man had, and was afterwards so sorry for it that he ought to have been let off. Comes swift to comfort me, the Pantomime—stupendous Phenomenon!—when clowns are shot from loaded mortars into the great chandelier, bright constellation that it is; when Harlequins, covered all over with scales of pure gold, twist and sparkle, like amazing fish; when Pantaloon (whom I deem it no irreverence to compare in my own mind to my grandfather) puts red-hot pokers in his pocket, and cries "Here's somebody coming!" or taxes the Clown with petty larceny,

by saying, " Now, I sawed you do it! " when Everything is
capable, with the greatest ease, of being changed into Anything; and " Nothing is, but thinking makes it so." Now,
too, I perceive my first experience of the dreary sensation—
often to return in after-life—of being unable, next day, to
get back to the dull, settled world; of wanting to live for
ever in the bright atmosphere I have quitted; of doting on
the little Fairy, with the wand like a celestial Barber's Pole,
and pining for a Fairy immortality along with her. Ah, she
comes back, in many shapes, as my eye wanders down the
branches of my Christmas Tree, and goes as often, and has
never yet stayed by me!

Out of this delight springs the toy-theatre,—there it is,
with its familiar proscenium, and ladies in feathers, in the
boxes!—and all its attendant occupation with paste and
glue, and gum, and water colours, in the getting-up of The
Miller and his Men, and Elizabeth, or the Exile of Siberia.
In spite of a few besetting accidents and failures (particularly
an unreasonable disposition in the respectable Kelmar, and
some others, to become faint in the legs, and double up, at
exciting points of the drama), a teeming world of fancies so
suggestive and all-embracing, that, far below it on my Christmas Tree, I see dark, dirty, real Theatres in the day-time,
adorned with these associations as with the freshest garlands
of the rarest flowers, and charming me yet.

But hark! The Waits are playing, and they break my
childish sleep! What images do I associate with the Christmas music as I see them set forth on the Christmas Tree?
Known before all the others, keeping far apart from all the
others, they gather round my little bed. An angel, speaking
to a group of shepherds in a field; some travellers, with eyes
uplifted, following a star; a baby in a manger; a child in a
spacious temple, talking with grave men; a solemn figure,
with a mild and beautiful face, raising a dead girl by the hand;
again, near a city gate, calling back the son of a widow, on
his bier, to life; a crowd of people looking through the

opened roof of a chamber where he sits, and letting down a sick person on a bed, with ropes; the same, in a tempest, walking on the water to a ship; again, on a sea-shore, teaching a great multitude; again, with a child upon his knee, and other children round; again, restoring sight to the blind, speech to the dumb, hearing to the deaf, health to the sick, strength to the lame, knowledge to the ignorant; again, dying upon a Cross, watched by armed soldiers, a thick darkness coming on, the earth beginning to shake, and only one voice heard, "Forgive them, for they know not what they do."

Still, on the lower and maturer branches of the Tree, Christmas associations cluster thick. School-books shut up; Ovid and Virgil silenced; the Rule of Three, with its cool impertinent inquiries, long disposed of; Terence and Plautus acted no more, in an arena of huddled desks and forms, all chipped, and notched, and inked; cricket-bats, stumps, and balls, left higher up, with the smell of trodden grass and the softened noise of shouts in the evening air; the tree is still fresh, still gay. If I no more come home at Christmas-time, there will be boys and girls (thank Heaven!) while the World lasts; and they do! Yonder they dance and play upon the branches of my Tree, God bless them, merrily, and my heart dances and plays too!

And I *do* come home at Christmas. We all do, or we all should. We all come home, or ought to come home, for a short holiday—the longer, the better—from the great boarding-school, where we are for ever working at our arithmetical slates, to take, and give a rest. As to going a visiting, where can we not go, if we will; where have we not been, when we would; starting our fancy from our Christmas Tree!

Away into the winter prospect. There are many such upon the tree! On, by low-lying, misty grounds, through fens and fogs, up long hills, winding dark as caverns between thick plantations, almost shutting out the sparkling stars; so, out on broad heights, until we stop at last, with sudden silence, at an avenue. The gate-bell has a deep, half-awful sound in the frosty air; the gate swings open on its hinges; and, as we drive up to a great house, the glancing lights grow larger in the windows, and the opposing rows of trees seem to fall solemnly back on either side, to give us place. At intervals, all day, a frightened hare has shot across this whitened turf; or the distant clatter of a herd of deer trampling the hard frost, has, for the minute, crushed the silence too. Their watchful eyes beneath the fern may be shining now, if we could see them, like the icy dewdrops on the leaves; but they are still, and all is still. And so, the lights growing larger, and the trees falling back before us, and closing up again behind us, as if to forbid retreat, we come to the house.

There is probably a smell of roasted chestnuts and other good comfortable things all the time, for we are telling Winter Stories—Ghost Stories, or more shame for us—round the Christmas fire; and we have never stirred, except to draw a little nearer to it. But, no matter for that. We came to the house, and it is an old house, full of great chimneys where wood is burnt on ancient dogs upon the hearth, and grim portraits (some of them with grim legends, too) lower distrustfully from the oaken panels of the walls. We are a middle-aged nobleman, and we make a generous supper with our host and hostess and their guests—it being Christmas-time, and the old house full of company—and then we go to bed. Our room is a very old room. It is hung with tapestry. We don't like the portrait of a cavalier in green, over the fireplace. There are great black beams in the ceiling, and there is a great black bedstead, supported at the foot by two great black figures, who seem to have come off a couple of tombs in the old baronial church in the park, for our particular accommodation. But, we are not a superstitious nobleman, and we don't mind. Well! we dismiss our servant, lock the door, and sit before the fire in our dressing-gown, musing about a great many things. At length we go to bed. Well! we can't sleep. We toss and tumble, and

can't sleep. The embers on the hearth burn fitfully and make
the room look ghostly. We can't help peeping out over
the counterpane, at the two black figures and the cavalier—
that wicked-looking cavalier—in green. In the flickering
light they seem to advance and retire: which, though we are
not by any means a superstitious nobleman, is not agreeable.
Well! we get nervous—more and more nervous. We say
"This is very foolish, but we can't stand this; we'll pretend to be ill, and knock up somebody." Well! we are just
going to do it, when the locked door opens, and there comes
in a young woman, deadly pale, and with long fair hair, who
glides to the fire, and sits down in the chair we have left there,
wringing her hands. Then, we notice that her clothes are
wet. Our tongue cleaves to the roof of our mouth, and we
can't speak; but, we observe her accurately. Her clothes
are wet; her long hair is dabbled with moist mud; she is
dressed in the fashion of two hundred years ago; and she
has at her girdle a bunch of rusty keys. Well! there she
sits, and we can't even faint, we are in such a state about it.
Presently she gets up, and tries all the locks in the room
with the rusty keys, which won't fit one of them; then, she
fixes her eyes on the portrait of the cavalier in green, and
says, in a low, terrible voice, "The stags know it!" After
that, she wrings her hands again, passes the bedside, and
goes out at the door. We hurry on our dressing-gown, seize
our pistols (we always travel with pistols), and are following,
when we find the door locked. We turn the key, look out
into the dark gallery; no one there. We wander away,
and try to find our servant. Can't be done. We pace the
gallery till daybreak; then return to our deserted room, fall
asleep, and are awakened by our servant (nothing ever haunts
him) and the shining sun. Well! we make a wretched breakfast, and all the company say we look queer. After breakfast,
we go over the house with our host, and then we take him
to the portrait of the cavalier in green, and then it all comes
out. He was false to a young housekeeper once attached to

that family, and famous for her beauty, who drowned herself in a pond, and whose body was discovered, after a long time, because the stags refused to drink of the water. Since which, it has been whispered that she traverses the house at midnight (but goes especially to that room where the cavalier in green was wont to sleep), trying the old locks with the rusty keys. Well! we tell our host of what we have seen, and a shade comes over his features, and he begs it may be hushed up; and so it is. But, it's all true; and we said so, before we died (we are dead now) to many responsible people.

There is no end to the old houses, with resounding galleries, and dismal state-bedchambers, and haunted wings shut up for many years, through which we may ramble, with an agreeable creeping up our back, and encounter any number of ghosts, but (it is worthy of remark perhaps) reducible to a very few general types and classes; for, ghosts have little originality, and "walk" in a beaten track. Thus, it comes to pass, that a certain room in a certain old hall, where a certain bad lord, baronet, knight, or gentleman, shot himself, has certain planks in the floor from which the blood *will not* be taken out. You may scrape and scrape, as the present owner has done, or plane and plane, as his father did, or scrub and scrub, as his grandfather did, or burn and burn with strong acids, as his great-grandfather did, but, there the blood will still be—no redder and no paler—no more and no less—always just the same. Thus, in such another house there is a haunted door, that never will keep open; or another door that never will keep shut; or a haunted sound of a spinning-wheel, or a hammer, or a foot-step, or a cry, or a sigh, or a horse's tramp, or the rattling of a chain. Or else, there is a turret-clock, which, at the midnight hour, strikes thirteen when the head of the family is going to die; or a shadowy, immovable black carriage which at such a time is always seen by somebody, waiting near the great gates in the stable-yard. Or thus, it came to pass how Lady Mary went to pay a visit at a large

wild house in the Scottish Highlands, and, being fatigued
with her long journey, retired to bed early, and innocently
said, next morning, at the breakfast-table, "How odd, to
have so late a party last night, in this remote place, and
not to tell me of it, before I went to bed!" Then, every
one asked Lady Mary what she meant? Then, Lady Mary
replied, "Why, all night long, the carriages were driving
round and round the terrace, underneath my window!"
Then, the owner of the house turned pale, and so did his
Lady, and Charles Macdoodle of Macdoodle signed to Lady
Mary to say no more, and every one was silent. After
breakfast, Charles Macdoodle told Lady Mary that it was a
tradition in the family that those rumbling carriages on the
terrace betokened death. And so it proved, for, two months
afterwards, the Lady of the mansion died. And Lady Mary,
who was a Maid of Honour at Court, often told this story
to the old Queen Charlotte; by this token that the old
King always said, "Eh, eh? What, what? Ghosts, ghosts?
No such thing, no such thing!" And never left off saying
so, until he went to bed.

Or, a friend of somebody's whom most of us know, when
he was a young man at college, had a particular friend, with
whom he made the compact that, if it were possible for the
Spirit to return to this earth after its separation from the
body, he of the twain who first died, should reappear to
the other. In course of time, this compact was forgotten by
our friend; the two young men having progressed in life, and
taken diverging paths that were wide asunder. But, one
night, many years afterwards, our friend being in the North
of England, and staying for the night in an inn, on the
Yorkshire Moors, happened to look out of bed; and there,
in the moonlight, leaning on a bureau near the window,
steadfastly regarding him, saw his old college friend! The
appearance being solemnly addressed, replied, in a kind of
whisper, but very audibly, "Do not come near me. I am
dead. I am here to redeem my promise. I come from

another world, but may not disclose its secrets!" Then, the whole form becoming paler, melted, as it were, into the moonlight, and faded away.

Or, there was the daughter of the first occupier of the picturesque Elizabethan house, so famous in our neighbourhood. You have heard about her? No! Why, *She* went out one summer evening at twilight, when she was a beautiful girl, just seventeen years of age, to gather flowers in the garden; and presently came running, terrified, into the hall to her father, saying, "Oh, dear father, I have met myself!" He took her in his arms, and told her it was fancy, but she said, "Oh no! I met myself in the broad walk, and I was pale and gathering withered flowers, and I turned my head, and held them up!" And, that night, she died; and a picture of her story was begun, though never finished, and they say it is somewhere in the house to this day, with its face to the wall.

Or, the uncle of my brother's wife was riding home on horseback, one mellow evening at sunset, when, in a green lane close to his own house, he saw a man standing before him, in the very centre of a narrow way. "Why does that man in the cloak stand there!" he thought. "Does he want me to ride over him?" But the figure never moved. He felt a strange sensation at seeing it so still, but slackened his trot and rode forward. When he was so close to it, as almost to touch it with his stirrup, his horse shied, and the figure glided up the bank, in a curious, unearthly manner—backward, and without seeming to use its feet—and was gone. The uncle of my brother's wife, exclaiming, "Good Heaven! It's my cousin Harry, from Bombay!" put spurs to his horse, which was suddenly in a profuse sweat, and, wondering at such strange behaviour, dashed round to the front of his house. There, he saw the same figure, just passing in at the long French window of the drawing-room, opening on the ground. He threw his bridle to a servant, and hastened in after it. His sister was sitting there, alone. "Alice, where's my cousin Harry?" "Your cousin Harry, John?" "Yes. From Bombay. I met him in the lane just now, and saw him enter here, this instant." Not a creature had been seen by any one; and in that hour and minute, as it afterwards appeared, this cousin died in India.

Or, it was a certain sensible old maiden lady, who died at ninety-nine, and retained her faculties to the last, who really did see the Orphan Boy; a story which has often been incorrectly told, but, of which the real truth is this—because it is, in fact, a story belonging to our family—and she was a connexion of our family. When she was about forty years of age, and still an uncommonly fine woman (her lover died young, which was the reason why she never married, though she had many offers), she went to stay at a place in Kent, which her brother, an Indian-Merchant, had newly bought. There was a story that this place had once been held in trust, by the guardian of a young boy; who was himself the next heir, and who killed the young boy by harsh and cruel treatment. She knew nothing of that. It has been said that there was a Cage in her bedroom in which the guardian used to put the boy. There was no such thing. There was only a closet. She went to bed, made no alarm whatever in the night, and in the morning said composedly to her maid when she came in, "Who is the pretty forlorn-looking child who has been peeping out of that closet all night?" The maid replied by giving a loud scream, and instantly decamping. She was surprised; but she was a woman of remarkable strength of mind, and she dressed herself and went downstairs, and closeted herself with her brother. "Now, Walter," she said, "I have been disturbed all night by a pretty, forlorn-looking boy, who has been constantly peeping out of that closet in my room, which I can't open. This is some trick." "I am afraid not, Charlotte," said he, "for it is the legend of the house. It is the Orphan Boy. What did he do?" "He opened the door softly," said she, "and peeped out. Sometimes, he came a step or two into the room. Then,

I called to him, to encourage him, and he shrunk, and
shuddered, and crept in again, and shut the door." "The
closet has no communication, Charlotte," said her brother,
"with any other part of the house, and it's nailed up."
This was undeniably true, and it took two carpenters a whole
forenoon to get it open, for examination. Then, she was
satisfied that she had seen the Orphan Boy. But, the wild
and terrible part of the story is, that he was also seen by
three of her brother's sons, in succession, who all died young.
On the occasion of each child being taken ill, he came home
in a heat, twelve hours before, and said, Oh, Mamma, he
had been playing under a particular oak-tree, in a certain
meadow, with a strange boy—a pretty, forlorn-looking boy,
who was very timid, and made signs! From fatal experience,
the parents came to know that this was the Orphan Boy,
and that the course of that child whom he chose for his
little playmate was surely run.

Legion is the name of the German castles, where we sit
up alone to wait for the Spectre—where we are shown into
a room, made comparatively cheerful for our reception—
where we glance round at the shadows, thrown on the blank
walls by the crackling fire—where we feel very lonely when
the village innkeeper and his pretty daughter have retired,
after laying down a fresh store of wood upon the hearth, and
setting forth on the small table such supper-cheer as a cold
roast capon, bread, grapes, and a flask of old Rhine wine—
where the reverberating doors close on their retreat, one after
another, like so many peals of sullen thunder—and where,
about the small hours of the night, we come into the knowledge of divers supernatural mysteries. Legion is the name of
the haunted German students, in whose society we draw yet
nearer to the fire, while the schoolboy in the corner opens his
eyes wide and round, and flies off the footstool he has chosen
for his seat, when the door accidentally blows open. Vast is
the crop of such fruit, shining on our Christmas Tree; in
blossom, almost at the very top; ripening all down the boughs!

Among the later toys and fancies hanging there—as idle often and less pure—be the images once associated with the sweet old Waits, the softened music in the night, ever unalterable! Encircled by the social thoughts of Christmas-time, still let the benignant figure of my childhood stand unchanged! In every cheerful image and suggestion that the season brings, may the bright star that rested above the poor roof, be the star of all the Christian World! A moment's pause, O vanishing tree, of which the lower boughs are dark to me as yet, and let me look once more! I know there are blank spaces on thy branches, where eyes that I have loved, have shone and smiled; from which they are departed. But, far above, I see the raiser of the dead girl, and the Widow's Son; and God is good! If Age be hiding for me in the unseen portion of thy downward growth, O may I, with a grey head, turn a child's heart to that figure yet, and a child's trustfulness and confidence!

Now, the tree is decorated with bright merriment, and song, and dance, and cheerfulness. And they are welcome. Innocent and welcome be they ever held, beneath the branches of the Christmas Tree, which cast no gloomy shadow! But, as it sinks into the ground, I hear a whisper going through the leaves. "This, in commemoration of the law of love and kindness, mercy and compassion. This, in remembrance of Me!"

WHAT CHRISTMAS IS AS WE GROW OLDER

[1851]

WHAT CHRISTMAS IS AS WE GROW OLDER.

TIME was, with most of us, when Christmas Day encircling all our limited world like a magic ring, left nothing out for us to miss or seek; bound together all our home enjoyments, affections, and hopes; grouped everything and every one around the Christmas fire; and made the little picture shining in our bright young eyes, complete.

Time came, perhaps, all so soon, when our thoughts over-leaped that narrow boundary; when there was some one (very dear, we thought then, very beautiful, and absolutely perfect) wanting to the fulness of our happiness; when we were wanting too (or we thought so, which did just as well) at the Christmas hearth by which that some one sat; and when we intertwined with every wreath and garland of our life that some one's name.

That was the time for the bright visionary Christmases which have long arisen from us to show faintly, after summer rain, in the palest edges of the rainbow! That was the time for the beatified enjoyment of the things that were to be, and never were, and yet the things that were so real in our resolute hope that it would be hard to say, now, what realities achieved since, have been stronger!

What! Did that Christmas never really come when we and the priceless pearl who was our young choice were received, after the happiest of totally impossible marriages, by the two united families previously at daggers-drawn on our account? When brothers and sisters in law who had always been rather cool to us before our relationship was effected, perfectly doted on us, and when fathers and mothers overwhelmed us with unlimited incomes? Was that Christmas dinner never really eaten, after which we arose, and generously and eloquently rendered honour to our late rival, present in the company, then and there exchanging friendship and forgiveness, and founding an attachment, not to be surpassed in Greek or Roman story, which subsisted until death? Has that same rival long ceased to care for that same priceless pearl, and married for money, and become usurious? Above all, do we really know, now, that we should probably have been miserable if we had won and worn the pearl, and that we are better without her?

That Christmas when we had recently achieved so much fame; when we had been carried in triumph somewhere, for doing something great and good; when we had won an honoured and ennobled name, and arrived and were received at home in a shower of tears of joy; is it possible that *that* Christmas has not come yet?

And is our life here, at the best, so constituted that, pausing as we advance at such a noticeable mile-stone in the track as this great birthday, we look back on the things that never were, as naturally and full as gravely as on the things that have been and are gone, or have been and still are? If it be so, and so it seems to be, must we come to the conclusion that life is little better than a dream, and little worth the loves and strivings that we crowd into it?

No! Far be such miscalled philosophy from us, dear Reader, on Christmas Day! Nearer and closer to our hearts be the Christmas spirit, which is the spirit of active usefulness, perseverance, cheerful discharge of duty, kindness and forbear- ance! It is in the last virtues especially, that we are, or should be, strengthened by the unaccomplished visions of our youth; for, who shall say that they are not our teachers to deal gently even with the impalpable nothings of the earth!

Therefore, as we grow older, let us be more thankful that the circle of our Christmas associations and of the lessons that they bring, expands! Let us welcome every one of them, and summon them to take their places by the Christmas hearth.

Welcome, old aspirations, glittering creatures of an ardent fancy, to your shelter underneath the holly! We know you, and have not outlived you yet. Welcome, old projects and old loves, however fleeting, to your nooks among the steadier lights that burn around us. Welcome, all that was ever real to our hearts; and for the earnestness that made you real, thanks to Heaven! Do we build no Christmas castles in the clouds now? Let our thoughts, fluttering like butterflies among these flowers of children, bear witness! Before this boy, there stretches out a Future, brighter than we ever looked on in our old romantic time, but bright with honour and with truth. Around this little head on which the sunny curls lie heaped, the graces sport, as prettily, as airily, as when there was no scythe within the reach of Time to shear away the curls of our first-love. Upon another girl's face near it—placider but smiling bright—a quiet and contented little face, we see Home fairly written. Shining from the word, as rays shine from a star, we see how, when our graves are old, other hopes than ours are young, other hearts than ours are moved; how other ways are smoothed; how other happiness blooms, ripens, and decays—no, not decays, for other homes and other bands of children, not yet in being nor for ages yet to be, arise, and bloom and ripen to the end of all!

Welcome, everything! Welcome, alike what has been, and what never was, and what we hope may be, to your shelter underneath the holly, to your places round the Christmas fire, where what is sits open-hearted! In yonder shadow, do we see obtruding furtively upon the blaze, an

enemy's face? By Christmas Day we do forgive him! If
the injury he has done us may admit of such companion-
ship, let him come here and take his place. If otherwise,
unhappily, let him go hence, assured that we will never
injure nor accuse him.

On this day we shut out Nothing!

"Pause," says a low voice. "Nothing? Think!"

"On Christmas Day, we will shut out from our fireside,
Nothing."

"Not the shadow of a vast City where the withered leaves
are lying deep?" the voice replies. "Not the shadow that
darkens the whole globe? Not the shadow of the City of
the Dead?"

Not even that. Of all days in the year, we will turn our
faces towards that City upon Christmas Day, and from its
silent hosts bring those we loved, among us. City of the
Dead, in the blessed name wherein we are gathered together
at this time, and in the Presence that is here among us
according to the promise, we will receive, and not dismiss,
thy people who are dear to us!

Yes. We can look upon these children angels that alight,
so solemnly, so beautifully among the living children by the
fire, and can bear to think how they departed from us.
Entertaining angels unawares, as the Patriarchs did, the
playful children are unconscious of their guests; but we can
see them—can see a radiant arm around one favourite neck,
as if there were a tempting of that child away. Among the
celestial figures there is one, a poor mis-shapen boy on earth,
of a glorious beauty now, of whom his dying mother said it
grieved her much to leave him here, alone, for so many years
as it was likely would elapse before he came to her—being
such a little child. But he went quickly, and was laid upon
her breast, and in her hand she leads him.

There was a gallant boy, who fell, far away, upon a
burning sand beneath a burning sun, and said, "Tell them
at home, with my last love, how much I could have wished

to kiss them once, but that I died contented and had done
my duty!" Or there was another, over whom they read the
words, "Therefore we commit his body to the deep," and so
consigned him to the lonely ocean and sailed on. Or there
was another, who lay down to his rest in the dark shadow of
great forests, and, on earth, awoke no more. O shall they
not, from sand and sea and forest, be brought home at such
a time!

There was a dear girl—almost a woman—never to be one
—who made a mourning Christmas in a house of joy, and
went her trackless way to the silent City. Do we recollect
her, worn out, faintly whispering what could not be heard,
and falling into that last sleep for weariness? O look upon
her now! O look upon her beauty, her serenity, her change-
less youth, her happiness! The daughter of Jairus was
recalled to life, to die; but she, more blest, has heard the
same voice, saying unto her, "Arise for ever!"

We had a friend who was our friend from early days, with
whom we often pictured the changes that were to come upon
our lives, and merrily imagined how we would speak, and
walk, and think, and talk, when we came to be old. His
destined habitation in the City of the Dead received him in
his prime. Shall he be shut out from our Christmas remembrance? Would his love have so excluded us? Lost friend,
lost child, lost parent, sister, brother, husband, wife, we
will not so discard you! You shall hold your cherished
places in our Christmas hearts, and by our Christmas fires;
and in the season of immortal hope, and on the birthday of
immortal mercy, we will shut out Nothing!

The winter sun goes down over town and village; on the
sea it makes a rosy path, as if the Sacred tread were fresh
upon the water. A few more moments, and it sinks, and
night comes on, and lights begin to sparkle in the prospect.
On the hill-side beyond the shapelessly-diffused town, and in
the quiet keeping of the trees that gird the village-steeple,
remembrances are cut in stone, planted in common flowers,

growing in grass, entwined with lowly brambles around many a mound of earth. In town and village, there are doors and windows closed against the weather, there are flaming logs heaped high, there are joyful faces, there is healthy music of voices. Be all ungentleness and harm excluded from the temples of the Household Gods, but be those remembrances admitted with tender encouragement! They are of the time and all its comforting and peaceful reassurances; and of the history that re-united even upon earth the living and the dead; and of the broad beneficence and goodness that too many men have tried to tear to narrow shreds.

THE POOR RELATION'S STORY

[1852]

THE
POOR RELATION'S STORY.

HE was very reluctant to take precedence of so many respected members of the family, by beginning the round of stories they were to relate as they sat in a goodly circle by the Christmas fire; and he modestly suggested that it would be more correct if "John our esteemed host" (whose health he begged to drink) would have the kindness to begin. For as to himself, he said, he was so little used to lead the way that really—— But as they all cried out here, that he must begin, and agreed with one voice that he might, could, would, and should begin, he left off rubbing his hands, and took his legs out from under his arm-chair, and did begin.

I have no doubt (said the poor relation) that I shall surprise the assembled members of our family, and particularly John our esteemed host to whom we are so much indebted for the great hospitality with which he has this day entertained us, by the confession I am going to make. But, if you do me the honour to be surprised at anything that falls from a person so unimportant in the family as I am, I can only say that I shall be scrupulously accurate in all I relate.

I am not what I am supposed to be. I am quite another thing. Perhaps before I go further, I had better glance at what I *am* supposed to be.

It is supposed, unless I mistake—the assembled members of our family will correct me if I do, which is very likely (here the poor relation looked mildly about him for contradiction); that I am nobody's enemy but my own. That I never met with any particular success in anything. That I failed in business because I was unbusiness-like and credulous —in not being prepared for the interested designs of my partner. That I failed in love, because I was ridiculously trustful—in thinking it impossible that Christiana could deceive me. That I failed in my expectations from my uncle Chill, on account of not being as sharp as he could have wished in worldly matters. That, through life, I have been rather put upon and disappointed in a general way. That I am at present a bachelor of between fifty-nine and sixty years of age, living on a limited income in the form of a quarterly allowance, to which I see that John our esteemed host wishes me to make no further allusion.

The supposition as to my present pursuits and habits is to the following effect.

I live in a lodging in the Clapham Road—a very clean back room, in a very respectable house—where I am expected not to be at home in the day-time, unless poorly; and which I usually leave in the morning at nine o'clock, on pretence of going to business. I take my breakfast—my roll and butter, and my half-pint of coffee—at the old-established coffee-shop near Westminster Bridge; and then I go into the City—I don't know why—and sit in Garraway's Coffee House, and on 'Change, and walk about, and look into a few offices and counting-houses where some of my relations or acquaintance are so good as to tolerate me, and where I stand by the fire if the weather happens to be cold. I get through the day in this way until five o'clock, and then I dine: at a cost, on the average, of one and threepence. Having still a little money to spend on my evening's entertainment, I look into the old-established coffee-shop as I go home, and take my cup of tea, and perhaps my bit of toast. So, as the large hand of the clock makes its way round to the morning hour again, I make my way round to the Clapham Road again, and go to bed when I get to my lodging—fire being expensive, and being objected to by the family on account of its giving trouble and making a dirt.

Sometimes, one of my relations or acquaintances is so obliging as to ask me to dinner. Those are holiday occasions, and then I generally walk in the Park. I am a solitary man, and seldom walk with anybody. Not that I am avoided because I am shabby; for I am not at all shabby, having always a very good suit of black on (or rather Oxford mixture, which has . the appearance of black and wears much better); but I have got into a habit of speaking low, and being rather silent, and my spirits are not high, and I am sensible that I am not an attractive companion.

The only exception to this general rule is the child of my first cousin, Little Frank. I have a particular affection for that child, and he takes very kindly to me. He is a diffident boy by nature; and in a crowd he is soon run over, as I may say, and forgotten. He and I, however, get on exceedingly well. I have a fancy that the poor child will in time succeed to my peculiar position in the family. We talk but little; still, we understand each other. We walk about, hand in hand; and without much speaking he knows what I mean, and I know what he means. When he was very little indeed, I used to take him to the windows of the toy-shops, and show him the toys inside. It is surprising how soon he found out that I would have made him a great many presents if I had been in circumstances to do it.

Little Frank and I go and look at the outside of the Monument—he is very fond of the Monument—and at the Bridges, and at all the sights that are free. On two of my birthdays, we have dined on à-la-mode beef, and gone at half-price to the play, and been deeply interested. I was once walking with him in Lombard Street, which we often

visit on account of my having mentioned to him that there
are great riches there—he is very fond of Lombard Street—
when a gentleman said to me as he passed by, "Sir, your
little son has dropped his glove." I assure you, if you will
excuse my remarking on so trivial a circumstance, this
accidental mention of the child as mine, quite touched my
heart and brought the foolish tears into my eyes.

When Little Frank is sent to school in the country, I shall
be very much at a loss what to do with myself, but I have
the intention of walking down there once a month and seeing
him on a half holiday. I am told he will then be at play
upon the Heath; and if my visits should be objected to, as
unsettling the child, I can see him from a distance without
his seeing me, and walk back again. His mother comes of a
highly genteel family, and rather disapproves, I am aware, of
our being too much together. I know that I am not calculated to improve his retiring disposition; but I think he
would miss me beyond the feeling of the moment if we were
wholly separated.

When I die in the Clapham Road, I shall not leave much
more in this world than I shall take out of it; but, I happen
to have a miniature of a bright-faced boy, with a curling
head, and an open shirt-frill waving down his bosom (my
mother had it taken for me, but I can't believe that it was
ever like), which will be worth nothing to sell, and which I
shall beg may be given to Frank. I have written my dear
boy a little letter with it, in which I have told him that I
felt very sorry to part from him, though bound to confess
that I knew no reason why I should remain here. I have
given him some short advice, the best in my power, to take
warning of the consequences of being nobody's enemy but his
own; and I have endeavoured to comfort him for what I fear
he will consider a bereavement, by pointing out to him, that
I was only a superfluous something to every one but him;
and that having by some means failed to find a place in this
great assembly, I am better out of it.

Such (said the poor relation, clearing his throat and beginning to speak a little louder) is the general impression about me. Now, it is a remarkable circumstance which forms the aim and purpose of my story, that this is all wrong. This is not my life, and these are not my habits. I do not even live in the Clapham Road. Comparatively speaking, I am very seldom there. I reside, mostly, in a—I am almost ashamed to say the word, it sounds so full of pretension—in a Castle. I do not mean that it is an old baronial habitation, but still it is a building always known to every one by the name of a Castle. In it, I preserve the particulars of my history; they run thus:

It was when I first took John Spatter (who had been my clerk) into partnership, and when I was still a young man of not more than five-and-twenty, residing in the house of my uncle Chill, from whom I had considerable expectations, that I ventured to propose to Christiana. I had loved Christiana a long time. She was very beautiful, and very winning in all respects. I rather mistrusted her widowed mother, who I feared was of a plotting and mercenary turn of mind; but, I thought as well of her as I could, for Christiana's sake. I never had loved any one but Christiana, and she had been all the world, and O far more than all the world, to me, from our childhood!

Christiana accepted me with her mother's consent, and I was rendered very happy indeed. My life at my uncle Chill's was of a spare dull kind, and my garret chamber was as dull, and bare, and cold, as an upper prison room in some stern northern fortress. But, having Christiana's love, I wanted nothing upon earth. I would not have changed my lot with any human being.

Avarice was, unhappily, my uncle Chill's master-vice. Though he was rich, he pinched, and scraped, and clutched, and lived miserably. As Christiana had no fortune, I was for some time a little fearful of confessing our engagement to him; but, at length I wrote him a letter, saying how it

all truly was.   I put it into his hand one night, on going
to bed.

As I came down-stairs next morning, shivering in the cold
December air; colder in my uncle's unwarmed house than in
the street, where the winter sun did sometimes shine, and
which was at all events enlivened by cheerful faces and voices
passing along; I carried a heavy heart towards the long, low
breakfast-room in which my uncle sat.   It was a large room
with a small fire, and there was a great bay window in it
which the rain had marked in the night as if with the tears
of houseless people.   It stared upon a raw yard, with a cracked
stone pavement, and some rusted iron railings half uprooted,
whence an ugly out-building that had once been a dissecting-
room (in the time of the great surgeon who had mortgaged
the house to my uncle), stared at it.

We rose so early always, that at that time of the year we
breakfasted by candle-light.   When I went into the room,
my uncle was so contracted by the cold, and so huddled
together in his chair behind the one dim candle, that I did
not see him until I was close to the table.

As I held out my hand to him, he caught up his stick
(being infirm, he always walked about the house with a stick),
and made a blow at me, and said, "You fool!"

"Uncle," I returned, "I didn't expect you to be so angry
as this."   Nor had I expected it, though he was a hard and
angry old man.

"You didn't expect!" said he; "when did you ever
expect?   When did you ever calculate, or look forward, you
contemptible dog?"

"These are hard words, uncle!"

"Hard words?   Feathers, to pelt such an idiot as you
with," said he.   "Here! Betsy Snap!   Look at him!"

Betsy Snap was a withered, hard-favoured, yellow old
woman—our only domestic—always employed, at this time
of the morning, in rubbing my uncle's legs.   As my uncle
adjured her to look at me, he put his lean grip on the

crown of her head, she kneeling beside him, and turned her face towards me. An involuntary thought connecting them both with the Dissecting Room, as it must often have been in the surgeon's time, passed across my mind in the midst of my anxiety.

"Look at the snivelling milksop!" said my uncle. "Look at the baby! This is the gentleman who, people say, is nobody's enemy but his own. This is the gentleman who can't say no. This is the gentleman who was making such large profits in his business that he must needs take a partner, t'other day. This is the gentleman who is going to marry a wife without a penny, and who falls into the hands of Jezabels who are speculating on my death!"

I knew, now, how great my uncle's rage was; for nothing short of his being almost beside himself would have induced him to utter that concluding word, which he held in such repugnance that it was never spoken or hinted at before him on any account.

"On my death," he repeated, as if he were defying me by defying his own abhorrence of the word. "On my death—death—Death! But I'll spoil the speculation. Eat your last under this roof, you feeble wretch, and may it choke you!"

You may suppose that I had not much appetite for the breakfast to which I was bidden in these terms; but, I took my accustomed seat. I saw that I was repudiated henceforth by my uncle; still I could bear that very well, possessing Christiana's heart.

He emptied his basin of bread and milk as usual, only that he took it on his knees with his chair turned away from the table where I sat. When he had done, he carefully snuffed out the candle; and the cold, slate-coloured, miserable day looked in upon us.

"Now, Mr. Michael," said he, "before we part, I should like to have a word with these ladies in your presence."

"As you will, sir," I returned; "but you deceive yourself,

and wrong us, cruelly, if you suppose that there is any feeling
at stake in this contract but pure, disinterested, faithful love."

To this, he only replied, "You lie!" and not one other
word.

We went, through half-thawed snow and half-frozen rain,
to the house where Christiana and her mother lived. My
uncle knew them very well. They were sitting at their
breakfast, and were surprised to see us at that hour.

"Your servant, ma'am," said my uncle to the mother.
"You divine the purpose of my visit, I dare say, ma'am.
I understand there is a world of pure, disinterested, faithful
love cooped up here. I am happy to bring it all it wants,
to make it complete. I bring you your son-in-law, ma'am
—and you, your husband, miss. The gentleman is a perfect
stranger to me, but I wish him joy of his wise bargain."

He snarled at me as he went out, and I never saw him
again.

It is altogether a mistake (continued the poor relation)
to suppose that my dear Christiana, over-persuaded and
influenced by her mother, married a rich man, the dirt from
whose carriage wheels is often, in these changed times, thrown
upon me as she rides by. No, no. She married me.

The way we came to be married rather sooner than we
intended, was this. I took a frugal lodging and was saving
and planning for her sake, when, one day, she spoke to me
with great earnestness, and said:

"My dear Michael, I have given you my heart. I have
said that I loved you, and I have pledged myself to be your
wife. I am as much yours through all changes of good and
evil as if we had been married on the day when such words
passed between us. I know you well, and know that if we
should be separated and our union broken off, your whole
life would be shadowed, and all that might, even now, be
stronger in your character for the conflict with the world
would then be weakened to the shadow of what it is!"

"God help me, Christiana!" said I. "You speak the truth."

"Michael!" said she, putting her hand in mine, in all maidenly devotion, "let us keep apart no longer. It is but for me to say that I can live contented upon such means as you have, and I well know you are happy. I say so from my heart. Strive no more alone; let us strive together. My dear Michael, it is not right that I should keep secret from you what you do not suspect, but what distresses my whole life. My mother: without considering that what you have lost, you have lost for me, and on the assurance of my faith: sets her heart on riches, and urges another suit upon me, to my misery. I cannot bear this, for to bear it is to be untrue to you. I would rather share your struggles than look on. I want no better home than you can give me. I know that you will aspire and labour with a higher courage if I am wholly yours, and let it be so when you will!"

I was blest indeed, that day, and a new world opened to me. We were married in a very little while, and I took my wife to our happy home. That was the beginning of the residence I have spoken of; the Castle we have ever since inhabited together, dates from that time. All our children have been born in it. Our first child—now married—was a little girl, whom we called Christiana. Her son is so like Little Frank, that I hardly know which is which.

The current impression as to my partner's dealings with me is also quite erroneous. He did not begin to treat me coldly, as a poor simpleton, when my uncle and I so fatally quarrelled; nor did he afterwards gradually possess himself of our business and edge me out. On the contrary, he behaved to me with the utmost good faith and honour.

Matters between us took this turn:—On the day of my separation from my uncle, and even before the arrival at our counting-house of my trunks (which he sent after me, *not* carriage paid), I went down to our room of business, on our

little wharf, overlooking the river; and there I told John
Spatter what had happened. John did not say, in reply, that
rich old relatives were palpable facts, and that love and
sentiment were moonshine and fiction. He addressed me
thus:

"Michael," said John, "we were at school together, and I
generally had the knack of getting on better than you, and
making a higher reputation."

"You had, John," I returned.

"Although," said John, "I borrowed your books and lost
them; borrowed your pocket-money, and never repaid it; got
you to buy my damaged knives at a higher price than I had
given for them new; and to own to the windows that I had
broken."

"All not worth mentioning, John Spatter," said I, "but
certainly true."

"When you were first established in this infant business,
which promises to thrive so well," pursued John, "I came
to you, in my search for almost any employment, and you
made me your clerk."

"Still not worth mentioning, my dear John Spatter," said
I; "still, equally true."

"And finding that I had a good head for business, and
that I was really useful to the business, you did not like to
retain me in that capacity, and thought it an act of justice
soon to make me your partner."

"Still less worth mentioning than any of those other little
circumstances you have recalled, John Spatter," said I; "for I
was, and am, sensible of your merits and my deficiencies."

"Now, my good friend," said John, drawing my arm through
his, as he had had a habit of doing at school; while two
vessels outside the windows of our counting-house—which
were shaped like the stern windows of a ship—went lightly
down the river with the tide, as John and I might then be
sailing away in company, and in trust and confidence, on our
voyage of life; "let there, under these friendly circumstances,

be a right understanding between us. You are too easy, Michael. You are nobody's enemy but your own. If I were to give you that damaging character among our connexion, with a shrug, and a shake of the head, and a sigh; and if I were further to abuse the trust you place in me—— "

"But you never will abuse it at all, John," I observed.

"Never!" said he; "but I am putting a case—I say, and if I were further to abuse that trust by keeping this piece of our common affairs in the dark, and this other piece in the light, and again this other piece in the twilight, and so on, I should strengthen my strength, and weaken your weakness, day by day, until at last I found myself on the high road to fortune, and you left behind on some bare common, a hopeless number of miles out of the way."

"Exactly so," said I.

"To prevent this, Michael," said John Spatter, "or the remotest chance of this, there must be perfect openness between us. Nothing must be concealed, and we must have but one interest."

"My dear John Spatter," I assured him, "that is precisely what I mean."

"And when you are too easy," pursued John, his face glowing with friendship, "you must allow me to prevent that imperfection in your nature from being taken advantage of, by any one; you must not expect me to humour it—— "

"My dear John Spatter," I interrupted, "I *don't* expect you to humour it. I want to correct it."

"And I, too," said John.

"Exactly so!" cried I. "We both have the same end in view; and, honourably seeking it, and fully trusting one another, and having but one interest, ours will be a prosperous and happy partnership."

"I am sure of it!" returned John Spatter. And we shook hands most affectionately.

I took John home to my Castle, and we had a very happy day. Our partnership throve well. My friend and partner

supplied what I wanted, as I had foreseen that he would;
and by improving both the business and myself, amply
acknowledged any little rise in life to which I had helped
him.

I am not (said the poor relation, looking at the fire as he
slowly rubbed his hands) very rich, for I never cared to be
that; but I have enough, and am above all moderate wants
and anxieties. My Castle is not a splendid place, but it is
very comfortable, and it has a warm and cheerful air, and
is quite a picture of Home.

Our eldest girl, who is very like her mother, married John
Spatter's eldest son. Our two families are closely united in
other ties of attachment. It is very pleasant of an evening,
when we are all assembled together—which frequently happens
—and when John and I talk over old times, and the one
interest there has always been between us.

I really do not know, in my Castle, what loneliness is.
Some of our children or grandchildren are always about it,
and the young voices of my descendants are delightful—O,
how delightful!—to me to hear. My dearest and most
devoted wife, ever faithful, ever loving, ever helpful and sus-
taining and consoling, is the priceless blessing of my house;
from whom all its other blessings spring. We are rather a
musical family, and when Christiana sees me, at any time, a
little weary or depressed, she steals to the piano and sings
a gentle air she used to sing when we were first betrothed.
So weak a man am I, that I cannot bear to hear it from any
other source. They played it once, at the Theatre, when I
was there with Little Frank; and the child said wondering,
"Cousin Michael, whose hot tears are these that have fallen
on my hand!"

Such is my Castle, and such are the real particulars of my
life therein preserved. I often take Little Frank home there.
He is very welcome to my grandchildren, and they play
together. At this time of the year—the Christmas and New

Year time—I am seldom out of my Castle. For, the associations of the season seem to hold me there, and the precepts of the season seem to teach me that it is well to be there.

"And the Castle is——" observed a grave, kind voice among the company.

"Yes. My Castle," said the poor relation, shaking his head as he still looked at the fire, "is in the Air. John our esteemed host suggests its situation accurately. My Castle is in the Air! I have done. Will you be so good as to pass the story?"

THE CHILD'S STORY

[1852]

THE CHILD'S STORY.

Once upon a time, a good many years ago, there was a traveller, and he set out upon a journey. It was a magic journey, and was to seem very long when he began it, and very short when he got half way through.

He travelled along a rather dark path for some little time, without meeting anything, until at last he came to a beautiful child. So he said to the child, "What do you do here?" And the child said, "I am always at play. Come and play with me!"

So, he played with that child, the whole day long, and they were very merry. The sky was so blue, the sun was so bright, the water was so sparkling, the leaves were so green, the flowers were so lovely, and they heard such singing-birds and saw so many butterflies, that everything was beautiful. This was in fine weather. When it rained, they loved to watch the falling drops, and to smell the fresh scents. When it blew, it was delightful to listen to the wind, and fancy what it said, as it came rushing from its home—where was that, they wondered!—whistling and howling, driving the clouds before it, bending the trees, rumbling in the chimneys, shaking the house, and making the sea roar in fury. But, when it snowed, that was best of all; for, they liked nothing so well as to look up at the white flakes falling fast and thick, like down from the breasts of millions of white birds;

and to see how smooth and deep the drift was; and to listen
to the hush upon the paths and roads.

They had plenty of the finest toys in the world, and
the most astonishing picture-books: all about scimitars
and slippers and turbans, and dwarfs and giants and genii
and fairies, and blue-beards and bean-stalks and riches and
caverns and forests and Valentines and Orsons: and all new
and all true.

But, one day, of a sudden, the traveller lost the child.
He called to him over and over again, but got no answer.
So, he went upon his road, and went on for a little while
without meeting anything, until at last he came to a handsome boy. So, he said to the boy, " What do you do here ? "
And the boy said, " I am always learning. Come and learn
with me."

So he learned with that boy about Jupiter and Juno, and
the Greeks and the Romans, and I don't know what, and
learned more than I could tell—or he either, for he soon
forgot a great deal of it. But, they were not always learning; they had the merriest games that ever were played.
They rowed upon the river in summer, and skated on the ice
in winter; they were active afoot, and active on horseback;
at cricket, and all games at ball; at prisoners' base, hare and
hounds, follow my leader, and more sports than I can think
of; nobody could beat them. They had holidays too, and
Twelfth cakes, and parties where they danced till midnight,
and real Theatres where they saw palaces of real gold and
silver rise out of the real earth, and saw all the wonders of
the world at once. As to friends, they had such dear friends
and so many of them, that I want the time to reckon them
up. They were all young, like the handsome boy, and were
never to be strange to one another all their lives through.

Still, one day, in the midst of all these pleasures, the traveller
lost the boy as he had lost the child, and, after calling to
him in vain, went on upon his journey. So he went on for
a little while without seeing anything, until at last he came

to a young man. So, he said to the young man, "What do you do here?" And the young man said, "I am always in love. Come and love with me."

So, he went away with that young man, and presently they came to one of the prettiest girls that ever was seen—just like Fanny in the corner there—and she had eyes like Fanny, and hair like Fanny, and dimples like Fanny's, and she laughed and coloured just as Fanny does while I am talking about her. So, the young man fell in love directly—just as Somebody I won't mention, the first time he came here, did with Fanny. Well! he was teased sometimes—just as Somebody used to be by Fanny; and they quarrelled sometimes—just as Somebody and Fanny used to quarrel; and they made it up, and sat in the dark, and wrote letters every day, and never were happy asunder, and were always looking out for one another and pretending not to, and were engaged at Christmas-time, and sat close to one another by the fire, and were going to be married very soon—all exactly like Somebody I won't mention, and Fanny!

But, the traveller lost them one day, as he had lost the rest of his friends, and, after calling to them to come back, which they never did, went on upon his journey. So, he went on for a little while without seeing anything, until at last he came to a middle-aged gentleman. So, he said to the gentleman, "What are you doing here?" And his answer was, "I am always busy. Come and be busy with me!"

So, he began to be very busy with that gentleman, and they went on through the wood together. The whole journey was through a wood, only it had been open and green at first, like a wood in spring; and now began to be thick and dark, like a wood in summer; some of the little trees that had come out earliest, were even turning brown. The gentleman was not alone, but had a lady of about the same age with him, who was his Wife; and they had children, who were with them too. So, they all went on together through the wood, cutting down the trees, and making a path through the branches and the fallen leaves, and carrying burdens, and working hard.

Sometimes, they came to a long green avenue that opened into deeper woods. Then they would hear a very little distant voice crying, "Father, father, I am another child! Stop for me!" And presently they would see a very little figure, growing larger as it came along, running to join them. When it came up, they all crowded round it, and kissed and welcomed it; and then they all went on together.

Sometimes, they came to several avenues at once, and then they all stood still, and one of the children said, "Father, I am going to sea," and another said, "Father, I am going to India," and another, "Father, I am going to seek my fortune where I can," and another, "Father, I am going to Heaven!" So, with many tears at parting, they went, solitary, down those avenues, each child upon its way; and the child who went to Heaven, rose into the golden air and vanished.

Whenever these partings happened, the traveller looked at the gentleman, and saw him glance up at the sky above the trees, where the day was beginning to decline, and the sunset to come on. He saw, too, that his hair was turning grey. But, they never could rest long, for they had their journey to perform, and it was necessary for them to be always busy.

At last, there had been so many partings that there were no children left, and only the traveller, the gentleman, and the lady, went upon their way in company. And now the wood was yellow; and now brown; and the leaves, even of the forest trees, began to fall.

So, they came to an avenue that was darker than the rest, and were pressing forward on their journey without looking down it when the lady stopped.

"My husband," said the lady. "I am called."

They listened, and they heard a voice a long way down the avenue, say, "Mother, mother!"

It was the voice of the first child who had said, "I am

going to Heaven!" and the father said, "I pray not yet.
The sunset is very near. I pray not yet!"

But, the voice cried, "Mother, mother!" without minding
him, though his hair was now quite white, and tears were on
his face.

Then, the mother, who was already drawn into the shade
of the dark avenue and moving away with her arms still
round his neck, kissed him, and said, "My dearest, I am
summoned, and I go!" And she was gone. And the traveller
and he were left alone together.

And they went on and on together, until they came to
very near the end of the wood: so near, that they could see
the sunset shining red before them through the trees.

Yet, once more, while he broke his way among the branches,
the traveller lost his friend. He called and called, but there
was no reply, and when he passed out of the wood, and saw
the peaceful sun going down upon a wide purple prospect,
he came to an old man sitting on a fallen tree. So, he said
to the old man, "What do you do here?" And the old
man said with a calm smile, "I am always remembering.
Come and remember with me!"

So the traveller sat down by the side of that old man, face
to face with the serene sunset; and all his friends came softly
back and stood around him. The beautiful child, the handsome boy, the young man in love, the father, mother, and
children: every one of them was there, and he had lost
nothing. So, he loved them all, and was kind and forbearing
with them all, and was always pleased to watch them all,
and they all honoured and loved him. And I think the
traveller must be yourself, dear Grandfather, because this
is what you do to us, and what we do to you.

THE SCHOOLBOY'S STORY

[1853]

THE SCHOOLBOY'S STORY.

BEING rather young at present—I am getting on in years, but still I am rather young—I have no particular adventures of my own to fall back upon. It wouldn't much interest anybody here, I suppose, to know what a screw the Reverend is, or what a griffin *she* is, or how they do stick it into parents—particularly hair-cutting, and medical attendance. One of our fellows was charged in his half's account twelve and sixpence for two pills—tolerably profitable at six and threepence a-piece, I should think—and he never took them either, but put them up the sleeve of his jacket.

As to the beef, it's shameful. It's *not* beef. Regular beef isn't veins. You can chew regular beef. Besides which, there's gravy to regular beef, and you never see a drop to ours. Another of our fellows went home ill, and heard the family doctor tell his father that he couldn't account for his complaint unless it was the beer. Of course it was the beer, and well it might be!

However, beef and Old Cheeseman are two different things. So is beer. It was Old Cheeseman I meant to tell about; not the manner in which our fellows get their constitutions destroyed for the sake of profit.

Why, look at the pie-crust alone. There's no flakiness in it. It's solid—like damp lead. Then our fellows get nightmares, and are bolstered for calling out and waking other fellows. Who can wonder!

Old Cheeseman one night walked in his sleep, put his hat on over his night-cap, got hold of a fishing-rod and a cricket-bat, and went down into the parlour, where they naturally thought from his appearance he was a Ghost. Why, he never would have done that if his meals had been wholesome. When we all begin to walk in our sleeps, I suppose they'll be sorry for it.

Old Cheeseman wasn't second Latin Master then; he was a fellow himself. He was first brought there, very small, in a post-chaise, by a woman who was always taking snuff and shaking him—and that was the most he remembered about it. He never went home for the holidays. His accounts (he never learnt any extras) were sent to a Bank, and the Bank paid them; and he had a brown suit twice a-year, and went into boots at twelve. They were always too big for him, too.

In the Midsummer holidays, some of our fellows who lived within walking distance, used to. come back and climb the trees outside the playground wall, on purpose to look at Old Cheeseman reading there by himself. He was always as mild as the tea—and *that's* pretty mild, I should hope!—so when they whistled to him, he looked up and nodded; and when they said, "Halloa, Old Cheeseman, what have you had for dinner?" he said, "Boiled mutton;" and when they said, "An't it solitary, Old Cheeseman?" he said, "It is a little dull sometimes:" and then they said, "Well good-bye, Old Cheeseman!" and climbed down again. Of course it was imposing on Old Cheeseman to give him nothing but boiled mutton through a whole Vacation, but that was just like the system. When they didn't give him boiled mutton, they gave him rice pudding, pretending it was a treat. And saved the butcher.

So Old Cheeseman went on. The holidays brought him into other trouble besides the loneliness; because when the fellows began to come back, not wanting to, he was always glad to see them; which was aggravating when they were

not at all glad to see him, and so he got his head knocked
against walls, and that was the way his nose bled. But he
was a favourite in general. Once a subscription was raised
for him; and, to keep up his spirits, he was presented before
the holidays with two white mice, a rabbit, a pigeon, and a
beautiful puppy. Old Cheeseman cried about it—especially
soon afterwards, when they all ate one another.

Of course Old Cheeseman used to be called by the names
of all sorts of cheeses—Double Glo'sterman, Family Cheshire-
man, Dutchman, North Wiltshireman, and all that. But he
never minded it. And I don't mean to say he was old in
point of years—because he wasn't—only he was called from
the first, Old Cheeseman.

At last, Old Cheeseman was made second Latin Master.
He was brought in one morning at the beginning of a new
half, and presented to the school in that capacity as "Mr.
Cheeseman." Then our fellows all agreed that Old Cheeseman
was a spy, and a deserter, who had gone over to the enemy's
camp, and sold himself for gold. It was no excuse for him
that he had sold himself for very little gold—two pound ten
a quarter and his washing, as was reported. It was decided
by a Parliament which sat about it, that Old Cheeseman's
mercenary motives could alone be taken into account, and that
he had "coined our blood for drachmas." The Parliament
took the expression out of the quarrel scene between Brutus
and Cassius.

When it was settled in this strong way that Old Cheeseman was a tremendous traitor, who had wormed himself into
our fellows' secrets on purpose to get himself into favour by
giving up everything he knew, all couragrous fellows were
invited to come forward and enrol themselves in a Society
for making a set against him. The President of the Society
was First boy, named Bob Tarter. His father was in the
West Indies, and he owned, himself, that his father was
worth Millions. He had great power among our fellows,
and he wrote a parody, beginning—

> " Who made believe to be so meek
> That we could hardly hear him speak,
> Yet turned out an Informing Sneak?
> Old Cheeseman."

—and on in that way through more than a dozen verses, which he used to go and sing, every morning, close by the new master's desk. He trained one of the low boys, too, a rosy-cheeked little Brass who didn't care what he did, to go up to him with his Latin Grammar one morning, and say it so : *Nominativus pronominum*—Old Cheeseman, *raro exprimitur*— was never suspected, *nisi distinctionis*—of being an informer, *aut emphasis gratiâ*—until he proved one. *Ut*—for instance, *Vos damnastis*—when he sold the boys. *Quasi*—as though, *dicat*—he should say, *Pretærea nemo*—I'm a Judas! All this produced a great effect on Old Cheeseman. He had never had much hair; but what he had, began to get thinner and thinner every day. He grew paler and more worn; and sometimes of an evening he was seen sitting at his desk with a precious long snuff to his candle, and his hands before his face, crying. But no member of the Society could pity him, even if he felt inclined, because the President said it was Old Cheeseman's conscience.

So Old Cheeseman went on, and didn't he lead a miserable life ! Of course the Reverend turned up his nose at him, and of course *she* did—because both of them always do that at all the masters—but he suffered from the fellows most, and he suffered from them constantly. He never told about it, that the Society could find out; but he got no credit for that, because the President said it was Old Cheeseman's cowardice.

He had only one friend in the world, and that one was almost as powerless as he was, for it was only Jane. Jane was a sort of wardrobe woman to our fellows, and took care of the boxes. She had come at first, I believe, as a kind of apprentice—some of our fellows say from a Charity, but *I* don't know—and after her time was out, had stopped at so much a year. So little a year, perhaps I ought to say, for

it is far more likely. However, she had put some pounds in
the Savings' Bank, and she was a very nice young woman.
She was not quite pretty; but she had a very frank, honest,
bright face, and all our fellows were fond of her. She was
uncommonly neat and cheerful, and uncommonly comfortable
and kind. And if anything was the matter with a fellow's
mother, he always went and showed the letter to Jane.

Jane was Old Cheeseman's friend. The more the Society
went against him, the more Jane stood by him. She used
to give him a good-humoured look out of her still-room
window, sometimes, that seemed to set him up for the day.
She used to pass out of the orchard and the kitchen garden
(always kept locked, I believe you!) through the playground,
when she might have gone the other way, only to give a
turn of her head, as much as to say "Keep up your spirits!"
to Old Cheeseman. His slip of a room was so fresh and
orderly that it was well known who looked after it while he
was at his desk; and when our fellows saw a smoking hot
dumpling on his plate at dinner, they knew with indignation
who had sent it up.

Under these circumstances, the Society resolved, after a
quantity of meeting and debating, that Jane should be
requested to cut Old Cheeseman dead; and that if she
refused, she must be sent to Coventry herself. So a deputation, headed by the President, was appointed to wait on Jane,
and inform her of the vote the Society had been under the
painful necessity of passing. She was very much respected
for all her good qualities, and there was a story about her
having once waylaid the Reverend in his own study, and
got a fellow off from severe punishment, of her own kind
comfortable heart. So the deputation didn't much like the
job. However, they went up, and the President told Jane
all about it. Upon which Jane turned very red, burst into
tears, informed the President and the deputation, in a way
not at all like her usual way, that they were a parcel of
malicious young savages, and turned the whole respected body

out of the room. Consequently it was entered in the Society's book (kept in astronomical cypher for fear of detection), that all communication with Jane was interdicted: and the President addressed the members on this convincing instance of Old Cheeseman's undermining.

But Jane was as true to Old Cheeseman as Old Cheeseman was false to our fellows—in their opinion, at all events—and steadily continued to be his only friend. It was a great exasperation to the Society, because Jane was as much a loss to them as she was a gain to him; and being more inveterate against him than ever, they treated him worse than ever. At last, one morning, his desk stood empty, his room was peeped into, and found to be vacant, and a whisper went about among the pale faces of our fellows that Old Cheeseman, unable to bear it any longer, had got up early and drowned himself.

The mysterious looks of the other masters after breakfast, and the evident fact that old Cheeseman was not expected, confirmed the Society in this opinion. Some began to discuss whether the President was liable to hanging or only transportation for life, and the President's face showed a great anxiety to know which. However, he said that a jury of his country should find him game; and that in his address he should put it to them to lay their hands upon their hearts and say whether they as Britons approved of informers, and how they thought they would like it themselves. Some of the Society considered that he had better run away until he found a forest where he might change clothes with a wood-cutter, and stain his face with blackberries; but the majority believed that if he stood his ground, his father—belonging as he did to the West Indies, and being worth millions—could buy him off.

All our fellows' hearts beat fast when the Reverend came in, and made a sort of a Roman, or a Field Marshal, of himself with the ruler; as he always did before delivering an address. But their fears were nothing to their astonishment

when he came out with the story that Old Cheeseman, "so
long our respected friend and fellow-pilgrim in the pleasant
plains of knowledge," he called him—O yes! I dare say! Much
of that!—was the orphan child of a disinherited young lady
who had married against her father's wish, and whose young
husband had died, and who had died of sorrow herself, and
whose unfortunate baby (Old Cheeseman) had been brought
up at the cost of a grandfather who would never consent to
see it, baby, boy, or man: which grandfather was now dead,
and serve him right—that's my putting in—and which grandfather's large property, there being no will, was now, and all
of a sudden and for ever, Old Cheeseman's! Our so long
respected friend and fellow-pilgrim in the pleasant plains of
knowledge, the Reverend wound up a lot of bothering quo-
tations by saying, would "come among us once more" that
day fortnight, when he desired to take leave of us himself,
in a more particular manner. With these words, he stared
severely round at our fellows, and went solemnly out.

There was precious consternation among the members of
the Society, now. Lots of them wanted to resign, and lots
more began to try to make out that they had never belonged
to it. However, the President stuck up, and said that they
must stand or fall together, and that if a breach was made
it should be over his body—which was meant to encourage
the Society: but it didn't. The President further said, he
would consider the position in which they stood, and would
give them his best opinion and advice in a few days. This
was eagerly looked for, as he knew a good deal of the world
on account of his father's being in the West Indies.

After days and days of hard thinking, and drawing armies
all over his slate, the President called our fellows together,
and made the matter clear. He said it was plain than when
Old Cheeseman came on the appointed day, his first revenge
would be to impeach the Society, and have it flogged all
round. After witnessing with joy the torture of his enemies,
and gloating over the cries which agony would extort from

them, the probability was that he would invite the Reverend, on pretence of conversation, into a private room—say the parlour into which Parents were shown, where the two great globes were which were never used—and would there reproach him with the various frauds and oppressions he had endured at his hands. At the close of his observations he would make a signal to a Prizefighter concealed in the passage, who would then appear and pitch into the Reverend, till he was left insensible. Old Cheeseman would then make Jane a present of from five to ten pounds, and would leave the establishment in fiendish triumph.

The President explained that against the parlour part, or the Jane part, of these arrangements he had nothing to say; but, on the part of the Society, he counselled deadly resistance. With this view he recommended that all available desks should be filled with stones, and that the first word of the complaint should be the signal to every fellow to let fly at Old Cheeseman. The bold advice put the Society in better spirits, and was unanimously taken. A post about Old Cheeseman's size was put up in the playground, and all our fellows practised at it till it was dinted all over.

When the day came, and Places were called, every fellow sat down in a tremble. There had been much discussing and disputing as to how Old Cheeseman would come; but it was the general opinion that he would appear in a sort of triumphal car drawn by four horses, with two livery servants in front, and the Prizefighter in disguise up behind. So, all our fellows sat listening for the sound of wheels. But no wheels were heard, for Old Cheeseman walked after all, and came into the school without any preparation. Pretty much as he used to be, only dressed in black.

"Gentlemen," said the Reverend, presenting him, "our so long respected friend and fellow-pilgrim in the pleasant plains of knowledge, is desirous to offer a word or two. Attention, gentlemen, one and all!"

Every fellow stole his hand into his desk and looked at

the President. The President was all ready, and taking aim at Old Cheeseman with his eyes.

What did Old Cheeseman then, but walk up to his old desk, look round him with a queer smile as if there was a tear in his eye, and begin in a quavering mild voice, "My dear companions and old friends!"

Every fellow's hand came out of his desk, and the President suddenly began to cry.

"My dear companions and old friends," said Old Cheeseman, "you have heard of my good fortune. I have passed so many years under this roof—my entire life so far, I may say—that I hope you have been glad to hear of it for my sake. I could never enjoy it without exchanging congratulations with you. If we have ever misunderstood one another at all, pray, my dear boys, let us forgive and forget. I have a great tenderness for you, and I am sure you return it. I want in the fulness of a grateful heart to shake hands with you every one. I have come back to do it, if you please, my dear boys."

Since the President had begun to cry, several other fellows had broken out here and there: but now, when Old Cheeseman began with him as first boy, laid his left hand affectionately on his shoulder and gave him his right; and when the President said "Indeed, I don't deserve it, sir; upon my honour I don't;" there was sobbing and crying all over the school. Every other fellow said he didn't deserve it, much in the same way; but Old Cheeseman, not minding that a bit, went cheerfully round to every boy, and wound up with every master—finishing off the Reverend last.

Then a snivelling little chap in a corner, who was always under some punishment or other, set up a shrill cry of "Success to Old Cheeseman! Hooray!" The Reverend glared upon him, and said, "Mr. Cheeseman, sir." But, Old Cheeseman protesting that he liked his old name a great deal better than his new one, all our fellows took up the cry; and, for I don't know how many minutes, there was such a thundering

of feet and hands, and such a roaring of Old Cheeseman, as
never was heard.

After that, there was a spread in the dining-room of the
most magnificent kind. Fowls, tongues, preserves, fruits,
confectionaries, jellies, neguses, barley-sugar temples, trifles,
crackers—eat all you can and pocket what you like—all at
Old Cheeseman's expense. After that, speeches, whole holiday, double and treble sets of all manners of things for all
manners of games, donkeys, pony-chaises and drive yourself,
dinner for all the masters at the Seven Bells (twenty pounds
a-head our fellows estimated it at), an annual holiday and
feast fixed for that day every year, and another on Old
Cheeseman's birthday—Reverend bound down before the
fellows to allow it, so that he could never back out—all at
Old Cheeseman's expense.

And didn't our fellows go down in a body and cheer
outside the Seven Bells? O no!

But there's something else besides. Don't look at the next
story-teller, for there's more yet. Next day, it was resolved
that the Society should make it up with Jane, and then be
dissolved. What do you think of Jane being gone, though!
"What? Gone for ever?" said our fellows, with long faces.
"Yes, to be sure," was all the answer they could get. None
of the people about the house would say anything more. At
length, the first boy took upon himself to ask the Reverend
whether our old friend Jane was really gone? The Reverend
(he has got a daughter at home—turn-up nose, and red)
replied severely, "Yes, sir, Miss Pitt is gone." The idea of
calling Jane, Miss Pitt! Some said she had been sent away
in disgrace for taking money from Old Cheeseman; others
said she had gone into Old Cheeseman's service at a rise of
ten pounds a year. All that our fellows knew, was, she
was gone.

It was two or three months afterwards, when, one afternoon, an open carriage stopped at the cricket field, just
outside bounds, with a lady and gentleman in it, who looked

at the game a long time and stood up to see it played.
Nobody thought much about them, until the same little
snivelling chap came in, against all rules, from the post
where he was Scout, and said, "It's Jane!" Both Elevens
forgot the game directly, and ran crowding round the carriage. It was Jane! In such a bonnet! And if you'll
believe me, Jane was married to Old Cheeseman.

It soon became quite a regular thing when our fellows
were hard at it in the playground, to see a carriage at the
low part of the wall where it joins the high part, and a lady
and gentleman standing up in it, looking over. The gentleman was always Old Cheeseman, and the lady was always
Jane.

The first time I ever saw them, I saw them in that way.
There had been a good many changes among our fellows
then, and it had turned out that Bob Tarter's father wasn't
worth Millions! He wasn't worth anything. Bob had gone
for a soldier, and Old Cheeseman had purchased his discharge.
But that's not the carriage. The carriage stopped, and all
our fellows stopped as soon as it was seen.

"So you have never sent me to Coventry after all!" said
the lady, laughing, as our fellows swarmed up the wall to
shake hands with her. "Are you never going to do it?"

"Never! never! never!" on all sides.

I didn't understand what she meant then, but of course I
do now. I was very much pleased with her face though, and
with her good way, and I couldn't help looking at her—and
at him too—with all our fellows clustering so joyfully about
them.

They soon took notice of me as a new boy, so I thought I
might as well swarm up the wall myself, and shake hands
with them as the rest did. I was quite as glad to see them
as the rest were, and was quite as familiar with them in a
moment.

"Only a fortnight now," said Old Cheeseman, "to the
holidays. Who stops? Anybody?"

A good many fingers pointed at me, and a good many voices cried "He does!" For it was the year when you were all away; and rather low I was about it, I can tell you.

"Oh!" said Old Cheeseman. "But it's solitary here in the holiday time. He had better come to us."

So I went to their delightful house, and was as happy as I could possibly be. They understand how to conduct themselves towards boys, *they* do. When they take a boy to the play, for instance, they *do* take him. They don't go in after it's begun, or come out before it's over. They know how to bring a boy up, too. Look at their own! Though he is very little as yet, what a capital boy he is! Why, my next favourite to Mrs. Cheeseman and Old Cheeseman, is young Cheeseman.

So, now I have told you all I know about Old Cheeseman. And it's not much after all, I am afraid. Is it?

NOBODY'S STORY

NOBODY'S STORY.

HE lived on the bank of a mighty river, broad and deep,
which was always silently rolling on to a vast undiscovered
ocean. It had rolled on, ever since the world began. It had
changed its course sometimes, and turned into new channels,
leaving its old ways dry and barren; but it had ever been
upon the flow, and ever was to flow until Time should be
no more. Against its strong, unfathomable stream, nothing
made head. No living creature, no flower, no leaf, no particle of animate or inanimate existence, ever strayed back
from the undiscovered ocean. The tide of the river set
resistlessly towards it; and the tide never stopped, any more
than the earth stops in its circling round the sun.

He lived in a busy place, and he worked very hard to live.
He had no hope of ever being rich enough to live a month
without hard work, but he was quite content, GOD knows, to
labour with a cheerful will. He was one of an immense
family, all of whose sons and daughters gained their daily
bread by daily work, prolonged from their rising up betimes
until their lying down at night. Beyond this destiny he had
no prospect, and he sought none.

There was over-much drumming, trumpeting, and speech-
making, in the neighbourhood where he dwelt; but he had
nothing to do with that. Such clash and uproar came from
the Bigwig family, at the unaccountable proceedings of which

race, he marvelled much. They set up the strangest statues, in iron, marble, bronze, and brass, before his door; and darkened his house with the legs and tails of uncouth images of horses. He wondered what it all meant, smiled in a rough good-humoured way he had, and kept at his hard work.

The Bigwig family (composed of all the stateliest people thereabouts, and all the noisiest) had undertaken to save him the trouble of thinking for himself, and to manage him and his affairs. "Why truly," said he, "I have little time upon my hands; and if you will be so good as to take care of me, in return for the money I pay over"—for the Bigwig family were not above his money—"I shall be relieved and much obliged, considering that you know best." Hence the drumming, trumpeting, and speech-making, and the ugly images of horses which he was expected to fall down and worship.

"I don't understand all this," said he, rubbing his furrowed brow confusedly. "But it *has* a meaning, maybe, if I could find it out."

"It means," returned the Bigwig family, suspecting some-thing of what he said, "honour and glory in the highest, to the highest merit."

"Oh!" said he. And he was glad to hear that.

But, when he looked among the images in iron, marble, bronze, and brass, he failed to find a rather meritorious countryman of his, once the son of a Warwickshire wool-dealer, or any single countryman whomsoever of that kind. He could find none of the men whose knowledge had rescued him and his children from terrific and disfiguring disease, whose boldness had raised his forefathers from the condition of serfs, whose wise fancy had opened a new and high existence to the humblest, whose skill had filled the working man's world with accumulated wonders. Whereas, he did find others whom he knew no good of, and even others whom he knew much ill of.

"Humph!" said he. "I don't quite understand it."

So, he went home, and sat down by his fireside to get it out of his mind.

Now, his fireside was a bare one, all hemmed in by blackened streets; but it was a precious place to him. The hands of his wife were hardened with toil, and she was old before her time; but she was dear to him. His children, stunted in their growth, bore traces of unwholesome nurture; but they had beauty in his sight. Above all other things, it was an earnest desire of this man's soul that his children should be taught. "If I am sometimes misled," said he, "for want of knowledge, at least let them know better, and avoid my mistakes. If it is hard to me to reap the harvest of pleasure and instruction that is stored in books, let it be easier to them."

But, the Digwig family broke out into violent family quarrels concerning what it was lawful to teach to this man's children. Some of the family insisted on such a thing being primary and indispensable above all other things; and others of the family insisted on such another thing being primary and indispensable above all other things; and the Digwig family, rent into factions, wrote pamphlets, held convocations, delivered charges, orations, and all varieties of discourses; impounded one another in courts Lay and courts Ecclesiastical; threw dirt, exchanged pummelings, and fell together by the ears in unintelligible animosity. Meanwhile, this man, in his short evening snatches at his fireside, saw the demon Ignorance arise there, and take his children to itself. He saw his daughter perverted into a heavy slatternly drudge; he saw his son go moping down the ways of low sensuality, to brutality and crime; he saw the dawning light of intelligence in the eyes of his babies so changing into cunning and suspicion, that he could have rather wished them idiots.

"I don't understand this any the better," said he; "but I think it cannot be right. Nay, by the clouded Heaven above me, I protest against this as my wrong!"

Becoming peaceable again (for his passion was usually

short-lived, and his nature kind), he looked about him on his
Sundays and holidays, and he saw how much monotony and
weariness there was, and thence how drunkenness arose with
all its train of ruin. Then he appealed to the Bigwig family,
and said, " We are a labouring people, and I have a glimmering suspicion in me that labouring people of whatever condition were made—by a higher intelligence than yours, as I
poorly understand it—to be in need of mental refreshment
and recreation. See what we fall into, when we rest without
it. Come! Amuse me harmlessly, show me something, give
me an escape ! "

But, here the Bigwig family fell into a state of uproar
absolutely deafening. When some few voices were faintly
heard, proposing to show him the wonders of the world, the
greatness of creation, the mighty changes of time, the work-
ings of nature and the beauties of art—to show him these
things, that is to say, at any period of his life when he could
look upon them—there arose among the Bigwigs such roaring
and raving, such pulpiting and petitioning, such maunder-
ing and memorialising, such name-calling and dirt-throwing,
such a shrill wind of parliamentary questioning and feeble
replying—where "I dare not" waited on "I would "—that
the poor fellow stood aghast, staring wildly around.

" Have I provoked all this," said he, with his hands to his
affrighted ears, "by what was meant to be an innocent
request, plainly arising out of my familiar experience, and
the common knowledge of all men who choose to open their
eyes? I don't understand, and I am not understood. What
is to come of such a state of things ! "

He was bending over his work, often asking himself the
question, when the news began to spread that a pestilence
had appeared among the labourers, and was slaying them by
thousands. Going forth to look about him, he soon found
this to be true. The dying and the dead were mingled in
the close and tainted houses among which his life was passed.
New poison was distilled into the always murky, always

sickening air. The robust and the weak, old age and infancy, the father and the mother, all were stricken down alike.

What means of flight had he? He remained there, where he was, and saw those who were dearest to him die. A kind preacher came to him, and would have said some prayers to soften his heart in his gloom, but he replied:

"O what avails it, missionary, to come to me, a man condemned to residence in this fœtid place, where every sense bestowed upon me for my delight becomes a torment, and where every minute of my numbered days is new mire added to the heap under which I lie oppressed! But, give me my first glimpse of Heaven, through a little of its light and air; give me pure water; help me to be clean; lighten this heavy atmosphere and heavy life, in which our spirits sink, and we become the indifferent and callous creatures you too often see us; gently and kindly take the bodies of those who die among us, out of the small room where we grow to be so familiar with the awful change that even ITS sanctity is lost to us; and, Teacher, then I will hear—none know better than you, how willingly—of Him whose thoughts were so much with the poor, and who had compassion for all human sorrow!"

He was at work again, solitary and sad, when his Master came and stood near to him dressed in black. He, also, had suffered heavily. His young wife, his beautiful and good young wife, was dead; so, too, his only child.

"Master, 'tis hard to bear—I know it—but be comforted. I would give you comfort, if I could."

The Master thanked him from his heart, but, said he, "O you labouring men! The calamity began among you. If you had but lived more healthily and decently, I should not be the widowed and bereft mourner that I am this day."

"Master," returned the other, shaking his head, "I have begun to understand a little that most calamities will come from us, as this one did, and that none will stop at our poor doors, until we are united with that great squabbling family yonder, to do the things that are right. We cannot live

healthily and decently, unless they who undertook to manage
us provide the means. We cannot be instructed unless they
will teach us; we cannot be rationally amused, unless they
will amuse us; we cannot but have some false gods of our
own, while they set up so many of theirs in all the public
places. The evil consequences of imperfect instruction, the
evil consequences of pernicious neglect, the evil consequences
of unnatural restraint and the denial of humanising enjoyments, will all come from us, and none of them will stop with
us. They will spread far and wide. They always do; they
always have done—just like the pestilence. I understand so
much, I think, at last."

But the Master said again, "O you labouring men! How
seldom do we ever hear of you, except in connection with
some trouble!"

"Master," he replied, "I am Nobody, and little likely to
be heard of (nor yet much wanted to be heard of, perhaps),
except when there *is* some trouble. But it never begins with
me, and it never can end with me. As sure as Death, it
comes down to me, and it goes up from me."

There was so much reason in what he said, that the Bigwig
family, getting wind of it, and being horribly frightened by
the late desolation, resolved to unite with him to do the
things that were right—at all events, so far as the said things
were associated with the direct prevention, humanly speaking,
of another pestilence. But, as their fear wore off, which it
soon began to do, they resumed their falling out among
themselves, and did nothing. Consequently the scourge
appeared again—low down as before—and spread avengingly
upward as before, and carried off vast numbers of the brawlers.
But not a man among them ever admitted, if in the least
degree he ever perceived, that he had anything to do with it.

So Nobody lived and died in the old, old, old way; and
this, in the main, is the whole of Nobody's story.

Had he no name, you ask? Perhaps it was Legion. It
matters little what his name was. Let us call him Legion.

If you were ever in the Belgian villages near the field of Waterloo, you will have seen, in some quiet little church, a monument erected by faithful companions in arms to the memory of Colonel A, Major B, Captains C, D and E, Lieutenants F and G, Ensigns H, I and J, seven non-commissioned officers, and one hundred and thirty rank and file, who fell in the discharge of their duty on the memorable day. The story of Nobody is the story of the rank and file of the earth. They bear their share of the battle; they have their part in the victory; they fall; they leave no name but in the mass. The march of the proudest of us, leads to the dusty way by which they go. O! Let us think of them this year at the Christmas fire, and not forget them when it is burnt out.

THE SEVEN POOR TRAVELLERS

[1854]

THE
SEVEN POOR TRAVELLERS.

In Three Chapters.

CHAPTER I.

IN THE OLD CITY OF ROCHESTER.

STRICTLY speaking, there were only six Poor Travellers; but, being a Traveller myself, though an idle one, and being withal as poor as I hope to be, I brought the number up to seven. This word of explanation is due at once, for what says the inscription over the quaint old door?

RICHARD WATTS, Esq.
by his Will, dated 22 Aug. 1579,
founded this Charity
for Six poor Travellers,
who not being Rogues, or Proctors,
May receive gratis for one Night,
Lodging, Entertainment,
and Fourpence each.

It was in the ancient little city of Rochester in Kent, of all the good days in the year upon a Christmas-eve, that I stood reading this inscription over the quaint old door in question. I had been wandering about the neighbouring Cathedral, and had seen the tomb of Richard Watts, with the effigy of worthy Master Richard starting out of it like a ship's figure-head; and I had felt that I could do no less, as I gave the Verger his fee, than inquire the way to Watts's Charity. The way being very short and very plain, I had come prosperously to the inscription and the quaint old door.

"Now," said I to myself, as I looked at the knocker, "I know I am not a Proctor; I wonder whether I am a Rogue!"

Upon the whole, though Conscience reproduced two or three pretty faces which might have had smaller attraction for a moral Goliath than they had had for me, who am but a Tom Thumb in that way, I came to the conclusion that I was not a Rogue. So, beginning to regard the establishment as in some sort my property, bequeathed to me and divers co-legatees, share and share alike, by the Worshipful Master Richard Watts, I stepped backward into the road to survey my inheritance.

I found it to be a clean white house, of a staid and venerable air, with the quaint old door already three times mentioned (an arched door), choice little long low lattice-windows, and a roof of three gables. The silent High-street of Rochester is full of gables, with old beams and timbers carved into strange faces. It is oddly garnished with a queer old clock that projects over the pavement out of a grave red-brick building, as if Time carried on business there, and hung out his sign. Sooth to say, he did an active stroke of work in Rochester, in the old days of the Romans, and the Saxons, and the Normans; and down to the times of King John, when the rugged castle—I will not undertake to say how many hundreds of years old then—was abandoned to the centuries of weather which have so defaced the dark apertures in its walls, that the ruin looks as if the rooks and daws had pecked its eyes out.

I was very well pleased, both with my property and its situation. While I was yet surveying it with growing content, I espied, at one of the upper lattices which stood open, a decent body, of a wholesome matronly appearance, whose eyes I caught inquiringly addressed to mine. They said so plainly, "Do you wish to see the house?" that I answered aloud, "Yes, if you please." And within a minute the old door opened, and I bent my head, and went down two steps into the entry.

"This," said the matronly presence, ushering me into a low room on the right, "is where the Travellers sit by the fire, and cook what bits of suppers they buy with their four-pences."

"O! Then they have no Entertainment?" said I. For the inscription over the outer door was still running in my head, and I was mentally repeating, in a kind of tune, "Lodging, entertainment, and fourpence each."

"They have a fire provided for 'em," returned the matron,—a mighty civil person, not, as I could make out, overpaid; "and these cooking utensils. And this what's painted on a board is the rules for their behaviour. They have their fourpences when they get their tickets from the steward over the way,—for I don't admit 'em myself, they must get their tickets first,—and sometimes one buys a rasher of bacon, and another a herring, and another a pound of potatoes, or what not. Sometimes two or three of 'em will club their fourpences together, and make a supper that way. But not much of anything is to be got for fourpence, at present, when provisions is so dear."

"True indeed," I remarked. I had been looking about the room, admiring its snug fireside at the upper end, its glimpse of the street through the low mullioned window, and its beams overhead. "It is very comfortable," said I.

"Ill-conwenient," observed the matronly presence.

I liked to hear her say so; for it showed a commendable anxiety to execute in no niggardly spirit the intentions of

Master Richard Watts. But the room was really so well adapted to its purpose that I protested, quite enthusiastically, against her disparagement.

"Nay, ma'am," said I, "I am sure it is warm in winter and cool in summer. It has a look of homely welcome and soothing rest. It has a remarkably cosy fireside, the very blink of which, gleaming out into the street upon a winter night, is enough to warm all Rochester's heart. And as to the convenience of the six Poor Travellers——"

"I don't mean them," returned the presence. "I speak of its being an ill-convenience to myself and my daughter, having no other room to sit in of a night."

This was true enough, but there was another quaint room of corresponding dimensions on the opposite side of the entry: so I stepped across to it, through the open doors of both rooms, and asked what this chamber was for.

"This," returned the presence, "is the Board Room. Where the gentlemen meet when they come here."

Let me see. I had counted from the street six upper windows besides these on the ground-story. Making a perplexed calculation in my mind, I rejoined, "Then the six Poor Travellers sleep upstairs?"

My new friend shook her head. "They sleep," she answered, "in two little outer galleries at the back, where their beds has always been, ever since the Charity was founded. It being so very ill-convenient to me as things is at present, the gentlemen are going to take off a bit of the back yard, and make a slip of a room for 'em there, to sit in before they go to bed."

"And then the six Poor Travellers," said I, "will be entirely out of the house?"

"Entirely out of the house," assented the presence, comfortably smoothing her hands. "Which is considered much better for all parties, and much more convenient."

I had been a little startled, in the Cathedral, by the emphasis with which the effigy of Master Richard Watts was bursting out of his tomb; but I began to think, now, that it might be expected to come across the High-street some stormy night, and make a disturbance here.

Howbeit, I kept my thoughts to myself, and accompanied the presence to the little galleries at the back. I found them on a tiny scale, like the galleries in old inn-yards; and they were very clean. While I was looking at them, the matron gave me to understand that the prescribed number of Poor Travellers were forthcoming every night from year's end to year's end; and that the beds were always occupied. My questions upon this, and her replies, brought us back to the Board Room so essential to the dignity of "the gentlemen," where she showed me the printed accounts of the Charity hanging up by the window. From them I gathered that the greater part of the property bequeathed by the Worshipful Master Richard Watts for the maintenance of this foundation was, at the period of his death, mere marshland; but that, in course of time, it had been reclaimed and built upon, and was very considerably increased in value. I found, too, that about a thirtieth part of the annual revenue was now expended on the purposes commemorated in the inscription over the door; the rest being handsomely laid out in Chancery, law expenses, collectorship, receivership, poundage, and other appendages of management, highly complimentary to the importance of the six Poor Travellers. In short, I made the not entirely new discovery that it may be said of an establishment like this, in dear old England, as of the fat oyster in the American story, that it takes a good many men to swallow it whole.

"And pray, ma'am," said I, sensible that the blankness of my face began to brighten as the thought occurred to me, "could one see these Travellers?"

"Well!" she returned dubiously, "no!"

"Not to-night, for instance!" said I.

"Well!" she returned more positively, "no. Nobody ever asked to see them, and nobody ever did see them."

As I am not easily baulked in a design when I am set upon it, I urged to the good lady that this was Christmas-eve; that Christmas comes but once a year,—which is unhappily too true, for when it begins to stay with us the whole year round we shall make this earth a very different place; that I was possessed by the desire to treat the Travellers to a supper and a temperate glass of hot Wassail; that the voice of Fame had been heard in that land, declaring my ability to make hot Wassail; that if I were permitted to hold the feast, I should be found conformable to reason, sobriety, and good hours; in a word, that I could be merry and wise myself, and had been even known at a pinch to keep others so, although I was decorated with no badge or medal, and was not a Brother, Orator, Apostle, Saint, or Prophet of any denomination whatever. In the end I prevailed, to my great joy. It was settled that at nine o'clock that night a Turkey and a piece of Roast Beef should smoke upon the board; and that I, faint and unworthy minister for once of Master Richard Watts, should preside as the Christmas-supper host of the six Poor Travellers.

I went back to my inn to give the necessary directions for the Turkey and Roast Beef, and, during the remainder of the day, could settle to nothing for thinking of the Poor Travellers. When the wind blew hard against the windows, —it was a cold day, with dark gusts of sleet alternating with periods of wild brightness, as if the year were dying fitfully,—I pictured them advancing towards their resting-place along various cold roads, and felt delighted to think how little they foresaw the supper that awaited them. I painted their portraits in my mind, and indulged in little heightening touches. I made them footsore; I made them weary; I made them carry packs and bundles; I made them stop by finger-posts and milestones, leaning on their bent sticks, and looking wistfully at what was written there; I made them lose their way; and filled their five wits with apprehensions of lying out all night, and being frozen to death. I took up my hat, and went out, climbed to the top of the Old Castle, and looked over the windy hills that slope down to the Medway, almost believing that I could descry some of my Travellers in the distance. After it fell dark, and the Cathedral bell was heard in the invisible steeple— quite a bower of frosty rime when I had last seen it— striking five, six, seven, I became so full of my Travellers that I could eat no dinner, and felt constrained to watch them still in the red coals of my fire. They were all arrived by this time, I thought, had got their tickets, and were gone in.—There my pleasure was dashed by the reflection that probably some Travellers had come too late and were shut out.

After the Cathedral bell had struck eight, I could smell a delicious savour of Turkey and Roast Beef rising to the window of my adjoining bedroom, which looked down into the inn-yard just where the lights of the kitchen reddened a massive fragment of the Castle Wall. It was high time to make the Wassail now; therefore I had up the materials (which, together with their proportions and combinations, I must decline to impart, as the only secret of my own I was ever known to keep), and made a glorious jorum. Not in a bowl; for a bowl anywhere but on a shelf is a low superstition, fraught with cooling and slopping; but in a brown earthenware pitcher, tenderly suffocated, when full, with a coarse cloth. It being now upon the stroke of nine, I set out for Watts's Charity, carrying my brown beauty in my arms. I would trust Ben, the waiter, with untold gold; but there are strings in the human heart which must never be sounded by another, and drinks that I make myself are those strings in mine.

The Travellers were all assembled, the cloth was laid, and Ben had brought a great billet of wood, and had laid it artfully on the top of the fire, so that a touch or two of the poker after supper should make a roaring blaze. Having deposited my brown beauty in a red nook of the hearth, inside the fender, where she soon began to sing like an ethereal cricket, diffusing at the same time odours as of ripe vineyards, spice forests, and orange groves,—I say, having stationed my beauty in a place of security and improvement, I introduced myself to my guests by shaking hands all round, and giving them a hearty welcome.

I found the party to be thus composed. Firstly, myself. Secondly, a very decent man indeed, with his right arm in a sling, who had a certain clean agreeable smell of wood about him, from which I judged him to have something to do with shipbuilding. Thirdly, a little sailor-boy, a mere child, with a profusion of rich dark brown hair, and deep womanly-looking eyes. Fourthly, a shabby-genteel personage in a threadbare black suit, and apparently in very bad circum-stances, with a dry suspicious look ; the absent buttons on his waistcoat cked out with red tape ; and a bundle of extraordinarily tattered papers sticking out of an inner breast-pocket. Fifthly, a foreigner by birth, but an English-man in speech, who carried his pipe in the band of his hat, and lost no time in telling me, in an easy, simple, engaging way, that he was a watchmaker from Geneva, and travelled all about the Continent, mostly on foot, working as a journeyman, and seeing new countries,—possibly (I thought) also smuggling a watch or so, now and then. Sixthly, a little widow, who had been very pretty and was still very young, but whose beauty had been wrecked in some great misfortune, and whose manner was remarkably timid, scared, and solitary. Seventhly and lastly, a Traveller of a kind familiar to my boyhood, but now almost obsolete,—a Book-Pedler, who had a quantity of Pamphlets and Numbers with him, and who presently boasted that he could repeat more verses in an evening than he could sell in a twelvemonth.

All these I have mentioned in the order in which they sat at table. I presided, and the matronly presence faced me. We were not long in taking our places, for the supper had arrived with me, in the following procession :

Myself with the pitcher.
Ben with Beer.
Inattentive Boy with hot plates.   Inattentive Boy with hot
plates.

THE TURKEY.

Female carrying sauces to be heated on the spot.

THE BEEF.

Man with Tray on his head, containing Vegetables and
Sundries.
Volunteer Hostler from Hotel, grinning,
And rendering no assistance.

As we passed along the High-street, comet-like, we left a
long tail of fragrance behind us which caused the public
to stop, sniffing in wonder. We had previously left at the
corner of the inn-yard a wall-eyed young man connected with
the Fly department, and well accustomed to the sound of a
railway whistle which Ben always carries in his pocket, whose
instructions were, so soon as he should hear the whistle
blown, to dash into the kitchen, seize the hot plum-pudding
and mince-pies, and speed with them to Watts's Charity,
where they would be received (he was further instructed) by
the sauce-female, who would be provided with brandy in a
blue state of combustion.

All these arrangements were executed in the most exact
and punctual manner. I never saw a finer turkey, finer beef,
or greater prodigality of sauce and gravy; and my Travellers
did wonderful justice to everything set before them. It
made my heart rejoice to observe how their wind and frost
hardened faces softened in the clatter of plates and knives
and forks, and mellowed in the fire and supper heat. While
their hats and caps and wrappers, hanging up, a few small
bundles on the ground in a corner, and in another corner
three or four old walking-sticks, worn down at the end to
mere fringe, linked this snug interior with the bleak outside
in a golden chain.

When supper was done, and my brown beauty had been elevated on the table, there was a general requisition to me to "take the corner;" which suggested to me comfortably enough how much my friends here made of a fire,—for when had *I* ever thought so highly of the corner, since the days when I connected it with Jack Horner? However, as I declined, Ben, whose touch on all convivial instruments is perfect, drew the table apart, and instructing my Travellers to open right and left on either side of me, and form round the fire, closed up the centre with myself and my chair, and preserved the order we had kept at table. He had already, in a tranquil manner, boxed the ears of the inattentive boys until they had been by imperceptible degrees boxed out of the room; and he now rapidly skirmished the sauce-female into the High-street, disappeared, and softly closed the door.

This was the time for bringing the poker to bear on the billet of wood. I tapped it three times, like an enchanted talisman, and a brilliant host of merry-makers burst out of it, and sported off by the chimney,—rushing up the middle in a fiery country dance, and never coming down again. Meanwhile, by their sparkling light, which threw our lamp into the shade, I filled the glasses, and gave my Travellers, CHRISTMAS!—CHRISTMAS-EVE, my friends, when the shepherds, who were Poor Travellers, too, in their way, heard the Angels sing, "On earth, peace. Good-will towards men!"

I don't know who was the first among us to think that we ought to take hands as we sat, in deference to the toast, or whether any one of us anticipated the others, but at any rate we all did it. We then drank to the memory of the good Master Richard Watts. And I wish his Ghost may never have had worse usage under that roof than it had from us.

It was the witching time for Story-telling. "Our whole life, Travellers," said I, "is a story more or less intelligible, —generally less; but we shall read it by a clearer light when it is ended. I, for one, am so divided this night between

fact and fiction, that I scarce know which is which. Shall I
beguile the time by telling you a story as we sit here?"

They all answered, yes. I had little to tell them, but I
was bound by my own proposal. Therefore, after looking for
awhile at the spiral column of smoke wreathing up from my
brown beauty, through which I could have almost sworn I
saw the effigy of Master Richard Watts less startled than
usual, I fired away.

CHAPTER II.

IN the year one thousand seven hundred and ninety-nine, a relative of mine came limping down, on foot, to this town of Chatham. I call it this town, because if anybody present knows to a nicety where Rochester ends and Chatham begins, it is more than I do. He was a poor traveller, with not a farthing in his pocket. He sat by the fire in this very room, and he slept one night in a bed that will be occupied to-night by some one here.

My relative came down to Chatham to enlist in a cavalry regiment, if a cavalry regiment would have him; if not, to take King George's shilling from any corporal or sergeant who would put a bunch of ribbons in his hat. His object was to get shot; but he thought he might as well ride to death as be at the trouble of walking.

My relative's Christian name was Richard, but he was better known as Dick. He dropped his own surname on the road down, and took up that of Doubledick. He was passed as Richard Doubledick; age, twenty-two; height, five foot ten; native place, Exmouth, which he had never been near in his life. There was no cavalry in Chatham when he limped over the bridge here with half a shoe to his dusty feet, so he enlisted into a regiment of the line, and was glad to get drunk and forget all about it.

You are to know that this relative of mine had gone wrong,

and run wild. His heart was in the right place, but it was
sealed up. He had been betrothed to a good and beautiful
girl, whom he had loved better than she—or perhaps even
he—believed; but in an evil hour he had given her cause to
say to him solemnly, "Richard, I will never marry another
man. I will live single for your sake, but Mary Marshall's
lips"—her name was Mary Marshall—"never address another
word to you on earth. Go, Richard! Heaven forgive you!"
This finished him. This brought him down to Chatham.
This made him Private Richard Doubledick, with a determination to be shot.

There was not a more dissipated and reckless soldier in
Chatham barracks, in the year one thousand seven hundred
and ninety-nine, than Private Richard Doubledick. He
associated with the dregs of every regiment; he was as
seldom sober as he could be, and was constantly under
punishment. It became clear to the whole barracks that
Private Richard Doubledick would very soon be flogged.

Now the Captain of Richard Doubledick's company was a
young gentleman not above five years his senior, whose eyes
had an expression in them which affected Private Richard
Doubledick in a very remarkable way. They were bright,
handsome, dark eyes,—what are called laughing eyes generally,
and, when serious, rather steady than severe,—but they were
the only eyes now left in his narrowed world that Private
Richard Doubledick could not stand. Unabashed by evil
report and punishment, defiant of everything else and
everybody else, he had but to know that those eyes looked
at him for a moment, and he felt ashamed. He could not
so much as salute Captain Taunton in the street like any
other officer. He was reproached and confused,—troubled
by the mere possibility of the captain's looking at him. In
his worst moments, he would rather turn back, and go any
distance out of his way, than encounter those two handsome,
dark, bright eyes.

One day, when Private Richard Doubledick came out of

the Black hole, where he had been passing the last eight-and-forty hours, and in which retreat he spent a good deal of his time, he was ordered to betake himself to Captain Taunton's quarters. In the stale and squalid state of a man just out of the Black hole, he had less fancy than ever for being seen by the Captain; but he was not so mad yet as to disobey orders, and consequently went up to the terrace overlooking the parade-ground, where the officers' quarters were; twisting and breaking in his hands, as he went along, a bit of the straw that had formed the decorative furniture of the Black hole.

"Come in!" cried the Captain, when he knocked with his knuckles at the door. Private Richard Doubledick pulled off his cap, took a stride forward, and felt very conscious that he stood in the light of the dark, bright eyes.

There was a silent pause. Private Richard Doubledick had put the straw in his mouth, and was gradually doubling it up into his windpipe and choking himself.

"Doubledick," said the Captain, "do you know where you are going to?"

"To the Devil, sir?" faltered Doubledick.

"Yes," returned the Captain. "And very fast."

Private Richard Doubledick turned the straw of the Black hole in his mouth, and made a miserable salute of acquiescence.

"Doubledick," said the Captain, "since I entered his Majesty's service, a boy of seventeen, I have been pained to see many men of promise going that road; but I have never been so pained to see a man determined to make the shameful journey as I have been, ever since you joined the regiment, to see you."

Private Richard Doubledick began to find a film stealing over the floor at which he looked; also to find the legs of the Captain's breakfast-table turning crooked, as if he saw them through water.

"I am only a common soldier, sir," said he. "It signifies very little what such a poor brute comes to."

"You are a man," returned the Captain, with grave indignation, "of education and superior advantages; and if you say that, meaning what you say, you have sunk lower than I had believed. How low that must be, I leave you to consider, knowing what I know of your disgrace, and seeing what I see."

"I hope to get shot soon, sir," said Private Richard Doubledick; "and then the regiment and the world together will be rid of me."

The legs of the table were becoming very crooked. Doubledick, looking up to steady his vision, met the eyes that had so strong an influence over him. He put his hand before his own eyes, and the breast of his disgrace-jacket swelled as if it would fly asunder.

"I would rather," said the young Captain, "see this in you, Doubledick, than I would see five thousand guineas counted out upon this table for a gift to my good mother. Have you a mother?"

"I am thankful to say she is dead, sir."

"If your praises," returned the Captain, "were sounded from mouth to mouth through the whole regiment, through the whole army, through the whole country, you would wish she had lived to say, with pride and joy, 'He is my son!'"

"Spare me, sir," said Doubledick. "She would never have heard any good of me. She would never have had any pride and joy in owning herself my mother. Love and compassion she might have had, and would have always had, I know; but not—Spare me, sir! I am a broken wretch, quite at your mercy!" And he turned his face to the wall, and stretched out his imploring hand.

"My friend——" began the Captain.

"God bless you, sir!" sobbed Private Richard Doubledick.

"You are at the crisis of your fate. Hold your course unchanged a little longer, and you know what must happen. I know even better than you can imagine, that, after that has happened, you are lost. No man who could shed those tears could bear those marks."

"I fully believe it, sir," in a low, shivering voice said Private Richard Doubledick.

"But a man in any station can do his duty," said the young Captain, "and, in doing it, can earn his own respect, even if his case should be so very unfortunate and so very rare that he can earn no other man's. A common soldier, poor brute though you called him just now, has this advantage in the stormy times we live in, that he always does his duty before a host of sympathising witnesses. Do you doubt that he may so do it as to be extolled through a whole regiment, through a whole army, through a whole country? Turn while you may yet retrieve the past, and try."

"I will! I ask for only one witness, sir," cried Richard, with a bursting heart.

"I understand you. I will be a watchful and a faithful one."

I have heard from Private Richard Doubledick's own lips, that he dropped down upon his knee, kissed that officer's hand, arose, and went out of the light of the dark, bright eyes, an altered man.

In that year, one thousand seven hundred and ninety-nine, the French were in Egypt, in Italy, in Germany, where not? Napoleon Bonaparte had likewise begun to stir against us in India, and most men could read the signs of the great troubles that were coming on. In the very next year, when we formed an alliance with Austria against him, Captain Taunton's regiment was on service in India. And there was not a finer non-commissioned officer in it,—no, nor in the whole line—than Corporal Richard Doubledick.

In eighteen hundred and one, the Indian army were on the coast of Egypt. Next year was the year of the proclamation of the short peace, and they were recalled. It had then become well known to thousands of men, that wherever Captain Taunton, with the dark, bright eyes, led, there, close to him, ever at his side, firm as a rock, true as the sun, and brave as Mars, would be certain to be found, while life beat in their hearts, that famous soldier, Sergeant Richard Doubledick.

Eighteen hundred and five, besides being the great year of Trafalgar, was a year of hard fighting in India. That year saw such wonders done by a Sergeant-Major, who cut his way single-handed through a solid mass of men, recovered the colours of his regiment, which had been seized from the hand of a poor boy shot through the heart, and rescued his wounded Captain, who was down, and in a very jungle of horses' hoofs and sabres,—saw such wonders done, I say, by this brave Sergeant-Major, that he was specially made the bearer of the colours he had won; and Ensign Richard Doubledick had risen from the ranks.

Surely cut up in every battle, but always reinforced by the bravest of men,—for the fame of following the old colours, shot through and through, which Ensign Richard Doubledick had saved, inspired all breasts,—this regiment fought its way through the Peninsular war, up to the investment of Badajos in eighteen hundred and twelve. Again and again it had been cheered through the British ranks until the tears had sprung into men's eyes at the mere hearing of the mighty British voice, so exultant in their valour; and there was not a drummer-boy but knew the legend, that wherever the two friends, Major Taunton, with the dark, bright eyes, and Ensign Richard Doubledick, who was devoted to him, were seen to go, there the boldest spirits in the English army became wild to follow.

One day, at Badajos,—not in the great storming, but in repelling a hot sally of the besieged upon our men at work in the trenches, who had given way,—the two officers found themselves hurrying forward, face to face, against a party of French infantry, who made a stand. There was an officer at their head, encouraging his men,—a courageous, handsome, gallant officer of five-and-thirty, whom Doubledick saw hurriedly, almost momentarily, but saw well. He particularly noticed this officer waving his sword, and rallying his men with au eager and excited cry, when they fired in obedience to his gesture, and Major Taunton dropped.

It was over in ten minutes more, and Doubledick returned to the spot where he had laid the best friend man ever had on a coat spread upon the wet clay. Major Taunton's uniform was opened at the breast, and on his shirt were three little spots of blood.

"Dear Doubledick," said he, "I am dying."

"For the love of Heaven, no!" exclaimed the other, kneeling down beside him, and passing his arm round his neck to raise his head. "Taunton! My preserver, my guardian angel, my witness! Dearest, truest, kindest of human beings! Taunton! For God's sake!"

The bright, dark eyes—so very, very dark now, in the pale face—smiled upon him; and the hand he had kissed thirteen years ago laid itself fondly on his breast.

"Write to my mother. You will see Home again. Tell her how we became friends. It will comfort her, as it comforts me."

He spoke no more, but faintly signed for a moment towards his hair as it fluttered in the wind. The Ensign understood him. He smiled again when he saw that, and, gently turning his face over on the supporting arm as if for rest, died, with his hand upon the breast in which he had revived a soul.

No dry eye looked on Ensign Richard Doubledick that melancholy day. He buried his friend on the field, and became a lone, bereaved man. Beyond his duty he appeared to have but two remaining cares in life,—one, to preserve the little packet of hair he was to give to Taunton's mother; the other, to encounter that French officer who had rallied the men under whose fire Taunton fell. A new legend now began to circulate among our troops; and it was, that when he and the French officer came face to face once more, there would be weeping in France.

The war went on—and through it went the exact picture of the French officer on the one side, and the bodily reality upon the other—until the Battle of Toulouse was fought. In the returns sent home appeared these words: "Severely wounded, but not dangerously, Lieutenant Richard Doubledick."

At Midsummer-time, in the year eighteen hundred and fourteen, Lieutenant Richard Doubledick, now a browned soldier, seven-and-thirty years of age, came home to England invalided. He brought the hair with him, near his heart. Many a French officer had he seen since that day; many a dreadful night, in searching with men and lanterns for his wounded, had he relieved French officers lying disabled; but the mental picture and the reality had never come together.

Though he was weak and suffered pain, he lost not an hour in getting down to Frome in Somersetshire, where Taunton's mother lived. In the sweet, compassionate words that naturally present themselves to the mind to-night, "he was the only son of his mother, and she was a widow."

It was a Sunday evening, and the lady sat at her quiet garden-window, reading the Bible; reading to herself, in a trembling voice, that very passage in it, as I have heard him tell. He heard the words: "Young man, I say unto thee, arise!"

He had to pass the window; and the bright, dark eyes of his debased time seemed to look at him. Her heart told her who he was; she came to the door quickly, and fell upon his neck.

"He saved me from ruin, made me a human creature, won me from infamy and shame. O, God for ever bless him! As He will, He will!"

"He will!" the lady answered. "I know he is in Heaven!" Then she piteously cried, "But O, my darling boy, my darling boy!"

Never from the hour when Private Richard Doubledick

enlisted at Chatham had the Private, Corporal, Sergeant, Sergeant-Major, Ensign, or Lieutenant breathed his right name, or the name of Mary Marshall, or a word of the story of his life, into any ear except his reclaimer's. That previous scene in his existence was closed. He had firmly resolved that his expiation should be to live unknown; to disturb no more the peace that had long grown over his old offences; to let it be revealed, when he was dead, that he had striven and suffered, and had never forgotten; and then, if they could forgive him and believe him—well, it would be time enough—time enough!

But that night, remembering the words he had cherished for two years, "Tell her how we became friends. It will comfort her, as it comforts me," he related everything. It gradually seemed to him as if in his maturity he had recovered a mother; it gradually seemed to her as if in her bereavement she had found a son. During his stay in England, the quiet garden into which he had slowly and painfully crept, a stranger, became the boundary of his home; when he was able to rejoin his regiment in the spring, he left the garden, thinking was this indeed the first time he had ever turned his face towards the old colours with a woman's blessing!

He followed them—so ragged, so scarred and pierced now, that they would scarcely hold together—to Quatre Bras and Ligny. He stood beside them, in an awful stillness of many men, shadowy through the mist and drizzle of a wet June forenoon, on the field of Waterloo. And down to that hour the picture in his mind of the French officer had never been compared with the reality.

The famous regiment was in action early in the battle, and received its first check in many an eventful year, when he was seen to fall. But it swept on to avenge him, and left behind it no such creature in the world of consciousness as Lieutenant Richard Doubledick.

Through pits of mire, and pools of rain; along deep

ditches, once roads, that were pounded and ploughed to
pieces by artillery, heavy waggons, tramp of men and horses,
and the struggle of every wheeled thing that could carry
wounded soldiers; jolted among the dying and the dead, so
disfigured by blood and mud as to be hardly recognisable
for humanity; undisturbed by the moaning of men and the
shrieking of horses, which, newly taken from the peaceful
pursuits of life, could not endure the sight of the stragglers
lying by the wayside, never to resume their toilsome journey;
dead, as to any sentient life that was in it, and yet alive,—
the form that had been Lieutenant Richard Doubledick, with
whose praises England rang, was conveyed to Brussels.
There it was tenderly laid down in hospital; and there it
lay, week after week, through the long bright summer
days, until the harvest, spared by war, had ripened and was
gathered in.

Over and over again the sun rose and set upon the crowded
city; over and over again the moonlight nights were quiet
on the plains of Waterloo: and all that time was a blank to
what had been Lieutenant Richard Doubledick. Rejoicing
troops marched into Brussels, and marched out; brothers and
fathers, sisters, mothers, and wives, came thronging thither,
drew their lots of joy or agony, and departed; so many times
a day the bells rang; so many times the shadows of the great
buildings changed; so many lights sprang up at dusk; so
many feet passed here and there upon the pavements; so
many hours of sleep and cooler air of night succeeded:
indifferent to all, a marble face lay on a bed, like the face
of a recumbent statue on the tomb of Lieutenant Richard
Doubledick.

Slowly labouring, at last, through a long heavy dream of
confused time and place, presenting faint glimpses of army
surgeons whom he knew, and of faces that had been familiar
to his youth,—dearest and kindest among them, Mary
Marshall's, with a solicitude upon it more like reality than
anything he could discern,—Lieutenant Richard Doubledick

came back to life. To the beautiful life of a calm autumn evening sunset, to the peaceful life of a fresh quiet room with a large window standing open; a balcony beyond, in which were moving leaves and sweet-smelling flowers; beyond, again, the clear sky, with the sun full in his sight, pouring its golden radiance on his bed.

It was so tranquil and so lovely that he thought he had passed into another world. And he said in a faint voice, "'Taunton, are you near me?"

A face bent over him. Not his, his mother's.

"I came to nurse you. We have nursed you many weeks. You were moved here long ago. Do you remember nothing?"

"Nothing."

The lady kissed his cheek, and held his hand, soothing him.

"Where is the regiment? What has happened? Let me call you mother. What has happened, mother?"

"A great victory, dear. The war is over, and the regiment was the bravest in the field."

His eyes kindled, his lips trembled, he sobbed, and the tears ran down his face. He was very weak, too weak to move his hand.

"Was it dark just now?" he asked presently.

"No."

"It was only dark to me? Something passed away, like a black shadow. But as it went, and the sun—O the blessed sun, how beautiful it is!—touched my face, I thought I saw a light white cloud pass out at the door. Was there nothing that went out?"

She shook her head, and in a little while he fell asleep, she still holding his hand, and soothing him.

From that time, he recovered. Slowly, for he had been desperately wounded in the head, and had been shot in the body, but making some little advance every day. When he had gained sufficient strength to converse as he lay in bed, he soon began to remark that Mrs. Taunton always brought him

back to his own history. Then he recalled his preserver's
dying words, and thought, "It comforts her."

One day he awoke out of a sleep, refreshed, and asked her
to read to him. But the curtain of the bed, softening the
light, which she always drew back when he awoke, that she
might see him from her table at the bedside where she sat
at work, was held undrawn; and a woman's voice spoke,
which was not hers.

"Can you bear to see a stranger?" it said softly. "Will
you like to see a stranger?"

"Stranger!" he repeated. The voice awoke old memories,
before the days of Private Richard Doubledick.

"A stranger now, but not a stranger once," it said in tones
that thrilled him. "Richard, dear Richard, lost through so
many years, my name——"

He cried out her name, "Mary," and she held him in her
arms, and his head lay on her bosom.

"I am not breaking a rash vow, Richard. These are not
Mary Marshall's lips that speak. I have another name."

She was married.

"I have another name, Richard. Did you ever hear it?"

"Never!"

He looked into her face, so pensively beautiful, and
wondered at the smile upon it through her tears.

"Think again, Richard. Are you sure you never heard
my altered name?"

"Never!"

"Don't move your head to look at me, dear Richard.
Let it lie here, while I tell my story. I loved a generous,
noble man; loved him with my whole heart; loved him for
years and years; loved him faithfully, devotedly; loved him
with no hope of return; loved him, knowing nothing of his
highest qualities—not even knowing that he was alive. He
was a brave soldier. He was honoured and beloved by
thousands of thousands, when the mother of his dear friend
found me, and showed me that in all his triumphs he had

never forgotten me. He was wounded in a great battle.
He was brought, dying, here, into Brussels. I came to watch
and tend him, as I would have joyfully gone, with such a
purpose, to the dreariest ends of the earth. When he knew
no one else, he knew me. When he suffered most, he bore
his sufferings barely murmuring, content to rest his head
where yours rests now. When he lay at the point of death,
he married me, that he might call me Wife before he died.
And the name, my dear love, that I took on that forgotten
night——"

"I know it now!" he sobbed. "The shadowy remembrance
strengthens. It is come back. I thank Heaven that my
mind is quite restored! My Mary, kiss me; lull this weary
head to rest, or I shall die of gratitude. His parting words
were fulfilled. I see Home again!"

Well! They were happy. It was a long recovery, but
they were happy through it all. The snow had melted
on the ground, and the birds were singing in the leafless
thickets of the early spring, when those three were first
able to ride out together, and when people flocked about the
open carriage to cheer and congratulate Captain Richard
Doubledick.

But even then it became necessary for the Captain, instead
of returning to England, to complete his recovery in the
climate of Southern France. They found a spot upon the
Rhône, within a ride of the old town of Avignon, and within
view of its broken bridge, which was all they could desire;
they lived there, together, six months; then returned to
England. Mrs. Taunton, growing old after three years—
though not so old as that her bright, dark eyes were dimmed
—and remembering that her strength had been benefited
by the change, resolved to go back for a year to those
parts. So she went with a faithful servant, who had often
carried her son in his arms; and she was to be rejoined
and escorted home, at the year's end, by Captain Richard
Doubledick.

She wrote regularly to her children (as she called them
now), and they to her. She went to the neighbourhood of
Aix; and there, in their own château near the farmer's house
she rented, she grew into intimacy with a family belonging
to that part of France. The intimacy began in her often
meeting among the vineyards a pretty child, a girl with a
most compassionate heart, who was never tired of listening
to the solitary English lady's stories of her poor son and
the cruel wars. The family were as gentle as the child, and
at length she came to know them so well that she accepted
their invitation to pass the last month of her residence
abroad under their roof. All this intelligence she wrote
home, piecemeal as it came about, from time to time; and
at last enclosed a polite note, from the head of the château,
soliciting, on the occasion of his approaching mission to
that neighbourhood, the honour of the company of cet
homme si justement célèbre, Monsieur le Capitaine Richard
Doubledick.

Captain Doubledick, now a hardy, handsome man in the
full vigour of life, broader across the chest and shoulders
than he had ever been before, despatched a courteous reply,
and followed it in person. Travelling through all that
extent of country after three years of Peace, he blessed the
better days on which the world had fallen. The corn was
golden, not drenched in unnatural red; was bound in sheaves
for food, not trodden underfoot by men in mortal fight.
The smoke rose up from peaceful hearths, not blazing ruins.
The carts were laden with the fair fruits of the earth, not
with wounds and death. To him who had so often seen the
terrible reverse, these things were beautiful indeed; and they
brought him in a softened spirit to the old château near Aix
upon a deep blue evening.

It was a large château of the genuine old ghostly kind,
with round towers, and extinguishers, and a high leaden roof,
and more windows than Aladdin's Palace. The lattice blinds
were all thrown open after the heat of the day, and there

were glimpses of rambling walls and corridors within. Then
there were immense out-buildings fallen into partial decay,
masses of dark trees, terrace-gardens, balustrades; tanks of
water, too weak to play and too dirty to work; statues,
weeds, and thickets of iron railing that seemed to have overgrown themselves like the shrubberies, and to have branched
out in all manner of wild shapes. The entrance doors stood
open, as doors often do in that country when the heat of
the day is past; and the Captain saw no bell or knocker,
and walked in.

He walked into a lofty stone hall, refreshingly cool and
gloomy after the glare of a Southern day's travel. Extending
along the four sides of this hall was a gallery, leading to
suites of rooms; and it was lighted from the top. Still no
bell was to be seen.

"Faith," said the Captain halting, ashamed of the clanking
of his boots, "this is a ghostly beginning!"

He started back, and felt his face turn white. In the
gallery, looking down at him, stood the French officer—the
officer whose picture he had carried in his mind so long
and so far. Compared with the original, at last—in every
lineament how like it was!

He moved, and disappeared, and Captain Richard Doubledick heard his steps coming quickly down into the hall. He
entered through an archway. There was a bright, sudden
look upon his face, much such a look as it had worn in that
fatal moment.

Monsieur le Capitaine Richard Doubledick? Enchanted
to receive him! A thousand apologies! The servants were
all out in the air. There was a little fête among them in
the garden. In effect, it was the fête day of my daughter,
the little cherished and protected of Madame Taunton.

He was so gracious and so frank that Monsieur le Capitaine
Richard Doubledick could not withhold his hand. "It is
the hand of a brave Englishman," said the French officer,
retaining it while he spoke. "I could respect a brave

Englishman, even as my foe, how much more as my friend!
I also am a soldier."

"He has not remembered me, as I have remembered him;
he did not take such note of my face, that day, as I took
of his," thought Captain Richard Doubledick. "How shall
I tell him?"

The French officer conducted his guest into a garden and
presented him to his wife, an engaging and beautiful woman,
sitting with Mrs. Taunton in a whimsical old-fashioned
pavilion. His daughter, her fair young face beaming with
joy, came running to embrace him; and there was a boy-
baby to tumble down among the orange trees on the broad
steps, in making for his father's legs. A multitude of
children visitors were dancing to sprightly music; and all
the servants and peasants about the château were dancing
too. It was a scene of innocent happiness that might have
been invented for the climax of the scenes of peace which
had soothed the Captain's journey.

He looked on, greatly troubled in his mind, until a resounding bell rang, and the French officer begged to show him his
rooms. They went up-stairs into the gallery from which
the officer had looked down; and Monsieur le Capitaine
Richard Doubledick was cordially welcomed to a grand outer
chamber, and a smaller one within, all clocks and draperies,
and hearths, and brazen dogs, and tiles, and cool devices,
and elegance, and vastness.

"You were at Waterloo," said the French officer.

"I was," said Captain Richard Doubledick. "And at
Badajos."

Left alone with the sound of his own stern voice in his
ears, he sat down to consider, What shall I do, and how
shall I tell him? At that time, unhappily, many deplorable
duels had been fought between English and French officers,
arising out of the recent war; and these duels, and how to
avoid this officer's hospitality, were the uppermost thoughts
in Captain Richard Doubledick's mind.

He was thinking, and letting the time run out in which
he should have dressed for dinner, when Mrs. Taunton spoke
to him outside the door, asking if he could give her the
letter he had brought from Mary. "His mother, above all,"
the Captain thought. "How shall I tell *her*?"

"You will form a friendship with your host, I hope," said
Mrs. Taunton, whom he hurriedly admitted, "that will last
for life. He is so true-hearted and so generous, Richard, that
you can hardly fail to esteem one another. If He had been
spared," she kissed (not without tears) the locket in which
she wore his hair, "he would have appreciated him with his
own magnanimity, and would have been truly happy that the
evil days were past which made such a man his enemy."

She left the room; and the Captain walked, first to one
window, whence he could see the dancing in the garden, then
to another window, whence he could see the smiling prospect
and the peaceful vineyards.

"Spirit of my departed friend," said he, "is it through
thee these better thoughts are rising in my mind? Is it
thou who hast shown me, all the way I have been drawn to
meet this man, the blessings of the altered time? Is it thou
who hast sent thy stricken mother to me, to stay my angry
hand? Is it from thee the whisper comes, that this man
did his duty as thou didst,—and as I did, through thy
guidance, which has wholly saved me here on earth,—and
that he did no more?"

He sat down, with his head buried in his hands, and, when
he rose up, made the second strong resolution of his life,—
that neither to the French officer, nor to the mother of his
departed friend, nor to any soul, while either of the two was
living, would he breathe what only he knew. And when he
touched that French officer's glass with his own, that day at
dinner, he secretly forgave him in the name of the Divine
Forgiver of injuries.

Here I ended my story as the first Poor Traveller. But, if

I had told it now, I could have added that the time has since come when the son of Major Richard Doubledick, and the son of that French officer, friends as their fathers were before them, fought side by side in one cause, with their respective nations, like long-divided brothers whom the better times have brought together, fast united.

CHAPTER III.

My story being finished, and the Wassail too, we broke up as the Cathedral bell struck 'Twelve. I did not take leave of my travellers that night; for it had come into my head to reappear, in conjunction with some hot coffee, at seven in the morning.

As I passed along the High-street, I heard the Waits at a distance, and struck off to find them. They were playing near one of the old gates of the City, at the corner of a wonderfully quaint row of red-brick tenements, which the clarionet obligingly informed me were inhabited by the Minor-Canons. They had odd little porches over the doors, like sounding-boards over old pulpits; and I thought I should like to see one of the Minor-Canons come out upon his top step, and favour us with a little Christmas discourse about the poor scholars of Rochester; taking for his text the words of his Master relative to the devouring of Widows' houses.

The clarionet was so communicative, and my inclinations were (as they generally are) of so vagabond a tendency, that I accompanied the Waits across an open green called the Vines, and assisted—in the French sense—at the performance of two waltzes, two polkas, and three Irish melodies, before I thought of my inn any more. However, I returned to it then, and found a fiddle in the kitchen, and Ben, the wall-eyed young man, and two chambermaids, circling round the great deal table with the utmost animation.

I had a very bad night. It cannot have been owing to the turkey or the beef,—and the Wassail is out of the question,—but in every endeavour that I made to get to sleep I failed most dismally. I was never asleep; and in whatsoever unreasonable direction my mind rambled, the effigy of Master Richard Watts perpetually embarrassed it.

In a word, I only got out of the Worshipful Master Richard Watts's way by getting out of bed in the dark at six o'clock, and tumbling, as my custom is, into all the cold water that could be accumulated for the purpose. The outer air was dull and cold enough in the street, when I came down there; and the one candle in our supper-room at Watts's Charity looked as pale in the burning as if it had had a bad night too. But my Travellers had all slept soundly, and they took to the hot coffee, and the piles of bread-and-butter, which Ben had arranged like deals in a timber-yard, as kindly as I could desire.

While it was yet scarcely daylight, we all came out into the street together, and there shook hands. The widow took the little sailor towards Chatham, where he was to find a steamboat for Sheerness; the lawyer, with an extremely knowing look, went his own way, without committing himself by announcing his intentions; two more struck off by the cathedral and old castle for Maidstone; and the book-pedler accompanied me over the bridge. As for me, I was going to walk by Cobham Woods, as far upon my way to London as I fancied.

When I came to the stile and footpath by which I was to diverge from the main road, I bade farewell to my last remaining Poor Traveller, and pursued my way alone. And now the mists began to rise in the most beautiful manner, and the sun to shine; and as I went on through the bracing air, seeing the hoar-frost sparkle everywhere, I felt as if all Nature shared in the joy of the great Birthday.

Going through the woods, the softness of my tread upon the mossy ground and among the brown leaves enhanced the

Christmas sacredness by which I felt surrounded. As the whitened stems environed me, I thought how the Founder of the time had never raised his benignant hand, save to bless and heal, except in the case of one unconscious tree.   By Cobham Hall, I came to the village, and the churchyard where the dead had been quietly buried, "in the sure and certain hope" which Christmas-time inspired.   What children could I see at play, and not be loving of, recalling who had loved them!   No garden that I passed was out of unison with the day, for I remembered that the tomb was in a garden, and that "she, supposing him to be the gardener," had said, "Sir, if thou have borne him hence, tell me where thou hast laid him, and I will take him away."   In time, the distant river with the ships came full in view, and with it pictures of the poor fishermen, mending their nets, who arose and followed him,—of the teaching of the people from a ship pushed off a little way from shore, by reason of the multitude, —of a majestic figure walking on the water, in the loneliness of night.   My very shadow on the ground was eloquent of Christmas; for did not the people lay their sick where the mere shadows of the men who had heard and seen him might fall as they passed along?

Thus Christmas begirt me, far and near, until I had come to Blackheath, and had walked down the long vista of gnarled old trees in Greenwich Park, and was being steam-rattled through the mists now closing in once more, towards the lights of London.   Brightly they shone, but not so brightly as my own fire, and the brighter faces around it, when we came together to celebrate the day.   And there I told of worthy Master Richard Watts, and of my supper with the Six Poor Travellers who were neither Rogues nor Proctors, and from that hour to this I have never seen one of them again.

THE HOLLY-TREE

[1855]

THE HOLLY-TREE.

Three Branches.

FIRST BRANCH.

MYSELF.

I HAVE kept one secret in the course of my life. I am a bashful man. Nobody would suppose it, nobody ever does suppose it, nobody ever did suppose it, but I am naturally a bashful man. This is the secret which I have never breathed until now.

I might greatly move the reader by some account of the innumerable places I have not been to, the innumerable people I have not called upon or received, the innumerable social evasions I have been guilty of, solely because I am by original constitution and character a bashful man. But I will leave the reader unmoved, and proceed with the object before me.

That object is to give a plain account of my travels and discoveries in the Holly-Tree Inn; in which place of good entertainment for man and beast I was once snowed up.

It happened in the memorable year when I parted for ever from Angela Leath, whom I was shortly to have married, on making the discovery that she preferred my bosom friend. From our school-days I had freely admitted Edwin, in my own mind, to be far superior to myself; and, though I was

grievously wounded at heart, I felt the preference to be
natural, and tried to forgive them both. It was under these
circumstances that I resolved to go to America—on my way
to the Devil.

Communicating my discovery neither to Angela nor to
Edwin, but resolving to write each of them an affecting
letter conveying my blessing and forgiveness, which the steam-
tender for shore should carry to the post when I myself
should be bound for the New World, far beyond recall,—I
say, locking up my grief in my own breast, and consoling
myself as I could with the prospect of being generous, I
quietly left all I held dear, and started on the desolate
journey I have mentioned.

The dead winter-time was in full dreariness when I left
my chambers for ever, at five o'clock in the morning. I had
shaved by candle-light, of course, and was miserably cold,
and experienced that general all-pervading sensation of
getting up to be hanged which I have usually found inseparable from untimely rising under such circumstances.

How well I remember the forlorn aspect of Fleet-street
when I came out of the Temple! The street-lamps flickering
in the gusty north-east wind, as if the very gas were contorted
with cold; the white-topped houses; the bleak, star-lighted
sky; the market people and other early stragglers, trotting
to circulate their almost frozen blood; the hospitable light
and warmth of the few coffee-shops and public-houses that
were open for such customers; the hard, dry, frosty rime with
which the air was charged (the wind had already beaten it into
every crevice), and which lashed my face like a steel whip.

It wanted nine days to the end of the month, and end of
the year. The Post-office packet for the United States was
to depart from Liverpool, weather permitting, on the first of
the ensuing month, and I had the intervening time on my
hands. I had taken this into consideration, and had resolved
to make a visit to a certain spot (which I need not name) on
the farther borders of Yorkshire. It was endeared to me by

my having first seen Angela at a farmhouse in that place, and my melancholy was gratified by the idea of taking a wintry leave of it before my expatriation. I ought to explain, that, to avoid being sought out before my resolution should have been rendered irrevocable by being carried into full effect, I had written to Angela overnight, in my usual manner, lamenting that urgent business, of which she should know all particulars by-and-by—took me unexpectedly away from her for a week or ten days.

There was no Northern Railway at that time, and in its place there were stage-coaches; which I occasionally find myself, in common with some other people, affecting to lament now, but which everybody dreaded as a very serious penance then. I had secured the box-seat on the fastest of these, and my business in Fleet-street was to get into a cab with my portmanteau, so to make the best of my way to the Peacock at Islington, where I was to join this coach. But when one of our Temple watchmen, who carried my portmanteau into Fleet-street for me, told me about the huge blocks of ice that had for some days past been floating in the river, having closed up in the night, and made a walk from the Temple Gardens over to the Surrey shore, I began to ask myself the question, whether the box-seat would not be likely to put a sudden and a frosty end to my unhappiness. I was heart-broken, it is true, and yet I was not quite so far gone as to wish to be frozen to death.

When I got up to the Peacock,—where I found everybody drinking hot purl, in self-preservation,—I asked if there were an inside seat to spare. I then discovered that, inside or out, I was the only passenger. This gave me a still livelier idea of the great inclemency of the weather, since that coach always loaded particularly well. However, I took a little purl (which I found uncommonly good), and got into the coach. When I was seated, they built me up with straw to the waist, and, conscious of making a rather ridiculous appearance, I began my journey.

It was still dark when we left the Peacock. For a little while, pale, uncertain ghosts of houses and trees appeared and vanished, and then it was hard, black, frozen day. People were lighting their fires; smoke was mounting straight up high into the rarefied air; and we were rattling for Highgate Archway over the hardest ground I have ever heard the ring of iron shoes on. As we got into the country, everything seemed to have grown old and gray. The roads, the trees, thatched roofs of cottages and homesteads, the ricks in farmers' yards. Out-door work was abandoned, horse-troughs at roadside inns were frozen hard, no stragglers lounged about, doors were close shut, little turnpike houses had blazing fires inside, and children (even turnpike people have children, and seem to like them) rubbed the frost from the little panes of glass with their chubby arms, that their bright eyes might catch a glimpse of the solitary coach going by. I don't know when the snow began to set in; but I know that we were changing horses somewhere when I heard the guard remark, "That the old lady up in the sky was picking her geese pretty hard to-day." Then, indeed, I found the white down falling fast and thick.

The lonely day wore on, and I dozed it out, as a lonely traveller does. I was warm and valiant after eating and drinking,—particularly after dinner; cold and depressed at all other times. I was always bewildered as to time and place, and always more or less out of my senses. The coach and horses seemed to execute in chorus Auld Lang Syne, without a moment's intermission. They kept the time and tune with the greatest regularity, and rose into the swell at the beginning of the Refrain, with a precision that worried me to death. While we changed horses, the guard and coach-man went stumping up and down the road, printing off their shoes in the snow, and poured so much liquid consolation into themselves without being any the worse for it, that I began to confound them, as it darkened again, with two great white casks standing on end. Our horses tumbled down in solitary places, and we got them up,—which was the pleasantest variety I had, for it warmed me. And it snowed and snowed, and still it snowed, and never left off snowing. All night long we went on in this manner. Thus we came round the clock, upon the Great North Road, to the performance of Auld Lang Syne all day again. And it snowed and snowed, and still it snowed, and never left off snowing.

I forget now where we were at noon on the second day, and where we ought to have been; but I know that we were scores of miles behindhand, and that our case was growing worse every hour. The drift was becoming prodigiously deep; landmarks were getting snowed out; the road and the fields were all one; instead of having fences and hedge-rows to guide us, we went crunching on over an unbroken surface of ghastly white that might sink beneath us at any moment and drop us down a whole hillside. Still the coachman and guard—who kept together on the box, always in council, and looking well about them—made out the track with astonishing sagacity.

When we came in sight of a town, it looked, to my fancy, like a large drawing on a slate, with abundance of slate-pencil expended on the churches and houses where the snow lay thickest. When we came within a town, and found the church clocks all stopped, the dial-faces choked with snow, and the inn-signs blotted out, it seemed as if the whole place were overgrown with white moss. As to the coach, it was a mere snowball; similarly, the men and boys who ran along beside us to the town's end, turning our clogged wheels and encouraging our horses, were men and boys of snow; and the bleak wild solitude to which they at last dismissed us was a snowy Sahara. One would have thought this enough: notwithstanding which, I pledge my word that it snowed and snowed, and still it snowed, and never left off snowing.

We performed Auld Lang Syne the whole day; seeing nothing, out of towns and villages, but the track of stoats, hares, and foxes, and sometimes of birds. At nine o'clock at night, on a Yorkshire moor, a cheerful burst from our horn, and a welcome sound of talking, with a glimmering and moving about of lanterns, roused me from my drowsy state. I found that we were going to change.

They helped me out, and I said to a waiter, whose bare head became as white as King Lear's in a single minute, "What Inn is this?"

"The Holly-Tree, sir," said he.

"Upon my word, I believe," said I, apologetically, to the guard and coachman, "that I must stop here."

Now the landlord, and the landlady, and the ostler, and the postboy, and all the stable authorities, had already asked the coachman, to the wide-eyed interest of all the rest of the establishment, if he meant to go on. The coachman had already replied, "Yes, he'd take her through it,"—meaning by Her the coach,—"if so be as George would stand by him." George was the guard, and he had already sworn that he _would_ stand by him. So the helpers were already getting the horses out.

My declaring myself beaten, after this parley, was not an announcement without preparation. Indeed, but for the way to the announcement being smoothed by the parley, I more than doubt whether, as an innately bashful man, I should have had the confidence to make it. As it was, it received the approval even of the guard and coachman. Therefore, with many confirmations of my inclining, and many remarks from one bystander to another, that the gentleman could go for'ard by the mail to-morrow, whereas to-night he would only be froze, and where was the good of a gentleman being froze,—ah, let alone buried alive (which latter clause was added by a humorous helper as a joke at my expense, and was extremely well received), I saw my portmanteau got out stiff, like a frozen body; did the handsome thing by the guard and coachman; wished them good-night and a prosperous journey; and, a little ashamed of myself, after all, for leaving them to fight it out alone, followed the landlord, landlady, and waiter of the Holly-Tree up-stairs.

I thought I had never seen such a large room as that into which they showed me. It had five windows, with dark red curtains that would have absorbed the light of a general illumination; and there were complications of drapery at the top of the curtains, that went wandering about the wall in a most extraordinary manner. I asked for a smaller room, and they told me there was no smaller room. They could screen me in, however, the landlord said. They brought a great old japanned screen, with natives (Japanese, I suppose) engaged in a variety of idiotic pursuits all over it; and left me roasting whole before an immense fire.

My bedroom was some quarter of a mile off, up a great staircase at the end of a long gallery; and nobody knows what a misery this is to a bashful man who would rather not meet people on the stairs. It was the grimmest room I have ever had the nightmare in; and all the furniture, from the four posts of the bed to the two old silver candlesticks, was tall, high-shouldered, and spindle-waisted. Below, in my sitting-room, if I looked round my screen, the wind rushed at me like a mad bull; if I stuck to my arm-chair, the fire scorched me to the colour of a new brick. The chimney-piece was very high, and there was a bad glass— what I may call a wavy glass—above it, which, when I stood up, just showed me my anterior phrenological developments, —and these never look well, in any subject, cut short off at the eyebrow. If I stood with my back to the fire, a gloomy vault of darkness above and beyond the screen insisted on being looked at; and, in its dim remoteness, the drapery of the ten curtains of the five windows went twisting and creeping about, like a nest of gigantic worms.

I suppose that what I observe in myself must be observed by some other men of similar character in *themselves;* therefore I am emboldened to mention, that, when I travel, I never arrive at a place but I immediately want to go away from it. Before I had finished my supper of broiled fowl and mulled port, I had impressed upon the waiter in detail

my arrangements for departure in the morning. Breakfast
and bill at eight. Fly at nine. Two horses, or, if needful,
even four.

Tired though I was, the night appeared about a week
long. In oases of nightmare, I thought of Angela, and felt
more depressed than ever by the reflection that I was on
the shortest road to Gretna Green. What had *I* to do with
Gretna Green? I was not going *that* way to the Devil, but
by the American route, I remarked in my bitterness.

In the morning I found that it was snowing still, that it
had snowed all night, and that I was snowed up. Nothing
could get out of that spot on the moor, or could come at it,
until the road had been cut out by labourers from the
market-town. When they might cut their way to the Holly-
Tree nobody could tell me.

It was now Christmas-eve. I should have had a dismal
Christmas-time of it anywhere, and consequently that did
not so much matter; still, being snowed up was like dying
of frost, a thing I had not bargained for. I felt very lonely.
Yet I could no more have proposed to the landlord and
landlady to admit me to their society (though I should have
liked it very much) than I could have asked them to present
me with a piece of plate. Here my great secret, the real
bashfulness of my character, is to be observed. Like most
bashful men, I judge of other people as if they were bashful
too. Besides being far too shamefaced to make the proposal
myself, I really had a delicate misgiving that it would be in
the last degree disconcerting to them.

Trying to settle down, therefore, in my solitude, I first of
all asked what books there were in the house. The waiter
brought me a *Book of Roads*, two or three old Newspapers,
a little Song-Book, terminating in a collection of Toasts and
Sentiments, a little Jest-Book, an odd volume of *Peregrine
Pickle*, and the *Sentimental Journey*. I knew every word of
the two last already, but I read them through again, then
tried to hum all the songs (Auld Lang Syne was among

them); went entirely through the jokes,—in which I found
a fund of melancholy adapted to my state of mind; proposed
all the toasts, enunciated all the sentiments, and mastered
the papers. The latter had nothing in them but stock
advertisements, a meeting about a county rate, and a highway
robbery. As I am a greedy reader, I could not make this
supply hold out until night; it was exhausted by tea-time.
Being then entirely cast upon my own resources, I got
through an hour in considering what to do next. Ultimately,
it came into my head (from which I was anxious by any
means to exclude Angela and Edwin), that I would endeavour
to recall my experience of Inns, and would try how long it
lasted me. I stirred the fire, moved my chair a little to one
side of the screen,—not daring to go far, for I knew the wind
was waiting to make a rush at me, I could hear it growling,
—and began.

My first impressions of an Inn dated from the Nursery;
consequently I went back to the Nursery for a starting-point,
and found myself at the knee of a sallow woman with a fishy
eye, an aquiline nose, and a green gown, whose specialty
was a dismal narrative of a landlord by the roadside, whose
visitors unaccountably disappeared for many years, until it
was discovered that the pursuit of his life had been to convert
them into pies. For the better devotion of himself to this
branch of industry, he had constructed a secret door behind
the head of the bed; and when the visitor (oppressed with
pie) had fallen asleep, this wicked landlord would look softly
in with a lamp in one hand and a knife in the other, would
cut his throat, and would make him into pies; for which
purpose he had coppers, underneath a trap-door, always
boiling; and rolled out his pastry in the dead of the night.
Yet even he was not insensible to the stings of conscience, for
he never went to sleep without being heard to mutter, "Too
much pepper!" which was eventually the cause of his being
brought to justice. I had no sooner disposed of this criminal
than there started up another of the same period, whose

profession was originally housebreaking; in the pursuit of which art he had had his right ear chopped off one night, as he was burglariously getting in at a window, by a brave and lovely servant-maid (whom the aquiline-nosed woman, though not at all answering the description, always mysteriously implied to be herself). After several years, this brave and lovely servant-maid was married to the landlord of a country Inn; which landlord had this remarkable characteristic, that he always wore a silk nightcap, and never would on any consideration take it off. At last, one night, when he was fast asleep, the brave and lovely woman lifted up his silk nightcap on the right side, and found that he had no ear there; upon which she sagaciously perceived that he was the clipped housebreaker, who had married her with the intention of putting her to death. She immediately heated the poker and terminated his career, for which she was taken to King George upon his throne, and received the compliments of royalty on her great discretion and valour. This same narrator, who had a Ghoulish pleasure, I have long been persuaded, in terrifying me to the utmost confines of my reason, had another authentic anecdote within her own experience, founded, I now believe, upon *Raymond and Agnes, or the Bleeding Nun.* She said it happened to her brother-in-law, who was immensely rich,—which my father was not; and immensely tall,—which my father was not. It was always a point with this Ghoul to present my dearest relations and friends to my youthful mind under circumstances of disparaging contrast. The brother-in-law was riding once through a forest on a magnificent horse (we had no magnificent horse at our house), attended by a favourite and valuable Newfoundland dog (we had no dog), when he found himself benighted, and came to an Inn. A dark woman opened the door, and he asked her if he could have a bed there. She answered yes, and put his horse in the stable, and took him into a room where there were two dark men. While he was at supper, a parrot in the room began to talk, saying,

"Blood, blood! · Wipe up the blood!" Upon which one of the dark men wrung the parrot's neck, and said he was fond of roasted parrots, and he meant to have this one for breakfast in the morning. After eating and drinking heartily, the immensely rich, tall brother-in-law went up to bed; but he was rather vexed, because they had shut his dog in the stable, saying that they never allowed dogs in the house. He sat very quiet for more than an hour, thinking and thinking, when, just as his candle was burning out, he heard a scratch at the door. He opened the door, and there was the Newfoundland dog! The dog came softly in, smelt about him, went straight to some straw in the corner which the dark men had said covered apples, tore the straw away, and disclosed two sheets steeped in blood. Just at that moment the candle went out, and the brother-in-law, looking through a chink in the door, saw the two dark men stealing up-stairs; one armed with a dagger that long (about five feet); the other carrying a chopper, a sack, and a spade. Having no remembrance of the close of this adventure, I suppose my faculties to have been always so frozen with terror at this stage of it, that the power of listening stagnated within me for some quarter of an hour.

These barbarous stories carried me, sitting there on the Holly-Tree hearth, to the Roadside Inn, renowned in my time in a sixpenny book with a folding plate, representing in a central compartment of oval form the portrait of Jonathan Bradford, and in four corner compartments four incidents of the tragedy with which the name is associated, —coloured with a hand at once so free and economical, that the bloom of Jonathan's complexion passed without any pause into the breeches of the ostler, and, smearing itself off into the next division, became rum in a bottle. Then I remembered how the landlord was found at the murdered traveller's bedside, with his own knife at his feet, and blood upon his hand; how he was hanged for the murder, notwithstanding his protestation that he had indeed come there to kill the traveller for his saddle-bags, but had been stricken motionless on finding him already slain; and how the ostler, years afterwards, owned the deed. By this time I had made myself quite uncomfortable. I stirred the fire, and stood with my back to it as long as I could bear the heat, looking up at the darkness beyond the screen, and at the wormy curtains creeping in and creeping out, like the worms in the ballad of Alonzo the Brave and the Fair Imogene.

There was an Inn in the cathedral town where I went to school, which had pleasanter recollections about it than any of these. I took it next. It was the Inn where friends used to put up, and where we used to go to see parents, and to have salmon and fowls, and be tipped. It had an ecclesiastical sign,—the Mitre,—and a bar that seemed to be the next best thing to a bishopric, it was so snug. I loved the landlord's youngest daughter to distraction,—but let that pass. It was in this Inn that I was cried over by my rosy little sister, because I had acquired a black eye in a fight. And though she had been, that Holly-Tree night, for many a long year where all tears are dried, the Mitre softened me yet.

"To be continued to-morrow," said I, when I took my candle to go to bed. But my bed took it upon itself to continue the train of thought that night. It carried me away, like the enchanted carpet, to a distant place (though still in England), and there, alighting from a stage-coach at another Inn in the snow, as I had actually done some years before, I repeated in my sleep a curious experience I had really had here. More than a year before I made the journey in the course of which I put up at that Inn, I had lost a very near and dear friend by death. Every night since, at home or away from home, I had dreamed of that friend; sometimes as still living; sometimes as returning from the world of shadows to comfort me; always as being beautiful, placid, and happy, never in association with any approach to fear or distress. It was at a lonely Inn in a wide moorland place, that I halted to pass the night. When I had looked

from my bedroom window over the waste of snow on which
the moon was shining, I sat down by my fire to write a
letter. I had always, until that hour, kept it within my
own breast that I dreamed every night of the dear lost one.
But in the letter that I wrote I recorded the circumstance,
and added that I felt much interested in proving whether
the subject of my dream would still be faithful to me, travel-
tired, and in that remote place. No. I lost the beloved
figure of my vision in parting with the secret. My sleep has
never looked upon it since, in sixteen years, but once. I
was in Italy, and awoke (or seemed to awake), the well-
remembered voice distinctly in my ears, conversing with it.
I entreated it, as it rose above my bed and soared up to
the vaulted roof of the old room, to answer me a question I
had asked touching the Future Life. My hands were still
outstretched towards it as it vanished, when I heard a bell
ringing by the garden wall, and a voice in the deep stillness
of the night calling on all good Christians to pray for the
souls of the dead; it being All Souls' Eve.

To return to the Holly-Tree. When I awoke next day,
it was freezing hard, and the lowering sky threatened more
snow. My breakfast cleared away, I drew my chair into its
former place, and, with the fire getting so much the better
of the landscape that I sat in twilight, resumed my Inn
remembrances.

That was a good Inn down in Wiltshire where I put up
once, in the days of the hard Wiltshire ale, and before all
beer was bitterness. It was on the skirts of Salisbury Plain,
and the midnight wind that rattled my lattice window came
moaning at me from Stonehenge. There was a hanger-on
at that establishment (a supernaturally preserved Druid I
believe him to have been, and to be still), with long white
hair, and a flinty blue eye always looking afar off; who
claimed to have been a shepherd, and who seemed to be ever
watching for the reappearance, on the verge of the horizon,
of some ghostly flock of sheep that had been mutton for

many ages.   He was a man with a weird belief in him that
no one could count the stones of Stonehenge twice, and make
the same number of them; likewise, that any one who
counted them three times nine times, and then stood in the
centre and said, "I dare!" would behold a tremendous
apparition, and be stricken dead.   He pretended to have
seen a bustard (I suspect him to have been familiar with the
dodo), in manner following: He was out upon the plain at
the close of a late autumn day, when he dimly discerned,
going on before him at a curious fitfully bounding pace,
what he at first supposed to be a gig-umbrella that had been
blown from some conveyance, but what he presently believed
to be a lean dwarf man upon a little pony.   Having followed
this object for some distance without gaining on it, and
having called to it many times without receiving any answer,
he pursued it for miles and miles, when, at length coming up
with it, he discovered it to be the last bustard in Great
Britain, degenerated into a wingless state, and running along
the ground.   Resolved to capture him or perish in the
attempt, he closed with the bustard; but the bustard, who
had formed a counter-resolution that he should do neither,
threw him, stunned him, and was last seen making off due
west.   This weird man, at that stage of metempsychosis, may
have been a sleep-walker or an enthusiast or a robber; but
I awoke one night to find him in the dark at my bedside,
repeating the Athanasian Creed in a terrific voice.   I paid
my bill next day, and retired from the county with all
possible precipitation.

That was not a commonplace story which worked itself
out at a little Inn in Switzerland, while I was staying there.
It was a very homely place, in a village of one narrow zigzag
street, among mountains, and you went in at the main door
through the cow-house, and among the mules and the dogs
and the fowls, before ascending a great bare staircase to the
rooms; which were all of unpainted wood, without plastering
or papering,—like rough packing-cases.   Outside there was

nothing but the straggling street, a little toy church with a
copper-coloured steeple, a pine forest, a torrent, mists, and
mountain-sides. A young man belonging to this Inn had
disappeared eight weeks before (it was winter-time), and was
supposed to have had some undiscovered love affair, and to
have gone for a soldier. He had got up in the night, and
dropped into the village street from the loft in which he
slept with another man; and he had done it so quietly, that
his companion and fellow-labourer had heard no movement
when he was awakened in the morning, and they said,
"Louis, where is Henri?" They looked for him high and
low, in vain, and gave him up. Now, outside this Inn, there
stood, as there stood outside every dwelling in the village, a
stack of firewood; but the stack belonging to the Inn was
higher than any of the rest, because the Inn was the richest
house, and burnt the most fuel. It began to be noticed,
while they were looking high and low, that a Bantam cock,
part of the live stock of the Inn, put himself wonderfully
out of his way to get to the top of this wood-stack; and
that he would stay there for hours and hours, crowing, until
he appeared in danger of splitting himself. Five weeks went
on,—six weeks,—and still this terrible Bantam, neglecting his
domestic affairs, was always on the top of the wood-stack,
crowing the very eyes out of his head. By this time it was
perceived that Louis had become inspired with a violent
animosity towards the terrible Bantam, and one morning he
was seen by a woman, who sat nursing her goître at a little
window in a gleam of sun, to catch up a rough billet of
wood, with a great oath, hurl it at the terrible Bantam
crowing on the wood-stack, and bring him down dead. Hereupon the woman, with a sudden light in her mind, stole
round to the back of the wood-stack, and, being a good
climber, as all those women are, climbed up, and soon was
seen upon the summit, screaming, looking down the hollow
within, and crying, "Seize Louis, the murderer! Ring the
church bell! Here is the body!" I saw the murderer that

day, and I saw him as I sat by my fire at the Holly-Tree
Inn, and I see him now, lying shackled with cords on the
stable litter, among the mild eyes and the smoking breath of
the cows, waiting to be taken away by the police, and stared
at by the fearful village. A heavy animal,—the dullest
animal in the stables,—with a stupid head, and a lumpish
face devoid of any trace of sensibility, who had been, within
the knowledge of the murdered youth, an embezzler of certain
small moneys belonging to his master, and who had taken
this hopeful mode of putting a possible accuser out of his way.
All of which he confessed next day, like a sulky wretch who
couldn't be troubled any more, now that they had got hold
of him, and meant to make an end of him. I saw him once
again, on the day of my departure from the Inn. In that
Canton the headsman still does his office with a sword; and
I came upon this murderer sitting bound to a chair, with
his eyes bandaged, on a scaffold in a little market-place. In
that instant, a great sword (loaded with quicksilver in the
thick part of the blade) swept round him like a gust of wind
or fire, and there was no such creature in the world. My
wonder was, not that he was so suddenly despatched, but
that any head was left unreaped, within a radius of fifty
yards of that tremendous sickle.

That was a good Inn, too, with the kind, cheerful landlady
and the honest landlord, where I lived in the shadow of Mont
Blanc, and where one of the apartments has a zoological
papering on the walls, not so accurately joined but that the
elephant occasionally rejoices in a tiger's hind legs and tail,
while the lion puts on a trunk and tusks, and the bear,
moulting as it were, appears as to portions of himself like a
leopard. I made several American friends at that Inn, who
all called Mont Blanc Mount Blank,—except one good-
humoured gentleman, of a very sociable nature, who became
on such intimate terms with it that he spoke of it familiarly
as "Blank;" observing, at breakfast, "Blank looks pretty
tall this morning;" or considerably doubting in the courtyard

in the evening, whether there warn't some go-ahead naters in our country, sir, that would make out the top of Blank in a couple of hours from first start—now!

Once I passed a fortnight at an Inn in the North of England, where I was haunted by the ghost of a tremendous pie. It was a Yorkshire pie, like a fort,—an abandoned fort with nothing in it; but the waiter had a fixed idea that it was a point of ceremony at every meal to put the pie on the table. After some days I tried to hint, in several delicate ways, that I considered the pie done with; as, for example, by emptying fag-ends of glasses of wine into it; putting cheese-plates and spoons into it, as into a basket; putting wine-bottles into it, as into a cooler; but always in vain, the pie being invariably cleaned out again and brought up as before. At last, beginning to be doubtful whether I was not the victim of a spectral illusion, and whether my health and spirits might not sink under the horrors of an imaginary pie, I cut a triangle out of it, fully as large as the musical instrument of that name in a powerful orchestra. Human prevision could not have foreseen the result—but the waiter mended the pie. With some effectual species of cement, he adroitly fitted the triangle in again, and I paid my reckoning and fled.

The Holly-Tree was getting rather dismal. I made an overland expedition beyond the screen, and penetrated as far as the fourth window. Here I was driven back by stress of weather. Arrived at my winter-quarters once more, I made up the fire, and took another Inn.

It was in the remotest part of Cornwall. A great annual Miner's Feast was being holden at the Inn, when I and my travelling companions presented ourselves at night among the wild crowd that were dancing before it by torchlight. We had had a break-down in the dark, on a stony morass some miles away; and I had the honour of leading one of the unharnessed post-horses. If any lady or gentleman, on perusal of the present lines, will take any very tall post-horse with his traces hanging about his legs, and will conduct him by the bearing-rein into the heart of a country dance of a hundred and fifty couples, that lady or gentleman will then, and only then, form an adequate idea of the extent to which that post-horse will tread on his conductor's toes. Over and above which, the post-horse, finding three hundred people whirling about him, will probably rear, and also lash out with his hind legs, in a manner incompatible with dignity or self-respect on his conductor's part. With such little drawbacks on my usually impressive aspect, I appeared at this Cornish Inn, to the unutterable wonder of the Cornish Miners. It was full, and twenty times full, and nobody could be received but the post-horse,—though to get rid of that noble animal was something. While my fellow-travellers and I were discussing how to pass the night and so much of the next day as must intervene before the jovial blacksmith and the jovial wheelwright would be in a condition to go out on the morass and mend the coach, an honest man stepped forth from the crowd and proposed his unlet floor of two rooms, with supper of eggs and bacon, ale and punch. We joyfully accompanied him home to the strangest of clean houses, where we were well entertained to the satisfaction of all parties. But the novel feature of the entertainment was, that our host was a chair-maker, and that the chairs assigned to us were mere frames, altogether without bottoms of any sort; so that we passed the evening on perches. Nor was this the absurdest consequence; for when we unbent at supper, and any one of us gave way to laughter, he forgot the peculiarity of his position, and instantly disappeared. I myself, doubled up into an attitude from which self-extrication was impossible, was taken out of my frame, like a clown in a comic pantomime who has tumbled into a tub, five times by the taper's light during the eggs and bacon.

The Holly-Tree was fast reviving within me a sense of loneliness. I began to feel conscious that my subject would never carry on until I was dug out. I might be a week here,—weeks!

There was a story with a singular idea in it, connected with an Inn I once passed a night at in a picturesque old town on the Welsh border. In a large double-bedded room of this Inn there had been a suicide committed by poison, in one bed, while a tired traveller slept unconscious in the other. After that time, the suicide bed was never used, but the other constantly was; the disused bedstead remaining in the room empty, though as to all other respects in its old state. The story ran, that whosoever slept in this room, though never so entire a stranger, from never so far off, was invariably observed to come down in the morning with an impression that he smelt Laudanum, and that his mind always turned upon the subject of suicide; to which, whatever kind of man he might be, he was certain to make some reference if he conversed with any one. This went on for years, until it at length induced the landlord to take the disused bedstead down, and bodily burn it,—bed, hangings, and all. The strange influence (this was the story) now changed to a fainter one, but never changed afterwards. The occupant of that room, with occasional but very rare exceptions, would come down in the morning, trying to recall a forgotten dream he had had in the night. The landlord, on his mentioning his perplexity, would suggest various commonplace subjects, not one of which, as he very well knew, was the true subject. But the moment the landlord suggested "Poison," the traveller started, and cried, "Yes!" He never failed to accept that suggestion, and he never recalled any more of the dream.

This reminiscence brought the Welsh Inns in general before me; with the women in their round hats, and the harpers with their white beards (venerable, but humbugs, I am afraid), playing outside the door while I took my dinner. The transition was natural to the Highland Inns, with the oatmeal bannocks, the honey, the venison steaks, the trout

from the loch, the whisky, and perhaps (having the
materials so temptingly at hand) the Athol brose. Once
was I coming south from the Scottish Highlands in hot
haste, hoping to change quickly at the station at the
bottom of a certain wild historical glen, when these eyes did
with mortification see the landlord come out with a telescope
and sweep the whole prospect for the horses; which horses
were away picking up their own living, and did not heave in
sight under four hours. Having thought of the loch-trout,
I was taken by quick association to the Anglers' Inns of
England (I have assisted at innumerable feats of angling by
lying in the bottom of the boat, whole summer days, doing
nothing with the greatest perseverance; which I have
generally found to be as effectual towards the taking of fish
as the finest tackle and the utmost science), and to the
pleasant white, clean, flower-pot-decorated bedrooms of those
inns, overlooking the river, and the ferry, and the green ait,
and the church-spire, and the country bridge; and to the
peerless Emma with the bright eyes and the pretty smile,
who waited, bless her! with a natural grace that would have
converted Blue-Beard. Casting my eyes upon my Holly-Tree
fire, I next discerned among the glowing coals the pictures
of a score or more of those wonderful English posting-inns
which we are all so sorry to have lost, which were so large
and so comfortable, and which were such monuments of
British submission to rapacity and extortion. He who
would see these houses pining away, let him walk from
Basingstoke, or even Windsor, to London, by way of
Hounslow, and moralise on their perishing remains; the
stables crumbling to dust; unsettled labourers and wanderers
bivouacking in the outhouses; grass growing in the yards;
the rooms, where erst so many hundred beds of down were
made up, let off to Irish lodgers at eighteenpence a week; a
little ill-looking beer-shop shrinking in the tap of former
days, burning coach-house gates for firewood, having one of
its two windows bunged up, as if it had received punishment

in a fight with the Railroad; a low, bandy-legged, brick-making bulldog standing in the doorway. What could I next see in my fire so naturally as the new railway-house of these times near the dismal country station; with nothing particular on draught but cold air and damp, nothing worth mentioning in the larder but new mortar, and no business doing beyond a conceited affectation of luggage in the hall? Then I came to the Inns of Paris, with the pretty apartment of four pieces up one hundred and seventy-five waxed stairs, the privilege of ringing the bell all day long without influencing anybody's mind or body but your own, and the not-too-much-for-dinner, considering the price. Next to the provincial Inns of France, with the great church-tower rising above the courtyard, the horse-bells jingling merrily up and down the street beyond, and the clocks of all descriptions in all the rooms, which are never right, unless taken at the precise minute when, by getting exactly twelve hours too fast or too slow, they uninten-tionally become so. Away I went, next, to the lesser road-side Inns of Italy; where all the dirty clothes in the house (not in wear) are always lying in your anteroom; where the mosquitoes make a raisin pudding of your face in summer, and the cold bites it blue in winter; where you get what you can, and forget what you can't; where I should again like to be boiling my tea in a pocket-handkerchief dumpling, for want of a teapot. So to the old palace Inns and old monastery Inns, in towns and cities of the same bright country; with their massive quadrangular staircases, whence you may look from among clustering pillars high into the blue vault of heaven; with their stately banqueting-rooms, and vast refec-tories; with their labyrinths of ghostly bedchambers, and their glimpses into gorgeous streets that have no appearance of reality or possibility. So to the close little Inns of the Malaria districts, with their pale attendants, and their peculiar smell of never letting in the air. So to the immense fantastic Inns of Venice, with the cry of the gondolier below,

as he skims the corner; the grip of the watery odours on one
particular little bit of the bridge of your nose (which is never
released while you stay there); and the great bell of St. Mark's
Cathedral tolling midnight. Next I put up for a minute
at the restless Inns upon the Rhine, where your going to bed,
no matter at what hour, appears to be the tocsin for everybody else's getting up; and where, in the table-d'hôte room
at the end of the long table (with several Towers of Babel
on it at the other end, all made of white plates), one knot of
stoutish men, entirely dressed in jewels and dirt, and having
nothing else upon them, *will* remain all night, clinking glasses,
and singing about the river that flows, and the grape that
grows, and Rhine wine that beguiles, and Rhine woman that
smiles and hi drink drink my friend and ho drink drink my
brother, and all the rest of it. I departed thence, as a matter
of course, to other German Inns, where all the eatables are
soddened down to the same flavour, and where the mind is
disturbed by the apparition of hot puddings, and boiled
cherries, sweet and slab, at awfully unexpected periods of the
repast. After a draught of sparkling beer from a foaming
glass jug, and a glance of recognition through the windows
of the student beer-houses at Heidelberg and elsewhere, I
put out to sea for the Inns of America, with their four
hundred beds apiece, and their eight or nine hundred ladies
and gentlemen at dinner every day. Again I stood in the
bar-rooms thereof, taking my evening cobbler, julep, sling,
or cocktail. Again I listened to my friend the General,—
whom I had known for five minutes, in the course of which
period he had made me intimate for life with two Majors,
who again had made me intimate for life with three Colonels,
who again had made me brother to twenty-two civilians,—
again, I say, I listened to my friend the General, leisurely
expounding the resources of the establishment, as to gentlemen's morning-room, sir; ladies' morning-room, sir; gentlemen's evening-room, sir; ladies' evening-room, sir; ladies' and
gentlemen's evening reuniting-room, sir; music-room, sir;

reading-room, sir; over four hundred sleeping-rooms, sir; and
the entire planned and finited within twelve calendar months
from the first clearing off of the old encumbrances on the
plot, at a cost of five hundred thousand dollars, sir. Again
I found, as to my individual way of thinking, that the
greater, the more gorgeous, and the more dollarous the
establishment was, the less desirable it was. Nevertheless,
again I drank my cobbler, julep, sling, or cocktail, in all
good-will, to my friend the General, and my friends the
Majors, Colonels, and civilians all; full well knowing that,
whatever little motes my beamy eyes may have descried in
theirs, they belong to a kind, generous, large-hearted, and
great people.

I had been going on lately at a quick pace to keep my
solitude out of my mind; but here I broke down for good,
and gave up the subject. What was I to do? What was to
become of me? Into what extremity was I submissively to
sink? Supposing that, like Baron Trenck, I looked out for a
mouse or spider, and found one, and beguiled my imprison-
ment by training it? Even that might be dangerous with
a view to the future. I might be so far gone when the
road did come to be cut through the snow, that, on my
way forth, I might burst into tears, and beseech, like the
prisoner who was released in his old age from the Bastille, to
be taken back again to the five windows, the ten curtains,
and the sinuous drapery.

A desperate idea came into my head. Under any other
circumstances I should have rejected it; but, in the strait
at which I was, I held it fast. Could I so far overcome the
inherent bashfulness which withheld me from the landlord's
table and the company I might find there, as to call up the
Boots, and ask him to take a chair,—and something in a
liquid form,—and talk to me? I could. I would. I did.

SECOND BRANCH.

WHERE had he been in his time? he repeated, when I asked him the question. Lord, he had been everywhere! And what had he been? Bless you, he had been everything you could mention a'most!

Seen a good deal? Why, of course he had. I should say so, he could assure me, if I only knew about a twentieth part of what had come in *his* way. Why, it would be easier for him, he expected, to tell what he hadn't seen than what he had. Ah! A deal, it would.

What was the curiousest thing he had seen? Well! He didn't know. He couldn't momently name what was the curiousest thing he had seen,—unless it was a Unicorn,—and he see *him* once at a Fair. But supposing a young gentleman not eight year old was to run away with a fine young woman of seven, might I think *that* a queer start? Certainly. Then that was a start as he himself had had his blessed eyes on, and he had cleaned the shoes they run away in—and they was so little that he couldn't get his hand into 'em.

Master Harry Walmers' father, you see, he lived at the Elmses, down away by Shooter's Hill there, six or seven miles from Lunnon. He was a gentleman of spirit, and good-looking, and held his head up when he walked, and had what you may call Fire about him. He wrote poetry, and he rode, and he ran, and he cricketed, and he danced, and he acted, and he done it all equally beautiful. He was uncommon proud of Master Harry as was his only child; but he didn't spoil him neither. He was a gentleman that had a will of his own and a eye of his own, and that would be minded. Consequently, though he made quite a companion of the fine bright boy, and was delighted to see him so fond of reading his fairy books, and was never tired of hearing him say my name is Norval, or hearing him sing his songs about Young May Moons is beaming love, and When he as adores thee has left but the name, and that; still he kept the command over the child, and the child *was* a child, and it's to be wished more of 'em was!

How did Boots happen to know all this? Why, through being under-gardener. Of course he couldn't be under-gardener, and be always about, in the summer-time, near the windows on the lawn, a mowing, and sweeping, and weeding, and pruning, and this and that, without getting acquainted with the ways of the family. Even supposing Master Harry hadn't come to him one morning early, and said, "Cobbs, how should you spell Norah, if you was asked?" and then began cutting it in print all over the fence.

He couldn't say he had taken particular notice of children before that; but really it was pretty to see them two mites a going about the place together, deep in love. And the courage of the boy! Bless your soul, he'd have throwed off his little hat, and tucked up his little sleeves, and gone in at a Lion, he would, if they had happened to meet one, and she had been frightened of him. One day he stops, along with her, where Boots was hoeing weeds in the gravel, and says, speaking up, "Cobbs," he says, "I like *you*." "Do you, sir? I'm proud to hear it." "Yes, I do, Cobbs. Why do I like you, do you think, Cobbs?" "Don't know, Master Harry, I am sure." "Because Norah likes you, Cobbs." "Indeed, sir? That's very gratifying." "Gratifying, Cobbs? It's better than millions of the brightest diamonds to be liked by Norah." "Certainly, sir." "You're going away, ain't you, Cobbs?" "Yes, sir." "Would you like another situation, Cobbs?" "Well, sir, I shouldn't object, if it was a good 'un." "Then, Cobbs," says he, "you shall be our Head Gardener when we are married." And he tucks her, in her little sky-blue mantle, under his arm, and walks away.

Boots could assure me that it was better than a picter, and equal to a play, to see them babies, with their long, bright, curling hair, their sparkling eyes, and their beautiful light tread, a rambling about the garden, deep in love. Boots was of opinion that the birds believed they was birds, and kept up with 'em, singing to please 'em. Sometimes they would creep under the Tulip-tree, and would sit there with their arms round one another's necks, and their soft cheeks touching, a reading about the Prince and the Dragon, and the good and bad enchanters, and the king's fair daughter. Sometimes he would hear them planning about having a house in a forest, keeping bees and a cow, and living entirely on milk and honey. Once he came upon them by the pond, and heard Master Harry say, "Adorable Norah, kiss me, and say you love me to distraction, or I'll jump in head-foremost." And Boots made no question he would have done it if she hadn't complied. On the whole, Boots said it had a tendency to make him feel as if he was in love himself—only he didn't exactly know who with.

"Cobbs," said Master Harry, one evening, when Cobbs was watering the flowers, "I am going on a visit, this present Midsummer, to my grandmamma's at York."

"Are you indeed, sir? I hope you'll have a pleasant time. I am going into Yorkshire, myself, when I leave here."

"Are you going to your grandmamma's, Cobbs?"

"No, sir. I haven't got such a thing."

"Not as a grandmamma, Cobbs?"

"No, sir."

The boy looked on at the watering of the flowers for a little while, and then said, "I shall be very glad indeed to go, Cobbs,—Norah's going."

"You'll be all right then, sir," says Cobbs, "with your beautiful sweetheart by your side."

"Cobbs," returned the boy, flushing, "I never let anybody joke about it, when I can prevent them."

"It wasn't a joke, sir," says Cobbs, with humility,—"wasn't so meant."

"I am glad of that, Cobbs, because I like you, you know, and you're going to live with us.—Cobbs!"

"Sir."

"What do you think my grandmamma gives me when I go down there?"

"I couldn't so much as make a guess, sir."

"A Bank of England five-pound note, Cobbs."

"Whew!" says Cobbs, "that's a spanking sum of money, Master Harry."

"A person could do a good deal with such a sum of money as that,—couldn't a person, Cobbs?"

"I believe you, sir!"

"Cobbs," said the boy, "I'll tell you a secret. At Norah's house, they have been joking her about me, and pretending to laugh at our being engaged,—pretending to make game of it, Cobbs!"

"Such, sir," says Cobbs, "is the depravity of human natur."

The boy, looking exactly like his father, stood for a few minutes with his glowing face towards the sunset, and then departed with, "Good-night, Cobbs. I'm going in."

If I was to ask Boots how it happened that he was a going to leave that place just at that present time, well, he couldn't rightly answer me. He did suppose he might have stayed there till now if he had been anyways inclined. But, you see, he was younger then, and he wanted change. That's what he wanted,—change. Mr. Walmers, he said to him when he gave him notice of his intentions to leave, "Cobbs," he says, "have you anythink to complain of? I make the inquiry because if I find that any of my people really has anythink to complain of, I wish to make it right if I can." "No, sir," says Cobbs; "thanking you, sir, I find myself as well sitiwated here as I could hope to be anywheres. The truth is, sir, that I'm a-going to seek my fortun'." "O, indeed, Cobbs!" he says; "I hope you may find it." And Boots could assure me—which he did, touching his hair with his bootjack, as a salute in the way of his present calling—that he hadn't found it yet.

Well, sir! Boots left the Elmses when his time was up, and Master Harry, he went down to the old lady's at York, which old lady would have given that child the teeth out of her head (if she had had any), she was so wrapped up in him. What does that Infant do,—for Infant you may call him and be within the mark,—but cut away from that old lady's with his Norah, on a expedition to go to Gretna Green and be married!

Sir, Boots was at this identical Holly-Tree Inn (having left it several times since to better himself, but always come back through one thing or another), when, one summer afternoon, the coach drives up, and out of the coach gets them two children. The Guard says to our Governor, "I don't quite make out these little passengers, but the young gentleman's words was, that they was to be brought here." The young gentleman gets out; hands his lady out; gives the Guard something for himself; says to our Governor, "We're to stop here to-night, please. Sitting-room and two bedrooms will be required. Chops and cherry-pudding for two!" and tucks her, in her little sky-blue mantle, under his arm, and walks into the house much bolder than Brass.

Boots leaves me to judge what the amazement of that establishment was, when these two tiny creatures all alone by themselves was marched into the Angel,—much more so, when he, who had seen them without their seeing him, give the

Governor his views of the expedition they was upon. "Cobbs,"
says the Governor, "if this is so, I must set off myself to
York, and quiet their friends' minds. In which case you
must keep your eye upon 'em, and humour 'em, till I come
back. But before I take these measures, Cobbs, I should
wish you to find from themselves whether your opinion is
correct. "Sir, to you," says Cobbs, "that shall be done
directly."

So Boots goes up-stairs to the Angel, and there he finds
Master Harry on a e-normous sofa,—immense at any time,
but looking like the Great Bed of Ware, compared with him,
—a drying the eyes of Miss Norah with his pocket-hankecher.
Their little legs was entirely off the ground, of course, and
it really is not possible for Boots to express to me how small
them children looked.

"It's Cobbs! It's Cobbs!" cried Master Harry, and comes
running to him, and catching hold of his hand. Miss Norah
comes running to him on t'other side and catching hold of
his t'other hand, and they both jump for joy.

"I see you a getting out, sir," says Cobbs. "I thought It
was you. I thought I couldn't be mistaken in your height
and figure. What's the object of your journey, sir?—
Matrimonial?"

"We are going to be married, Cobbs, at Gretna Green,"
returned the boy. "We have run away on purpose. Norah
has been in rather low spirits, Cobbs; but she'll be happy,
now we have found you to be our friend."

"Thank you, sir, and thank you, miss," says Cobbs, "for
your good opinion. Did you bring any luggage with you,
sir?"

If I will believe Boots when he gives me his word and
honour upon it, the lady had got a parasol, a smelling-
bottle, a round and a half of cold buttered toast, eight
peppermint drops, and a hair-brush,—seemingly a doll's.
The gentleman had got about half a dozen yards of string,
a knife, three or four sheets of writing-paper folded up

surprising small, a orange, and a Chaney mug with his name upon it.

"What may be the exact natur of your plans, sir?" says Cobbs.

"To go on," replied the boy,—which the courage of that boy was something wonderful!—"in the morning, and be married to-morrow."

"Just so, sir," says Cobbs. "Would it meet your views, sir, if I was to accompany you?"

When Cobbs said this, they both jumped for joy again, and cried out, "Oh, yes, yes, Cobbs! Yes!"

"Well, sir," says Cobbs. "If you will excuse my having the freedom to give an opinion, what I should recommend would be this. I'm acquainted with a pony, sir, which, put in a pheayton that I could borrow, would take you and Mrs. Harry Walmers, Junior, (myself driving, if you approved,) to the end of your journey in a very short space of time. I am not altogether sure, sir, that this pony will be at liberty to-morrow, but even if you had to wait over to-morrow for him, it might be worth your while. As to the small account here, sir, in case you was to find yourself running at all short, that don't signify; because I'm a part proprietor of this inn, and it could stand over."

Boots assures me that when they clapped their hands, and jumped for joy again, and called him "Good Cobbs!" and "Dear Cobbs!" and bent across him to kiss one another in the delight of their confiding hearts, he felt himself the meanest rascal for deceiving 'em that ever was born.

"Is there anything you want just at present, sir?" says Cobbs, mortally ashamed of himself.

"We should like some cakes after dinner," answered Master Harry, folding his arms, putting out one leg, and looking straight at him, "and two apples,—and jam. With dinner we should like to have toast-and-water. But Norah has always been accustomed to half a glass of currant wine at dessert. And so have I."

"It shall be ordered at the bar, sir," says Cobbs; and away he went.

Boots has the feeling as fresh upon him at this minute of speaking as he had then, that he would far rather have had it out in half a dozen rounds with the Governor than have combined with him; and that he wished with all his heart there was any impossible place where those two babies could make an impossible marriage, and live impossibly happy ever afterwards. However, as it couldn't be, he went into the Governor's plans, and the Governor set off for York in half an hour.

The way in which the women of that house—without exception—every one of 'em—married *and* single—took to that boy when they heard the story, Boots considers surprising. It was as much as he could do to keep 'em from dashing into the room and kissing him. They climbed up all sorts of places, at the risk of their lives, to look at him through a pane of glass. They was seven deep at the keyhole. They was out of their minds about him and his bold spirit.

In the evening, Boots went into the room to see how the runaway couple was getting on. The gentleman was on the window-seat, supporting the lady in his arms. She had tears upon her face, and was lying, very tired and half asleep, with her head upon his shoulder.

"Mrs. Harry Walmers, Junior, fatigued, sir?" says Cobbs.

"Yes, she is tired, Cobbs; but she is not used to be away from home, and she has been in low spirits again. Cobbs, do you think you could bring a biffin, please?"

"I ask your pardon, sir," says Cobbs. "What was it you——?"

"I think a Norfolk biffin would rouse her, Cobbs. She is very fond of them."

Boots withdrew in search of the required restorative, and, when he brought it in, the gentleman handed it to the lady, and fed her with a spoon, and took a little himself; the lady being heavy with sleep, and rather cross. "What

should you think, sir," says Cobbs, "of a chamber candlestick?" The gentleman approved; the chambermaid went
first, up the great staircase; the lady, in her sky-blue mantle,
followed, gallantly escorted by the gentleman; the gentleman
embraced her at her door, and retired to his own apartment,
where Boots softly locked him up.

Boots couldn't but feel with increased acuteness what a base
deceiver he was, when they consulted him at breakfast (they
had ordered sweet milk-and-water, and toast and currant jelly,
overnight) about the pony. It really was as much as he
could do, he don't mind confessing to me, to look them two
young things in the face, and think what a wicked old father
of lies he had grown up to be. Howsomever, he went on a
lying like a Trojan about the pony. He told 'em that it
did so unfort'nately happen that the pony was half clipped,
you see, and that he couldn't be taken out in that state, for
fear it should strike to his inside. But that he'd be finished
clipping in the course of the day, and that to-morrow
morning at eight o'clock the pheayton would be ready. Boots's
view of the whole case, looking back on it in my room, is,
that Mrs. Harry Walmers, Junior, was beginning to give in.
She hadn't had her hair curled when she went to bed, and
she didn't seem quite up to brushing it herself, and its
getting in her eyes put her out. But nothing put out
Master Harry. He sat behind his breakfast-cup, a tearing
away at the jelly, as if he had been his own father.

After breakfast, Boots is inclined to consider that they
drawed soldiers,—at least, he knows that many such was
found in the fireplace, all on horseback. In the course of
the morning, Master Harry rang the bell,—it was surprising
how that there boy did carry on,—and said, in a sprightly
way, "Cobbs, is there any good walks in this neighbourhood?"

"Yes, sir," says Cobbs. "There's Love-lane."

"Get out with you, Cobbs!"—that was that there boy's
expression,—"you're joking."

"Begging your pardon, sir," says Cobbs, "there really is

Love-lane. And a pleasant walk it is, and proud shall I be to show it to yourself and Mrs. Harry Walmers, Junior."

"Norah, dear," said Master Harry, "this is curious. We really ought to see Love-lane. Put on your bonnet, my sweetest darling, and we will go there with Cobbs."

Boots leaves me to judge what a Beast he felt himself to be, when that young pair told him, as they all three jogged along together, that they had made up their minds to give him two thousand guineas a year as head-gardener, on accounts of his being so true a friend to 'em. Boots could have wished at the moment that the earth would have opened and swallowed him up, he felt so mean, with their beaming eyes a looking at him, and believing him. Well, sir, he turned the conversation as well as he could, and he took 'em down Love-lane to the water-meadows, and there Master Harry would have drowned himself in half a moment more, a getting out a water-lily for her,—but nothing daunted that boy. Well, sir, they was tired out. All being so new and strange to 'em, they was tired as tired could be. And they laid down on a bank of daisies, like the children in the wood, leastways meadows, and fell asleep.

Boots don't know—perhaps I do,—but never mind, it don't signify either way—why it made a man fit to make a fool of himself to see them two pretty babies a lying there in the clear still sunny day, not dreaming half so hard when they was asleep as they done when they was awake. But, Lord! when you come to think of yourself, you know, and what a game you have been up to ever since you was in your own cradle, and what a poor sort of a chap you are, and how it's always either Yesterday with you, or else To-morrow, and never To-day, that's where it is!

Well, sir, they woke up at last, and then one thing was getting pretty clear to Boots, namely, that Mrs. Harry Walmerses, Junior's, temper was on the move. When Master Harry took her round the waist, she said he "teased her so;" and when he says, "Norah, my young May Moon, your

Harry tease you?" she tells him, "Yes; and I want to go home!"

A biled fowl, and baked bread-and-butter pudding, brought Mrs. Walmers up a little; but Boots could have wished, he must privately own to me, to have seen her more sensible of the voice of love, and less abandoning of herself to currants. However, Master Harry, he kept up, and his noble heart was as fond as ever. Mrs. Walmers turned very sleepy about dusk, and began to cry. Therefore, Mrs. Walmers went off to bed as per yesterday; and Master Harry ditto repeated.

About eleven or twelve at night comes back the Governor in a chaise, along with Mr. Walmers and a elderly lady. Mr. Walmers looks amused and very serious, both at once, and says to our missis, "We are much indebted to you, ma'am, for your kind care of our little children, which we can never sufficiently acknowledge. Pray, ma'am, where is my boy?" Our missis says, "Cobbs has the dear child in charge, sir. Cobbs, show Forty!" Then he says to Cobbs, "Ah, Cobbs, I am glad to see you! I understood you was here!" And Cobbs says, "Yes, sir. Your most obedient, sir."

I may be surprised to hear Boots say it, perhaps; but Boots assures me that his heart beat like a hammer, going up-stairs. "I beg your pardon, sir," says he, while unlocking the door; "I hope you are not angry with Master Harry. For Master Harry is a fine boy, sir, and will do you credit and honour." And Boots signifies to me, that, if the fine boy's father had contradicted him in the daring state of mind in which he then was, he thinks he should have "fetched him a crack," and taken the consequences.

But Mr. Walmers only says, "No, Cobbs. No, my good fellow. Thank you!" And, the door being opened, goes in.

Boots goes in too, holding the light, and he sees Mr. Walmers go up to the bedside, bend gently down, and kiss the little sleeping face. Then he stands looking at it for a minute, looking wonderfully like it (they do say he ran away with Mrs. Walmers); and then he gently shakes the little shoulder.

"Harry, my dear boy! Harry!"

Master Harry starts up and looks at him. Looks at Cobbs too. Such is the honour of that mite, that he looks at Cobbs, to see whether he has brought him into trouble.

"I am not angry, my child. I only want you to dress yourself and come home."

"Yes, pa."

Master Harry dresses himself quickly. His breast begins to swell when he has nearly finished, and it swells more and more as he stands, at last, a looking at his father: his father standing a looking at him, the quiet image of him.

"Please may I"—the spirit of that little creatur, and the way he kept his rising tears down!—"please, dear pa—may I—kiss Norah before I go?"

"You may, my child."

So he takes Master Harry in his hand, and Boots leads the way with the candle, and they come to that other bed-room, where the elderly lady is seated by the bed, and poor little Mrs. Harry Walmers, Junior, is fast asleep. There the father lifts the child up to the pillow, and he lays his little face down for an instant by the little warm face of poor unconscious little Mrs. Harry Walmers, Junior, and gently draws it to him,—a sight so touching to the chambermaids who are peeping through the door, that one of them calls out, "It's a shame to part 'em!" But this chambermaid was always, as Boots informs me, a soft-hearted one. Not that there was any harm in that girl. Far from it.

Finally, Boots says, that's all about it. Mr. Walmers drove away in the chaise, having hold of Master Harry's hand. The elderly lady and Mrs. Harry Walmers, Junior, that was never to be (she married a Captain long afterwards, and died in India), went off next day. In conclusion, Boots put it to me whether I hold with him in two opinions:

firstly, that there are not many couples on their way to be married who are half as innocent of guile as those two children; secondly, that it would be a jolly good thing for a great many couples on their way to be married, if they could only be stopped in time, and brought back separately.

THIRD BRANCH.

THE BILL.

I HAD been snowed up a whole week. The time had hung so lightly on my hands, that I should have been in great doubt of the fact but for a piece of documentary evidence that lay upon my table.

The road had been dug out of the snow on the previous day, and the document in question was my bill. It testified emphatically to my having eaten and drunk, and warmed myself, and slept among the sheltering branches of the Holly-Tree, seven days and nights.

I had yesterday allowed the road twenty-four hours to improve itself, finding that I required that additional margin of time for the completion of my task. I had ordered my Bill to be upon the table, and a chaise to be at the door, "at eight o'clock to-morrow evening." It was eight o'clock to-morrow evening when I buckled up my travelling writing-desk in its leather case, paid my Bill, and got on my warm coats and wrappers. Of course, no time now remained for my travelling on to add a frozen tear to the icicles which were doubtless hanging plentifully about the farmhouse where I had first seen Angela. What I had to do was to get across to Liverpool by the shortest open road, there to meet my heavy baggage and embark. It was quite enough to do, and I had not an hour too much time to do it in.

I had taken leave of all my Holly-Tree friends—almost,

for the time being, of my bashfulness too—and was standing for half a minute at the Inn door watching the ostler as he took another turn at the cord which tied my portmanteau on the chaise, when I saw lamps coming down towards the Holly-Tree. The road was so padded with snow that no wheels were audible; but all of us who were standing at the Inn door saw lamps coming on, and at a lively rate too, between the walls of snow that had been heaped up on either side of the track. The chambermaid instantly divined how the case stood, and called to the ostler, " Tom, this is a Gretna job!" The ostler, knowing that her sex instinctively scented a marriage, or anything in that direction, rushed up the yard bawling, "Next four out!" and in a moment the whole establishment was thrown into commotion.

I had a melancholy interest in seeing the happy man who loved and was beloved; and therefore, instead of driving off at once, I remained at the Inn door when the fugitives drove up. A bright-eyed fellow, muffled in a mantle, jumped out so briskly that he almost overthrew me. He turned to apologise, and, by Heaven, it was Edwin!

"Charley!" said he, recoiling. "Gracious powers, what do you do here?"

"Edwin," said I, recoiling, "gracious powers, what do *you* do here?" I struck my forehead as I said it, and an insupportable blaze of light seemed to shoot before my eyes.

He hurried me into the little parlour (always kept with a slow fire in it and no poker), where posting company waited while their horses were putting to, and, shutting the door, said:

"Charley, forgive me!"

"Edwin!" I returned. "Was this well? When I loved her so dearly! When I had garnered up my heart so long!" I could say no more.

He was shocked when he saw how moved I was, and made the cruel observation, that he had not thought I should have taken it so much to heart.

I looked at him. I reproached him no more. But I looked at him.

"My dear, dear Charley," said he, "don't think ill of me, I beseech you! I know you have a right to my utmost confidence, and, believe me, you have ever had it until now. I abhor secrecy. Its meanness is intolerable to me. But I and my dear girl have observed it for your sake."

He and his dear girl! It steeled me.

"You have observed it for my sake, sir?" said I, wondering how his frank face could face it out so.

"Yes!—and Angela's," said he.

I found the room reeling round in an uncertain way, like a labouring humming-top. "Explain yourself," said I, holding on by one hand to an arm-chair.

"Dear old darling Charley!" returned Edwin, in his cordial manner, "consider! When you were going on so happily with Angela, why should I compromise you with the old gentleman by making you a party to our engagement, and (after he had declined my proposals) to our secret intention? Surely it was better that you should be able honourably to say, 'He never took counsel with me, never told me, never breathed a word of it.' If Angela suspected it, and showed me all the favour and support she could—God bless her for a precious creature and a priceless wife!—I couldn't help that. Neither I nor Emmeline ever told her, any more than we told you. And for the same good reason, Charley; trust me, for the same good reason, and no other upon earth!"

Emmeline was Angela's cousin. Lived with her. Had been brought up with her. Was her father's ward. Had property.

"Emmeline is in the chaise, my dear Edwin!" said I, embracing him with the greatest affection.

"My good fellow!" said he, "do you suppose I should be going to Gretna Green without her?"

I ran out with Edwin, I opened the chaise door, I took Emmeline in my arms, I folded her to my heart. She was wrapped in soft white fur, like the snowy landscape: but was warm, and young, and lovely. I put their leaders to with my own hands, I gave the boys a five-pound note apiece, I cheered them as they drove away, I drove the other way myself as hard as I could pelt.

I never went to Liverpool, I never went to America, I went straight back to London, and I married Angela. I have never until this time, even to her, disclosed the secret of my character, and the mistrust and the mistaken journey into which it led me. When she, and they, and our eight children and their seven—I mean Edwin's and Emmeline's, whose eldest girl is old enough now to wear white for herself, and to look very like her mother in it—come to read these pages, as of course they will, I shall hardly fail to be found out at last. Never mind! I can bear it. I began at the Holly-Tree, by idle accident, to associate the Christmas-time of year with human interest, and with some inquiry into, and some care for, the lives of those by whom I find myself surrounded. I hope that I am none the worse for it, and that no one near me or afar off is the worse for it. And I say, May the green Holly-Tree flourish, striking its roots deep into our English ground, and having its germinating qualities carried by the birds of Heaven all over the world!

THE WRECK OF THE GOLDEN MARY

MARY

[1856]

THE WRECK OF THE GOLDEN MARY.

THE WRECK.

I was apprenticed to the Sea when I was twelve years old, and I have encountered a great deal of rough weather, both literal and metaphorical. It has always been my opinion since I first possessed such a thing as an opinion, that the man who knows only one subject is next tiresome to the man who knows no subject. Therefore, in the course of my life I have taught myself whatever I could, and although I am not an educated man, I am able, I am thankful to say, to have an intelligent interest in most things.

A person might suppose, from reading the above, that I am in the habit of holding forth about number one. That is not the case. Just as if I was to come into a room among strangers, and must either be introduced or introduce myself, so I have taken the liberty of passing these few remarks, simply and plainly that it may be known who and what I am. I will add no more of the sort than that my name is William George Ravender, that I was born at Penrith half a year after my own father was drowned, and that I am on the second day of this present blessed Christmas week of one thousand eight hundred and fifty-six, fifty-six years of age.

When the rumour first went flying up and down that there was gold in California—which, as most people know, was before it was discovered in the British colony of Australia— I was in the West Indies, trading among the Islands. Being in command and likewise part-owner of a smart schooner, I had my work cut out for me, and I was doing it. Consequently, gold in California was no business of mine.

But, by the time when I came home to England again, the thing was as clear as your hand held up before you at noon-day. There was Californian gold in the museums and in the goldsmiths' shops, and the very first time I went upon 'Change, I met a friend of mine (a seafaring man like myself), with a Californian nugget hanging to his watch-chain. I handled it. It was as like a peeled walnut with bits unevenly broken off here and there, and then electrotyped all over, as ever I saw anything in my life.

I am a single man (she was too good for this world and for me, and she died six weeks before our marriage-day), so when I am ashore, I live in my house at Poplar. My house at Poplar is taken care of and kept ship-shape by an old lady who was my mother's maid before I was born. She is as handsome and as upright as any old lady in the world. She is as fond of me as if she had ever had an only son, and I was he. Well do I know wherever I sail that she never lays down her head at night without having said, "Merciful Lord! bless and preserve William George Ravender, and send him safe home, through Christ our Saviour!" I have thought of it in many a dangerous moment, when it has done me no harm, I am sure.

In my house at Poplar, along with this old lady, I lived quiet for best part of a year: having had a long spell of it among the Islands, and having (which was very uncommon in me) taken the fever rather badly. At last, being strong and hearty, and having read every book I could lay hold of, right out, I was walking down Leadenhall Street in the City of London, thinking of turning-to again, when I met

what I call Smithick and Watersby of Liverpool. I chanced
to lift up my eyes from looking in at a ship's chrono-
meter in a window, and I saw him bearing down upon me,
head on.

It is, personally, neither Smithick, nor Watersby, that I
here mention, nor was I ever acquainted with any man of
either of those names, nor do I think that there has been
any one of either of those names in that Liverpool House
for years back. But, it is in reality the House itself that I
refer to; and a wiser merchant or a truer gentleman never
stepped.

"My dear Captain Ravender," says he. "Of all the men
on earth, I wanted to see you most. I was on my way to
you."

"Well!" says I. "That looks as if you were to see me,
don't it?" With that I put my arm in his, and we walked
on towards the Royal Exchange, and when we got there,
walked up and down at the back of it where the Clock-
Tower is. We walked an hour and more, for he had much
to say to me. He had a scheme for chartering a new ship of
their own to take out cargo to the diggers and emigrants
in California, and to buy and bring back gold. Into the
particulars of that scheme I will not enter, and I have no
right to enter. All I say of it is, that it was a very original
one, a very fine one, a very sound one, and a very lucrative
one beyond doubt.

He imparted it to me as freely as if I had been a part of
himself. After doing so, he made me the handsomest sharing
offer that ever was made to me, boy or man—or I believe
to any other captain in the Merchant Navy—and he took
this round turn to finish with:

"Ravender, you are well aware that the lawlessness of that
coast and country at present, is as special as the circumstances
in which it is placed. Crews of vessels outward-bound, desert
as soon as they make the land; crews of vessels homeward-
bound, ship at enormous wages, with the express intention of

murdering the captain and seizing the gold freight; no man
can trust another, and the devil seems let loose. Now," says
he, "you know my opinion of you, and you know I am only
expressing it, and with no singularity, when I tell you that
you are almost the only man on whose integrity, discretion,
and energy—" &c., &c. For, I don't want to repeat what he
said, though I was and am sensible of it.

Notwithstanding my being, as I have mentioned, quite
ready for a voyage, still I had some doubts of this voyage.
Of course I knew, without being told, that there were
peculiar difficulties and dangers in it, a long way over and
above those which attend all voyages. It must not be supposed that I was afraid to face them; but, in my opinion a
man has no manly motive or sustainment in his own breast
for facing dangers, unless he has well considered what they
are, and is able quietly to say to himself, "None of these
perils can now take me by surprise; I shall know what to
do for the best in any of them; all the rest lies in the higher
and greater hands to which I humbly commit myself." On
this principle I have so attentively considered (regarding it
as my duty) all the hazards I have ever been able to think
of, in the ordinary way of storm, shipwreck, and fire at sea,
that I hope I should be prepared to do, in any of those
cases, whatever could be done, to save the lives intrusted to
my charge.

As I was thoughtful, my good friend proposed that he
should leave me to walk there as long as I liked, and that I
should dine with him by-and-by at his club in Pall Mall.
I accepted the invitation and I walked up and down there,
quarter-deck fashion, a matter of a couple of hours; now
and then looking up at the weathercock as I might have
looked up aloft; and now and then taking a look into
Cornhill, as I might have taken a look over the side.

All dinner-time, and all after dinner-time, we talked it
over again. I gave him my views of his plan, and he very
much approved of the same. I told him I had nearly decided,

but not quite. "Well, well," says he, "come down to Liverpool to-morrow with me, and see the Golden Mary." I liked the name (her name was Mary, and she was golden, if golden stands for good), so I began to feel that it was almost done when I said I would go to Liverpool. On the next morning but one we were on board the Golden Mary. I might have known, from his asking me to come down and see her, what she was. I declare her to have been the completest and most exquisite Beauty that ever I set my eyes upon.

We had inspected every timber in her, and had come back to the gangway to go ashore from the dock-basin, when I put out my hand to my friend. "Touch upon it," says I, "and touch heartily. I take command of this ship, and I am hers and yours, if I can get John Steadiman for my chief mate."

John Steadiman had sailed with me four voyages. The first voyage John was third mate out to China, and came home second. The other three voyages he was my first officer. At this time of chartering the Golden Mary, he was aged thirty-two. A brisk, bright, blue-eyed fellow, a very neat figure and rather under the middle size, never out of the way and never in it, a face that pleased everybody and that all children took to, a habit of going about singing as cheerily as a blackbird, and a perfect sailor.

We were in one of those Liverpool hackney-coaches in less than a minute, and we cruised about in her upwards of three hours, looking for John. John had come home from Van Diemen's Land barely a month before, and I had heard of him as taking a frisk in Liverpool. We asked after him, among many other places, at the two boarding-houses he was fondest of, and we found he had had a week's spell at each of them; but, he had gone here and gone there, and had set off "to lay out on the main-to'-gallant-yard of the highest Welsh mountain" (so he had told the people of the house), and where he might be then, or when he might come

back, nobody could tell us. But it was surprising, to be
sure, to see how every face brightened the moment there
was mention made of the name of Mr. Steadiman.

We were taken aback at meeting with no better luck, and
we had wore ship and put her head for my friends, when as
we were jogging through the streets, I clap my eyes on John
himself coming out of a toyshop! He was carrying a little
boy, and conducting two uncommon pretty women to their
coach, and he told me afterwards that he had never in his
life seen one of the three before, but that he was so taken
with them on looking in at the toyshop while they were
buying the child a cranky Noah's Ark, very much down
by the head, that he had gone in and asked the ladies'
permission to treat him to a tolerably correct Cutter there
was in the window, in order that such a handsome boy might
not grow up with a lubberly idea of naval architecture.

We stood off and on until the ladies' coachman began to
give way, and then we hailed John. On his coming aboard
of us, I told him, very gravely, what I had said to my friend.
It struck him, as he said himself, amidships. He was quite
shaken by it. "Captain Ravender," were John Steadiman's
words, "such an opinion from you is true commendation,
and I'll sail round the world with you for twenty years if
you hoist the signal, and stand by you for ever!" And
now indeed I felt that it was done, and that the Golden Mary
was afloat.

Grass never grew yet under the feet of Smithick and
Watersby. The riggers were out of that ship in a fortnight's
time, and we had begun taking in cargo. John was always
aboard, seeing everything stowed with his own eyes; and
whenever I went aboard myself early or late, whether he was
below in the hold, or on deck at the hatchway, or overhauling
his cabin, nailing up pictures in it of the Blush Roses of
England, the Blue Belles of Scotland, and the female Sham-
rock of Ireland: of a certainty I heard John singing like a
blackbird.

We had room for twenty passengers. Our sailing advertise-
ment was no sooner out, than we might have taken these
twenty times over. In entering our men, I and John (both
together) picked them, and we entered none but good hands
—as good as were to be found in that port. And so, in a
good ship of the best build, well owned, well arranged, well
officered, well manned, well found in all respects, we parted
with our pilot at a quarter past four o'clock in the afternoon
of the seventh of March, one thousand eight hundred and
fifty-one, and stood with a fair wind out to sea.

It may be easily believed that up to that time I had had
no leisure to be intimate with my passengers. The most of
them were then in their berths sea-sick; however, in going
among them, telling them what was good for them, persuading
them not to be there, but to come up on deck and feel the
breeze, and in rousing them with a joke, or a comfortable
word, I made acquaintance with them, perhaps, in a more
friendly and confidential way from the first, than I might
have done at the cabin table.

Of my passengers, I need only particularise, just at present,
a bright-eyed blooming young wife who was going out to join
her husband in California, taking with her their only child,
a little girl of three years old, whom he had never seen; a
sedate young woman in black, some five years older (about
thirty as I should say), who was going out to join a brother;
and an old gentleman, a good deal like a hawk if his eyes
had been better and not so red, who was always talking,
morning, noon, and night, about the gold discovery. But,
whether he was making the voyage, thinking his old arms
could dig for gold, or whether his speculation was to buy it,
or to barter for it, or to cheat for it, or to snatch it anyhow
from other people, was his secret. He kept his secret.

These three and the child were the soonest well. The
child was a most engaging child, to be sure, and very fond
of me: though I am bound to admit that John Steadiman
and I were borne on her pretty little books in reverse order,

and that he was captain there, and I was mate. It was
beautiful to watch her with John, and it was beautiful to
watch John with her. Few would have thought it possible,
to see John playing at bo-peep round the mast, that he was
the man who had caught up an iron bar and struck a Malay
and a Maltese dead, as they were gliding with their knives
down the cabin stair aboard the barque Old England, when
the captain lay ill in his cot, off Saugar Point. But he was;
and give him his back against a bulwark, he would have done
the same by half a dozen of them. The name of the young
mother was Mrs. Atherfield, the name of the young lady in
black was Miss Coleshaw, and the name of the old gentleman
was Mr. Rarx.

As the child had a quantity of shining fair hair, clustering in curls all about her face, and as her name was Lucy,
Steadiman gave her the name of the Golden Lucy. So,
we had the Golden Lucy and the Golden Mary; and
John kept up the idea to that extent as he and the child
went playing about the decks, that I believe she used to
think the ship was alive somehow—a sister or companion,
going to the same place as herself. She liked to be by the
wheel, and in fine weather, I have often stood by the man
whose trick it was at the wheel, only to hear her, sitting near
my feet, talking to the ship. Never had a child such a doll
before, I suppose; but she made a doll of the Golden Mary,
and used to dress her up by tying ribbons and little bits of
finery to the belaying-pins; and nobody ever moved them,
unless it was to save them from being blown away.

Of course I took charge of the two young women, and I
called them "my dear," and they never minded, knowing
that whatever I said was said in a fatherly and protecting
spirit. I gave them their places on each side of me at dinner,
Mrs. Atherfield on my right and Miss Coleshaw on my left;
and I directed the unmarried lady to serve out the breakfast, and the married lady to serve out the tea. Likewise I
said to my black steward in their presence, "Tom Snow,

these two ladies are equally the mistresses of this house, and
do you obey their orders equally;" at which Tom laughed,
and they all laughed.

Old Mr. Rarx was not a pleasant man to look at, nor yet to
talk to, or to be with, for no one could help seeing that he was
a sordid and selfish character, and that he had warped further
and further out of the straight with time. Not but what he
was on his best behaviour with us, as everybody was; for we
had no bickering among us, for'ard or aft. I only mean to
say, he was not the man one would have chosen for a messmate.
If choice there had been, one might even have gone a few
points out of one's course, to say, "No! Not him!" But,
there was one curious inconsistency in Mr. Rarx. That was,
that he took an astonishing interest in the child. He looked,
and I may add, he was, one of the last of men to care at all
for a child, or to care much for any human creature. Still,
he went so far as to be habitually uneasy, if the child was
long on deck, out of his sight. He was always afraid of her
falling overboard, or falling down a hatchway, or of a block
or what not coming down upon her from the rigging in the
working of the ship, or of her getting some hurt or other.
He used to look at her and touch her, as if she was something
precious to him. He was always solicitous about her not
injuring her health, and constantly entreated her mother to
be careful of it. This was so much the more curious, because
the child did not like him, but used to shrink away from him,
and would not even put out her hand to him without coaxing
from others. I believe that every soul on board frequently
noticed this, and not one of us understood it. However, it
was such a plain fact, that John Steadiman said more than
once when old Mr. Rarx was not within earshot, that if the
Golden Mary felt a tenderness for the dear old gentleman
she carried in her lap, she must be bitterly jealous of the
Golden Lucy.

Before I go any further with this narrative, I will state that
our ship was a barque of three hundred tons, carrying a crew

of eighteen men, a second mate in addition to John, a
carpenter, an armourer or smith, and two apprentices (one a
Scotch boy, poor little fellow). We had three boats; the Long-
boat, capable of carrying twenty-five men; the Cutter, capable
of carrying fifteen; and the Surf-boat, capable of carrying ten.
I put down the capacity of these boats according to the
numbers they were really meant to hold.

We had tastes of bad weather and head-winds, of course;
but, on the whole we had as fine a run as any reasonable
man could expect, for sixty days. I then began to enter two
remarks in the ship's Log and in my Journal; first, that there
was an unusual and amazing quantity of ice; second, that the
nights were most wonderfully dark, in spite of the ice.

For five days and a half, it seemed quite useless and hopeless to alter the ship's course so as to stand out of the way
of this ice. I made what southing I could; but, all that
time, we were beset by it. Mrs. Atherfield after standing by
me on deck once, looking for some time in an awed manner
at the great bergs that surrounded us, said in a whisper,
"O! Captain Ravender, it looks as if the whole solid earth
had changed into ice, and broken up!" I said to her,
laughing, "I don't wonder that it does, to your inexperi-
enced eyes, my dear." But I had never seen a twentieth
part of the quantity, and, in reality, I was pretty much of
her opinion.

However, at two P.M. on the afternoon of the sixth day,
that is to say, when we were sixty-six days out, John Steadiman who had gone aloft, sang out from the top, that the sea
was clear ahead. Before four P.M. a strong breeze springing
up right astern, we were in open water at sunset. The
breeze then freshening into half a gale of wind, and the
Golden Mary being a very fast sailer, we went before the
wind merrily, all night.

I had thought it impossible that it could be darker than
it had been, until the sun, moon, and stars should fall out
of the Heavens, and Time should be destroyed; but, it had

been next to light, in comparison with what it was now.
The darkness was so profound, that looking into it was painful and oppressive—like looking, without a ray of light, into
a dense black bandage put as close before the eyes as it
could be, without touching them. I doubled the look-out,
and John and I stood in the bow side-by-side, never leaving
it all night. Yet I should no more have known that he was
near me when he was silent, without putting out my arm
and touching him, than I should if he had turned in and
been fast asleep below. We were not so much looking out,
all of us, as listening to the utmost, both with our eyes
and ears.

Next day, I found that the mercury in the barometer,
which had risen steadily since we cleared the ice, remained
steady. I had had very good observations, with now and
then the interruption of a day or so, since our departure. I
got the sun at noon, and found that we were in Lat. 58° S.,
Long. 60° W., off New South Shetland; in the neighbourhood
of Cape Horn. We were sixty-seven days out, that day.
The ship's reckoning was accurately worked and made up.
The ship did her duty admirably, all on board were well,
and all hands were as smart, efficient, and contented, as it
was possible to be.

When the night came on again as dark as before, it was
the eighth night I had been on deck. Nor had I taken more
than a very little sleep in the day-time, my station being
always near the helm, and often at it, while we were among
the ice. Few but those who have tried it can imagine the
difficulty and pain of only keeping the eyes open—physically
open—under such circumstances, in such darkness. They get
struck by the darkness, and blinded by the darkness. They
make patterns in it, and they flash in it, as if they had gone
out of your head to look at you. On the turn of midnight,
John Steadiman, who was alert and fresh (for I had always
made him turn in by day), said to me, "Captain Ravender,
I entreat of you to go below. I am sure you can hardly

stand, and your voice is getting weak, sir. Go below, and take a little rest. I'll call you if a block chafes." I said to John in answer, "Well, well, John! Let us wait till the turn of one o'clock, before we talk about that." I had just had one of the ship's lanterns held up, that I might see how the night went by my watch, and it was then twenty minutes after twelve.

At five minutes before one, John sang out to the boy to bring the lantern again, and when I told him once more what the time was, entreated and prayed of me to go below. "Captain Ravender," says he, "all's well; we can't afford to have you laid up for a single hour; and I respectfully and earnestly beg of you to go below." The end of it was, that I agreed to do so, on the understanding that if I failed to come up of my own accord within three hours, I was to be punctually called. Having settled that, I left John in charge. But I called him to me once afterwards, to ask him a question. I had been to look at the barometer, and had seen the mercury still perfectly steady, and had come up the companion again to take a last look about me—if I can use such a word in reference to such darkness—when I thought that the waves, as the Golden Mary parted them and shook them off, had a hollow sound in them; something that I fancied was a rather unusual reverberation. I was standing by the quarter-deck rail on the starboard side, when I called John aft to me, and bade him listen. He did so with the greatest attention. Turning to me he then said, "Rely upon it, Captain Ravender, you have been without rest too long, and the novelty is only in the state of your sense of hearing." I thought so too by that time, and I think so now, though I can never know for absolute certain in this world, whether it was or not.

When I left John Steadiman in charge, the ship was still going at a great rate through the water. The wind still blew right astern. Though she was making great way, she was under shortened sail, and had no more than she could easily carry. All was snug, and nothing complained. There was a pretty sea running, but not a very high sea neither, nor at all a confused one.

I turned in, as we seamen say, all standing. The meaning of that is, I did not pull my clothes off—no, not even so much as my coat: though I did my shoes, for my feet were badly swelled with the deck. There was a little swing-lamp alight in my cabin. I thought, as I looked at it before shutting my eyes, that I was so tired of darkness, and troubled by darkness, that I could have gone to sleep best in the midst of a million of flaming gas-lights. That was the last thought I had before I went off, except the prevailing thought that I should not be able to get to sleep at all.

I dreamed that I was back at Penrith again, and was trying to get round the church, which had altered its shape very much since I last saw it, and was cloven all down the middle of the steeple in a most singular manner. Why I wanted to get round the church I don't know; but I was as anxious to do it as if my life depended on it. Indeed, I believe it did in the dream. For all that, I could not get round the church. I was still trying, when I came against it with a violent shock, and was flung out of my cot against the ship's side. Shrieks and a terrific outcry struck me far harder than the bruising timbers, and amidst sounds of grinding and crashing, and a heavy rushing and breaking of water—sounds I understood too well—I made my way on deck. It was not an easy thing to do, for the ship heeled over frightfully, and was beating in a furious manner.

I could not see the men as I went forward, but I could hear that they were hauling in sail, in disorder. I had my trumpet in my hand, and, after directing and encouraging them in this till it was done, I hailed first John Steadiman, and then my second mate, Mr. William Rames. Both answered clearly and steadily. Now, I had practised them and all my crew, as I have ever made it a custom to practise all who sail with me, to take certain stations and wait my

orders, in case of any unexpected crisis. When my voice
was heard hailing, and their voices were heard answering, I
was aware, through all the noises of the ship and sea, and
all the crying of the passengers below, that there was a
pause. "Are you ready, Rames?"—"Ay, ay, sir!"—"Then
light up, for God's sake!" In a moment he and another
were burning blue-lights, and the ship and all on board
seemed to be enclosed in a mist of light, under a great black
dome.

The light shone up so high that I could see the huge
Iceberg upon which we had struck, cloven at the top and
down the middle, exactly like Penrith Church in my dream.
At the same moment I could see the watch last relieved,
crowding up and down on deck; I could see Mrs. Atherfield
and Miss Coleshaw thrown about on the top of the companion
as they struggled to bring the child up from below; I could
see that the masts were going with the shock and the beating
of the ship; I could see the frightful breach stove in on the
starboard side, half the length of the vessel, and the sheath-
ing and timbers spirting up; I could see that the Cutter was
disabled, in a wreck of broken fragments; and I could see
every eye turned upon me. It is my belief that if there had
been ten thousand eyes there, I should have seen them all,
with their different looks. And all this in a moment. But
you must consider what a moment.

I saw the men, as they looked at me, fall towards their
appointed stations, like good men and true. If she had not
righted, they could have done very little there or anywhere
but die—not that it is little for a man to die at his post—I
mean they could have done nothing to save the passengers
and themselves. Happily, however, the violence of the shock
with which we had so determinedly borne down direct on
that fatal Iceberg, as if it had been our destination instead
of our destruction, had so smashed and pounded the ship
that she got off in this same instant and righted. I did not
want the carpenter to tell me she was filling and going

down; I could see and hear that. I gave Rames the word
to lower the Long-boat and the Surf-boat, and I myself told
off the men for each duty. Not one hung back, or came
before the other. I now whispered to John Steadiman,
"John, I stand at the gangway here, to see every soul on
board safe over the side. You shall have the next post of
honour, and shall be the last but one to leave the ship.
Bring up the passengers, and range them behind me; and
put what provision and water you can get at, in the boats.
Cast your eye for'ard, John, and you'll see you have not a
moment to lose."

My noble fellows got the boats over the side as orderly as
I ever saw boats lowered with any sea running, and, when
they were launched, two or three of the nearest men in them
as they held on, rising and falling with the swell, called out,
looking up at me, "Captain Ravender, if anything goes
wrong with us, and you are saved, remember we stood by
you!"—"We'll all stand by one another ashore, yet, please
God, my lads!" says I. "Hold on bravely, and be tender
with the women."

The women were an example to us. They trembled very
much, but they were quiet and perfectly collected. "Kiss
me, Captain Ravender," says Mrs. Atherfield, "and God in
heaven bless you, you good man!" "My dear," says I,
"those words are better for me than a life-boat." I held
her child in my arms till she was in the boat, and then
kissed the child and handed her safe down. I now said to
the people in her, "You have got your freight, my lads, all
but me, and I am not coming yet awhile. Pull away from
the ship, and keep off!"

That was the Long-boat. Old Mr. Rarx was one of her
complement, and he was the only passenger who had greatly
misbehaved since the ship struck. Others had been a little
wild, which was not to be wondered at, and not very
blamable; but, he had made a lamentation and uproar which
it was dangerous for the people to hear, as there is always

contagion in weakness and selfishness. His incessant cry had been that he must not be separated from the child, that he couldn't see the child, and that he and the child must go together. He had even tried to wrest the child out of my arms, that he might keep her in his. "Mr. Rarx," said I to him when it came to that, "I have a loaded pistol in my pocket; and if you don't stand out of the gangway, and keep perfectly quiet, I shall shoot you through the heart, if you have got one." Says he, "You won't do murder, Captain Ravender!" "No, sir," says I, "I won't murder forty-four people to humour you, but I'll shoot you to save them." After that he was quiet, and stood shivering a little way off, until I named him to go over the side.

The Long-boat being cast off, the Surf-boat was soon filled. There only remained aboard the Golden Mary, John Mullion the man who had kept on burning the blue-lights (and who had lighted every new one at every old one before it went out, as quietly as if he had been at an illumination); John Steadiman; and myself. I hurried those two into the Surf-boat, called to them to keep off, and waited with a grateful and relieved heart for the Long-boat to come and take me in, if she could. I looked at my watch, and it showed me, by the blue-light, ten minutes past two. They lost no time. As soon as she was near enough, I swung myself into her, and called to the men, "With a will, lads! She's reeling!" We were not an inch too far out of the inner vortex of her going down, when, by the blue-light which John Mullion still burnt in the bow of the Surf-boat, we saw her lurch, and plunge to the bottom head-foremost. The child cried, weeping wildly, "O the dear Golden Mary! O look at her! Save her! Save the poor Golden Mary!" And then the light burnt out, and the black dome seemed to come down upon us.

I suppose if we had all stood a-top of a mountain, and seen the whole remainder of the world sink away from under us, we could hardly have felt more shocked and solitary than we did when we knew we were alone on the wide ocean, and that the beautiful ship in which most of us had been securely asleep within half an hour was gone for ever. There was an awful silence in our boat, and such a kind of palsy on the rowers and the man at the rudder, that I felt they were scarcely keeping her before the sea. I spoke out then, and said, "Let every one here thank the Lord for our preservation!" All the voices answered (even the child's), "We thank the Lord!" I then said the Lord's Prayer, and all hands said it after me with a solemn murmuring. Then I gave the word "Cheerily, O men, Cheerily!" and I felt that they were handling the boat again as a boat ought to be handled.

The Surf-boat now burnt another blue-light to show us where they were, and we made for her, and laid ourselves as nearly alongside of her as we dared. I had always kept my boats with a coil or two of good stout stuff in each of them, so both boats had a rope at hand. We made a shift, with much labour and trouble, to get near enough to one another to divide the blue-lights (they were no use after that night, for the sea-water soon got at them), and to get a tow-rope out between us. All night long we kept together, sometimes obliged to cast off the rope, and sometimes getting it out again, and all of us wearying for the morning—which appeared so long in coming that old Mr. Rarx screamed out, in spite of his fears of me, "The world is drawing to an end, and the sun will never rise any more!"

When the day broke, I found that we were all huddled together in a miserable manner. We were deep in the water; being, as I found on mustering, thirty-one in number, or at least six too many. In the Surf-boat they were fourteen in number, being at least four too many. The first thing I did, was to get myself passed to the rudder—which I took from that time—and to get Mrs. Atherfield, her child, and Miss Coleshaw, passed on to sit next me. As to old Mr. Rarx, I put him in the bow, as far from us as I could.

And I put some of the best men near us in order that if I
should drop there might be a skilful hand ready to take the
helm.

The sea moderating as the sun came up, though the sky
was cloudy and wild, we spoke the other boat, to know what
stores they had, and to overhaul what we had. I had a
compass in my pocket, a small telescope, a double-barrelled
pistol, a knife, and a fire-box and matches. Most of my
men had knives, and some had a little tobacco: some, a pipe
as well. We had a mug among us, and an iron spoon. As
to provisions, there were in my boat two bags of biscuit,
one piece of raw beef, one piece of raw pork, a bag of coffee,
roasted but not ground (thrown in, I imagine, by mistake,
for something else), two small casks of water, and about half-
a-gallon of rum in a keg. The Surf-boat, having rather
more rum than we, and fewer to drink it, gave us, as I
estimated, another quart into our keg. In return, we gave
them three double handfuls of coffee, tied up in a piece of a
handkerchief; they reported that they had aboard besides, a
bag of biscuit, a piece of beef, a small cask of water, a small
box of lemons, and a Dutch cheese. It took a long time to
make these exchanges, and they were not made without risk
to both parties; the sea running quite high enough to make
our approaching near to one another very hazardous. In the
bundle with the coffee, I conveyed to John Steadiman (who
had a ship's compass with him), a paper written in pencil,
and torn from my pocket-book, containing the course I meant
to steer, in the hope of making land, or being picked up by
some vessel—I say in the hope, though I had little hope of
either deliverance. I then sang out to him, so as all might
hear, that if we two boats could live or die together, we
would; but, that if we should be parted by the weather, and
join company no more, they should have our prayers and
blessings, and we asked for theirs. We then gave them
three cheers, which they returned, and I saw the men's heads
droop in both boats as they fell to their oars again.

These arrangements had occupied the general attention advantageously for all, though (as I expressed in the last sentence) they ended in a sorrowful feeling. I now said a few words to my fellow-voyagers on the subject of the small stock of food on which our lives depended if they were preserved from the great deep, and on the rigid necessity of our eking it out in the most frugal manner. One and all replied that whatever allowance I thought best to lay down should be strictly kept to. We made a pair of scales out of a thin strap of iron-plating and some twine, and I got together for weights such of the heaviest buttons among us as I calculated made up some fraction over two ounces. This was the allowance of solid food served out once a-day to each, from that time to the end; with the addition of a coffee-berry, or sometimes half a one, when the weather was very fair, for breakfast. We had nothing else whatever, but half a pint of water each per day, and sometimes, when we were coldest and weakest, a teaspoonful of rum each, served out as a dram. I know how learnedly it can be shown that rum is poison, but I also know that in this case, as in all similar cases I have ever read of—which are numerous—no words can express the comfort and support derived from it. Nor have I the least doubt that it saved the lives of far more than half our number. Having mentioned half a pint of water as our daily allowance, I ought to observe that sometimes we had less, and sometimes we had more; for much rain fell, and we caught it in a canvas stretched for the purpose.

Thus, at that tempestuous time of the year, and in that tempestuous part of the world, we shipwrecked people rose and fell with the waves. It is not my intention to relate (if I can avoid it) such circumstances appertaining to our doleful condition as have been better told in many other narratives of the kind than I can be expected to tell them. I will only note, in so many passing words, that day after day and night after night, we received the sea upon our backs to prevent it from swamping the boat; that one party was always kept baling, and that every hat and cap among us soon got worn out, though patched up fifty times, as the only vessels we had for that service; that another party lay down in the bottom of the boat, while a third rowed; and that we were soon all in boils and blisters and rags.

The other boat was a source of such anxious interest to all of us that I used to wonder whether, if we were saved, the time could ever come when the survivors in this boat of ours could be at all indifferent to the fortunes of the survivors in that. We got out a tow-rope whenever the weather permitted, but that did not often happen, and how we two parties kept within the same horizon, as we did, He, who mercifully permitted it to be so for our consolation, only knows. I never shall forget the looks with which, when the morning light came, we used to gaze about us over the stormy waters, for the other boat. We once parted company for seventy-two hours, and we believed them to have gone down, as they did us. The joy on both sides when we came within view of one another again, had something in a manner Divine in it; each was so forgetful of individual suffering, in tears of delight and sympathy for the people in the other boat.

I have been wanting to get round to the individual or personal part of my subject, as I call it, and the foregoing incident puts me in the right way. The patience and good disposition aboard of us, was wonderful. I was not surprised by it in the women; for all men born of women know what great qualities they will show when men will fail; but, I own I was a little surprised by it in some of the men. Among one-and-thirty people assembled at the best of times, there will usually, I should say, be two or three uncertain tempers. I knew that I had more than one rough temper with me among my own people, for I had chosen those for the Long-boat that I might have them under my eye. But, they

softened under their misery, and were as considerate of the
ladies, and as compassionate of the child, as the best among
us, or among men—they could not have been more so. I
heard scarcely any complaining. The party lying down would
moan a good deal in their sleep, and I would often notice a
man—not always the same man, it is to be understood, but
nearly all of them at one time or other—sitting moaning
at his oar, or in his place, as he looked mistily over the sea.
When it happened to be long before I could catch his eye, he
would go on moaning all the time in the dismallest manner;
but, when our looks met, he would brighten and leave off.
I almost always got the impression that he did not know
what sound he had been making, but that he thought he
had been humming a tune.

Our sufferings from cold and wet were far greater than
our sufferings from hunger. We managed to keep the child
warm; but, I doubt if any one else among us ever was warm
for five minutes together; and the shivering, and the chattering
of teeth, were sad to hear. The child cried a little at first
for her lost playfellow, the Golden Mary; but hardly ever
whimpered afterwards; and when the state of the weather
made it possible, she used now and then to be held up in
the arms of some of us, to look over the sea for John
Steadiman's boat. I see the golden hair and the innocent
face now, between me and the driving clouds, like an angel
going to fly away.

It had happened on the second day, towards night, that
Mrs. Atherfield, in getting Little Lucy to sleep, sang her a
song. She had a soft, melodious voice, and, when she had
finished it, our people up and begged for another. She
sang them another, and after it had fallen dark ended with
the Evening Hymn. From that time, whenever anything
could be heard above the sea and wind, and while she had
any voice left, nothing would serve the people but that she
should sing at sunset. She always did, and always ended
with the Evening Hymn. We mostly took up the last line,

and shed tears when it was done, but not miserably. We had a prayer night and morning, also, when the weather allowed of it.

Twelve nights and eleven days we had been driving in the boat, when old Mr. Rarx began to be delirious, and to cry out to me to throw the gold overboard or it would sink us, and we should all be lost. For days past the child had been declining, and that was the great cause of his wildness. He had been over and over again shrieking out to me to give her all the remaining meat, to give her all the remaining rum, to save her at any cost, or we should all be ruined. At this time, she lay in her mother's arms at my feet. One of her little hands was almost always creeping about her mother's neck or chin. I had watched the wasting of the little hand, and I knew it was nearly over.

The old man's cries were so discordant with the mother's love and submission, that I called out to him in an angry voice, unless he held his peace on the instant, I would order him to be knocked on the head and thrown overboard. He was mute then, until the child died, very peacefully, an hour afterwards: which was known to all in the boat by the mother's breaking out into lamentations for the first time since the wreck—for, she had great fortitude and constancy, though she was a little gentle women. Old Mr. Rarx then became quite ungovernable, tearing what rags he had on him, raging in imprecations, and calling to me that if I had thrown the gold overboard (always the gold with him!) I might have saved the child. "And now," says he, in a terrible voice, "we shall founder, and all go to the Devil, for our sins will sink us, when we have no innocent child to bear us up!" We so discovered with amazement, that this old wretch had only cared for the life of the pretty little creature dear to all of us, because of the influence he superstitiously hoped she might have in preserving him! Altogether it was too much for the smith or armourer, who was sitting next the old man, to bear. He took him by the throat and rolled him under the thwarts, where he lay still enough for hours afterwards.

All that thirteenth night, Miss Coleshaw, lying across my knees as I kept the helm, comforted and supported the poor mother. Her child, covered with a pea-jacket of mine, lay in her lap. It troubled me all night to think that there was no Prayer-Book among us, and that I could remember but very few of the exact words of the burial service. When I stood up at broad day, all knew what was going to be done, and I noticed that my poor fellows made the motion of uncovering their heads, though their heads had been stark bare to the sky and sea for many a weary hour. There was a long heavy swell on, but otherwise it was a fair morning, and there were broad fields of sunlight on the waves in the east. I said no more than this: "I am the Resurrection and the Life, saith the Lord. He raised the daughter of Jairus the ruler, and said she was not dead but slept. He raised the widow's son. He arose Himself, and was seen of many. He loved little children, saying, Suffer them to come unto Me and rebuke them not, for of such is the kingdom of heaven. In His name, my friends, and committed to His merciful goodness!" With those words I laid my rough face softly on the placid little forehead, and buried the Golden Lucy in the grave of the Golden Mary.

Having had it on my mind to relate the end of this dear little child, I have omitted something from its exact place, which I will supply here. It will come quite as well here as anywhere else.

Foreseeing that if the boat lived through the stormy weather, the time must come, and soon come, when we should have absolutely no morsel to eat, I had one momentous point often in my thoughts. Although I had, years before that, fully satisfied myself that the instances in which human beings in the last distress have fed upon each other, are exceedingly few, and have very seldom indeed (if ever) occurred when the people in distress, however dreadful their extremity, have been accustomed to moderate forbearance and restraint; I say, though I had long before quite satisfied my mind on this topic, I felt doubtful whether there might not have been in former cases some harm and danger from keeping it out of sight and pretending not to think of it. I felt doubtful whether some minds, growing weak with fasting and exposure and having such a terrific idea to dwell upon in secret, might not magnify it until it got to have an awful attraction about it. This was not a new thought of mine, for it had grown out of my reading. However, it came over me stronger than it had ever done before—as it had reason for doing—in the boat, and on the fourth day I decided that I would bring out into the light that unformed fear which must have been more or less darkly in every brain among us. Therefore, as a means of beguiling the time and inspiring hope, I gave them the best summary in my power of Bligh's voyage of more than three thousand miles, in an open boat, after the Mutiny of the Bounty, and of the wonderful preservation of that boat's crew. They listened throughout with great interest, and I concluded by telling them, that, in my opinion, the happiest circumstance in the whole narrative was, that Bligh, who was no delicate man either, had solemnly placed it on record therein that he was sure and certain that under no conceivable circumstances whatever would that emaciated party, who had gone through all the pains of famine, have preyed on one another. I cannot describe the visible relief which this spread through the boat, and how the tears stood in every eye. From that time I was as well convinced as Bligh himself that there was no danger, and that this phantom, at any rate, did not haunt us.

Now, it was a part of Bligh's experience that when the people in his boat were most cast down, nothing did them so much good as hearing a story told by one of their number. When I mentioned that, I saw that it struck the general attention as much as it did my own, for I had not thought

of it until I came to it in my summary. This was on the·
day after Mrs. Atherfield first sang to us. I proposed that,
whenever the weather would permit, we should have a story
two hours after dinner (I always issued the allowance I have
mentioned at one o'clock, and called it by that name), as
well as our song at sunset. The proposal was received with
a cheerful satisfaction that warmed my heart within me; and
I do not say too much when I say that those two periods
in the four-and-twenty hours were expected with positive
pleasure, and were really enjoyed by all hands. Spectres as
we soon were in our bodily wasting, our imaginations did
not perish like the gross flesh upon our bones. Music and
Adventure, two of the great gifts of Providence to mankind,
could charm us long after that was lost.

The wind was almost always against us after the second
day; and for many days together we could not nearly hold
our own. We had all varieties of bad weather. We had
rain, hail, snow, wind, mist, thunder and lightning. Still
the boats lived through the heavy seas, and still we perishing
people rose and fell with the great waves.

Sixteen nights and fifteen days, twenty nights and nineteen
days, twenty-four nights and twenty-three days. So the time
went on. Disheartening as I knew that our progress, or
want of progress, must be, I never deceived them as to my
calculations of it. In the first place, I felt that we were all
too near eternity for deceit; in the second place, I knew
that if I failed, or died, the man who followed me must
have a knowledge of the true state of things to begin upon.
When I told them at noon, what I reckoned we had made
or lost, they generally received what I said in a tranquil and
resigned manner, and always gratefully towards me. It was
not unusual at any time of the day for some one to burst
out weeping loudly without any new cause; and, when the
burst was over, to calm down a little better than before. I
had seen exactly the same thing in a house of mourning.

During the whole of this time, old Mr. Rarx had had his

fits of calling out to me to throw the gold (always the gold!) overboard, and of heaping violent reproaches upon me for not having saved the child; but now, the food being all gone, and I having nothing left to serve out but a bit of coffee-berry now and then, he began to be too weak to do this, and consequently fell silent. Mrs. Atherfield and Miss Coleshaw generally lay, each with an arm across one of my knees, and her head upon it. They never complained at all. Up to the time of her child's death, Mrs. Atherfield had bound up her own beautiful hair every day; and I took particular notice that this was always before she sang her song at night, when every one looked at her. But she never did it after the loss of her darling; and it would have been now all tangled with dirt and wet, but that Miss Coleshaw was careful of it long after she was herself, and would sometimes smooth it down with her weak thin hands.

We were past mustering a story now; but one day, at about this period, I reverted to the superstition of old Mr. Rarx, concerning the Golden Lucy, and told them that nothing vanished from the eye of God, though much might pass away from the eyes of men. "We were all of us," says I, "children once; and our baby feet have strolled in green woods ashore; and our baby hands have gathered flowers in gardens, where the birds were singing. The children that we were, are not lost to the great knowledge of our Creator. Those innocent creatures will appear with us before Him, and plead for us. What we were in the best time of our generous youth will arise and go with us too. The purest part of our lives will not desert us at the pass to which all of us here present are gliding. What we were then, will be as much in existence before Him, as what we are now." They were no less comforted by this consideration, than I was myself; and Miss Coleshaw, drawing my ear nearer to her lips, said, "Captain Ravender, I was on my way to marry a disgraced and broken man, whom I dearly loved when he was honourable and good. Your words seem to have come out of my own poor heart." She pressed my hand upon it, smiling.

Twenty-seven nights and twenty-six days. We were in no want of rain-water, but we had nothing else. And yet, even now, I never turned my eyes upon a waking face but it tried to brighten before mine. O, what a thing it is, in a time of danger and in the presence of death, the shining of a face upon a face! I have heard it broached that orders should be given in great new ships by electric telegraph. I admire machinery as much as any man, and am as thankful to it as any man can be for what it does for us. But it will never be a substitute for the face of a man, with his soul in it, encouraging another man to be brave and true. Never try it for that. It will break down like a straw.

I now began to remark certain changes in myself which I did not like. They caused me much disquiet. I often saw the Golden Lucy in the air above the boat. I often saw her I have spoken of before, sitting beside me. I saw the Golden Mary go down, as she really had gone down, twenty times in a day. And yet the sea was mostly, to my thinking, not sea neither, but moving country and extraordinary mountainous regions, the like of which have never been beheld. I felt it time to leave my last words regarding John Steadiman, in case any lips should last out to repeat them to any living ears. I said that John had told me (as he had on deck) that he had sung out "Breakers ahead!" the instant they were audible, and had tried to wear ship, but she struck before it could be done. (His cry, I dare say, had made my dream.) I said that the circumstances were altogether without warning, and out of any course that could have been guarded against; that the same loss would have happened if I had been in charge; and that John was not to blame, but from first to last had done his duty nobly, like the man he was. I tried to write it down in my pocket-book, but could make no words, though I knew what the words were that I wanted to make. When it had come to that, her hands—though she was dead so long—laid me down gently in the bottom of the boat, and she and the Golden Lucy swung me to sleep.

All that follows, was written by John Steadiman, Chief Mate :

On the twenty-sixth day after the foundering of the Golden Mary at sea, I, John Steadiman, was sitting in my place in the stern-sheets of the Surf-boat, with just sense enough left in me to steer—that is to say, with my eyes strained, wide-awake, over the bows of the boat, and my brains fast asleep and dreaming—when I was roused upon a sudden by our second mate, Mr. William Rames.

"Let me take a spell in your place," says he. "And look you out for the Long-boat astern. The last time she rose on the crest of a wave, I thought I made out a signal flying aboard her."

We shifted our places, clumsily and slowly enough, for we were both of us weak and dazed with wet, cold, and hunger. I waited some time, watching the heavy rollers astern, before the Long-boat rose a-top of one of them at the same time with us. At last, she was heaved up for a moment well in view, and there, sure enough, was the signal flying aboard of her—a strip of rag of some sort, rigged to an oar, and hoisted in her bows.

"What does it mean?" says Rames to me in a quavering, trembling sort of voice. "Do they signal a sail in sight?"

"Hush, for God's sake!" says I, clapping my hand over his mouth. "Don't let the people hear you. They'll all go mad together if we mislead them about that signal. Wait a bit, till I have another look at it."

I held on by him, for he had set me all of a tremble with his notion of a sail in sight, and watched for the Long-boat again. Up she rose on the top of another roller. I made out the signal clearly, that second time, and saw that it was rigged half-mast high.

"Rames," says I, "it's a signal of distress. Pass the word forward to keep her before the sea, and no more. We must get the Long-boat within hailing distance of us, as soon as possible."

I dropped down into my old place at the tiller without another word—for the thought went through me like a knife that something had happened to Captain Ravender. I should consider myself unworthy to write another line of this statement, if I had not made up my mind to speak the truth, the whole truth, and nothing but the truth—and I must, therefore, confess plainly that now, for the first time, my heart sank within me. This weakness on my part was produced in some degree, as I take it, by the exhausting effects of previous anxiety and grief.

Our provisions—if I may give that name to what we had left—were reduced to the rind of one lemon and about a couple of handsfull of coffee-berries. Besides these great distresses, caused by the death, the danger, and the suffering among my crew and passengers, I had had a little distress of my own to shake me still more, in the death of the child whom I had got to be very fond of on the voyage out—so fond that I was secretly a little jealous of her being taken in the Long-boat instead of mine when the ship foundered. It used to be a great comfort to me, and I think to those with me also, after we had seen the last of the Golden Mary, to see the Golden Lucy, held up by the men in the Long-boat, when the weather allowed it, as the best and brightest sight they had to show. She looked, at the distance we saw her from, almost like a little white bird in the air. To miss her for the first time, when the weather lulled a little again, and we all looked out for our white bird and looked in vain, was a sore disappointment. To see the men's heads bowed down and the captain's hand pointing into the sea when we hailed the Long-boat, a few days after, gave me as heavy a shock and as sharp a pang of heartache to bear as ever I remember suffering in all my life. I only mention these

things to show that if I did give way a little at first,
under the dread that our captain was lost to us, it was not
without having been a good deal shaken beforehand by
more trials of one sort or another than often fall to one
man's share.

I had got over the choking in my throat with the help
of a drop of water, and had steadied my mind again so as
to be prepared against the worst, when I heard the hail
(Lord help the poor fellows, how weak it sounded!)—

"Surf-boat, ahoy!"

I looked up, and there were our companions in misfortune
tossing abreast of us; not so near that we could make out
the features of any of them, but near enough, with some
exertion for people in our condition, to make their voices
heard in the intervals when the wind was weakest.

I answered the hail, and waited a bit, and heard nothing,
and then sung out the captain's name. The voice that
replied did not sound like his; the words that reached us
were :

"Chief-mate wanted on board!"

Every man of my crew knew what that meant as well as I
did. As second officer in command, there could be but one
reason for wanting me on board the Long-boat. A groan
went all round us, and my men looked darkly in each other's
faces, and whispered under their breaths :

"The captain is dead!"

I commanded them to be silent, and not to make too sure
of bad news, at such a pass as things had now come to with
us. Then, hailing the Long-boat, I signified that I was ready
to go on board when the weather would let me—stopped a
bit to draw a good long breath—and then called out as loud
as I could the dreadful question :

"Is the captain dead?"

The black figures of three or four men in the after-part of
the Long-boat all stooped down together as my voice reached
them. They were lost to view for about a minute; then

appeared again—one man among them was held up on his feet by the rest, and he hailed back the blessed words (a very faint hope went a very long way with people in our desperate situation): "Not yet!"

The relief felt by me, and by all with me, when we knew that our captain, though unfitted for duty, was not lost to us, it is not in words—at least, not in such words as a man like me can command—to express. I did my best to cheer the men by telling them what a good sign it was that we were not as badly off yet as we had feared; and then communicated what instructions I had to give, to William Rames, who was to be left in command in my place when I took charge of the Long-boat. After that, there was nothing to be done, but to wait for the chance of the wind dropping at sunset, and the sea going down afterwards, so as to enable our weak crews to lay the two boats alongside of each other, without undue risk—or, to put it plainer, without saddling ourselves with the necessity for any extraordinary exertion of strength or skill. Both the one and the other had now been starved out of us for days and days together.

At sunset the wind suddenly dropped, but the sea, which had been running high for so long a time past, took hours after that before it showed any signs of getting to rest. The moon was shining, the sky was wonderfully clear, and it could not have been, according to my calculations, far off midnight, when the long, slow, regular swell of the calming ocean fairly set in, and I took the responsibility of lessening the distance between the Long-boat and ourselves.

It was, I dare say, a delusion of mine; but I thought I had never seen the moon shine so white and ghastly anywhere, either at sea or on land, as she shone that night while we were approaching our companions in misery. When there was not much more than a boat's length between us, and the white light streamed cold and clear over all our faces, both crews rested on their oars with one great shudder, and stared over the gunwale of either boat, panic-stricken at the first sight of each other.

"Any lives lost among you?" I asked, in the midst of that frightful silence.

The men in the Long-boat huddled together like sheep at the sound of my voice.

"None yet, but the child, thanks be to God!" answered one among them.

And at the sound of his voice, all my men shrank together like the men in the Long-boat. I was afraid to let the horror produced by our first meeting at close quarters after the dreadful changes that wet, cold, and famine had produced, last one moment longer than could be helped; so, without giving time for any more questions and answers, I commanded the men to lay the two boats close alongside of each other. When I rose up and committed the tiller to the hands of Rames, all my poor fellows raised their white faces imploringly to mine. "Don't leave us, sir," they said, "don't leave us." "I leave you," says I, "under the command and the guidance of Mr. William Rames, as good a sailor as I am, and as trusty and kind a man as ever stepped. Do your duty by him, as you have done it by me; and remember to the last, that while there is life there is hope. God bless and help you all!" With those words I collected what strength I had left, and caught at two arms that were held out to me, and so got from the stern-sheets of one boat into the stern-sheets of the other.

"Mind where you step, sir," whispered one of the men who had helped me into the Long-boat. I looked down as he spoke. Three figures were huddled up below me, with the moonshine falling on them in ragged streaks through the gaps between the men standing or sitting above them. The first face I made out was the face of Miss Coleshaw; her eyes were wide open and fixed on me. She seemed still to keep her senses, and, by the alternate parting and closing of her lips, to be trying to speak, but I could not hear that she

uttered a single word. On her shoulder rested the head of
Mrs. Atherfield. The mother of our poor little Golden
Lucy must, I think, have been dreaming of the child she
had lost; for there was a faint smile just ruffling the white
stillness of her face, when I first saw it turned upward, with
peaceful closed eyes towards the heavens. From her, I
looked down a little, and there, with his head on her lap,
and with one of her hands resting tenderly on his cheek—
there lay the Captain, to whose help and guidance, up to
this miserable time, we had never looked in vain,—there,
worn out at last in our service, and for our sakes, lay the
best and bravest man of all our company. I stole my hand
in gently through his clothes and laid it on his heart, and
felt a little feeble warmth over it, though my cold dulled
touch could not detect even the faintest beating. The two
men in the stern-sheets with me, noticing what I was doing
—knowing I loved him like a brother—and seeing, I suppose, more distress in my face than I myself was conscious
of its showing, lost command over themselves altogether,
and burst into a piteous moaning, sobbing lamentation
over him. One of the two drew aside a jacket from
his feet, and showed me that they were bare, except where
a wet, ragged strip of stocking still clung to one of them.
When the ship struck the Iceberg, he had run on deck
leaving his shoes in his cabin. All through the voyage in
the boat his feet had been unprotected; and not a soul had
discovered it until he dropped! As long as he could keep
his eyes open, the very look of them had cheered the men,
and comforted and upheld the women. Not one living
creature in the boat, with any sense about him, but had
felt the good influence of that brave man in one way or
another. Not one but had heard him, over and over again,
give the credit to others which was due only to himself;
praising this man for patience, and thanking that man for
help, when the patience and the help had really and truly,
as to the best part of both, come only from him. All this,

and much more, I heard pouring confusedly from the men's lips while they crouched down, sobbing and crying over their commander, and wrapping the jacket as warmly and tenderly as they could over his cold feet. It went to my heart to check them; but I knew that if this lamenting spirit spread any further, all chance of keeping alight any last sparks of hope and resolution among the boat's company would be lost for ever. Accordingly I sent them to their places, spoke a few encouraging words to the men forward, promising to serve out, when the morning came, as much as I dared, of any eatable thing left in the lockers; called to Rames, in my old boat, to keep as near us as he safely could; drew the garments and coverings of the two poor suffering women more closely about them; and, with a secret prayer to be directed for the best in bearing the awful responsibility now laid on my shoulders, took my Captain's vacant place at the helm of the Long-boat.

This, as well as I can tell it, is the full and true account of how I came to be placed in charge of the lost passengers and crew of the Golden Mary, on the morning of the twenty-seventh day after the ship struck the Iceberg, and foundered at sea.

THE PERILS OF CERTAIN
ENGLISH PRISONERS

[1857]

THE PERILS OF CERTAIN ENGLISH PRISONERS.

In Two Chapters.

CHAPTER I.

THE ISLAND OF SILVER-STORE.

It was in the year of our Lord one thousand seven hundred and forty-four, that I, Gill Davis to command, His Mark, having then the honour to be a private in the Royal Marines, stood a-leaning over the bulwarks of the armed sloop Christopher Columbus, in the South American waters off the Mosquito shore.

My lady remarks to me, before I go any further, that there is no such christian-name as Gill, and that her confident opinion is, that the name given to me in the baptism wherein I was made, &c., was Gilbert. She is certain to be right, but I never heard of it. I was a foundling child, picked up somewhere or another, and I always understood my christian-name to be Gill. It is true that I was called Gills when employed at Snorridge Bottom betwixt Chatham and Maidstone to frighten birds; but that had nothing to do with the Baptism wherein I was made, &c., and wherein a number of things were promised for me by somebody, who let me alone ever afterwards as to performing any of them, and who, I consider, must have been the Beadle. Such name of Gills was entirely owing to my cheeks, or gills, which at that time of my life were of a raspy description.

My lady stops me again, before I go any further, by laughing exactly in her old way and waving the feather of her pen at me. That action on her part, calls to my mind as I look at her hand with the rings on it——Well! I won't! To be sure it will come in, in its own place. But it's always strange to me, noticing the quiet hand, and noticing it (as I have done, you know, so many times) a-fondling children and grandchildren asleep, to think that when blood and honour were up—there! I won't! not at present!—Scratch it out.

She won't scratch it out, and quite honourable; because we have made an understanding that everything is to be taken down, and that nothing that is once taken down shall be scratched out. I have the great misfortune not to be able to read and write, and I am speaking my true and faithful account of those Adventures, and my lady is writing it, word for word.

I say, there I was, a-leaning over the bulwarks of the sloop Christopher Columbus in the South American waters off the Mosquito shore: a subject of his Gracious Majesty King George of England, and a private in the Royal Marines.

In those climates, you don't want to do much. I was doing nothing. I was thinking of the shepherd (my father, I wonder?) on the hill-sides by Snorridge Bottom, with a long staff, and with a rough white coat in all weathers all the year round, who used to let me lie in a corner of his hut by night, and who used to let me go about with him and his sheep by day when I could get nothing else to do, and who used to give me so little of his victuals and so much of his staff, that I ran away from him—which was what he wanted all along, I expect—to be knocked about the world in preference to Snorridge Bottom. I had been knocked about the world for nine-and-twenty years in all, when I stood looking along those bright blue South American Waters. Looking after the shepherd, I may say. Watching him in a half-waking dream, with my eyes half-shut, as he, and his flock of sheep, and his two dogs, seemed to move away from the ship's side, far away over the blue water, and go right down into the sky.

"It's rising out of the water, steady," a voice said close to me. I had been thinking on so, that it like woke me with a start, though it was no stranger voice than the voice of Harry Charker, my own comrade.

"What's rising out of the water, steady?" I asked my comrade.

"What?" says he. "The Island."

"O! The Island!" says I, turning my eyes towards it. "True. I forgot the Island."

"Forgot the port you're going to? That's odd, ain't it?"

"It is odd," says I.

"And odd," he said, slowly considering with himself, "ain't even. Is it, Gill?"

He had always a remark just like that to make, and seldom another. As soon as he had brought a thing round to what it was not, he was satisfied. He was one of the best of men, and, in a certain sort of a way, one with the least to say for himself. I qualify it, because, besides being able to read and write like a Quarter-master, he had always one most excellent idea in his mind. That was, Duty. Upon my soul, I don't believe, though I admire learning beyond everything, that he could have got a better idea out of all the books in the world, if he had learnt them every word, and been the cleverest of scholars.

My comrade and I had been quartered in Jamaica, and from there we had been drafted off to the British settlement of Belize, lying away West and North of the Mosquito coast. At Belize there had been great alarm of one cruel gang of pirates (there were always more pirates than enough in those Caribbean Seas), and as they got the better of our English cruisers by running into out-of-the-way creeks and shallows, and taking the land when they were hotly pressed, the governor of Belize had received orders from home to keep a sharp look-out for them along shore. Now, there was an armed sloop came once a-year from Port Royal, Jamaica, to the Island, laden with all manner of necessaries, to eat, and to drink, and to wear, and to use in various ways; and it was aboard of that sloop which had touched at Belize, that I was a-standing, leaning over the bulwarks.

The Island was occupied by a very small English colony. It had been given the name of Silver-Store. The reason of its being so called, was, that the English colony owned and worked a silver mine over on the mainland, in Honduras, and used this Island as a safe and convenient place to store their silver in, until it was annually fetched away by the sloop. It was brought down from the mine to the coast on the backs of mules, attended by friendly Indians and guarded by white men; from thence it was conveyed over to Silver-Store, when the weather was fair, in the canoes of that country; from Silver-Store, it was carried to Jamaica by the armed sloop once a-year, as I have already mentioned; from Jamaica, it went, of course, all over the world.

How I came to be aboard the armed sloop, is easily told. Four-and-twenty marines under command of a lieutenant— that officer's name was Linderwood—had been told off at Belize, to proceed to Silver-Store, in aid of boats and seamen stationed there for the chase of the Pirates. The Island was considered a good post of observation against the pirates, both by land and sea; neither the pirate ship nor yet her boats had been seen by any of us, but they had been so much heard of, that the reinforcement was sent. Of that party, I was one. It included a corporal and a sergeant. Charker was corporal, and the sergeant's name was Drooce. He was the most tyrannical non-commissioned officer in His Majesty's service.

The night came on, soon after I had had the foregoing words with Charker. All the wonderful bright colours went out of the sea and sky in a few minutes, and all the stars in

the Heavens seemed to shine out together, and to look down
at themselves in the sea, over one another's shoulders, millions
deep. Next morning, we cast anchor off the Island. There
was a snug harbour within a little reef; there was a sandy
beach; there were cocoa-nut trees with high straight stems,
quite bare, and foliage at the top like plumes of magnificent
green feathers; there were all the objects that are usually
seen in those parts, and I am not going to describe them,
having something else to tell about.

Great rejoicings, to be sure, were made on our arrival. All
the flags in the place were hoisted, all the guns in the place
were fired, and all the people in the place came down to look
at us. One of those Sambo fellows—they call those natives
Sambos, when they are half-negro and half-Indian—had come
off outside the reef, to pilot us in, and remained on board
after we had let go our anchor. He was called Christian
George King, and was fonder of all hands than anybody else
was. Now, I confess, for myself, that on that first day, if I
had been captain of the Christopher Columbus, instead of
private in the Royal Marines, I should have kicked Christian
George King—who was no more a Christian than he was a
King or a George—over the side, without exactly knowing
why, except that it was the right thing to do.

But, I must likewise confess, that I was not in a particularly pleasant humour, when I stood under arms that
morning, aboard the Christopher Columbus in the harbour of
the Island of Silver-Store. I had had a hard life, and the
life of the English on the Island seemed too easy and too
gay to please me. "Here you are," I thought to myself,
"good scholars and good livers; able to read what you like,
able to write what you like, able to eat and drink what you
like, and spend what you like, and do what you like; and
much you care for a poor, ignorant Private in the Royal
Marines! Yet it's hard, too, I think, that you should have
all the half-pence, and I all the kicks; you all the smooth,
and I all the rough; you all the oil, and I all the vinegar."

It was as envious a thing to think as might be, let alone its
being nonsensical; but, I thought it. I took it so much
amiss, that, when a very beautiful young English lady came
aboard, I grunted to myself, "Ah! *you* have got a lover, I'll
be bound!" As if there was any new offence to me in that,
if she had!

She was sister to the captain of our sloop, who had been
in a poor way for some time, and who was so ill then that
he was obliged to be carried ashore. She was the child of a
military officer, and had come out there with her sister, who
was married to one of the owners of the silver-mine, and who
had three children with her. It was easy to see that she
was the light and spirit of the Island. After I had got a
good look at her, I grunted to myself again, in an even
worse state of mind than before, "I'll be damned, if I don't
hate him, whoever he is!"

My officer, Lieutenant Linderwood, was as ill as the captain
of the sloop, and was carried ashore, too. They were both
young men of about my age, who had been delicate in the
West India climate. I even took *that* in bad part. I thought
I was much fitter for the work than they were, and that if
all of us had our deserts, I should be both of them rolled
into one. (It may be imagined what sort of an officer of
marines I should have made, without the power of reading a
written order. And as to any knowledge how to command the
sloop—Lord! I should have sunk her in a quarter of an hour!)

However, such were my reflections; and when we men
were ashore and dismissed, I strolled about the place along
with Charker, making my observations in a similar spirit.

It was a pretty place: in all its arrangements partly South
American and partly English, and very agreeable to look at
on that account, being like a bit of home that had got
chipped off and had floated away to that spot, accommo-
dating itself to circumstances as it drifted along. The huts
of the Sambos, to the number of five-and-twenty, perhaps,
were down by the beach to the left of the anchorage. On

the right was a sort of barrack, with a South American Flag
and the Union Jack, flying from the same staff, where the
little English colony could all come together, if they saw
occasion.   It was a walled square of building, with a sort of
pleasure-ground inside, and inside that again a sunken block
like a powder magazine, with a little square trench round it,
and steps down to the door. Charker and I were looking
in at the gate, which was not guarded; and I had said to
Charker, in reference to the bit like a powder magazine,
" That's where they keep the silver you see ; " and Charker had
said to me, after thinking it over, "And silver ain't gold.
Is it, Gill ?" when the beautiful young English lady I had
been so bilious about, looked out of a door, or a window—
at all events looked out, from under a bright awning.   She
no sooner saw us two in uniform, than she came out so
quickly that she was still putting on her broad Mexican hat
of plaited straw when we saluted.

" Would you like to come in," she said, "and see the
place?   It is rather a curious place."

We thanked the young lady, and said we didn't wish to
be troublesome ; but, she said it could be no trouble to an
English soldier's daughter, to show English soldiers how their
countrymen and countrywomen fared, so far away from England ; and consequently we saluted again, and went in.   Then,
as we stood in the shade, she showed us (being as affable as
beautiful), how the different families lived in their separate
houses, and how there was a general house for stores, and a
general reading-room, and a general room for music and
dancing, and a room for Church ; and how there were other
houses on the rising ground called the Signal Hill, where
they lived in the hotter weather.

" Your officer has been carried up there," she said, "and
my brother, too, for the better air.   At present, our few
residents are dispersed over both spots : deducting, that is
to say, such of our number as are always going to, or coming
from, or staying at, the Mine."

("*He* is among one of those parties," I thought, "and I wish somebody would knock his head off.")

"Some of our married ladies live here," she said, "during at least half the year, as lonely as widows, with their children."

"Many children here, ma'am?"

"Seventeen. There are thirteen married ladies, and there are eight like me."

There were not eight like her—there was not one like her —in the world. She meant single.

"Which, with about thirty Englishmen of various degrees," said the young lady, "form the little colony now on the Island. I don't count the sailors, for they don't belong to us. Nor the soldiers," she gave us a gracious smile when she spoke of the soldiers, "for the same reason."

"Nor the Sambos, ma'am," said I.

"No."

"Under your favour, and with your leave, ma'am," said I, "are they trustworthy?"

"Perfectly! We are all very kind to them, and they are very grateful to us."

"Indeed, ma'am? Now—Christian George King—— ?"

"Very much attached to us all. Would die for us."

She was, as in my uneducated way I have observed, very beautiful women almost always to be, so composed, that her composure gave great weight to what she said, and I believed it.

Then, she pointed out to us the building like a powder magazine, and explained to us in what manner the silver was brought from the mine, and was brought over from the mainland, and was stored there. The Christopher Columbus would have a rich lading, she said, for there had been a great yield that year, a much richer yield than usual, and there was a chest of jewels besides the silver.

When we had looked about us, and were getting sheepish, through fearing we were troublesome, she turned us over to a young woman, English born but West India bred, who served her as her maid. This young woman was the widow of a non-commissioned officer in a regiment of the line. She had got married and widowed at St. Vincent, with only a few months between the two events. She was a little saucy woman, with a bright pair of eyes, rather a neat little foot and figure, and rather a neat little turned-up nose. The sort of young woman, I considered at the time, who appeared to invite you to give her a kiss, and who would have slapped your face if you accepted the invitation.

I couldn't make out her name at first; for, when she gave it in answer to my inquiry, it sounded like Beltot, which didn't sound right. But, when we became better acquainted —which was while Charker and I were drinking sugar-cane sangaree, which she made in a most excellent manner—I found that her Christian name was Isabella, which they shortened into Bell, and that the name of the deceased non-commissioned officer was Tott. Being the kind of neat little woman it was natural to make a toy of—I never saw a woman so like a toy in my life—she had got the plaything name of Belltott. In short, she had no other name on the island. Even Mr. Commissioner Pordage (and *he* was a grave one!) formally addressed her as Mrs. Belltott. But, I shall come to Mr. Commissioner Pordage presently.

The name of the captain of the sloop was Captain Maryon, and therefore it was no news to hear from Mrs. Belltott, that his sister, the beautiful unmarried young English lady, was Miss Maryon. The novelty was, that her Christian name was Marion too. Marion Maryon. Many a time I have run off those two names in my thoughts, like a bit of verse. Oh many, and many, and many a time!

We saw out all the drink that was produced, like good men and true, and then took our leaves, and went down to the beach. The weather was beautiful; the wind steady, low, and gentle; the island, a picture; the sea, a picture; the sky, a picture. In that country there are two rainy seasons in the year. One sets in at about our English Midsummer; the other, about a fortnight after our English Michaelmas. It was the beginning of August at that time; the first of these rainy seasons was well over; and everything was in its most beautiful growth, and had its loveliest look upon it.

"They enjoy themselves here," I says to Charker, turning surly again. "This is better than private-soldiering."

We had come down to the beach, to be friendly with the boat's-crew who were camped and hutted there; and we were approaching towards their quarters over the sand, when Christian George King comes up from the landing-place at a wolf's-trot, crying, "Yup, So-Jeer!"—which was that Sambo Pilot's barbarous way of saying, Hallo, Soldier! I have stated myself to be a man of no learning, and, if I entertain prejudices, I hope allowance may be made. I will now confess to one. It may be a right one or it may be a wrong one; but, I never did like Natives, except in the form of oysters.

So, when Christian George King, who was individually unpleasant to me besides, comes a trotting along the sand, clucking, "Yup, So-Jeer!" I had a thundering good mind to let fly at him with my right. I certainly should have done it, but that it would have exposed me to reprimand.

"Yup, So-Jeer!" says he. "Bad job."

"What do you mean?" says I.

"Yup, So-Jeer!" says he, "Ship Leakee."

"Ship leaky?" says I.

"Iss," says he, with a nod that looked as if it was jerked out of him by a most violent hiccup—which is the way with those savages.

I cast my eyes at Charker, and we both heard the pumps going aboard the sloop, and saw the signal run up, "Come on board; hands wanted from the shore." In no time some of the sloop's liberty-men were already running down to the water's edge, and the party of seamen, under orders against the Pirates, were putting off to the Columbus in two boats.

"O Christian George King sar berry sorry!" says that Sambo vagabond, then. "Christian George King cry, English fashion!" His English fashion of crying was to screw his black knuckles into his eyes, howl like a dog, and roll himself on his back on the sand. It was trying not to kick him, but I gave Charker the word, "Double-quick, Harry!" and we got down to the water's edge, and got on board the sloop.

By some means or other, she had sprung such a leak, that no pumping would keep her free; and what between the two fears that she would go down in the harbour, and that, even if she did not, all the supplies she had brought for the little colony would be destroyed by the sea-water as it rose in her, there was great confusion. In the midst of it, Captain Maryon was heard hailing from the beach. He had been carried down in his hammock, and looked very bad; but he insisted on being stood there on his feet; and I saw him, myself, come off in the boat, sitting upright in the stern-sheets, as if nothing was wrong with him.

A quick sort of council was held, and Captain Maryon soon resolved that we must all fall to work to get the cargo out, and that when that was done, the guns and heavy matters must be got out, and that the sloop must be hauled ashore, and careened, and the leak stopped. We were all mustered (the Pirate-Chace party volunteering), and told off into parties, with so many hours of spell and so many hours of relief, and we all went at it with a will. Christian George King was entered one of the party in which I worked, at his own request, and he went at it with as good a will as any of the rest. He went at it with so much heartiness, to say the truth, that he rose in my good opinion almost as fast as the water rose in the ship. Which was fast enough, and faster.

Mr. Commissioner Pordage kept in a red-and-black japanned box, like a family lump-sugar box, some document or other, which some Sambo chief or other had got drunk and spilt some ink over (as well as I could understand the matter), and by that means had given up lawful possession of the

Island. Through having hold of this box, Mr. Pordage got
his title of Commissioner. He was styled Consul too, and
spoke of himself as "Government."

He was a stiff-jointed, high-nosed old gentleman, without
an ounce of fat on him, of a very angry temper and a very
yellow complexion. Mrs. Commissioner Pordage, making allowance for difference of sex, was much the same. Mr. Kitten,
a small, youngish, bald, botanical and mineralogical gentleman, also connected with the mine—but everybody there was
that, more or less—was sometimes called by Mr. Commissioner Pordage, his Vice-commissioner, and sometimes his
Deputy-consul. Or sometimes he spoke of Mr. Kitten, merely
as being "under Government."

The beach was beginning to be a lively scene with the
preparations for careening the sloop, and, with cargo, and
spars, and rigging, and water-casks, dotted about it, and
with temporary quarters for the men rising up there out of
such sails and odds and ends as could be best set on one
side to make them, when Mr. Commissioner Pordage comes
down in a high fluster, and asks for Captain Maryon. The
Captain, ill as he was, was slung in his hammock betwixt
two trees, that he might direct; and he raised his head, and
answered for himself.

"Captain Maryon," cries Mr. Commissioner Pordage, "this
is not official. This is not regular."

"Sir," says the Captain, "it hath been arranged with the
clerk and supercargo, that you should be communicated with,
and requested to render any little assistance that may lie in
your power. I am quite certain that hath been duly done."

"Captain Maryon," replies Mr. Commissioner Pordage,
"there hath been no written correspondence. No documents
have passed, no memoranda have been made, no minutes
have been made, no entries and counter-entries appear in
the official muniments. This is indecent. I call upon you,
sir, to desist, until all is regular, or Government will take
this up."

"Sir," says Captain Maryon, chafing a little, as he looked out of his hammock; "between the chances of Government taking this up, and my ship taking herself down, I much prefer to trust myself to the former."

"You do, sir?" cries Mr. Commissioner Pordage.

"I do, sir," says Captain Maryon, lying down again.

"Then, Mr. Kitten," says the Commissioner, "send up instantly for my Diplomatic coat."

He was dressed in a linen suit at that moment; but, Mr. Kitten started off himself and brought down the Diplomatic coat, which was a blue cloth one, gold-laced, and with a crown on the button.

"Now, Mr. Kitten," says Pordage, "I instruct you, as Vice-commissioner, and Deputy-consul of this place, to demand of Captain Maryon, of the sloop Christopher Columbus, whether he drives me to the act of putting this coat on?"

"Mr. Pordage," says Captain Maryon, looking out of his hammock again, "as I can hear what you say, I can answer it without troubling the gentleman. I should be sorry that you should be at the pains of putting on too hot a coat on my account; but, otherwise, you may put it on hind-side before, or inside-out, or with your legs in the sleeves, or your head in the skirts, for any objection that I have to offer to your thoroughly pleasing yourself."

"Very good, Captain Maryon," says Pordage, in a tremendous passion. "Very good, sir. Be the consequences on your own head! Mr. Kitten, as it has come to this, help me on with it."

When he had given that order, he walked off in the coat, and all our names were taken, and I was afterwards told that Mr. Kitten wrote from his dictation more than a bushel of large paper on the subject, which cost more before it was done with, than ever could be calculated, and which only got done with after all, by being lost.

Our work went on merrily, nevertheless, and the Christopher Columbus, hauled up, lay helpless on her side like a great fish out of water. While she was in that state, there was a feast, or a ball, or an entertainment, or more properly all three together, given us in honour of the ship, and the ship's company, and the other visitors. At that assembly, I believe, I saw all the inhabitants then upon the Island, without any exception. I took no particular notice of more than a few, but I found it very agreeable in that little corner of the world to see the children, who were of all ages, and mostly very pretty—as they mostly are. There was one handsome elderly lady, with very dark eyes and gray hair, that I inquired about. I was told that her name was Mrs. Venning; and her married daughter, a fair slight thing, was pointed out to me by the name of Fanny Fisher. Quite a child she looked, with a little copy of herself holding to her dress; and her husband, just come back from the mine, exceeding proud of her. They were a good-looking set of people on the whole, but I didn't like them. I was out of sorts; in conversation with Charker, I found fault with all of them. I said of Mrs. Venning, she was proud; of Mrs. Fisher, she was a delicate little baby-fool. What did I think of this one? Why, he was a fine gentleman. What did I say to that one? Why, she was a fine lady. What could you expect them to be (I asked Charker), nursed in that climate, with the tropical night shining for them, musical instruments playing to them, great trees bending over them, soft lamps lighting them, fire-flies sparkling in among them, bright flowers and birds brought into existence to please their eyes, delicious drinks to be had for the pouring out, delicious fruits to be got for the picking, and every one dancing and murmuring happily in the scented air, with the sea breaking low on the reef for a pleasant chorus.

"Fine gentlemen and fine ladies, Harry?" I says to Charker. "Yes, I think so! Dolls! Dolls! Not the sort of stuff for wear, that comes of poor private soldiering in the Royal Marines!"

However, I could not gainsay that they were very hospitable

people, and that they treated us uncommonly well. Every man of us was at the entertainment, and Mrs. Belltott had more partners than she could dance with: though she danced all night, too. As to Jack (whether of the Christopher Columbus, or of the Pirate pursuit party, it made no difference), he danced with his brother Jack, danced with himself, danced with the moon, the stars, the trees, the prospect, anything. I didn't greatly take to the chief-officer of that party, with his bright eyes, brown face, and easy figure. I didn't much like his way when he first happened to come where we were, with Miss Maryon on his arm. "O, Captain Carton," she says, "here are two friends of mine!" He says, "Indeed? These two Marines?"—meaning Charker and self. "Yes," says she, "I showed these two friends of mine when they first came, all the wonders of Silver-Store." He gave us a laughing look, and says he, "You are in luck, men. I would be disrated and go before the mast to-morrow, to be shown the way upward again by such a guide. You are in luck, men." When we had saluted, and he and the lady had waltzed away, I said, "You are a pretty fellow, too, to talk of luck. You may go to the Devil!"

Mr. Commissioner Pordage and Mrs. Commissioner, showed among the company on that occasion like the King and Queen of a much Greater Britain than Great Britain. Only two other circumstances in that jovial night made much separate impression on me. One was this. A man in our draft of marines, named Tom Packer, a wild unsteady young fellow, but the son of a respectable shipwright in Portsmouth Yard, and a good scholar who had been well brought up, comes to me after a spell of dancing, and takes me aside by the elbow, and says, swearing angrily:

"Gill Davis, I hope I may not be the death of Sergeant Drooce one day!"

Now, I knew Drooce had always borne particularly hard on this man, and I knew this man to be of a very hot temper: so, I said:

"'Tut, nonsense! don't talk so to me! If there's a man in the corps who scorns the name of an assassin, that man and Tom Packer are one."

Tom wipes his head, being in a mortal sweat, and says he: "I hope so, but I can't answer for myself when he lords it over me, as he has just now done, before a woman. I tell you what, Gill! Mark my words! It will go hard with Sergeant Drooce, if ever we are in an engagement together, and he has to look to me to save him. Let him say a prayer then, if he knows one, for it's all over with him, and he is on his Death-bed. Mark my words!"

I did mark his words, and very soon afterwards, too, as will shortly be taken down.

The other circumstance that I noticed at that ball, was, the gaiety and attachment of Christian George King. The innocent spirits that Sambo Pilot was in, and the impossibility he found himself under of showing all the little colony, but especially the ladies and children, how fond he was of them, how devoted to them, and how faithful to them for life and death, for present, future, and everlasting, made a great impression on me. If ever a man, Sambo or no Sambo, was trustful and trusted, to what may be called quite an infantine and sweetly beautiful extent, surely, I thought that morning when I did at last lie down to rest, it was that Sambo Pilot, Christian George King.

This may account for my dreaming of him. He stuck in my sleep, cornerwise, and I couldn't get him out. He was always flitting about me, dancing round me, and peeping in over my hammock, though I woke and dozed off again fifty times. At last, when I opened my eyes, there he really was, looking in at the open side of the little dark hut; which was made of leaves, and had Charker's hammock slung in it as well as mine.

"So—Jeer!" says he, in a sort of a low croak. "Yup!"

"Hallo!" says I, starting up. "What? You *are* there, are you?"

"Iss," says he. "Christian George King got news."

"What news has he got?"

"Pirates out!"

I was on my feet in a second. So was Charker. We were both aware that Captain Carton, in command of the boats, constantly watched the mainland for a secret signal, though, of course, it was not known to such as us what the signal was.

Christian George King had vanished before we touched the ground. But, the word was already passing from hut to hut to turn out quietly, and we knew that the nimble barbarian had got hold of the truth, or something near it.

In a space among the trees behind the encampment of us visitors, naval and military, was a snugly-screened spot, where we kept the stores that were in use, and did our cookery. The word was passed to assemble here. It was very quickly given, and was given (so far as we were concerned) by Sergeant Drooce, who was as good in a soldier point of view, as he was bad in a tyrannical one. We were ordered to drop into this space, quietly, behind the trees, one by one. As we assembled here, the seamen assembled too. Within ten minutes, as I should estimate, we were all here, except the usual guard upon the beach. The beach (we could see it through the wood) looked as it always had done in the hottest time of the day. The guard were in the shadow of the sloop's hull, and nothing was moving but the sea, and that moved very faintly. Work had always been knocked off at that hour, until the sun grew less fierce, and the sea-breeze rose; so that its being holiday with us, made no difference, just then, in the look of the place. But I may mention that it was a holiday, and the first we had had since our hard work began. Last night's ball had been given, on the leak's being repaired, and the careening done. The worst of the work was over, and to-morrow we were to begin to get the sloop afloat again.

We marines were now drawn up here under arms. The

chace-party were drawn up separate. The men of the Columbus were drawn up separate. The officers stepped out into the midst of the three parties, and spoke so as all might hear. Captain Carton was the officer in command, and he had a spy-glass in his hand. His coxswain stood by him with another spy-glass, and with a slate on which he seemed to have been taking down signals.

"Now, men!" says Captain Carton; "I have to let you know, for your satisfaction: Firstly, that there are ten pirate-boats, strongly manned and armed, lying hidden up a creek yonder on the coast, under the overhanging branches of the dense trees. Secondly, that they will certainly come out this night when the moon rises, on a pillaging and murdering expedition, of which some part of the mainland is the object. Thirdly—don't cheer, men!—that we will give chace, and, if we can get at them, rid the world of them, please God!"

Nobody spoke, that I heard, and nobody moved, that I saw. Yet there was a kind of ring, as if every man answered and approved with the best blood that was inside of him.

"Sir," says Captain Maryon, "I beg to volunteer on this service, with my boats. My people volunteer, to the ship's boys."

"In His Majesty's name and service," the other answers, touching his hat, "I accept your aid with pleasure. Lieutenant Linderwood, how will you divide your men?"

I was ashamed—I give it out to be written down as large and plain as possible—I was heart and soul ashamed of my thoughts of those two sick officers, Captain Maryon and Lieutenant Linderwood, when I saw them, then and there. The spirit in those two gentlemen beat down their illness (and very ill I knew them to be) like Saint George beating down the Dragon. Pain and weakness, want of ease and want of rest, had no more place in their minds than fear itself. Meaning now to express for my lady to write down, exactly what I felt then and there, I felt this: "You two brave fellows that I had been so grudgeful of, I know that if you were dying you would put it off to get up and do your best, and then you would be so modest that in lying down again to die, you would hardly say, ' I did it ! ' "

It did me good. It really did me good.

But, to go back to where I broke off. Says Captain Carton to Lieutenant Linderwood, "Sir, how will you divide your men? There is not room for all; and a few men should, in any case, be left here."

There was some debate about it. At last, it was resolved to leave eight Marines and four seamen on the Island, besides the sloop's two boys. And because it was considered that the friendly Sambos would only want to be commanded in case of any danger (though none at all was apprehended there), the officers were in favour of leaving the two non-commissioned officers, Drooce and Charker. It was a heavy disappointment to them, just as my being one of the left was a heavy disappointment to me—then, but not soon afterwards. We men drew lots for it, and I drew " Island." So did Tom Packer. So, of course, did four more of our rank and file.

When this was settled, verbal instructions were given to all hands to keep the intended expedition secret, in order that the women and children might not be alarmed, or the expedition put in a difficulty by more volunteers. The assembly was to be on that same spot at sunset. Every man was to keep up an appearance, meanwhile, of occupying himself in his usual way. That is to say, every man excepting four old trusty seamen, who were appointed, with an officer, to see to the arms and ammunition, and to muffle the rullocks of the boats, and to make everything as trim and swift and silent as it could be made.

The Sambo Pilot had been present all the while, in case of his being wanted, and had said to the officer in command, five hundred times over if he had said it once, that Christian George King would stay with the So-Jeers, and take care of the booffer ladies and the booffer childs—booffer being that native's expression for beautiful. He was now asked a few

questions concerning the putting off of the boats, and in
particular whether there was any way of embarking at the
back of the Island : which Captain Carton would have half
liked to do, and then have dropped round in its shadow and
slanted across to the main. But, "No," says Christian George
King. "No, no, no! Told you so, ten time. No, no, no!
All reef, all rock, all swim, all drown!" Striking out as
he said it, like a swimmer gone mad, and turning over on
his back on dry land, and spluttering himself to death, in a
manner that made him quite an exhibition.

The sun went down, after appearing to be a long time
about it, and the assembly was called. Every man answered
to his name, of course, and was at his post. It was not yet
black dark, and the roll was only just gone through, when up
comes Mr. Commissioner Pordage with his Diplomatic coat on.

"Captain Carton," says he, "Sir, what is this?"

"This, Mr. Commissioner" (he was very short with him),
"is an expedition against the Pirates. It is a secret expedition, so please to keep it a secret."

"Sir," says Commissioner Pordage, "I trust there is going
to be no unnecessary cruelty committed?"

"Sir," returns the officer, "I trust not."

"That is not enough, sir," cries Commissioner Pordage,
getting wroth. "Captain Carton, I give you notice. Government requires you to treat the enemy with great delicacy,
consideration, clemency, and forbearance."

"Sir," says Captain Carton, "I am an English officer,
commanding English Men, and I hope I am not likely to
disappoint the Government's just expectations. But, I
presume you know that these villains under their black flag
have despoiled our countrymen of their property, burnt their
homes, barbarously murdered them and their little children,
and worse than murdered their wives and daughters?"

"Perhaps I do, Captain Carton," answers Pordage, waving
his hand, with dignity; "perhaps I do not. It is not
customary, sir, for Government to commit itself."

"It matters very little, Mr. Pordage, whether or no.
Believing that I hold my commission by the allowance of
God, and not that I have received it direct from the Devil,
I shall certainly use it, with all avoidance of unnecessary
suffering and with all merciful swiftness of execution, to
exterminate these people from the face of the earth. Let
me recommend you to go home, air, and to keep out of the
night-air."

Never another syllable did that officer say to the Commissioner, but turned away to his men. The Commissioner
buttoned his Diplomatic coat to the chin, said, "Mr. Kitten,
attend me!" gasped, half choked himself, and took himself off.

It now fell very dark, indeed. I have seldom, if ever,
seen it darker, nor yet so dark. The moon was not due
until one in the morning, and it was but a little after nine
when our men lay down where they were mustered. It was
pretended that they were to take a nap, but everybody knew
that no nap was to be got under the circumstances. Though
all were very quiet, there was a restlessness among the people;
much what I have seen among the people on a race-course,
when the bell has rung for the saddling for a great race with
large stakes on it.

At ten, they put off; only one boat putting off at a time;
another following in five minutes; both then lying on their
oars until another followed. Ahead of all, paddling his own
outlandish little canoe without a sound, went the Sambo
pilot, to take them safely outside the reef. No light was
shown but once, and that was in the commanding officer's
own hand. I lighted the dark lantern for him, and he took
it from me when he embarked. They had blue lights and
such like with them, but kept themselves as dark as Murder.

The expedition got away with wonderful quietness, and
Christian George King soon came back dancing with joy.

"Yup, So-Jeer," says he to myself in a very objectionable
kind of convulsions, "Christian George King sar berry glad.
Pirates all be blown a-pieces. Yup! Yup!"

My reply to that cannibal was, "However glad you may be, hold your noise, and don't dance jigs and slap your knees about it, for I can't abear to see you do it."

I was on duty then; we twelve who were left being divided into four watches of three each, three hours' spell. I was relieved at twelve. A little before that time, I had challenged, and Miss Maryon and Mrs. Belltott had come in.

"Good Davis," says Miss Maryon, "what is the matter? Where is my brother?"

I told her what was the matter, and where her brother was.

"O Heaven help him!" says she, clasping her hands and looking up—she was close in front of me, and she looked most lovely to be sure; "he is not sufficiently recovered, not strong enough for such strife!"

"If you had seen him, miss," I told her, "as I saw him when he volunteered, you would have known that his spirit is strong enough for any strife. It will bear his body, miss, to wherever duty calls him. It will always bear him to an honourable life, or a brave death."

"Heaven bless you!" says she, touching my arm. "I know it. Heaven bless you!"

Mrs. Belltott surprised me by trembling and saying nothing. They were still standing looking towards the sea and listening, after the relief had come round. It continuing very dark, I asked to be allowed to take them back. Miss Maryon thanked me, and she put her arm in mine, and I did take them back. I have now got to make a confession that will appear singular. After I had left them, I laid myself down on my face on the beach, and cried for the first time since I had frightened birds as a boy at Snorridge Bottom, to think what a poor, ignorant, low-placed, private soldier I was.

It was only for half a minute or so. A man can't at all times be quite master of himself, and it was only for half a minute or so. Then I up and went to my hut, and turned into my hammock, and fell asleep with wet eyelashes, and a sore, sore heart. Just as I had often done when I was a child, and had been worse used than usual.

I slept (as a child under those circumstances might) very sound, and yet very sore at heart all through my sleep. I was awoke by the words, "He is a determined man." I had sprung out of my hammock, and had seized my firelock, and was standing on the ground, saying the words myself. "He is a determined man." But, the curiosity of my state was, that I seemed to be repeating them after somebody, and to have been wonderfully startled by hearing them.

As soon as I came to myself, I went out of the hut, and away to where the guard was. Charker challenged:

"Who goes there?"

"A friend."

"Not Gill?" says he, as he shouldered his piece.

"Gill," says I.

"Why, what the deuce do you do out of your hammock?" says he.

"Too hot for sleep," says I; "is all right?"

"Right!" says Charker, "yes, yes; all's right enough here; what should be wrong here? It's the boats that we want to know of. Except for fire-flies twinkling about, and the lonesome splashes of great creatures as they drop into the water, there's nothing going on here to ease a man's mind from the boats."

The moon was above the sea, and had risen, I should say, some half-an-hour. As Charker spoke, with his face towards the sea, I, looking landward, suddenly laid my right hand on his breast, and said, "Don't move. Don't turn. Don't raise your voice! You never saw a Maltese face here?"

"No. What do you mean?" he asks, staring at me.

"Nor yet an English face, with one eye and a patch across the nose?"

"No. What ails you? What do you mean?"

I had seen both, looking at us round the stem of a cocoa-nut tree, where the moon struck them. I had seen that

Sambo Pilot, with one hand laid on the stem of the tree, drawing them back into the heavy shadow. I had seen their naked cutlasses twinkle and shine, like bits of the moonshine in the water that had got blown ashore among the trees by the light wind. I had seen it all, in a moment. And I saw in a moment (as any man would), that the signalled move of the pirates on the mainland was a plot and a feint; that the leak had been made to disable the sloop; that the boats had been tempted away, to leave the Island unprotected; that the pirates had landed by some secreted way at the back; and that Christian George King was a double-dyed traitor, and a most infernal villain.

I considered, still all in one and the same moment, that Charker was a brave man, but not quick with his head; and that Sergeant Drooce, with a much better head, was close by. All I said to Charker was, "I am afraid we are betrayed. Turn your back full to the moonlight on the sea, and cover the stem of the cocoa-nut tree which will then be right before you, at the height of a man's heart. Are you right?"

"I am right," says Charker, turning instantly, and falling into the position with a nerve of iron; "and right ain't left. Is it, Gill?"

A few seconds brought me to Sergeant Drooce's hut. He was fast asleep, and being a heavy sleeper, I had to lay my hand upon him to rouse him. The instant I touched him he came rolling out of his hammock, and upon me like a tiger. And a tiger he was, except that he knew what he was up to, in his utmost heat, as well as any man.

I had to struggle with him pretty hard to bring him to his senses, panting all the while (for he gave me a breather), "Sergeant, I am Gill Davis! Treachery! Pirates on the Island!"

The last words brought him round, and he took his hands off. "I have seen two of them within this minute," said I. And so I told him what I had told Harry Charker.

His soldierly, though tyrannical, head was clear in an instant. He didn't waste one word, even of surprise. "Order the guard," says he, "to draw off quietly into the Fort." (They called the enclosure I have before mentioned, the Fort, though it was not much of that.) "Then get you to the Fort as quick as you can, rouse up every soul there, and fasten the gate. I will bring in all those who are up at the Signal Hill. If we are surrounded before we can join you, you must make a sally and cut us out if you can. The word among our men is, 'Women and children!'"

He burst away, like fire going before the wind over dry reeds. He roused up the seven men who were off duty, and had them bursting away with him, before they knew they were not asleep. I reported orders to Charker, and ran to the Fort, as I have never run at any other time in all my life: no, not even in a dream.

The gate was not fast, and had no good fastening: only a double wooden bar, a poor chain, and a bad lock. Those, I secured as well as they could be secured in a few seconds by one pair of hands, and so ran to that part of the building where Miss Maryon lived. I called to her loudly by her name until she answered. I then called loudly all the names I knew—Mrs. Macey (Miss Maryon's married sister), Mr. Macey, Mrs. Venning, Mr. and Mrs. Fisher, even Mr. and Mrs. Pordage. Then I called out, "All you gentlemen here, get up and defend the place! We are caught in a trap. Pirates have landed. We are attacked!"

At the terrible word "Pirates!"—for, those villains had done such deeds in those seas as never can be told in writing, and can scarcely be so much as thought of—cries and screams rose up from every part of the place. Quickly lights moved about from window to window, and the cries moved about with them, and men, women, and children came flying down into the square. I remarked to myself, even then, what a number of things I seemed to see at once. I noticed Mrs. Macey coming towards me, carrying all her three children together. I noticed Mr. Pordage in the greatest terror, in vain trying to get on his Diplomatic coat; and Mr. Kitten respectfully tying his pocket-handkerchief over Mrs. Pordage's nightcap. I noticed Mrs. Belltott run out screaming, and shrink upon the ground near me, and cover her face in her hands, and lie all of a bundle, shivering. But, what I noticed with the greatest pleasure was, the determined eyes with which those men of the Mine that I had thought fine gentlemen, came round me with what arms they had: to the full as cool and resolute as I could be, for my life—ay, and for my soul, too, into the bargain!

The chief person being Mr. Macey, I told him how the three men of the guard would be at the gate directly, if they were not already there, and how Sergeant Drooce and the other seven were gone to bring in the outlying part of the people of Silver-Store. I next urged him, for the love of all who were dear to him, to trust no Sambo, and, above all, if he could get any good chance at Christian George King, not to lose it, but to put him out of the world.

"I will follow your advice to the letter, Davis," says he; " what next?"

My answer was, "I think, sir, I would recommend you next, to order down such heavy furniture and lumber as can be moved, and make a barricade within the gate." ·

"That's good again," says he: "will you see it done?"

"I'll willingly help to do it," says I, "unless or until my superior, Sergeant Drooce, gives me other orders."

He shook me by the hand, and having told off some of his companions to help me, bestirred himself to look to the arms and ammunition. A proper quick, brave, steady, ready gentleman!

One of their three little children was deaf and dumb. Miss Maryon had been from the first with all the children, soothing them, and dressing them (poor little things, they had been brought out of their beds), and making them

believe that it was a game of play, so that some of them
were now even laughing. I had been working hard with the
others at the barricade, and had got up a pretty good
breastwork within the gate. Drooce and the seven had come
back, bringing in the people from the Signal Hill, and had
worked along with us: but, I had not so much as spoken a
word to Drooce, nor had Drooce so much as spoken a word
to me, for we were both too busy. The breastwork was now
finished, and I found Miss Maryon at my side, with a child
in her arms. Her dark hair was fastened round her head
with a band. She had a quantity of it, and it looked even
richer and more precious, put up hastily out of her way,
than I had seen it look when it was carefully arranged. She
was very pale, but extraordinarily quiet and still.

"Dear good Davis," said she, "I have been waiting to
speak one word to you."

I turned to her directly. If I had received a musket-ball
in the heart, and she had stood there, I almost believe I
should have turned to her before I dropped.

"This pretty little creature," said she, kissing the child in
her arms, who was playing with her hair and trying to pull
it down, "cannot hear what we say—can hear nothing. I
trust you so much, and have such great confidence in you,
that I want you to make me a promise."

"What is it, Miss?"

"That if we are defeated, and you are absolutely sure of
my being taken, you will kill me."

"I shall not be alive to do it, Miss. I shall have died
in your defence before it comes to that. They must step
across my body to lay a hand on you."

"But, if you are alive, you brave soldier." How she
looked at me! "And if you cannot save me from the
Pirates, living, you will save me, dead. Tell me so."

Well! I told her I would do that at the last, if all else
failed. She took my hand—my rough, coarse hand—and
put it to her lips. She put it to the child's lips, and the

child kissed it. I believe I had the strength of half a dozen men in me, from that moment, until the fight was over.

All this time, Mr. Commissioner Pordage had been wanting to make a Proclamation to the Pirates to lay down their arms and go away; and everybody had been hustling him about and tumbling over him, while he was calling for pen and ink to write it with. Mrs. Pordage, too, had some curious ideas about the British respectability of her nightcap (which had as many frills to it, growing in layers one inside another, as if it was a white vegetable of the artichoke sort), and she wouldn't take the nightcap off, and would be angry when it got crushed by the other ladies who were handing things about, and, in short, she gave as much trouble as her husband did. But, as we were now forming for the defence of the place, they were both poked out of the way with no ceremony. The children and ladies were got into the little trench which surrounded the silver-house (we were afraid of leaving them in any of the light buildings, lest they should be set on fire), and we made the best disposition we could. There was a pretty good store, in point of amount, of tolerable swords and cutlasses. Those were issued. There were, also, perhaps a score or so of spare muskets. Those were brought out. To my astonishment, little Mrs. Fisher that I had taken for a doll and a baby, was not only very active in that service, but volunteered to load the spare arms.

"For, I understand it well," says she, cheerfully, without a shake in her voice.

"I am a soldier's daughter and a sailor's sister, and I understand it too," says Miss Maryon, just in the same way.

Steady and busy behind where I stood, those two beautiful and delicate young women fell to handling the guns, hammering the flints, looking to the locks, and quietly directing others to pass up powder and bullets from hand to hand, as unflinching as the best of tried soldiers.

Sergeant Drooce had brought in word that the pirates were very strong in numbers—over a hundred was his estimate—and that they were not, even then, all landed; for, he had seen them in a very good position on the further side of the Signal Hill, evidently waiting for the rest of their men to come up. In the present pause, the first we had had since the alarm, he was telling this over again to Mr. Macey, when Mr. Macey suddenly cried out: "The signal! Nobody has thought of the signal!"

We knew of no signal, so we could not have thought of it.

"What signal may you mean, sir?" says Sergeant Drooce, looking sharp at him.

"There is a pile of wood upon the Signal Hill. If it could be lighted—which never has been done yet—it would be a signal of distress to the mainland."

Charker cries, directly: "Sergeant Drooce, dispatch me on that duty. Give me the two men who were on guard with me to-night, and I'll light the fire, if it can be done."

"And if it can't, Corporal——" Mr. Macey strikes in.

"Look at these ladies and children, sir!" says Charker. "I'd sooner *light myself*, than not try any chance to save them."

We gave him a Hurrah!—it burst from us, come of it what might—and he got his two men, and was let out at the gate, and crept away. I had no sooner come back to my place from being one of the party to handle the gate, than Miss Maryon said in a low voice behind me:

"Davis, will you look at this powder? This is not right."

I turned my head. Christian George King again, and treachery again! Sea-water had been conveyed into the magazine, and every grain of powder was spoiled!

"Stay a moment," said Sergeant Drooce, when I had told him, without causing a movement in a muscle of his face: "look to your pouch, my lad. You Tom Packer, look to your pouch, confound you! Look to your pouches, all you Marines."

The same artful savage had got at them, somehow or another, and the cartridges were all unserviceable. "Hum!"

says the Sergeant. "Look to your loading, men. You are right so far?"

Yes; we were right so far.

"Well, my lads, and gentlemen all," says the Sergeant, "this will be a hand-to-hand affair, and so much the better."

He treated himself to a pinch of snuff, and stood up, square-shouldered and broad-chested, in the light of the moon —which was now very bright—as cool as if he was waiting for a play to begin. He stood quiet, and we all stood quiet, for a matter of something like half-an-hour. I took notice from such whispered talk as there was, how little we that the silver did not belong to, thought about it, and how much the people that it did belong to, thought about it. At the end of the half-hour, it was reported from the gate that Charker and the two were falling back on us, pursued by about a dozen.

"Sally! Gate-party, under Gill Davis," says the Sergeant, "and bring 'em in! Like men, now!"

We were not long about it, and we brought them in. "Don't take me," says Charker, holding me round the neck, and stumbling down at my feet when the gate was fast, "don't take me near the ladies or the children, Gill. They had better not see Death, till it can't be helped. They'll see it soon enough."

"Harry!" I answered, holding up his head. "Comrade!"

He was cut to pieces. The signal had been secured by the first pirate party that landed; his hair was all singed off, and his face was blackened with the running pitch from a torch.

He made no complaint of pain, or of anything. "Good-bye, old chap," was all he said, with a smile. "I've got my death. And Death ain't life. Is it, Gill?"

Having helped to lay his poor body on one side, I went back to my post. Sergeant Drooce looked at me, with his eyebrows a little lifted. I nodded. "Close up here men, and gentlemen all!" said the Sergeant. "A place too many, in the line."

The Pirates were so close upon us at this time, that the foremost of them were already before the gate. More and more came up with a great noise, and shouting loudly. When we believed from the sound that they were all there, we gave three English cheers. The poor little children joined, and were so fully convinced of our being at play, that they enjoyed the noise, and were heard clapping their hands in the silence that followed.

Our disposition was this, beginning with the rear. Mrs. Venning, holding her daughter's child in her arms, sat on the steps of the little square trench surrounding the silver-house, encouraging and directing those women and children as she might have done in the happiest and easiest time of her life. Then, there was an armed line, under Mr. Maccy, across the width of the enclosure, facing that way and having their backs towards the gate, in order that they might watch the walls and prevent our being taken by surprise. Then there was a space of eight or ten feet deep, in which the spare arms were, and in which Miss Maryon and Mrs. Fisher, their hands and dresses blackened with the spoilt gunpowder, worked on their knees, tying such things as knives, old bayonets, and spear-heads, to the muzzles of the useless muskets. Then, there was a second armed line, under Sergeant Drooce, also across the width of the enclosure, but facing to the gate. Then came the breastwork we had made, with a zig-zag way through it for me and my little party to hold good in retreating, as long as we could, when we were driven from the gate. We all knew that it was impossible to hold the place long, and that our only hope was in the timely discovery of the plot by the boats, and in their coming back.

I and my men were now thrown forward to the gate. From a spy-hole, I could see the whole crowd of Pirates. There were Malays among them, Dutch, Maltese, Greeks, Sambos,

Negroes, and Convict Englishmen from the West India Islands; among the last, him with the one eye and the patch across the nose. There were some Portuguese, too, and a few Spaniards. The captain was a Portuguese; a little man with very large ear-rings under a very broad hat, and a great bright shawl twisted about his shoulders. They were all strongly armed, but like a boarding party, with pikes, swords, cutlasses, and axes. I noticed a good many pistols, but not a gun of any kind among them. This gave me to understand that they had considered that a continued roll of musketry might perhaps have been heard on the mainland; also, that for the reason that fire would be seen from the mainland they would not set the Fort in flames and roast us alive; which was one of their favourite ways of carrying on. I looked about for Christian George King, and if I had seen him I am much mistaken if he would not have received my one round of ball-cartridge in his head. But, no Christian George King was visible.

A sort of a wild Portuguese demon, who seemed either fierce-mad or fierce-drunk—but, they all seemed one or the other—came forward with the black flag, and gave it a wave or two. After that, the Portuguese captain called out in shrill English, "I say you! English fools! Open the gate! Surrender!

As we kept close and quiet, he said something to his men which I didn't understand, and when he had said it, the one-eyed English rascal with the patch (who had stepped out when he began), said it again in English. It was only this. "Boys of the black flag, this is to be quickly done. Take all the prisoners you can. If they don't yield, kill the children to make them. Forward!" Then, they all came on at the gate, and, in another half minute were smashing and splitting it in.

We struck at them through the gaps and shivers, and we dropped many of them, too; but, their very weight would have carried such a gate, if they had been unarmed. I soon found Sergeant Drooce at my side, forming us six remaining marines in line—Tom Packer next to me—and ordering us to fall back three paces, and, as they broke in, to give them our one little volley at short distance. "Then," says he, "receive them behind your breastwork on the bayonet, and at least let every man of you pin one of the cursed cockchafers through the body."

We checked them by our fire, slight as it was, and we checked them at the breastwork. However, they broke over it like swarms of devils—they were, really and truly, more devils than men—and then it was hand to hand, indeed.

We clubbed our muskets and laid about us; even then, those two ladies—always behind me—were steady and ready with the arms. I had a lot of Maltese and Malays upon me, and, but for a broadsword that Miss Maryon's own hand put in mine, should have got my end from them. But, was that all? No. I saw a heap of banded dark hair and a white dress come thrice between me and them, under my own raised right arm, which each time might have destroyed the wearer of the white dress; and each time one of the lot went down, struck dead.

Drooce was armed with a broadsword, too, and did such things with it, that there was a cry, in half-a-dozen languages, of "Kill that sergeant!" as I knew, by the cry being raised in English, and taken up in other tongues. I had received a severe cut across the left arm a few moments before, and should have known nothing of it, except supposing that some-body had struck me a smart blow, if I had not felt weak, and seen myself covered with spouting blood, and, at the same instant of time, seen Miss Maryon tearing her dress and binding it with Mrs. Fisher's help round the wound. They called to Tom Packer, who was scouring by, to stop and guard me for one minute, while I was bound, or I should bleed to death in trying to defend myself. Tom stopped directly, with a good sabre in his hand.

In that same moment—all things seem to happen in that

same moment, at such a time—half-a-dozen had rushed howling at Sergeant Drooce. The Sergeant, stepping back against the wall, stopped one howl for ever with such a terrible blow, and waited for the rest to come on, with such a wonderfully unmoved face, that they stopped and looked at him.

"See him now!" cried Tom Packer. "Now, when I could cut him out! Gill! Did I tell you to mark my words?"

I implored Tom Packer in the Lord's name, as well as I could in my faintness, to go to the Sergeant's aid.

"I hate and detest him," says Tom, moodily wavering. "Still, he is a brave man." Then he calls out, "Sergeant Drooce, Sergeant Drooce! Tell me you have driven me too hard, and are sorry for it."

The Sergeant, without turning his eyes from his assailants, which would have been instant death to him, answers:

"No. I won't."

"Sergeant Drooce!" cries Tom, in a kind of an agony. "I have passed my word that I would never save you from Death, if I could, but would leave you to die. Tell me you have driven me too hard and are sorry for it, and that shall go for nothing."

One of the group laid the Sergeant's bald bare head open. The Sergeant laid him dead.

"I tell you," says the Sergeant, breathing a little short, and waiting for the next attack, "no. I won't. If you are not man enough to strike for a fellow-soldier because he wants help, and because of nothing else, I'll go into the other world and look for a better man."

Tom swept upon them, and cut him out. Tom and he fought their way through another knot of them, and sent them flying, and came over to where I was beginning again to feel, with inexpressible joy, that I had got a sword in my hand.

They had hardly come to us, when I heard, above all the other noises, a tremendous cry of women's voices. I also saw Miss Maryon, with quite a new face, suddenly clap her two hands over Mrs. Fisher's eyes. I looked towards the silver-house, and saw Mrs. Venning—standing upright on the top of the steps of the trench, with her gray hair and her dark eyes—hide her daughter's child behind her, among the folds of her dress, strike a pirate with her other hand, and fall, shot by his pistol.

The cry arose again, and there was a terrible and confusing rush of the women into the midst of the struggle. In another moment, something came tumbling down upon me that I thought was the wall. It was a heap of Sambos who had come over the wall; and of four men who clung to my legs like serpents, one who clung to my right leg was Christian George King.

"Yup, So-Jeer," says he, "Christian George King sar berry glad So-Jeer a prisoner. Christian George King been waiting for So-Jeer sech long time. Yup, yup!"

What could I do, with five-and-twenty of them on me, but be tied hand and foot? So, I was tied hand and foot. It was all over now—boats not come back—all lost! When I was fast bound and was put up against the wall, the one-eyed English convict came up with the Portuguese Captain, to have a look at me.

"See!" says he. "Here's the determined man! If you had slept sounder, last night, you'd have slept your soundest last night, my determined man."

The Portuguese Captain laughed in a cool way, and with the flat of his cutlass, hit me crosswise, as if I was the bough of a tree that he played with: first on the face, and then across the chest and the wounded arm. I looked him steady in the face without tumbling while he looked at me, I am happy to say; but, when they went away, I fell, and lay there.

The sun was up, when I was roused and told to come down to the beach and be embarked. I was full of aches and pains, and could not at first remember; but, I remembered quite soon enough. The killed were lying about all over the place, and the Pirates were burying their dead, and taking away their wounded on hastily-made litters, to the back of the Island. As for us prisoners, some of their boats had come round to the usual harbour, to carry us off. We looked a wretched few, I thought, when I got down there; still, it was another sign that we had fought well, and made the enemy suffer.

The Portuguese Captain had all the women already embarked in the boat he himself commanded, which was just putting off when I got down. Miss Maryon sat on one side of him, and gave me a moment's look, as full of quiet courage, and pity, and confidence, as if it had been an hour long. On the other side of him was poor little Mrs. Fisher, weeping for her child and her mother. I was shoved into the same boat with Drooce and Packer, and the remainder of our party of marines: of whom we had lost two privates, besides Charker, my poor, brave comrade. We all made a melancholy passage, under the hot sun over to the mainland. There, we landed in a solitary place, and were mustered on the sea sand. Mr. and Mrs. Macey and their children were amongst us, Mr. and Mrs. Pordage, Mr. Kitten, Mr. Fisher, and Mrs. Belltott. We mustered only fourteen men, fifteen women, and seven children. Those were all that remained of the English who had lain down to sleep last night, unsuspecting and happy, on the Island of Silver-Store.

[The second chapter, which was not written by Mr. Dickens, describes the Prisoners (twenty-two women and children) taken into the interior by the Pirate Captain, who makes them the material guarantee for the precious metal and jewels left on the island; declaring that, if the latter be wrested by English ships from the pirates in charge, he will murder the captives. From their "Prison in the Woods," however (this being the title of the second chapter), they escape by means of rafts down the river; and the sequel is told in a third and concluding chapter by Mr. Dickens.]

CHAPTER III.

WE contrived to keep afloat all that night, and, the stream
running strong with us, to glide a long way down the river.
But, we found the night to be a dangerous time for such
navigation, on account of the eddies and rapids, and it was
therefore settled next day that in future we would bring-to
at sunset, and encamp on the shore. As we knew of no boats
that the Pirates possessed, up at the Prison in the Woods,
we settled always to encamp on the opposite side of the
stream, so as to have the breadth of the river between
our sleep and them. Our opinion was, that if they were
acquainted with any near way by land to the mouth of this
river, they would come up it in force, and retake us or kill
us, according as they could; but that if that was not the
case, and if the river ran by none of their secret stations,
we might escape.

When I say we settled this or that, I do not mean that
we planned anything with any confidence as to what might
happen an hour hence. So much had happened in one night,
and such great changes had been violently and suddenly made
in the fortunes of many among us, that we had got better
used to uncertainty, in a little while, than I dare say most
people do in the course of their lives.

The difficulties we soon got into, through the off-settings
and point-currents of the stream, made the likelihood of our

being drowned, alone—to say nothing of our being retaken—as broad and plain as the sun at noonday to all of us. But, we all worked hard at managing the rafts, under the direction of the seamen (of our own skill, I think we never could have prevented them from oversetting), and we also worked hard at making good the defects in their first hasty construction—which the water soon found out. While we humbly resigned ourselves to going down, if it was the will of Our Father that was in Heaven, we humbly made up our minds, that we would all do the best that was in us.

And so we held on, gliding with the stream. It drove us to this bank, and it drove us to that bank, and it turned us, and whirled us; but yet it carried us on. Sometimes much too slowly; sometimes much too fast, but yet it carried us on.

My little deaf and dumb boy slumbered a good deal now, and that was the case with all the children. They caused very little trouble to any one. They seemed, in my eyes, to get more like one another, not only in quiet manner, but in the face, too. The motion of the raft was usually so much the same, the scene was usually so much the same, the sound of the soft wash and ripple of the water was usually so much the same, that they were made drowsy, as they might have been by the constant playing of one tune. Even on the grown people, who worked hard and felt anxiety, the same things produced something of the same effect. Every day was so like the other, that I soon lost count of the days, myself, and had to ask Miss Maryon, for instance, whether this was the third or fourth? Miss Maryon had a pocket-book and pencil, and she kept the log; that is to say, she entered up a clear little journal of the time, and of the distances our seamen thought we had made, each night.

So, as I say, we kept afloat and glided on. All day long, and every day, the water, and the woods, and sky; all day long, and every day, the constant watching of both sides of the river, and far ahead at every bold turn and sweep it made, for any signs of Pirate-boats, or Pirate-dwellings. So, as I say, we kept afloat and glided on. The days melting themselves together to that degree, that I could hardly believe my ears when I asked "How many, now, Miss?" and she answered "Seven."

To be sure, poor Mr. Pordage had, by about now, got his Diplomatic coat into such a state as never was seen. What with the mud of the river, what with the water of the river, what with the sun, and the dews, and the tearing boughs, and the thickets, it hung about him in discoloured shreds like a mop. The sun had touched him a bit. He had taken to always polishing one particular button, which just held on to his left wrist, and to always calling for stationery. I suppose that man called for pens, ink, and paper, tape, and sealing-wax, upwards of one thousand times in four-and-twenty hours. He had an idea that we should never get out of that river unless we were written out of it in a formal Memorandum; and the more we laboured at navigating the rafts, the more he ordered us not to touch them at our peril, and the more he sat and roared for stationery.

Mrs. Pordage, similarly, persisted in wearing her nightcap. I doubt if any one but ourselves who had seen the progress of that article of dress, could by this time have told what it was meant for. It had got so limp and ragged that she couldn't see out of her eyes for it. It was so dirty, that whether it was vegetable matter out of a swamp, or weeds out of the river, or an old porter's-knot from England, I don't think any new spectator could have said. Yet, this unfortunate old woman had a notion that it was not only vastly genteel, but that it was the correct thing as to propriety. And she really did carry herself over the other ladies who had no nightcaps, and who were forced to tie up their hair how they could, in a superior manner that was perfectly amazing.

I don't know what she looked like, sitting in that blessed nightcap, on a log of wood, outside the hut or cabin upon

our raft. She would have rather resembled a fortune-teller
in one of the picture-books that used to be in the shop
windows in my boyhood, except for her stateliness. But,
Lord bless my heart, the dignity with which she sat and
moped, with her head in that bundle of tatters, was like
nothing else in the world! She was not on speaking terms
with more than three of the ladies. Some of them had, what
she called, "taken precedence" of her—in getting into, or out
of, that miserable little shelter!—and others had not called
to pay their respects, or something of that kind. So, there
she sat, in her own state and ceremony, while her husband
sat on the same log of wood, ordering us one and all to let
the raft go to the bottom, and to bring him stationery.

What with this noise on the part of Mr. Commissioner
Pordage, and what with the cries of Sergeant Drooce on the
raft astern (which were sometimes more than Tom Packer
could silence), we often made our slow way down the river,
anything but quietly. Yet, that it was of great importance
that no ears should be able to hear us from the woods on
the banks, could not be doubted. We were looked for, to a
certainty, and we might be retaken at any moment. It was
an anxious time; it was, indeed, indeed, an anxious time.

On the seventh night of our voyage on the rafts, we made
fast, as usual, on the opposite side of the river to that from
which we had started, in as dark a place as we could pick
out. Our little encampment was soon made, and supper was
eaten, and the children fell asleep. The watch was set, and
everything made orderly for the night. Such a starlight
night, with such blue in the sky, and such black in the places
of heavy shade on the banks of the great stream!

Those two ladies, Miss Maryon and Mrs. Fisher, had always
kept near me since the night of the attack. Mr. Fisher, who
was untiring in the work of our raft, had said to me:

"My dear little childless wife has grown so attached to
you, Davis, and you are such a gentle fellow, as well as
such a determined one;" our party had adopted that last

expression from the one-eyed English pirate, and I repeat
what Mr. Fisher said, only because he said it; "that it
takes a load off my mind to leave her in your charge."

I said to him: "Your lady is in far better charge than
mine, sir, having Miss Maryon to take care of her; but, you
may rely upon it, that I will guard them both—faithful and
true."

Says he: "I do rely upon it, Davis, and I heartily wish
all the silver on our old Island was yours."

That seventh starlight night, as I have said, we made our
camp, and got our supper, and set our watch, and the
children fell asleep. It was solemn and beautiful in those
wild and solitary parts, to see them, every night before they
lay down, kneeling under the bright sky, saying their little
prayers at women's laps. At that time we men all uncovered,
and mostly kept at a distance. When the innocent creatures
rose up, we murmured "Amen!" all together. For, though
we had not heard what they said, we knew it must be good
for us.

At that time, too, as was only natural, those poor mothers
in our company, whose children had been killed, shed many
tears. I thought the night seemed to console them while
it made them cry; but, whether I was right or wrong in
that, they wept very much. On this seventh night, Mrs.
Fisher had cried for her lost darling until she cried herself
asleep. She was lying on a little couch of leaves and such-
like (I made the best little couch I could for them every
night), and Miss Maryon had covered her, and sat by her,
holding her hand. The stars looked down upon them. As
for me, I guarded them.

"Davis!" says Miss Maryon. (I am not going to say
what a voice she had. I couldn't if I tried.)

"I am here, Miss."

"The river sounds as if it were swollen to-night."

"We all think, Miss, that we are coming near the sea."

"Do you believe now, we shall escape?"

"I do now, Miss, really believe it." I had always said I did; but, I had in my own mind been doubtful.

"How glad you will be, my good Davis, to see England again!"

I have another confession to make that will appear singular. When she said these words, something rose in my throat; and the stars I looked away at, seemed to break into sparkles that fell down my face and burnt it.

"England is not much to me, Miss, except as a name."

"O, so true an Englishman should not say that!—Are you not well to-night, Davis?" Very kindly, and with a quick change.

"Quite well, Miss."

"Are you sure? Your voice sounds altered in my hearing."

"No, Miss, I am a stronger man than ever. But, England is nothing to me."

Miss Maryon sat silent for so long a while, that I believed she had done speaking to me for one time. However, she had not; for by-and-by she said in a distinct clear tone:

"No, good friend; you must not say that England is nothing to you. It is to be much to you, yet—everything to you. You have to take back to England the good name you have earned here, and the gratitude and attachment and respect you have won here: and you have to make some good English girl very happy and proud, by marrying her; and I shall one day see her, I hope, and make her happier and prouder still, by telling her what noble services her husband's were in South America, and what a noble friend he was to me there."

Though she spoke these kind words in a cheering manner, she spoke them compassionately. I said nothing. It will appear to be another strange confession, that I paced to and fro, within call, all that night, a most unhappy man, reproaching myself all the night long. "You are as ignorant as any man alive; you are as obscure as any man alive; you

are as poor as any man alive; you are no better than the
mud under your foot." That was the way in which I went
on against myself until the morning.

With the day, came the day's labour. What I should
have done without the labour, I don't know. We were
afloat again at the usual hour, and were again making our
way down the river. It was broader, and clearer of obstruc-
tions than it had been, and it seemed to flow faster. This
was one of Drooce's quiet days; Mr. Pordage, besides being
sulky, had almost lost his voice; and we made good way,
and with little noise.

There was always a seaman forward on the raft, keeping
a bright look-out. Suddenly, in the full heat of the day,
when the children were slumbering, and the very trees and
reeds appeared to be slumbering, this man—it was Short—
holds up his hand, and cries with great caution: "Avast!
Voices ahead!"

We held on against the stream as soon as we could bring
her up, and the other raft followed suit. At first, Mr.
Macey, Mr. Fisher, and myself, could hear nothing; though
both the seamen aboard of us agreed that they could hear
voices and oars. After a little pause, however, we united in
thinking that we *could* hear the sound of voices, and the dip
of oars. But, you can hear a long way in those countries,
and there was a bend of the river before us, and nothing
was to be seen except such waters and such banks as we were
now in the eighth day (and might, for the matter of our
feelings, have been in the eightieth), of having seen with
anxious eyes.

It was soon decided to put a man ashore, who should creep
through the wood, see what was coming, and warn the rafts.
The rafts in the meantime to keep the middle of the stream.
The man to be put ashore, and not to swim ashore, as the
first thing could be more quickly done than the second. The
raft conveying him, to get back into mid-stream, and to hold
on along with the other, as well as it could, until signalled

by the man. In case of danger, the man to shift for himself until it should be safe to take him on board again. I volunteered to be the man.

We knew that the voices and oars must come up slowly against the stream; and our seamen knew, by the set of the stream, under which bank they would come. I was put ashore accordingly. The raft got off well, and I broke into the wood.

Steaming hot it was, and a tearing place to get through. So much the better for me, since it was something to contend against and do. I cut off the bend of the river, at a great saving of space, came to the water's edge again, and hid myself, and waited. I could now hear the dip of the oars very distinctly; the voices had ceased.

The sound came on in a regular tune, and as I lay hidden, I fancied the tune so played to be, "Chris'en—George—King! Chris'en—George—King! Chris'en—George—King!" over and over again, always the same, with the pauses always at the same places. I had likewise time to make up my mind that if these were the Pirates, I could and would (barring my being shot) swim off to my raft, in spite of my wound, the moment I had given the alarm, and hold my old post by Miss Maryon.

"Chris'en —George — King! Chris'en —George — King! Chris'en—George—King!" coming up, now, very near.

I took a look at the branches about me, to see where a shower of bullets would be most likely to do me least hurt; and I took a look back at the track I had made in forcing my way in; and now I was wholly prepared and fully ready for them.

"Chris'en —George — King! Chris'en —George — King! Chris'en—George—King!" Here they were!

Who were they? The barbarous Pirates, scum of all nations, headed by such men as the hideous little Portuguese monkey, and the one-eyed English convict with the gash across his face, that ought to have gashed his wicked head

off? The worst men in the world picked out from the
worst, to do the cruellest and most atrocious deeds that
ever stained it? The howling, murdering, black-flag waving,
mad, and drunken crowd of devils that had overcome us by
numbers and by treachery? No. These were English men in
English boats—good blue-jackets and red-coats—marines that
I knew myself, and sailors that knew our seamen! At the
helm of the first boat, Captain Carton, eager and steady.
At the helm of the second boat, Captain Maryon, brave
and bold. At the helm of the third boat, an old seaman,
with determination carved into his watchful face, like the
figure-head of a ship. Every man doubly and trebly armed
from head to foot. Every man lying-to at his work, with
a will that had all his heart and soul in it. Every man
looking out for any trace of friend or enemy, and burning
to be the first to do good or avenge evil. Every man with
his face on fire when he saw me, his countryman who had
been taken prisoner, and hailed me with a cheer, as Captain
Carton's boat ran in and took me on board.

I reported, "All escaped, sir! All well, all safe, all
here!"

God bless me—and God bless them—what a cheer! It
turned me weak, as I was passed on from hand to hand to
the stern of the boat: every hand patting me or grasping
me in some way or other, in the moment of my going by.

"Hold up, my brave fellow," says Captain Carton, clapping
me on the shoulder like a friend, and giving me a flask.
"Put your lips to that, and they'll be red again. Now, boys,
give way!"

The banks flew by us as if the mightiest stream that ever
ran was with us; and so it was, I am sure, meaning the
stream to those men's ardour and spirit. The banks flew by
us, and we came in sight of the rafts—the banks flew by us,
and we came alongside of the rafts—the banks stopped; and
there was a tumult of laughing and crying, and kissing and
shaking of hands, and catching up of children and setting

of them down again, and a wild hurry of thankfulness and joy that melted every one and softened all hearts.

I had taken notice, in Captain Carton's boat, that there was a curious and quite new sort of fitting on board. It was a kind of a little bower made of flowers, and it was set up behind the captain, and betwixt him and the rudder. Not only was this arbour, so to call it, neatly made of flowers, but it was ornamented in a singular way. Some of the men had taken the ribbons and buckles off their hats, and hung them among the flowers; others had made festoons and streamers of their handkerchiefs, and hung them there; others had intermixed such trifles as bits of glass and shining fragments of lockets and tobacco-boxes with the flowers; so that altogether it was a very bright and lively object in the sunshine. But why there, or what for, I did not understand.

Now, as soon as the first bewilderment was over, Captain Carton gave the order to land for the present. But this boat of his, with two hands left in her, immediately put off again when the men were out of her, and kept off, some yards from the shore. As she floated there, with the two hands gently backing water to keep her from going down the stream, this pretty little arbour attracted many eyes. None of the boat's crew, however, had anything to say about it, except that it was the captain's fancy.

The captain—with the women and children clustering round him, and the men of all ranks grouped outside them, and all listening—stood telling how the Expedition, deceived by its bad intelligence, had chased the light Pirate boats all that fatal night, and had still followed in their wake next day, and had never suspected until many hours too late that the great Pirate body had drawn off in the darkness when the chase began, and shot over to the Island. He stood telling how the Expedition, supposing the whole array of armed boats to be ahead of it, got tempted into shallows and went aground; but not without having its revenge upon the two decoy-boats, both of which it had come up with, overhand, and sent to the bottom with all on board. He stood telling how the Expedition, fearing then that the case stood as it did, got afloat again, by great exertion, after the loss of four more tides, and returned to the Island, where they found the sloop scuttled and the treasure gone. He stood telling how my officer, Lieutenant Linderwood, was left upon the Island, with as strong a force as could be got together hurriedly from the mainland, and how the three boats we saw before us were manned and armed and had come away, exploring the coast and inlets, in search of any tidings of us. He stood telling all this, with his face to the river; and, as he stood telling it, the little arbour of flowers floated in the sunshine before all the faces there.

Leaning on Captain Carton's shoulder, between him and Miss Maryon, was Mrs. Fisher, her head drooping on her arm. She asked him, without raising it, when he had told so much, whether he had found her mother?

"Be comforted! She lies," said the Captain gently, "under the cocoa-nut trees on the beach."

"And my child, Captain Carton, did you find my child, too? Does my darling rest with my mother?"

"No. Your pretty child sleeps," said the Captain, "under a shade of flowers."

His voice shook; but there was something in it that struck all the hearers. At that moment there sprung from the arbour in his boat a little creature, clapping her hands and stretching out her arms, and crying, "Dear papa! Dear mamma! I am not killed. I am saved. I am coming to kiss you. Take me to them, take me to them, good, kind sailors!"

Nobody who saw that scene has ever forgotten it, I am sure, or ever will forget it. The child had kept quite still, where her brave grandmamma had put her (first whispering in her ear, "Whatever happens to me, do not stir, my dear!"), and had remained quiet until the fort was deserted; she had then crept out of the trench, and gone into her mother's house; and there, alone on the solitary Island, in her mother's room, and asleep on her mother's bed, the Captain had found her. Nothing could induce her to be parted from him after he took her up in his arms, and he had brought her away with him, and the men had made the bower for her. To see those men now, was a sight. The joy of the women was beautiful; the joy of those women who had lost their own children, was quite sacred and divine; but, the ecstasies of Captain Carton's boat's crew, when their pet was restored to her parents, were wonderful for the tenderness they showed in the midst of roughness. As the Captain stood with the child in his arms, and the child's own little arms now clinging round his neck, now round her father's, now round her mother's, now round some one who pressed up to kiss her, the boat's crew shook hands with one another, waved their hats over their heads, laughed, sang, cried, danced—and all among themselves, without wanting to interfere with anybody—in a manner never to be represented. At last, I saw the coxswain and another, two very hard-faced men, with grizzled heads, who had been the heartiest of the hearty all along, close with one another, get each of them the other's head under his arm, and pommel away at it with his fist as hard as he could, in his excess of joy.

When we had well rested and refreshed ourselves—and very glad we were to have some of the heartening things to eat and drink that had come up in the boats—we recommenced our voyage down the river: rafts, and boats, and all. I said to myself, it was a very different kind of voyage now, from what it had been; and I fell into my proper place and station among my fellow-soldiers.

But, when we halted for the night, I found that Miss Maryon had spoken to Captain Carton concerning me. For, the Captain came straight up to me, and says he, "My brave fellow, you have been Miss Maryon's body-guard all along, and you shall remain so. Nobody shall supersede you in the distinction and pleasure of protecting that young lady." I thanked his honour in the fittest words I could find, and that night I was placed on my old post of watching the place where she slept. More than once in the night, I saw Captain Carton come out into the air, and stroll about there, to see that all was well. I have now this other singular confession to make, that I saw him with a heavy heart. Yes; I saw him with a heavy, heavy heart.

In the day-time, I had the like post in Captain Carton's boat. I had a special station of my own, behind Miss Maryon, and no hands but hers ever touched my wound. (It has been healed these many long years; but, no other hands have ever touched it.) Mr. Pordage was kept tolerably quiet now, with pen and ink, and began to pick up his senses a little. Seated in the second boat, he made documents with Mr. Kitten, pretty well all day; and he generally handed in a Protest about something whenever we stopped. The Captain, however, made so very light of these papers, that it grew into a saying among the men, when one of them wanted a match for his pipe, "Hand us over a Protest, Jack!" As to Mrs. Pordage, she still wore the nightcap, and she now had cut all the ladies on account of her not having been formally and separately rescued by Captain Carton before anybody else. The end of Mr. Pordage, to bring to an end all I know about him, was, that he got great compliments at home for his conduct on these trying occasions, and that he died of yellow jaundice, a Governor and a K.C.B.

Sergeant Drooce had fallen from a high fever into a low one. Tom Packer—the only man who could have pulled the Sergeant through it—kept hospital aboard the old raft, and Mrs. Belltott, as brisk as ever again (but the spirit of that little woman, when things tried it, was not equal to appearances), was head-nurse under his directions. Before we got down to the Mosquito coast, the joke had been made by one of our men, that we should see her gazetted Mrs. Tom Packer, *vice* Belltott exchanged.

When we reached the coast, we got native boats as

substitutes for the rafts; and we rowed along under the
land; and in that beautiful climate, and upon that beautiful water, the blooming days were like enchantment. Ah!
They were running away, faster than any sea or river, and
there was no tide to bring them back. We were coming
very near the settlement where the people of Silver-Store
were to be left, and from which we Marines were under
orders to return to Belize.

Captain Carton had, in the boat by him, a curious long-
barrelled Spanish gun, and he had said to Miss Maryon one
day that it was the best of guns, and had turned his head
to me, and said:

"Gill Davis, load her fresh with a couple of slugs, against
a chance of showing how good she is."

So, I had discharged the gun over the sea, and had loaded
her, according to orders, and there it had lain at the Captain's
feet, convenient to the Captain's hand.

The last day but one of our journey was an uncommonly
hot day. We started very early; but, there was no cool air
on the sea as the day got on, and by noon the heat was
really hard to bear, considering that there were women and
children to bear it. Now, we happened to open, just at that
time, a very pleasant little cove or bay, where there was a
deep shade from a great growth of trees. Now, the Captain,
therefore, made the signal to the other boats to follow him
in and lie by a while.

The men who were off duty went ashore, and lay down,
but were ordered, for caution's sake, not to stray, and to keep
within view. The others rested on their oars, and dozed.
Awnings had been made of one thing and another, in all the
boats, and the passengers found it cooler to be under them
in the shade, when there was room enough, than to be in
the thick woods. So, the passengers were all afloat, and
mostly sleeping. I kept my post behind Miss Maryon, and
she was on Captain Carton's right in the boat, and Mrs.
Fisher sat on her right again. The Captain had Mrs.

Fisher's daughter on his knee.   He and the two ladies were talking about the Pirates, and were talking softly; partly, because people do talk softly under such indolent circumstances, and partly because the little girl had gone off asleep.

I think I have before given it out for my Lady to write down, that Captain Carton had a fine bright eye of his own. All at once, he darted me a side look, as much as to say, "Steady—don't take on—I see something!"—and gave the child into her mother's arms.   That eye of his was so easy to understand, that I obeyed it by not so much as looking either to the right or to the left out of a corner of my own, or changing my attitude the least trifle.   The Captain went on talking in the same mild and easy way; but began —with his arms resting across his knees, and his head a little hanging forward, as if the heat were rather too much for him—began to play with the Spanish gun.

"They had laid their plans, you see," says the Captain, taking up the Spanish gun across his knees, and looking, lazily, at the inlaying on the stock, " with a great deal of art; and the corrupt or blundering local authorities were so easily deceived;" he ran his left hand idly along the barrel, but I saw, with my breath held, that he covered the action of cocking the gun with his right—" so easily deceived, that they summoned us out to come into the trap.   But my intention as to future operations——"   In a flash the Spanish gun was at his bright eye, and he fired.

All started up; innumerable echoes repeated the sound of the discharge; a cloud of bright-coloured birds flew out of the woods screaming; a handful of leaves were scattered in the place where the shot had struck; a crackling of branches was heard; and some lithe but heavy creature sprang into the air, and fell forward, head down, over the muddy bank.

" What is it?" cries Captain Maryon from his boat.   All silent then, but the echoes rolling away.

" It is a 'Traitor and a Spy," said Captain Carton, handing

me the gun to load again. "And I think the other name
of the animal is Christian George King!"

Shot through the heart. Some of the people ran round
to the spot, and drew him out, with the slime and wet
trickling down his face; but his face itself would never stir
any more to the end of time.

"Leave him hanging to that tree," cried Captain Carton;
his boat's crew giving way, and he leaping ashore. "But
first into this wood, every man in his place. And boats!
Out of gunshot!"

It was a quick change, well meant and well made, though
it ended in disappointment. No Pirates were there; no one
but the Spy was found. It was supposed that the Pirates,
unable to retake us, and expecting a great attack upon them
to be the consequence of our escape, had made from the
ruins in the Forest, taken to their ship along with the
Treasure, and left the Spy to pick up what intelligence he
could. In the evening we went away, and he was left hanging to the tree, all alone, with the red sun making a kind
of a dead sunset on his black face.

Next day, we gained the settlement on the Mosquito coast
for which we were bound. Having stayed there to refresh
seven days, and having been much commended, and highly
spoken of, and finely entertained, we Marines stood under
orders to march from the Town-Gate (it was neither much
of a town nor much of a gate), at five in the morning.

My officer had joined us before then. When we turned
out at the gate, all the people were there; in the front of
them all those who had been our fellow-prisoners, and all the
seamen.

"Davis," says Lieutenant Linderwood. "Stand out, my
friend!"

I stood out from the ranks, and Miss Maryon and Captain
Carton came up to me.

"Dear Davis," says Miss Maryon, while the tears fell fast
down her face, "your grateful friends, in most unwillingly

taking leave of you, ask the favour that, while you bear away with you their affectionate remembrance, which nothing can ever impair, you will also take this purse of money—far more valuable to you, we all know, for the deep attachment and thankfulness with which it is offered, than for its own contents, though we hope those may prove useful to you, too, in after life."

I got out, in answer, that I thankfully accepted the attachment and affection, but not the money. Captain Carton looked at me very attentively, and stepped back, and moved away. I made him my bow as he stepped back, to thank him for being so delicate.

"No, miss," said I, "I think it would break my heart to accept of money. But, if you could condescend to give to a man so ignorant and common as myself, any little thing you have worn—such as a bit of ribbon——"

She took a ring from her finger, and put it in my hand. And she rested her hand in mine, while she said these words:

"The brave gentlemen of old—but not one of them was braver, or had a nobler nature than you—took such gifts from ladies, and did all their good actions for the givers' sakes. If you will do yours for mine, I shall think with pride that I continue to have some share in the life of a gallant and generous man."

For the second time in my life she kissed my hand. I made so bold, for the first time, as to kiss hers; and I tied the ring at my breast, and I fell back to my place.

Then, the horse-litter went out at the gate with Sergeant Drooce in it; and the horse-litter went out at the gate with Mrs. Belltott in it; and Lieutenant Linderwood gave the word of command, "Quick march!" and, cheered and cried for, we went out of the gate too, marching along the level plain towards the serene blue sky, as if we were marching straight to Heaven.

When I have added here that the Pirate scheme was blown to shivers, by the Pirate-ship which had the Treasure on board being so vigorously attacked by one of His Majesty's cruisers, among the West India Keys, and being so swiftly boarded and carried, that nobody suspected anything about the scheme until three-fourths of the Pirates were killed, and the other fourth were in irons, and the Treasure was recovered; I come to the last singular confession I have got to make.

It is this. I well knew what an immense and hopeless distance there was between me and Miss Maryon; I well knew that I was no fitter company for her than I was for the angels; I well knew that she was as high above my reach as the sky over my head; and yet I loved her. What put it in my low heart to be so daring, or whether such a thing ever happened before or since, as that a man so uninstructed and obscure as myself got his unhappy thoughts lifted up to such a height, while knowing very well how presumptuous and impossible to be realised they were, I am unable to say; still, the suffering to me was just as great as if I had been a gentleman. I suffered agony—agony. I suffered hard, and I suffered long. I thought of her last words to me, however, and I never disgraced them. If it had not been for those dear words, I think I should have lost myself in despair and recklessness.

The ring will be found lying on my heart, of course, and will be laid with me wherever I am laid. I am getting on in years now, though I am able and hearty. I was recommended for promotion, and everything was done to reward me that could be done; but my total want of all learning stood in my way, and I found myself so completely out of the road to it, that I could not conquer any learning, though I tried. I was long in the service, and I respected it, and was respected in it, and the service is dear to me at this present hour.

At this present hour, when I give this out to my Lady to be written down, all my old pain has softened away, and I am as happy as a man can be, at this present fine old country-house of Admiral Sir George Carton, Baronet. It was my Lady Carton who herself sought me out, over a great many miles of the wide world, and found me in Hospital wounded, and brought me here. It is my Lady Carton who writes down my words. My Lady was Miss Maryon. And now, that I conclude what I had to tell, I see my Lady's honoured gray hair droop over her face, as she leans a little lower at her desk; and I fervently thank her for being so tender as I see she is, towards the past pain and trouble of her poor, old, faithful, humble soldier.

GOING INTO SOCIETY

[1858]

GOING INTO SOCIETY.

At one period of its reverses, the House fell into the
occupation of a Showman. He was found registered as its
occupier, on the parish books of the time when he rented
the House, and there was therefore no need of any clue to
his name. But, he himself was less easy to be found; for, he
had led a wandering life, and settled people had lost sight
of him, and people who plumed themselves on being respectable were shy of admitting that they had ever known anything
of him. At last, among the marsh lands near the river's
level, that lie about Deptford and the neighbouring market-
gardens, a Grizzled Personage in velveteen, with a face so cut
up by varieties of weather that he looked as if he had been
tattooed, was found smoking a pipe at the door of a wooden
house on wheels. The wooden house was laid up in ordinary
for the winter, near the mouth of a muddy creek; and everything near it, the foggy river, the misty marshes, and the
steaming market-gardens, smoked in company with the grizzled
man. In the midst of this smoking party, the funnel-
chimney of the wooden house on wheels was not remiss, but
took its pipe with the rest in a companionable manner.

On being asked if it were he who had once rented the
House to Let, Grizzled Velveteen looked surprised, and said
yes. Then his name was Magsman? That was it, Toby
Magsman—which lawfully christened Robert; but called in

the line, from a infant, Toby. There was nothing agin Toby
Magsman, he believed? If there was suspicion of such—
mention it!

'There was no suspicion of such, he might rest assured.
But, some inquiries were making about that House, and
would he object to say why he left it?

Not at all; why should he? He left it, along of a
Dwarf.

Along of a Dwarf?

Mr. Magsman repeated, deliberately and emphatically,
Along of a Dwarf.

Might it be compatible with Mr. Magsman's inclination
and convenience to enter, as a favour, into a few particulars?

Mr. Magsman entered into the following particulars.

It was a long time ago, to begin with ;—afore lotteries and
a deal more was done away with. Mr. Magsman was looking
about for a good pitch, and he see that house, and he says
to himself, "I'll have you, if you're to be had. If money'll
get you, I'll have you."

The neighbours cut up rough, and made complaints; but
Mr. Magsman don't know what they *would* have had. It
was a lovely thing. First of all, there was the canvass, representin the picter of the Giant, in Spanish trunks and a ruff,
who was himself half the heighth of the house, and was run
up with a line and pulley to a pole on the roof, so that his
Ed was coeval with the parapet. Then, there was the
canvass, representin the picter of the Albina lady, showing
her white air to the Army and Navy in correct uniform.
Then, there was the canvass, representin the picter of the
Wild Indian a scalpin a member of some foreign nation.
Then, there was the canvass, representin the picter of a child
of a British Planter, seized by two Boa Constrictors—not
that *we* never had no child, nor no Constrictors neither.
Similarly, there was the canvass, representin the picter of
the Wild Ass of the Prairies—not that *we* never had no wild
asses, nor wouldn't have had 'em at a gift. Last, there was

the canvass, representin the picter of the Dwarf, and like him too (considerin), with George the Fourth in such a state of astonishment at him as His Majesty couldn't with his utmost politeness and stoutness express. The front of the House was so covered with canvasses, that there wasn't a spark of day-light ever visible on that side. "MAGSMAN'S AMUSEMENTS," fifteen foot long by two foot high, ran over the front door and parlour winders. The passage was a Arbour of green baize and gardenstuff. A barrel-organ performed there unceasing. And as to respectability,—if threepence ain't respectable, what is?

But, the Dwarf is the principal article at present, and he was worth the money. He was wrote up as MAJOR TRSCHOFFKI, OF THE IMPERIAL BULGRADERIAN BRIGADE. Nobody couldn't pronounce the name, and it never was intended anybody should. The public always turned it, as a regular rule, into Chopski. In the line he was called Chops; partly on that account, and partly because his real name, if he ever had any real name (which was very dubious), was Stakes.

He was a un-common small man, he really was. Certainly not so small as he was made out to be, but where is your Dwarf as is? He was a most uncommon small man, with a most uncommon large Ed; and what he had inside that Ed, nobody never knowed but himself: even supposin himself to have ever took stock of it, which it would have been a stiff job for even him to do.

The kindest little man as never growed! Spirited, but not proud. When he travelled with the Spotted Baby—though he knowed himself to be a nat'ral Dwarf, and knowed the Baby's spots to be put upon him artificial, he nursed that Baby like a mother. You never heerd him give a ill-name to a Giant. He *did* allow himself to break out into strong language respectin the Fat Lady from Norfolk; but that was an affair of the 'art; and when a man's 'art has been trifled with by a lady, and the preference giv to a Indian, he ain't master of his actions.

He was always in love, of course; every human nat'ral phenomenon is. And he was always in love with a large woman; *I* never knowed the Dwarf as could be got to love a small one. Which helps to keep 'em the Curiosities they are.

One sing'ler idea he had in that Ed of his, which must have meant something, or it wouldn't have been there. It was always his opinion that he was entitled to property. He never would put his name to anything. He had been taught to write, by the young man without arms, who got his living with his toes (quite a writing master *he* was, and taught scores in the line), but Chops would have starved to death, afore he'd have gained a bit of bread by putting his hand to a paper. This is the more curious to bear in mind, because HE had no property, nor hope of property, except his house and a sarser. When I say his house, I mean the box, painted and got up outside like a reg'lar six-roomer, that he used to creep into, with a diamond ring (or quite as good to look at) on his forefinger, and ring a little bell out of what the Public believed to be the Drawing-room winder. And when I say a sarser, I mean a Chaney sarser in which he made a collection for himself at the end of every Entertainment. His cue for that, he took from me; "Ladies and gentlemen, the little man will now walk three times round the Cairawan, and retire behind the curtain." When he said anything important, in private life, he mostly wound it up with this form of words, and they was generally the last thing he said to me at night afore he went to bed.

He had what I consider a fine mind—a poetic mind. His ideas respectin his property never come upon him so strong as when he sat upon a barrel-organ and had the handle turned. Arter the wibration had run through him a little time, he would screech out, "Toby, I feel my property coming—grind away! I'm counting my guineas by thousands, Toby—grind away! Toby, I shall be a man of fortun! I feel the Mint a jingling in me, Toby, and I'm swelling out into the Bank

of England!" Such is the influence of music on a poetic
mind. Not that he was partial to any other music but a
barrel-organ; on the contrary, hated it.

He had a kind of a everlasting grudge agin the Public:
which is a thing you may notice in many phenomenons that
get their living out of it. What riled him most in the
nater of his occupation was, that it kep him out of Society.
He was continiwally saying, "Toby, my ambition is, to go
into Society. The curse of my position towards the Public
is, that it keeps me hout of Society. This don't signify to
a low beast of a Indian; he an't formed for Society. This
don't signify to a Spotted Baby; *he* an't formed for Society.
—I am."

Nobody never could make out what Chops done with his
money. He had a good salary, down on the drum every
Saturday as the day come round, besides having the run of
his teeth—and he was a Woodpecker to eat—but all Dwarfs
are. The sarser was a little income, bringing him in so many
halfpence that he'd carry 'em for a week together, tied up
in a pocket-handkercher. And yet he never had money.
And it couldn't be the Fat Lady from Norfolk, as was once
supposed; because it stands to reason that when you have a
animosity towards a Indian, which makes you grind your
teeth at him to his face, and which can hardly hold you
from Goosing him audible when he's going through his
War-Dance—it stands to reason you wouldn't under them
circumstances deprive yourself, to support that Indian in
the lap of luxury.

Most unexpected, the mystery come out one day at
Egham Races. The Public was shy of bein pulled in, and
Chops was ringin his little bell out of his drawing-room
winder, and was snarlin to me over his shoulder as he
kneeled down with his legs out at the back-door—for he
couldn't be shoved into his house without kneeling down,
and the premises wouldn't accommodate his legs—was snarlin,
"Here's a precious Public for you; why the Devil don't they

tumble up?" when a man in the crowd holds up a carrier-
pigeon, and cries out, "If there's any person here as has
got a ticket, the Lottery's just drawed, and the number as
has come up for the great prize is three, seven, forty-two!
Three, seven, forty-two!" I was givin the man to the Furies
myself, for calling off the Public's attention—for the Public
will turn away, at any time, to look at anything in preference
to the thing showed 'em; and if you doubt it, get 'em
together for any indiwidual purpose on the face of the earth,
and send only two people in late, and see if the whole
company an't far more interested in takin particular notice
of them two than of you—I say, I wasn't best pleased with
the man for callin out, and wasn't blessin him in my own
mind, when I see Chops's little bell fly out of winder at a
old lady, and he gets up and kicks his box over, exposin the
whole secret, and he catches hold of the calves of my legs
and he says to me, "Carry me into the wan, Toby, and
throw a pail of water over me or I'm a dead man, for I've
come into my property!"

Twelve thousand odd hundred pound, was Chops's winnins.
He had bought a half-ticket for the twenty-five thousand
prize, and it had come up. The first use he made of his
property, was, to offer to fight the Wild Indian for five
hundred pound a side, him with a poisoned darnin-needle
and the Indian with a club; but the Indian being in want
of backers to that amount, it went no further.

Arter he had been mad for a week—in a state of mind, in
short, in which, if I had let him sit on the organ for only
two minutes, I believe he would have bust—but we kep the
organ from him—Mr. Chops come round, and behaved liberal
and beautiful to all. He then sent for a young man he
knowed, as had a wery genteel appearance and was a Bonnet
at a gaming-booth (most respectable brought up, father
havin been imminent in the livery stable line but unfort'nate
in a commercial crisis, through paintin a old gray, ginger-
bay, and sellin him with a Pedigree), and Mr. Chops said

to this Bonnet, who said his name was Normandy, which it wasn't:

"Normandy, I'm a goin into Society. Will you go with me?"

Says Normandy: "Do I understand you, Mr. Chops, to hintimate that the 'ole of the expenses of that move will be borne by yourself?"

"Correct," says Mr. Chops. "And you shall have a Princely allowance too."

The Bonnet lifted Mr. Chops upon a chair, to shake hands with him, and replied in poetry, with his eyes seemingly full of tears

> "My boat is on the shore,
> And my bark is on the sea,
> And I do not ask for more,
> But I'll Go:—along with thee."

They went into Society, in a chay and four grays with silk jackets. They took lodgings in Pall Mall, London, and they blazed away.

In consequence of a note that was brought to Bartlemy Fair in the autumn of next year by a servant, most wonderful got up in milk-white cords and tops, I cleaned myself and went to Pall Mall, one evening appinted. The gentlemen was at their wine arter dinner, and Mr. Chops's eyes was more fixed in that Ed of his than I thought good for him. There was three of 'em (in company, I mean), and I knowed the third well. When last met, he had on a white Roman shirt, and a bishop's mitre covered with leopard-skin, and played the clarionet all wrong, in a band at a Wild Beast Show.

This gent took on not to know me, and Mr. Chops said: "Gentlemen, this is a old friend of former days:" and Normandy looked at me through a eye-glass, and said, "Magsman, glad to see you!"—which I'll take my oath he wasn't. Mr. Chops, to git him convenient to the table, had his chair on a throne (much of the form of George the Fourth's in the canvass), but he hardly appeared to me to

be King there in any other pint of view, for his two
gentlemen ordered about like Emperors. They was all
dressed like May-Day—gorgeous!—and as to Wine, they
swam in all sorts.

I made the round of the bottles, first separate (to say I
had done it), and then mixed 'em all together (to say I had
done it), and then tried two of 'em as half-and-half, and
then t'other two. Altogether, I passed a pleasin evenin, but
with a tendency to feel muddled, until I considered it good
manners to get up and say, " Mr. Chops, the best of friends
must part, I thank you for the wariety of foreign drains
you have stood so 'ansome, I looks towards you in red wine,
and I takes my leave." Mr. Chops replied, " If you'll just
hitch me out of this over your right arm, Magsman, and
carry me down-stairs, I'll see you out." I said I couldn't
think of such a thing, but he would have it, so I lifted him
off his throne. He smelt strong of Maidcary, and I couldn't
help thinking as I carried him down that it was like carrying
a large bottle full of wine, with a rayther ugly stopper, a
good deal out of proportion.

When I set him on the door-mat in the hall, he kep
me close to him by holding on to my coat-collar, and he
whispers:

" I ain't 'appy, Magsman."

" What's on your mind, Mr. Chops?"

" They don't use me well. They an't grateful to me.
They puts me on the mantel-piece when I won't have in
more Champagne-wine, and they locks me in the sideboard
when I won't give up my property."

" Get rid of 'em, Mr. Chops."

" I can't. We're in Society together, and what would
Society say?"

" Come out of Society!" says I.

" I can't. You don't know what you're talking about.
When you have once gone into Society, you mustn't come
out of it."

"Then if you'll excuse the freedom, Mr. Chops," were my remark, shaking my head grave, "I think it's a pity you ever went in."

Mr. Chops shook that deep Ed of his, to a surprisin extent, and slapped it half a dozen times with his hand, and with more Wice than I thought were in him. Then, he says, "You're a good fellow, but you don't understand. Good night, go along. Magsman, the little man will now walk three times round the Cairawan, and retire behind the curtain." The last I see of him on that occasion was his tryin, on the extremest werge of insensibility, to climb up the stairs, one by one, with his hands and knees. They'd have been much too steep for him, if he had been sober; but he wouldn't be helped.

It warn't long after that, that I read in the newspaper of Mr. Chops's being presented at court. It was printed, "It will be recollected"—and I've noticed in my life, that it is sure to be printed that it *will* be recollected, whenever it won't—"that Mr. Chops is the individual of small stature, whose brilliant success in the last State Lottery attracted so much attention." Well, I says to myself, Such is Life! He has been and done it in earnest at last! He has astonished George the Fourth!

(On account of which, I had that canvass new-painted, him with a bag of money in his hand, a presentin it to George the Fourth, and a lady in Ostrich Feathers fallin in love with him in a bag-wig, sword, and buckles correct.)

I took the House as is the subject of present inquiries—though not the honour of bein acquainted—and I run Magsman's Amusements in it thirteen months—sometimes one thing, sometimes another, sometimes nothin particular, but always all the canvasses outside. One night, when we had played the last company out, which was a shy company, through its raining Heavens hard, I was takin a pipe in the one pair back along with the young man with the toes, which I had taken on for a month (though he never drawed

—except on paper), and I heard a kickin at the street door. "Halloa!" I says to the young man, "what's up!" He rubs his eyebrows with his toes, and he says, "I can't imagine, Mr. Magsman"—which he never could imagine nothin, and was monotonous company.

The noise not leavin off, I laid down my pipe, and I took up a candle, and I went down and opened the door. I looked out into the street; but nothin could I see, and nothin was I aware of, until I turned round quick, because some creetur run between my legs into the passage. There was Mr. Chops!

"Magsman," he says, "take me, on the old terms, and you've got me; if it's done, say done!"

I was all of a maze, but I said, "Done, sir."

"Done to your done, and double done!" says he. "Have you got a bit of supper in the house?"

Bearin in mind them sparklin warieties of foreign drains as we'd guzzled away at in Pall Mall, I was ashamed to offer him cold sassages and gin-and-water; but he took 'em both and took 'em free; havin a chair for his table, and sittin down at it on a stool, like hold times. I, all of a maze all the while.

It was arter he had made a clean sweep of the sassages (beef, and to the best of my calculations two pound and a quarter), that the wisdom as was in that little man began to come out of him like perspiration.

"Magsman," he says, "look upon me! You see afore you, One as has both gone into Society and come out."

"O! You are out of it, Mr. Chops? How did you get out, sir?"

"SOLD OUT!" says he. You never saw the like of the wisdom as his Ed expressed, when he made use of them two words.

"My friend Magsman, I'll impart to you a discovery I've made. It's wallable; it's cost twelve thousand five hundred pound; it may do you good in life.—The secret of this

matter is, that it ain't so much that a person goes into
Society, as that Society goes into a person."

Not exactly keeping up with his meanin, I shook my head,
put on a deep look, and said, "You're right there, Mr.
Chops."

"Magsman," he says, twitchin me by the leg, "Society has
gone into me, to the tune of every penny of my property."

I felt that I went pale, and though nat'rally a bold
speaker, I couldn't hardly say, "Where's Normandy?"

"Bolted. With the plate," said Mr. Chops.

"And t'other one?" meaning him as formerly wore the
bishop's mitre.

"Bolted. With the jewels," said Mr. Chops.

I sat down and looked at him, and he stood up and looked
at me.

"Magsman," he says, and he seemed to myself to get wiser
as he got hoarser; "Society, taken in the lump, is all dwarfs.
At the court of St. James's, they was all a doing my old
business—all a goin three times round the Cairawan, in the
hold court-suits and properties. Elsewheres, they was most
of 'em ringin their little bells out of make-believes. Every-
wheres, the sarser was a goin round. Magsman, the sarser
is the universal Institution!"

I perceived, you understand, that he was soured by his
misfortuns, and I felt for Mr. Chops.

"As to Fat Ladies," says he, giving his head a tremendious
one agin the wall, "there's lots of *them* in Society, and
worse than the original. *Hers* was a outrage upon Taste—
simply a outrage upon Taste—awakenin contempt—carryin
its own punishment in the form of a Indian!" Here he giv
himself another tremendious one. "But *theirs*, Magsman,
theirs is mercenary outrages. Lay in Cashmeer shawls, buy
bracelets, strew 'em and a lot of 'andsome fans and things
about your rooms, let it be known that you give away like
water to all as come to admire, and the Fat Ladies that
don't exhibit for so much down upon the drum, will come

from all the pints of the compass to flock about you, whatever
you are. They'll drill holes in your 'art, Magsman, like a
Cullender. And when you've no more left to give, they'll
laugh at you to your face, and leave you to have your bones
picked dry by Wulturs, like the dead Wild Ass of the
Prairies that you deserve to be!" Here he giv himself the
most tremendious one of all, and dropped.

I thought he was gone. His Ed was so heavy, and he
knocked it so hard, and he fell so stoney, and the sassagerial
disturbance in him must have been so immense, that I
thought he was gone. But, he soon come round with care,
and he sat up on the floor, and he said to me, with wisdom
comin out of his eyes, if ever it come:

"Magsman! The most material difference between the
two states of existence through which your unappy friend
has passed;" he reached out his poor little hand, and his
tears dropped down on the moustachio which it was a
credit to him to have done his best to grow, but it is not
in mortals to command success,—"the difference is this.
When I was out of Society, I was paid light for being
seen. When I went into Society, I paid heavy for being
seen. I prefer the former, even if I wasn't forced upon
it. Give me out through the trumpet, in the hold way,
to-morrow."

Arter that, he slid into the line again as easy as if he had
been iled all over. But the organ was kep from him, and
no allusions was ever made, when a company was in, to his
property. He got wiser every day; his views of Society and
the Public was luminous, bewilderin, awful; and his Ed got
bigger and bigger as his Wisdom expanded it.

He took well, and pulled 'em in most excellent for nine
weeks. At the expiration of that period, when his Ed was
a sight, he expressed one evenin, the last Company havin
been turned out, and the door shut, a wish to have a
little music.

"Mr. Chops," I said (I never dropped the "Mr." with him;

the world might do it, but not me); "Mr. Chops, are you sure as you are in a state of mind and body to sit upon the organ?"

His answer was this: "Toby, when next met with on the tramp, I forgive her and the Indian. And I am."

It was with fear and trembling that I began to turn the handle; but he sat like a lamb. It will be my belief to my dying day, that I see his Ed expand as he sat; you may therefore judge how great his thoughts was. He sat out all the changes, and then he come off.

"Toby," he says, with a quiet smile, "the little man will now walk three times round the Cairawan, and retire behind the curtain."

When we called him in the morning, we found him gone into a much better Society than mine or Pall Mall's. I giv Mr. Chops as comfortable a funeral as lay in my power, followed myself as Chief, and had the George the Fourth canvass carried first, in the form of a banner. But, the House was so dismal arterwards, that I giv it up, and took to the Wan again.

———

"I don't triumph," said Jarber, folding up the second manuscript, and looking hard at Trottle. "I don't triumph over this worthy creature. I merely ask him if he is satisfied now?"

"How can he be anything else?" I said, answering for Trottle, who sat obstinately silent. "This time, Jarber, you have not only read us a delightfully amusing story, but you have also answered the question about the House. Of course it stands empty now. Who would think of taking it after it had been turned into a caravan?" I looked at Trottle, as I said those last words, and Jarber waved his hand indulgently in the same direction.

"Let this excellent person speak," said Jarber. "You were about to say, my good man——?"

"I only wished to ask, sir," said Trottle doggedly, "if you

could kindly oblige me with a date or two in connection
with that last story?"

"A date!" repeated Jarber. "What does the man want
with dates!"

"I should be glad to know, with great respect," persisted
Trottle, "if the person named Magsman was the last tenant
who lived in the House. It's my opinion—if I may be
excused for giving it—that he most decidedly was not."

With those words, Trottle made a low bow, and quietly
left the room.

There is no denying that Jarber, when we were left together,
looked sadly discomposed. He had evidently forgotten to
inquire about dates; and, in spite of his magnificent talk
about his series of discoveries, it was quite as plain that
the two stories he had just read, had really and truly
exhausted his present stock. I thought myself bound, in
common gratitude, to help him out of his embarrassment
by a timely suggestion. So I proposed that he should come
to tea again, on the next Monday evening, the thirteenth,
and should make such inquiries in the meantime, as might
enable him to dispose triumphantly of Trottle's objection.

He gallantly kissed my hand, made a neat little speech of
acknowledgment, and took his leave. For the rest of the
week I would not encourage Trottle by allowing him to refer
to the House at all. I suspected he was making his own
inquiries about dates, but I put no questions to him.

On Monday evening, the thirteenth, that dear unfortunate
Jarber came, punctual to the appointed time. He looked so
terribly harassed, that he was really quite a spectacle of
feebleness and fatigue. I saw, at a glance, that the question
of dates had gone against him, that Mr. Magsman had not
been the last tenant of the House, and that the reason of its
emptiness was still to seek.

"What I have gone through," said Jarber, "words are not
eloquent enough to tell. O Sophonisba, I have begun another
series of discoveries! Accept the last two as stories laid on

your shrine; and wait to blame me for leaving your curiosity unappeased, until you have heard Number Three." ·

Number Three looked like a very short manuscript, and I said as much. Jarber explained to me that we were to have some poetry this time. In the course of his investigations he had stepped into the Circulating Library, to seek for information on the one important subject. All the Library-people knew about the House was, that a female relative of the last tenant, as they believed, had, just after that tenant left, sent a little manuscript poem to them which she described as referring to events that had actually passed in the House; and which she wanted the proprietor of the Library to publish. She had written no address on her letter; and the proprietor had kept the manuscript ready to be given back to her (the publishing of poems not being in his line) when she might call for it. She had never called for it; and the poem had been lent to Jarber, at his express request, to read to me.

Before he began, I rang the bell for Trottle; being determined to have him present at the new reading, as a wholesome check on his obstinacy. To my surprise Peggy answered the bell, and told me that Trottle had stepped out without saying where. I instantly felt the strongest possible conviction that he was at his old tricks: and that his stepping out in the evening, without leave, meant—Philandering.

Controlling myself on my visitor's account, I dismissed Peggy, stifled my indignation, and prepared, as politely as might be, to listen to Jarber.

THE HAUNTED HOUSE

[1859]

THE HAUNTED HOUSE.

In Two Chapters.*

THE MORTALS IN THE HOUSE.

UNDER none of the accredited ghostly circumstances, and environed by none of the conventional ghostly surroundings, did I first make acquaintance with the house which is the subject of this Christmas piece. I saw it in the daylight, with the sun upon it. There was no wind, no rain, no lightning, no thunder, no awful or unwonted circumstance, of any kind, to heighten its effect. More than that: I had come to it direct from a railway station: it was not more than a mile distant from the railway station; and, as I stood outside the house, looking back upon the way I had come, I could see the goods train running smoothly along the embankment in the valley. I will not say that everything was utterly commonplace, because I doubt if anything can be that, except to utterly commonplace people—and there my vanity steps in; but, I will take it on myself to say that anybody might see the house as I saw it, any fine autumn morning.

The manner of my lighting on it was this.

* The original has eight chapters, which will be found in *All the Year Round*, vol. ii., old series; but those not printed here, excepting a page at the close, were not written by Mr. Dickens.

I was travelling towards London out of the North, intend-
ing to stop by the way, to look at the house. My health
required a temporary residence in the country; and a friend
of mine who knew that, and who had happened to drive past
the house, had written to me to suggest it as a likely place.
I had got into the train at midnight, and had fallen asleep,
and had woke up and had sat looking out of window at the
brilliant Northern Lights in the sky, and had fallen asleep
again, and had woke up again to find the night gone, with
the usual discontented conviction on me that I hadn't been to
sleep at all;—upon which question, in the first imbecility of
that condition, I am ashamed to believe that I would have
done wager by battle with the man who sat opposite me.
That opposite man had had, through the night—as that
opposite man always has—several legs too many, and all of
them too long. In addition to this unreasonable conduct
(which was only to be expected of him), he had had a pencil
and a pocket-book, and had been perpetually listening and
taking notes. It had appeared to me that these aggravating
notes related to the jolts and bumps of the carriage, and I
should have resigned myself to his taking them, under a
general supposition that he was in the civil-engineering way
of life, if he had not sat staring straight over my head
whenever he listened. He was a goggle-eyed gentleman of a
perplexed aspect, and his demeanour became unbearable.

It was a cold, dead morning (the sun not being up yet),
and when I had out-watched the paling light of the fires of
the iron country, and the curtain of heavy smoke that hung
at once between me and the stars and between me and the
day, I turned to my fellow-traveller and said:

" I *beg* your pardon, sir, but do you observe anything
particular in me?" For, really, he appeared to be taking
down, either my travelling-cap or my hair, with a minuteness
that was a liberty.

The goggle-eyed gentleman withdrew his eyes from behind
me, as if the back of the carriage were a hundred miles

off, and said, with a lofty look of compassion for my insignificance:

"In you, sir?—B."

"B, sir?" said I, growing warm.

"I have nothing to do with you, sir," returned the gentleman; "pray let me listen—O."

He enunciated this vowel after a pause, and noted it down.

At first I was alarmed, for an Express lunatic and no communication with the guard, is a serious position. The thought came to my relief that the gentleman might be what is popularly called a Rapper: one of a sect for (some of) whom I have the highest respect, but whom I don't believe in. I was going to ask him the question, when he took the bread out of my mouth.

"You will excuse me," said the gentleman contemptuously, "if I am too much in advance of common humanity to trouble myself at all about it. I have passed the night—as indeed I pass the whole of my time now—in spiritual intercourse."

"O!" said I, something snappishly.

"The conferences of the night began," continued the gentleman, turning several leaves of his note-book, "with this message: 'Evil communications corrupt good manners.'"

"Sound," said I; "but, absolutely new?"

"New from spirits," returned the gentleman.

I could only repeat my rather snappish "O!" and ask if I might be favoured with the last communication.

"'A bird in the hand,'" said the gentleman, reading his last entry with great solemnity, "'is worth two in the Bosh.'"

"Truly I am of the same opinion," said I; "but shouldn't it be Bush?"

"It came to me, Bosh," returned the gentleman.

The gentleman then informed me that the spirit of Socrates had delivered this special revelation in the course of the night. "My friend, I hope you are pretty well. There are two in this railway carriage. How do you do? There are seventeen thousand four hundred and seventy-nine spirits here, but you cannot see them. Pythagoras is here. He is not at liberty to mention it, but hopes you like travelling." Galileo likewise had dropped in, with this scientific intelligence. "I am glad to see you, *amico. Come sta?* Water will freeze when it is cold enough. *Addio!*" In the course of the night, also, the following phenomena had occurred. Bishop Butler had insisted on spelling his name, "Bubler," for which offence against orthography and good manners he had been dismissed as out of temper. John Milton (suspected of wilful mystification) had repudiated the authorship of Paradise Lost, and had introduced, as joint authors of that poem, two Unknown gentlemen, respectively named Grungers and Scadgingtone. And Prince Arthur, nephew of King John of England, had described himself as tolerably comfortable in the seventh circle, where he was learning to paint on velvet, under the direction of Mrs. Trimmer and Mary Queen of Scots.

If this should meet the eye of the gentleman who favoured me with these disclosures, I trust he will excuse my confessing that the sight of the rising sun, and the contemplation of the magnificent Order of the vast Universe, made me impatient of them. In a word, I was so impatient of them, that I was mightily glad to get out at the next station, and to exchange these clouds and vapours for the free air of Heaven.

By that time it was a beautiful morning. As I walked away among such leaves as had already fallen from the golden, brown, and russet trees; and as I looked around me on the wonders of Creation, and thought of the steady, unchanging, and harmonious laws by which they are sustained; the gentleman's spiritual intercourse seemed to me as poor a piece of journey-work as ever this world saw. In which heathen state of mind, I came within view of the house, and stopped to examine it attentively.

It was a solitary house, standing in a sadly neglected garden: a pretty even square of some two acres. It was a

house of about the time of George the Second; as stiff, as
cold, as formal, and in as bad taste, as could possibly be
desired by the most loyal admirer of the whole quartett of
Georges. It was uninhabited, but had, within a year or two,
been cheaply repaired to render it habitable; I say cheaply,
because the work had been done in a surface manner, and
was already decaying as to the paint and plaster, though the
colours were fresh. A lop-sided board drooped over the
garden wall, announcing that it was "to let on very reasonable terms, well furnished." It was much too closely and
heavily shadowed by trees, and, in particular, there were six
tall poplars before the front windows, which were excessively
melancholy, and the site of which had been extremely ill
chosen.

It was easy to see that it was an avoided house—a house
that was shunned by the village, to which my eye was guided
by a church spire some half a mile off—a house that nobody
would take. And the natural inference was, that it had the
reputation of being a haunted house.

No period within the four-and-twenty hours of day and
night is so solemn to me, as the early morning. In the
summer time, I often rise very early, and repair to my room
to do a day's work before breakfast, and I am always on
those occasions deeply impressed by the stillness and solitude
around me. Besides that there is something awful in the
being surrounded by familiar faces asleep—in the knowledge
that those who are dearest to us and to whom we are dearest,
are profoundly unconscious of us, in an impassive state,
anticipative of that mysterious condition to which we are all
tending—the stopped life, the broken threads of yesterday,
the deserted seat, the closed book, the unfinished but
abandoned occupation, all are images of Death. The tranquillity of the hour is the tranquillity of Death. The colour
and the chill have the same association. Even a certain air
that familiar household objects take upon them when they
first emerge from the shadows of the night into the morning,

of being newer, and as they used to be long ago, has its counterpart in the subsidence of the worn face of maturity or age, in death, into the old youthful look. Moreover, I once saw the apparition of my father, at this hour. He was alive and well, and nothing ever came of it, but I saw him in the daylight, sitting with his back towards me, on a seat that stood beside my bed. His head was resting on his hand, and whether he was slumbering or grieving, I could not discern. Amazed to see him there, I sat up, moved my position, leaned out of bed, and watched him. As he did not move, I spoke to him more than once. As he did not move then, I became alarmed and laid my hand upon his shoulder, as I thought—and there was no such thing.

For all these reasons, and for others less easily and briefly statable, I find the early morning to be my most ghostly time. Any house would be more or less haunted, to me, in the early morning; and a haunted house could scarcely address me to greater advantage than then.

I walked on into the village, with the desertion of this house upon my mind, and I found the landlord of the little inn, sanding his door-step. I bespoke breakfast, and broached the subject of the house.

"Is it haunted?" I asked.

The landlord looked at me, shook his head, and answered, "I say nothing."

"Then it *is* haunted?"

"Well!" cried the landlord, in an outburst of frankness that had the appearance of desperation—"I wouldn't sleep in it."

"Why not?"

"If I wanted to have all the bells in a house ring, with nobody to ring 'em; and all the doors in a house bang, with nobody to bang 'em; and all sorts of feet treading about, with no feet there; why, then," said the landlord, "I'd sleep in that house."

"Is anything seen there?"

The landlord looked at me again, and then, with his former appearance of desperation, called down his stable-yard for "Ikey!"

The call produced a high-shouldered young fellow, with a round red face, a short crop of sandy hair, a very broad humorous mouth, a turned-up nose, and a great sleeved waistcoat of purple bars, with mother-of-pearl buttons, that seemed to be growing upon him, and to be in a fair way— if it were not pruned—of covering his head and overrunning his boots.

"This gentleman wants to know," said the landlord, "if anything's seen at the Poplars."

"'Ooded woman with a howl," said Ikey, in a state of great freshness.

"Do you mean a cry?"

"I mean a bird, sir."

"A hooded woman with an owl. Dear me! Did you ever see her?"

"I seen the howl."

"Never the woman?"

"Not so plain as the howl, but they always keeps together."

"Has anybody ever seen the woman as plainly as the owl?"

"Lord bless you, sir! Lots."

"Who?"

"Lord bless you, sir! Lots."

"The general-dealer opposite, for instance, who is opening his shop?"

"Perkins? Bless you, Perkins wouldn't go a-nigh the place. No!" observed the young man, with considerable feeling; "he an't overwise, an't Perkins, but he an't such a fool as *that.*"

(Here, the landlord murmured his confidence in Perkins's knowing better.)

"Who is—or who was—the hooded woman with the owl? Do you know?"

"Well!" said Ikey, holding up his cap with one hand while he scratched his head with the other, "they say, in general, that she was murdered, and the howl he 'ooted the while."

This very concise summary of the facts was all I could learn, except that a young man, as hearty and likely a young man as ever I see, had been took with fits and held down in 'em, after seeing the hooded woman. Also, that a personage, dimly described as "a hold chap, a sort of one-eyed tramp, answering to the name of Joby, unless you challenged him as Greenwood, and then he said, 'Why not? and even if so, mind your own business,'" had encountered the hooded woman, a matter of five or six times. But, I was not materially assisted by these witnesses: inasmuch as the first was in California, and the last was, as Ikey said (and he was confirmed by the landlord), Anywheres.

Now, although I regard with a hushed and solemn fear, the mysteries, between which and this state of existence is interposed the barrier of the great trial and change that fall on all the things that live; and although I have not the audacity to pretend that I know anything of them; I can no more reconcile the mere banging of doors, ringing of bells, creaking of boards, and such-like insignificances, with the majestic beauty and pervading analogy of all the Divine rules that I am permitted to understand, than I had been able, a little while before, to yoke the spiritual intercourse of my fellow-traveller to the chariot of the rising sun. Moreover, I had lived in two haunted houses—both abroad. In one of these, an old Italian palace, which bore the reputation of being very badly haunted indeed, and which had recently been twice abandoned on that account, I lived eight months, most tranquilly and pleasantly: notwithstanding that the house had a score of mysterious bedrooms, which were never used, and possessed, in one large room in which I sat reading, times out of number at all hours, and next to which I slept, a haunted chamber of the first pretensions. I gently hinted

these considerations to the landlord. And as to this particular house having a bad name, I reasoned with him, Why,
how many things had bad names undeservedly, and how
easy it was to give bad names, and did he not think that if
he and I were persistently to whisper in the village that any
weird-looking old drunken tinker of the neighbourhood had
sold himself to the Devil, he would come in time to be
suspected of that commercial venture! All this wise talk
was perfectly ineffective with the landlord, I am bound to
confess, and was as dead a failure as ever I made in my life.

To cut this part of the story short, I was piqued about
the haunted house, and was already half resolved to take it.
So, after breakfast, I got the keys from Perkins's brother-in-
law (a whip and harness maker, who keeps the Post Office,
and is under submission to a most rigorous wife of the
Doubly Seceding Little Emmanuel persuasion), and went up
to the house, attended by my landlord and by Ikey.

Within, I found it, as I had expected, transcendently
dismal. The slowly changing shadows waved on it from the
heavy trees, were doleful in the last degree; the house was
ill-placed, ill-built, ill-planned, and ill-fitted. It was damp,
it was not free from dry rot, there was a flavour of rats in it,
and it was the gloomy victim of that indescribable decay
which settles on all the work of man's hands whenever it is
not turned to man's account. The kitchens and offices were
too large, and too remote from each other. Above stairs
and below, waste tracts of passage intervened between patches
of fertility represented by rooms; and there was a mouldy
old well with a green growth upon it, hiding like a murderous
trap, near the bottom of the back-stairs, under the double
row of bells. One of these bells was labelled, on a black
ground in faded white letters, MASTER B. This, they told
me, was the bell that rang the most.

"Who was Master B.?" I asked. "Is it known what he
did while the owl hooted?"

"Rang the bell," said Ikey.

I was rather struck by the prompt dexterity with which this young man pitched his fur cap at the bell, and rang it himself. It was a loud, unpleasant bell, and made a very disagreeable sound. The other bells were inscribed according to the names of the rooms to which their wires were conducted: as "Picture Room," "Double Room," "Clock Room," and the like. Following Master B.'s bell to its source, I found that young gentleman to have had but indifferent third-class accommodation in a triangular cabin under the cock-loft, with a corner fireplace which Master B. must have been exceedingly small if he were ever able to warm himself at, and a corner chimney-piece like a pyramidal staircase to the ceiling for Tom Thumb. The papering of one side of the room had dropped down bodily, with fragments of plaster adhering to it, and almost blocked up the door. It appeared that Master B., in his spiritual condition, always made a point of pulling the paper down. Neither the landlord nor Ikey could suggest why he made such a fool of himself.

Except that the house had an immensely large rambling loft at top, I made no other discoveries. It was moderately well furnished, but sparely. Some of the furniture—say, a third—was as old as the house; the rest was of various periods within the last half century. I was referred to a corn-chandler in the market-place of the county town to treat for the house. I went that day, and I took it for six months.

It was just the middle of October when I moved in with my maiden sister (I venture to call her eight-and-thirty, she is so very handsome, sensible, and engaging). We took with us, a deaf stable-man, my bloodhound Turk, two women servants, and a young person called an Odd Girl. I have reason to record of the attendant last enumerated, who was one of the Saint Lawrence's Union Female Orphans, that she was a fatal mistake and a disastrous engagement.

The year was dying early, the leaves were falling fast, it

was a raw cold day when we took possession, and the gloom
of the house was most depressing. The cook (an amiable
woman, but of a weak turn of intellect) burst into tears on
beholding the kitchen, and requested that her silver watch
might be delivered over to her sister (2 Tuppintock's Gardens,
Liggs's Walk, Clapham Rise), in the event of anything
happening to her from the damp. Streaker, the housemaid,
feigned cheerfulness, but was the greater martyr. The Odd
Girl, who had never been in the country, alone was pleased,
and made arrangements for sowing an acorn in the garden
outside the scullery window, and rearing an oak.

We went, before dark, through all the natural—as opposed
to supernatural—miseries incidental to our state. Dispiriting
reports ascended (like the smoke) from the basement in
volumes, and descended from the upper rooms. There was
no rolling-pin, there was no salamander (which failed to
surprise me, for I don't know what it is), there was nothing
in the house, what there was, was broken, the last people
must have lived like pigs, what could the meaning of the
landlord be? Through these distresses, the Odd Girl was
cheerful and exemplary. But within four hours after dark we
had got into a supernatural groove, and the Odd Girl had
seen "Eyes," and was in hysterics.

My sister and I had agreed to keep the haunting strictly
to ourselves, and my impression was, and still is, that I had
not left Ikey, when he helped to unload the cart, alone with
the women, or any one of them, for one minute. Nevertheless, as I say, the Odd Girl had "seen Eyes" (no other
explanation could ever be drawn from her), before nine, and
by ten o'clock had had as much vinegar applied to her as
would pickle a handsome salmon.

I leave a discerning public to judge of my feelings, when,
under these untoward circumstances, at about half-past ten
o'clock Master B.'s bell began to ring in a most infuriated
manner, and Turk howled until the house resounded with his
lamentations!

I hope I may never again be in a state of mind so unchristian as the mental frame in which I lived for some weeks, respecting the memory of Master B. Whether his bell was rung by rats, or mice, or bats, or wind, or what other accidental vibration, or sometimes by one cause, sometimes another, and sometimes by collusion, I don't know; but, certain it is, that it did ring two nights out of three, until I conceived the happy idea of twisting Master B.'s neck—in other words, breaking his bell short off—and silencing that young gentleman, as to my experience and belief, for ever.

But, by that time, the Odd Girl had developed such improving powers of catalepsy, that she had become a shining example of that very inconvenient disorder. She would stiffen, like a Guy Fawkes endowed with unreason, on the most irrelevant occasions. I would address the servants in a lucid manner, pointing out to them that I had painted Master B.'s room and balked the paper, and taken Master B.'s bell away and balked the ringing, and if they could suppose that that confounded boy had lived and died, to clothe himself with no better behaviour than would most unquestionably have brought him and the sharpest particles of a birch-broom into close acquaintance in the present imperfect state of existence, could they also suppose a mere poor human being, such as I was, capable by those contemptible means of counteracting and limiting the powers of the disembodied spirits of the dead, or of any spirits?—I say I would become emphatic and cogent, not to say rather complacent, in such an address, when it would all go for nothing by reason of the Odd Girl's suddenly stiffening from the toes upward, and glaring among us like a parochial petrifaction.

Streaker, the housemaid, too, had an attribute of a most discomfiting nature. I am unable to say whether she was of an unusually lymphatic temperament, or what else was the matter with her, but this young woman became a mere Distillery for the production of the largest and most transparent tears I ever met with. Combined with these characteristics, was a peculiar tenacity of hold in those specimens, so that they didn't fall, but hung upon her face and nose. In this condition, and mildly and deplorably shaking her head, her silence would throw me more heavily than the Admirable Crichton could have done in a verbal disputation for a purse of money. Cook, likewise, always covered me with confusion as with a garment, by neatly winding up the session with the protest that the Ouse was wearing her out, and by meekly repeating her last wishes regarding her silver watch.

As to our nightly life, the contagion of suspicion and fear was among us, and there is no such contagion under the sky. Hooded woman? According to the accounts, we were in a perfect Convent of hooded women. Noises? With that contagion down-stairs, I myself have sat in the dismal parlour, listening, until I have heard so many and such strange noises, that they would have chilled my blood if I had not warmed it by dashing out to make discoveries. Try this in bed, in the dead of the night; try this at your own comfortable fireside, in the life of the night. You can fill any house with noises, if you will, until you have a noise for every nerve in your nervous system.

I repeat; the contagion of suspicion and fear was among us, and there is no such contagion under the sky. The women (their noses in a chronic state of excoriation from smelling-salts) were always primed and loaded for a swoon, and ready to go off with hair-triggers. The two elder detached the Odd Girl on all expeditions that were considered doubly hazardous, and she always established the reputation of such adventures by coming back cataleptic. If Cook or Streaker went overhead after dark, we knew we should presently hear a bump on the ceiling; and this took place so constantly, that it was as if a fighting man were engaged to go about the house, administering a touch of his art which I believe is called The Auctioneer, to every domestic he met with.

It was in vain to do anything. It was in vain to be frightened, for the moment in one's own person, by a real

owl, and then to show the owl. It was in vain to discover,
by striking an accidental discord on the piano, that Turk
always howled at particular notes and combinations. It was
in vain to be a Rhadamanthus with the bells, and if an unfortunate bell rang without leave, to have it down inexorably
and silence it. It was in vain to fire up chimneys, let torches
down the well, charge furiously into suspected rooms and
recesses. We changed servants, and it was no better. The
new set ran away, and a third set came, and it was no better.
At last, our comfortable housekeeping got to be so disorganised
and wretched, that I one night dejectedly said to my sister:
"Patty, I begin to despair of our getting people to go on
with us here, and I think we must give this up."

My sister, who is a woman of immense spirit, replied, "No,
John, don't give it up. Don't be beaten, John. There is
another way."

"And what is that?" said I.

"John," returned my sister, "if we are not to be driven
out of this house, and that for no reason whatever, that is
apparent to you or me, we must help ourselves and take the
house wholly and solely into our own hands."

"But, the servants," said I.

"Have no servants," said my sister, boldly.

Like most people in my grade of life, I had never thought
of the possibility of going on without those faithful obstruc-
tions. The notion was so new to me when suggested, that I
looked very doubtful.

"We know they come here to be frightened and infect
one another, and we know they are frightened and do infect
one another," said my sister.

"With the exception of Bottles," I observed, in a medita-
tive tone.

(The deaf stable-man. I kept him in my service, and still
keep him, as a phenomenon of moroseness not to be matched
in England.)

"To be sure, John," assented my sister; "except Bottles.

And what does that go to prove? Bottles talks to nobody, and hears nobody unless he is absolutely roared at, and what alarm has Bottles ever given, or taken! None."

This was perfectly true; the individual in question having retired, every night at ten o'clock, to his bed over the coach-house, with no other company than a pitchfork and a pail of water. That the pail of water would have been over me, and the pitchfork through me, if I had put myself without announcement in Bottles's way after that minute, I had deposited in my own mind as a fact worth remembering. Neither had Bottles ever taken the least notice of any of our many uproars. An imperturbable and speechless man, he had sat at his supper, with Streaker present in a swoon, and the Odd Girl marble, and had only put another potato in his check, or profited by the general misery to help himself to beefsteak pie.

"And so," continued my sister, "I exempt Bottles. And considering, John, that the house is too large, and perhaps too lonely, to be kept well in hand by Bottles, you, and me, I propose that we cast about among our friends for a certain selected number of the most reliable and willing—form a Society here for three months—wait upon ourselves and one another—live cheerfully and socially—and see what happens."

I was so charmed with my sister, that I embraced her on the spot, and went into her plan with the greatest ardour.

We were then in the third week of November; but, we took our measures so vigorously, and were so well seconded by the friends in whom we confided, that there was still a week of the month unexpired, when our party all came down together merrily, and mustered in the haunted house.

I will mention, in this place, two small changes that I made while my sister and I were yet alone. It occurring to me as not improbable that Turk howled in the house at night, partly because he wanted to get out of it, I stationed him in his kennel outside, but unchained; and I seriously warned the village that any man who came in his way must not expect to leave him without a rip in his own throat. I then casually asked Ikey if he were a judge of a gun? On his saying, "Yes, sir, I knows a good gun when I sees her," I begged the favour of his stepping up to the house and looking at mine.

"*She's* a true one, sir," said Ikey, after inspecting a double-barrelled rifle that I bought in New York a few years ago. "No mistake about *her*, sir."

"Ikey," said I, "don't mention it; I have seen something in this house."

"No, sir?" he whispered, greedily opening his eyes. "'Ooded lady, sir?"

"Don't be frightened," said I. "It was a figure rather like you."

"Lord, sir?"

"Ikey!" said I, shaking hands with him warmly: I may say affectionately; "if there is any truth in these ghost-stories, the greatest service I can do you, is, to fire at that figure. And I promise you, by Heaven and earth, I will do it with this gun if I see it again!"

The young man thanked me, and took his leave with some little precipitation, after declining a glass of liquor. I imparted my secret to him, because I had never quite forgotten his throwing his cap at the bell; because I had, on another occasion, noticed something very like a fur cap, lying not far from the bell, one night when it had burst out ringing; and because I had remarked that we were at our ghostliest whenever he came up in the evening to comfort the servants. Let me do Ikey no injustice. He was afraid of the house, and believed in its being haunted; and yet he would play false on the haunting side, so surely as he got an opportunity. The Odd Girl's case was exactly similar. She went about the house in a state of real terror, and yet lied monstrously and wilfully, and invented many of the alarms she spread,

and made many of the sounds we heard. I had had my eye
on the two, and I know it. It is not necessary for me, here,
to account for this preposterous state of mind; I content
myself with remarking that it is familiarly known to every
intelligent man who has had fair medical, legal, or other
watchful experience; that it is as well established and as
common a state of mind as any with which observers are
acquainted; and that it is one of the first elements, above
all others, rationally to be suspected in, and strictly looked
for, and separated from, any question of this kind.

To return to our party. The first thing we did when we
were all assembled, was, to draw lots for bedrooms. That
done, and every bedroom, and, indeed, the whole house,
having been minutely examined by the whole body, we allotted
the various household duties, as if we had been on a gipsy
party, or a yachting party, or a hunting party, or were
shipwrecked.   I   then   recounted   the   floating   rumours
concerning the hooded lady, the owl, and Master B.: with
others, still more filmy, which had floated about during our
occupation, relative to some ridiculous old ghost of the female
gender who went up and down, carrying the ghost of a round
table; and also to an impalpable Jackass, whom nobody was
ever able to catch. Some of these ideas I really believe our
people below had communicated to one another in some
diseased way, without conveying them in words. We then
gravely called one another to witness, that we were not there
to be deceived, or to deceive—which we considered pretty
much the same thing—and that, with a serious sense of
responsibility, we would be strictly true to one another, and
would strictly follow out the truth. The understanding was
established, that any one who heard unusual noises in the
night, and who wished to trace them, should knock at my
door; lastly, that on Twelfth Night, the last night of holy
Christmas, all our individual experiences since that then
present hour of our coming together in the haunted house,
should be brought to light for the good of all; and that we

would hold our peace on the subject till then, unless on some remarkable provocation to break silence.

We were, in number and in character, as follows:

First—to get my sister and myself out of the way—there were we two. In the drawing of lots, my sister drew her own room, and I drew Master B.'s. Next, there was our first cousin John Herschel, so called after the great astronomer: than whom I suppose a better man at a telescope does not breathe. With him, was his wife: a charming creature to whom he had been married in the previous spring. I thought it (under the circumstances) rather imprudent to bring her, because there is no knowing what even a false alarm may do at such a time; but I suppose he knew his own business best, and I must say that if she had been *my* wife, I never could have left her endearing and bright face behind. They drew the Clock Room. Alfred Starling, an uncommonly agreeable young fellow of eight-and-twenty for whom I have the greatest liking, was in the Double Room; mine, usually, and designated by that name from having a dressing-room within it, with two large and cumbersome windows, which no wedges *I* was ever able to make, would keep from shaking, in any weather, wind or no wind. Alfred is a young fellow who pretends to be "fast" (another word for loose, as I understand the term), but who is much too good and sensible for that nonsense, and who would have distinguished himself before now, if his father had not unfortunately left him a small independence of two hundred a year, on the strength of which his only occupation in life has been to spend six. I am in hopes, however, that his Banker may break, or that he may enter into some speculation guaranteed to pay twenty per cent.; for, I am convinced that if he could only be ruined, his fortune is made. Belinda Bates, bosom friend of my sister, and a most intellectual, amiable, and delightful girl, got the Picture Room. She has a fine genius for poetry, combined with real business earnestness, and "goes in"—to use an expression of Alfred's—for Woman's mission,

Woman's rights, Woman's wrongs, and everything that is woman's with a capital W, or is not and ought to be, or is and ought not to be. "Most praiseworthy, my dear, and Heaven prosper you!" I whispered to her on the first night of my taking leave of her at the Picture-Room door, "but don't overdo it. And in respect of the great necessity there is, my darling, for more employments being within the reach of Woman than our civilisation has as yet assigned to her, don't fly at the unfortunate men, even those men who are at first sight in your way, as if they were the natural oppressors of your sex; for, trust me, Belinda, they do sometimes spend their wages among wives and daughters, sisters, mothers, aunts, and grandmothers; and the play is, really, not *all* Wolf and Red Riding-Hood, but has other parts in it." However, I digress.

Belinda, as I have mentioned, occupied the Picture Room. We had but three other chambers: the Corner Room, the Cupboard Room, and the Garden Room. My old friend, Jack Governor, "slung his hammock," as he called it, in the Corner Room. I have always regarded Jack as the finest-looking sailor that ever sailed. He is gray now, but as handsome as he was a quarter of a century ago—nay, handsomer. A portly, cheery, well-built figure of a broad-shouldered man, with a frank smile, a brilliant dark eye, and a rich dark eyebrow. I remember those under darker hair, and they look all the better for their silver setting. He has been wherever his Union namesake flies, has Jack, and I have met old shipmates of his, away in the Mediterranean and on the other side of the Atlantic, who have beamed and brightened at the casual mention of his name, and have cried, "You know Jack Governor? Then you know a prince of men!" That he is! And so unmistakably a naval officer, that if you were to meet him coming out of an Esquimaux snow-hut in seal's skin, you would be vaguely persuaded he was in full naval uniform.

Jack once had that bright clear eye of his on my sister;

but, it fell out that he married another lady and took her to South America, where she died. This was a dozen years ago or more. He brought down with him to our haunted house a little cask of salt beef; for, he is always convinced that all salt beef not of his own pickling, is mere carrion, and invariably, when he goes to London, packs a piece in his portmanteau. He had also volunteered to bring with him one "Nat Beaver," an old comrade of his, captain of a merchantman. Mr. Beaver, with a thick-set wooden face and figure, and apparently as hard as a block all over, proved to be an intelligent man, with a world of watery experiences in him, and great practical knowledge. At times, there was a curious nervousness about him, apparently the lingering result of some old illness; but, it seldom lasted many minutes. He got the Cupboard Room, and lay there next to Mr. Undery, my friend and solicitor: who came down, in an amateur capacity, "to go through with it," as he said, and who plays whist better than the whole Law List, from the red cover at the beginning to the red cover at the end.

I never was happier in my life, and I believe it was the universal feeling among us. Jack Governor, always a man of wonderful resources, was Chief Cook, and made some of the best dishes I ever ate, including unapproachable curries. My sister was pastrycook and confectioner. Starling and I were Cook's Mate, turn and turn about, and on special occasions the chief cook "pressed" Mr. Beaver. We had a great deal of out-door sport and exercise, but nothing was neglected within, and there was no ill-humour or misunderstanding among us, and our evenings were so delightful that we had at least one good reason for being reluctant to go to bed.

We had a few night alarms in the beginning. On the first night, I was knocked up by Jack with a most wonderful ship's lantern in his hand, like the gills of some monster of the deep, who informed me that he "was going aloft to the main truck," to have the weathercock down. It was a stormy night and I remonstrated; but Jack called my attention to its making a sound like a cry of despair, and said somebody would be "hailing a ghost" presently, if it wasn't done. So, up to the top of the house, where I could hardly stand for the wind, we went, accompanied by Mr. Beaver; and there Jack, lantern and all, with Mr. Beaver after him, swarmed up to the top of a cupola, some two dozen feet above the chimneys, and stood upon nothing particular, coolly knocking the weathercock off, until they both got into such good spirits with the wind and the height, that I thought they would never come down. Another night, they turned out again, and had a chimney-cowl off. Another night, they cut a sobbing and gulping water-pipe away. Another night, they found out something else. On several occasions, they both, in the coolest manner, simultaneously dropped out of their respective bedroom windows, hand over hand by their counterpanes, to "overhaul" something mysterious in the garden.

The engagement among us was faithfully kept, and nobody revealed anything. All we knew was, if any one's room were haunted, no one looked the worse for it.

THE GHOST IN MASTER B.'S ROOM.

WHEN I established myself in the triangular garret which
had gained so distinguished a reputation, my thoughts
naturally turned to Master B. My speculations about him
were uneasy and manifold. Whether his Christian name was
Benjamin, Bissextile (from his having been born in Leap
Year), Bartholomew, or Bill. Whether the initial letter
belonged to his family name, and that was Baxter, Black,
Brown, Barker, Buggins, Baker, or Bird. Whether he was
a foundling, and had been baptized B. Whether he was a
lion-hearted boy, and B. was short for Briton, or for Bull.
Whether he could possibly have been kith and kin to an
illustrious lady who brightened my own childhood, and had
come of the blood of the brilliant Mother Bunch?

With these profitless meditations I tormented myself much.
I also carried the mysterious letter into the appearance and
pursuits of the deceased; wondering whether he dressed in
Blue, wore Boots (he couldn't have been Bald), was a boy of
Brains, liked Books, was good at Bowling, had any skill as
a Boxer, even in his Buoyant Boyhood Bathed from a Bath-
ing-machine at Bognor, Bangor, Bournemouth, Brighton, or
Broadstairs, like a Bounding Billiard Ball?

So, from the first, I was haunted by the letter B.

It was not long before I remarked that I never by any
hazard had a dream of Master B., or of anything belonging
to him. But, the instant I awoke from sleep, at whatever
hour of the night, my thoughts took him up, and roamed

away, trying to attach his initial letter to something that
would fit it and keep it quiet.

For six nights, I had been worried thus in Master B.'s
room, when I began to perceive that things were going wrong.

The first appearance that presented itself was early in the
morning when it was but just daylight and no more. I was
standing shaving at my glass, when I suddenly discovered, to
my consternation and amazement, that I was shaving—not
myself—I am fifty—but a boy. Apparently Master B.!

I trembled and looked over my shoulder; nothing there.
I looked again in the glass, and distinctly saw the features
and expression of a boy, who was shaving, not to get rid of
a beard, but to get one. Extremely troubled in my mind,
I took a few turns in the room, and went back to the
looking-glass, resolved to steady my hand and complete the
operation in which I had been disturbed. Opening my eyes,
which I had shut while recovering my firmness, I now met
in the glass, looking straight at me, the eyes of a young man
of four or five and twenty. Terrified by this new ghost, I
closed my eyes, and made a strong effort to recover myself.
Opening them again, I saw, shaving his cheek in the glass,
my father, who has long been dead. Nay, I even saw my
grandfather too, whom I never did see in my life.

Although naturally much affected by these remarkable
visitations, I determined to keep my secret, until the time
agreed upon for the present general disclosure. Agitated by
a multitude of curious thoughts, I retired to my room, that
night, prepared to encounter some new experience of a spectral
character. Nor was my preparation needless, for, waking
from an uneasy sleep at exactly two o'clock in the morning,
what were my feelings to find that I was sharing my bed
with the skeleton of Master B.!

I sprang up, and the skeleton sprang up also. I then
heard a plaintive voice saying, "Where am I? What is
become of me?" and, looking hard in that direction,
perceived the ghost of Master B.

The young spectre was dressed in an obsolete fashion: or
rather, was not so much dressed as put into a case of inferior
pepper-and-salt cloth, made horrible by means of shining
buttons. I observed that these buttons went, in a double
row, over each shoulder of the young ghost, and appeared
to descend his back. He wore a frill round his neck. His
right hand (which I distinctly noticed to be inky) was laid
upon his stomach; connecting this action with some feeble
pimples on his countenance, and his general air of nausea,
I concluded this ghost to be the ghost of a boy who had
habitually taken a great deal too much medicine.

"Where am I?" said the little spectre, in a pathetic voice.
"And why was I born in the Calomel days, and why did I
have all that Calomel given me?"

I replied, with sincere earnestness, that upon my soul I
couldn't tell him.

"Where is my little sister," said the ghost, "and where
my angelic little wife, and where is the boy I went to school
with?"

I entreated the phantom to be comforted, and above all
things to take heart respecting the loss of the boy he went
to school with. I represented to him that probably that boy
never did, within human experience, come out well, when
discovered. I urged that I myself had, in later life, turned
up several boys whom I went to school with, and none of
them had at all answered. I expressed my humble belief
that that boy never did answer. I represented that he was
a mythic character, a delusion, and a snare. I recounted
how, the last time I found him, I found him at a dinner
party behind a wall of white cravat, with an inconclusive
opinion on every possible subject, and a power of silent
boredom absolutely Titanic. I related how, on the strength
of our having been together at "Old Doylance's," he had
asked himself to breakfast with me (a social offence of the
largest magnitude); how, fanning my weak embers of belief
in Doylance's boys, I had let him in; and how, he had

proved to be a fearful wanderer about the earth, pursuing
the race of Adam with inexplicable notions concerning the
currency, and with a proposition that the Bank of England
should, on pain of being abolished, instantly strike off and
circulate, God knows how many thousand millions of ten-
and-sixpenny notes.

The ghost heard me in silence, and with a fixed stare.
"Barber!" it apostrophised me when I had finished.

"Barber?" I repeated—for I am not of that profession.

"Condemned," said the ghost, "to shave a constant change
of customers—now, me—now, a young man—now, thyself as
thou art—now, thy father—now, thy grandfather; condemned,
too, to lie down with a skeleton every night, and to rise
with it every morning——"

(I shuddered on hearing this dismal announcement).

"Barber! Pursue me!"

I had felt, even before the words were uttered, that I was
under a spell to pursue the phantom. I immediately did
so, and was in Master B.'s room no longer.

Most people know what long and fatiguing night journeys
had been forced upon the witches who used to confess, and
who, no doubt, told the exact truth—particularly as they
were always assisted with leading questions, and the Torture
was always ready. I asseverate that, during my occupation
of Master B.'s room, I was taken by the ghost that haunted
it, on expeditions fully as long and wild as any of those.
Assuredly, I was presented to no shabby old man with a
goat's horns and tail (something between Pan and an old
clothesman), holding conventional receptions, as stupid as those
of real life and less decent; but, I came upon other things
which appeared to me to have more meaning.

Confident that I speak the truth and shall be believed, I
declare without hesitation that I followed the ghost, in the
first instance on a broom-stick, and afterwards on a rocking-
horse. The very smell of the animal's paint—especially
when I brought it out, by making him warm—I am ready

to swear to. I followed the ghost, afterwards, in a hackney coach; an institution with the peculiar smell of which, the present generation is unacquainted, but to which I am again ready to swear as a combination of stable, dog with the mange, and very old bellows. (In this, I appeal to previous generations to confirm or refute me.) I pursued the phantom, on a headless donkey: at least, upon a donkey who was so interested in the state of his stomach that his head was always down there, investigating it; on ponies, expressly born to kick up behind; on roundabouts and swings, from fairs; in the first cab—another forgotten institution where the fare regularly got into bed, and was tucked up with the driver.

Not to trouble you with a detailed account of all my travels in pursuit of the ghost of Master B., which were longer and more wonderful than those of Sinbad the Sailor, I will confine myself to one experience from which you may judge of many.

I was marvellously changed. I was myself, yet not myself. I was conscious of something within me, which has been the same all through my life, and which I have always recognised under all its phases and varieties as never altering, and yet I was not the I who had gone to bed in Master B.'s room. I had the smoothest of faces and the shortest of legs, and I had taken another creature like myself, also with the smoothest of faces and the shortest of legs, behind a door, and was confiding to him a proposition of the most astounding nature.

This proposition was, that we should have a Seraglio.

The other creature assented warmly. He had no notion of respectability, neither had I. It was the custom of the East, it was the way of the good Caliph Haroun Alraschid (let me have the corrupted name again for once, it is so scented with sweet memories!), the usage was highly laudable, and most worthy of imitation. "O, yes! Let us," said the other creature with a jump, "have a Seraglio."

It was not because we entertained the faintest doubts of

the meritorious character of the Oriental establishment we proposed to import, that we perceived it must be kept a secret from Miss Griffin. It was because we knew Miss Griffin to be bereft of human sympathies, and incapable of appreciating the greatness of the great Haroun. Mystery impenetrably shrouded from Miss Griffin then, let us entrust it to Miss Bule.

We were ten in Miss Griffin's establishment by Hampstead Ponds; eight ladies and two gentlemen. Miss Bule, whom I judge to have attained the ripe age of eight or nine, took the lead in society. I opened the subject to her in the course of the day, and proposed that she should become the Favourite.

Miss Bule, after struggling with the diffidence so natural to, and charming in, her adorable sex, expressed herself as flattered by the idea, but wished to know how it was proposed to provide for Miss Pipson? Miss Bule—who was understood to have vowed towards that young lady, a friendship, halves, and no secrets, until death, on the Church Service and Lessons complete in two volumes with case and lock—Miss Bule said she could not, as the friend of Pipson, disguise from herself, or me, that Pipson was not one of the common.

Now, Miss Pipson, having curly light hair and blue eyes (which was my idea of anything mortal and feminine that was called Fair), I promptly replied that I regarded Miss Pipson in the light of a Fair Circassian.

" And what then?" Miss Bule pensively asked.

I replied that she must be inveigled by a Merchant, brought to me veiled, and purchased as a slave.

[The other creature had already fallen into the second male place in the State, and was set apart for Grand Vizier. He afterwards resisted this disposal of events, but had his hair pulled until he yielded.]

" Shall I not be jealous?" Miss Bule inquired, casting down her eyes.

" Zobeide, no," I replied; " you will ever be the favourite

Sultana; the first place in my heart, and on my throne, will be ever yours."

Miss Bule, upon that assurance, consented to propound the idea to her seven beautiful companions. It occurring to me, in the course of the same day, that we knew we could trust a grinning and good-natured soul called Tabby, who was the serving drudge of the house, and had no more figure than one of the beds, and upon whose face there was always more or less black-lead, I slipped into Miss Bule's hand after supper, a little note to that effect: dwelling on the black-lead as being in a manner deposited by the finger of Providence, pointing Tabby out for Mesrour, the celebrated chief of the Blacks of the Hareem.

There were difficulties in the formation of the desired institution, as there are in all combinations. The other creature showed himself of a low character, and, when defeated in aspiring to the throne, pretended to have conscientious scruples about prostrating himself before the Caliph; wouldn't call him Commander of the Faithful; spoke of him slightingly and inconsistently as a mere "chap;" said he, the other creature, "wouldn't play"—Play!—and was otherwise coarse and offensive. This meanness of disposition was, however, put down by the general indignation of an united Seraglio, and I became blessed in the smiles of eight of the fairest of the daughters of men.

The smiles could only be bestowed when Miss Griffin was looking another way, and only then in a very wary manner, for there was a legend among the followers of the Prophet that she saw with a little round ornament in the middle of the pattern on the back of her shawl. But every day after dinner, for an hour, we were all together, and then the Favourite and the rest of the Royal Hareem competed who should most beguile the leisure of the Serene Haroun reposing from the cares of State—which were generally, as in most affairs of State, of an arithmetical character, the Commander of the Faithful being a fearful boggler at a sum.

On these occasions, the devoted Mesrour, chief of the Blacks of the Harem, was always in attendance (Miss Griffin usually ringing for that officer, at the same time, with great vehemence), but never acquitted himself in a manner worthy of his historical reputation. In the first place, his bringing a broom into the Divan of the Caliph, even when Haroun wore on his shoulders the red robe of anger (Miss Pipson's pelisse), though it might be got over for the moment, was never to be quite satisfactorily accounted for. In the second place, his breaking out into grinning exclamations of "Lork you pretties!" was neither Eastern nor respectful. In the third place, when specially instructed to say "Bismillah!" he always said "Hallelujah!" This officer, unlike his class, was too good-humoured altogether, kept his mouth open far too wide, expressed approbation to an incongruous extent, and even once—it was on the occasion of the purchase of the Fair Circassian for five hundred thousand purses of gold, and cheap, too—embraced the Slave, the Favourite, and the Caliph, all round. (Parenthetically let me say God bless Mesrour, and may there have been sons and daughters on that tender bosom, softening many a hard day since!)

Miss Griffin was a model of propriety, and I am at a loss to imagine what the feelings of the virtuous woman would have been, if she had known, when she paraded us down the Hampstead-road two and two, that she was walking with a stately step at the head of Polygamy and Mahomedanism. I believe that a mysterious and terrible joy with which the contemplation of Miss Griffin, in this unconscious state, inspired us, and a grim sense prevalent among us that there was a dreadful power in our knowledge of what Miss Griffin (who knew all things that could be learnt out of book) didn't know, were the mainspring of the preservation of our secret. It was wonderfully kept, but was once upon the verge of self-betrayal. The danger and escape occurred upon a Sunday. We were all ten ranged in a conspicuous part of the gallery at church, with Miss Griffin at our head—as we were every

Sunday—advertising the establishment in an unsecular sort of way—when the description of Solomon in his domestic glory happened to be read. The moment that monarch was thus referred to, conscience whispered me, "Thou, too, Haroun!" The officiating minister had a cast in his eye, and it assisted conscience by giving him the appearance of reading personally at me. A crimson blush, attended by a fearful perspiration, suffused my features. The Grand Vizier became more dead than alive, and the whole Seraglio reddened as if the sunset of Bagdad shone direct upon their lovely faces. At this portentous time the awful Griffin rose, and balefully surveyed the children of Islam. My own impression was, that Church and State had entered into a conspiracy with Miss Griffin to expose us, and that we should all be put into white sheets, and exhibited in the centre aisle. But, so Westerly—if I may be allowed the expression as opposite to Eastern associations—was Miss Griffin's sense of rectitude, that she merely suspected Apples, and we were saved.

I have called the Seraglio, united. Upon the question, solely, whether the Commander of the Faithful durst exercise a right of kissing in that sanctuary of the palace, were its peerless inmates divided. Zobeide asserted a counter-right in the Favourite to scratch, and the fair Circassian put her face, for refuge, into a green baize bag, originally designed for books. On the other hand, a young antelope of transcendent beauty from the fruitful plains of Camden-town (whence she had been brought, by traders, in the half-yearly caravan that crossed the intermediate desert after the holidays), held more liberal opinions, but stipulated for limiting the benefit of them to that dog, and son of a dog, the Grand Vizier—who had no rights, and was not in question. At length, the difficulty was compromised by the installation of a very youthful slave as Deputy. She, raised upon a stool, officially received upon her cheeks the salutes intended by the gracious Haroun for other Sultanas, and was privately rewarded from the coffers of the Ladies of the Hareem.

And now it was, at the full height of enjoyment of my bliss, that I became heavily troubled. I began to think of my mother, and what she would say to my taking home at Midsummer eight of the most beautiful of the daughters of men, but all unexpected. I thought of the number of beds we made up at our house, of my father's income, and of the baker, and my despondency redoubled. The Seraglio and malicious Vizier, divining the cause of their Lord's unhappiness, did their utmost to augment it. They professed unbounded fidelity, and declared that they would live and die with him. Reduced to the utmost wretchedness by these protestations of attachment, I lay awake, for hours at a time, ruminating on my frightful lot. In my despair, I think I might have taken an early opportunity of falling on my knees before Miss Griffin, avowing my resemblance to Solomon, and praying to be dealt with according to the outraged laws of my country, if an unthought-of means of escape had not opened before me.

One day, we were out walking, two and two—on which occasion the Vizier had his usual instructions to take note of the boy at the turnpike, and if he profanely gazed (which he always did) at the beauties of the Harem, to have him bowstrung in the course of the night—and it happened that our hearts were veiled in gloom. An unaccountable action on the part of the antelope had plunged the State into disgrace. That charmer, on the representation that the previous day was her birthday, and that vast treasures had been sent in a hamper for its celebration (both baseless assertions), had secretly but most pressingly invited thirty-five neighbouring princes and princesses to a ball and supper: with a special stipulation that they were "not to be fetched till twelve." This wandering of the antelope's fancy, led to the surprising arrival at Miss Griffin's door, in divers equipages and under various escorts, of a great company in full dress, who were deposited on the top step in a flush of high expectancy, and who were dismissed in tears. At the beginning of the double knocks attendant on these ceremonies, the antelope had retired to a back attic, and bolted herself in; and at every new arrival, Miss Griffin had gone so much more and more distracted, that at last she had been seen to tear her front. Ultimate capitulation on the part of the offender, had been followed by solitude in the linen-closet, bread and water and a lecture to all, of vindictive length, in which Miss Griffin had used expressions: Firstly, "I believe you all of you knew of it;" Secondly, "Every one of you is as wicked as another;" Thirdly, "A pack of little wretches."

Under these circumstances, we were walking drearily along; and I especially, with my Moosulmaun responsibilities heavy on me, was in a very low state of mind; when a strange man accosted Miss Griffin, and, after walking on at her side for a little while and talking with her, looked at me. Supposing him to be a minion of the law, and that my hour was come, I instantly ran away, with the general purpose of making for Egypt.

The whole Seraglio cried out, when they saw me making off as fast as my legs would carry me (I had an impression that the first turning on the left, and round by the public-house, would be the shortest way to the Pyramids), Miss Griffin screamed after me, the faithless Vizier ran after me, and the boy at the turnpike dodged me into a corner, like a sheep, and cut me off. Nobody scolded me when I was taken and brought back; Miss Griffin only said, with a stunning gentleness, This was very curious! Why had I run away when the gentleman looked at me?

If I had had any breath to answer with, I dare say I should have made no answer; having no breath, I certainly made none. Miss Griffin and the strange man took me between them, and walked me back to the palace in a sort of state; but not at all (as I couldn't help feeling, with astonishment), in culprit state.

When we got there, we went into a room by ourselves, and Miss Griffin called in to her assistance, Mesrour, chief of the dusky guards of the Harem. Mesrour, on being whispered to, began to shed tears.

"Bless you, my precious!" said that officer, turning to me; "your Pa's took bitter bad!"

I asked, with a fluttered heart, "Is he very ill?"

"Lord temper the wind to you, my lamb!" said the good Mesrour, kneeling down, that I might have a comforting shoulder for my head to rest on, "your Pa's dead!"

Haroun Alraschid took to flight at the words; the Seraglio vanished; from that moment, I never again saw one of the eight of the fairest of the daughters of men.

I was taken home, and there was Debt at home as well as Death, and we had a sale there. My own little bed was so superciliously looked upon by a Power unknown to me, hazily called "The Trade," that a brass coal-scuttle, a roasting-jack, and a birdcage, were obliged to be put into it to make a Lot of it, and then it went for a song. So I heard mentioned, and I wondered what song, and thought what a dismal song it must have been to sing!

Then, I was sent to a great, cold, bare, school of big boys; where everything to eat and wear was thick and clumpy, without being enough; where everybody, large and small, was cruel; where the boys knew all about the sale, before I got there, and asked me what I had fetched, and who had bought me, and hooted at me, "Going, going, gone!" I never whispered in that wretched place that I had been Haroun, or had had a Seraglio: for, I knew that if I mentioned my reverses, I should be so worried, that I should have to drown myself in the muddy pond near the playground, which looked like the beer.

Ah me, ah me! No other ghost has haunted the boy's room, my friends, since I have occupied it, than the ghost of my own childhood, the ghost of my own innocence, the ghost of my own airy belief. Many a time have I pursued the phantom: never with this man's stride of mine to come up with it, never with these man's hands of mine to touch it, never more to this man's heart of mine to hold it in its purity. And here you see me working out, as cheerfully and thankfully as I may, my doom of shaving in the glass a constant change of customers, and of lying down and rising up with the skeleton allotted to me for my mortal companion.

A MESSAGE FROM THE SEA

[1860]

A MESSAGE FROM THE SEA.

CHAPTER I.

THE VILLAGE.

"AND a mighty sing'lar and pretty place it is, as ever I saw in all the days of my life!" said Captain Jorgan, looking up at it.

Captain Jorgan had to look high to look at it, for the village was built sheer up the face of a steep and lofty cliff. There was no road in it, there was no wheeled vehicle in it, there was not a level yard in it. From the sea-beach to the cliff-top two irregular rows of white houses, placed opposite to one another, and twisting here and there, and there and here, rose, like the sides of a long succession of stages of crooked ladders, and you climbed up the village or climbed down the village by the staves between, some six feet wide or so, and made of sharp irregular stones. The old pack-saddle, long laid aside in most parts of England as one of the appendages of its infancy, flourished here intact. Strings of pack-horses and pack-donkeys toiled slowly up the staves of the ladders, bearing fish, and coal, and such other cargo as was unshipping at the pier from the dancing fleet of village boats, and from two or three little coasting traders. As the beasts of burden ascended laden, or descended light, they got so lost at intervals in the floating clouds of village

smoke, that they seemed to dive down some of the village
chimneys, and come to the surface again far off, high above
others.   No two houses in the village were alike, in chimney,
size, shape, door, window, gable, roof-tree, anything.   The
sides of the ladders were musical with water, running clear
and bright.   The staves were musical with the clattering
feet of the pack-horses and pack-donkeys, and the voices of
the fishermen urging them up, mingled with the voices of
the fishermen's wives and their many children.   The pier was
musical with the wash of the sea, the creaking of capstans
and windlasses, and the airy fluttering of little vanes and
sails.   The rough, sea-bleached boulders of which the pier
was made, and the whiter boulders of the shore, were brown
with drying nets.   The red-brown cliffs, richly wooded to
their extremest verge, had their softened and beautiful forms
reflected in the bluest water, under the clear North Devonshire sky of a November day without a cloud.   The village
itself was so steeped in autumnal foliage, from the houses lying
on the pier to the topmost round of the topmost ladder,
that one might have fancied it was out a bird's-nesting, and
was (as indeed it was) a wonderful climber.   And mentioning
birds, the place was not without some music from them too;
for the rook was very busy on the higher levels, and the gull
with his flapping wings was fishing in the bay, and the lusty
little robin was hopping among the great stone blocks and
iron rings of the break-water, fearless in the faith of his
ancestors, and the Children in the Wood.

Thus it came to pass that Captain Jorgan, sitting balancing
himself on the pier-wall, struck his leg with his open hand,
as some men do when they are pleased—and as he always did
when he was pleased—and said,—

"A mighty sing'lar and pretty place it is, as ever I saw
in all the days of my life!"

Captain Jorgan had not been through the village, but had
come down to the pier by a winding side-road, to have a
preliminary look at it from the level of his own natural

element. He had seen many things and places, and had
stowed them all away in a shrewd intellect and a vigorous
memory. He was an American born, was Captain Jorgan,
—a New-Englander,—but he was a citizen of the world, and
a combination of most of the best qualities of most of its
best countries.

For Captain Jorgan to sit anywhere in his long-skirted
blue coat and blue trousers, without holding converse with
everybody within speaking distance, was a sheer impossibility.
So the captain fell to talking with the fishermen, and to
asking them knowing questions about the fishery, and the
tides, and the currents, and the race of water off that point
yonder, and what you kept in your eye, and got into a line
with what else when you ran into the little harbour; and
other nautical profundities. Among the men who exchanged
ideas with the captain was a young fellow, who exactly hit
his fancy,—a young fisherman of two or three and twenty, in
the rough sea-dress of his craft, with a brown face, dark
curling hair, and bright, modest eyes under his Sou'wester
hat, and with a frank, but simple and retiring manner, which
the captain found uncommonly taking. "I'd bet a thousand
dollars," said the captain to himself, "that your father was
an honest man!"

"Might you be married now?" asked the captain, when
he had had some talk with this new acquaintance.

"Not yet."

"Going to be?" said the captain.

"I hope so."

The captain's keen glance followed the slightest possible
turn of the dark eye, and the slightest possible tilt of the
Sou'wester hat. The captain then slapped both his legs, and
said to himself,—

"Never knew such a good thing in all my life! There's
his sweetheart looking over the wall!"

There was a very pretty girl looking over the wall, from
a little platform of cottage, vine, and fuchsia; and she

certainly did not look as if the presence of this young
fisherman in the landscape made it any the less sunny and
hopeful for her.

Captain Jorgan, having doubled himself up to laugh with
that hearty good-nature which is quite exultant in the
innocent happiness of other people, had undoubled himself,
and was going to start a new subject, when there appeared
coming down the lower ladders of stones, a man whom
he hailed as "Tom Pettifer, Ho!" Tom Pettifer, Ho,
responded with alacrity, and in speedy course descended on
the pier.

"Afraid of a sun-stroke in England in November, Tom,
that you wear your tropical hat, strongly paid outside and
paper-lined inside, here?" said the captain, eyeing it.

"It's as well to be on the safe side, sir," replied Tom.

"Safe side!" repeated the captain, laughing. " You'd
guard against a sun-stroke, with that old hat, in an Ice Pack.
Wa'al! What have you made out at the Post-office?"

"It is the Post-office, sir."

"What's the Post-office?" said the captain.

"The name, sir. The name keeps the Post-office."

"A coincidence!" said the captain. "A lucky hit! Show
me where it is. Good-bye, shipmates, for the present! I
shall come and have another look at you, afore I leave, this
afternoon."

This was addressed to all there, but especially the young
fisherman; so all there acknowledged it, but especially the
young fisherman. "*He's* a sailor!" said one to another, as
they looked after the captain moving away. That he was;
and so outspeaking was the sailor in him, that although his
dress had nothing nautical about it, with the single exception
of its colour, but was a suit of a shore-going shape and form,
too long in the sleeves and too short in the legs, and too
unaccommodating everywhere, terminating earthward in a
pair of Wellington boots, and surmounted by a tall, stiff
hat, which no mortal could have worn at sea in any wind

unde.· heaven; nevertheless, a glimpse of his sagacious, weather-beaten face, or his strong, brown hand, would have established the captain's calling. Whereas Mr. Pettifer—a man of a certain plump neatness, with a curly whisker, and elaborately nautical in a jacket, and shoes, and all things correspondent—looked no more like a seaman, beside Captain Jorgan, than he looked like a sea-serpent.

The two climbed high up the village,—which had the most arbitrary turns and twists in it, so that the cobbler's house came dead across the ladder, and to have held a reasonable course, you must have gone through his house, and through him too, as he sat at his work between two little windows, with one eye microscopically on the geological formation of that part of Devonshire, and the other telescopically on the open sea,—the two climbed high up the village, and stopped before a quaint little house, on which was painted, "Mrs. RAYBROCK, DRAPER;" and also "POST-OFFICE." Before it, ran a rill of murmuring water, and access to it was gained by a little plank-bridge.

"Here's the name," said Captain Jorgan, "sure enough. You can come in if you like, Tom."

The captain opened the door, and passed into an odd little shop, about six feet high, with a great variety of beams and bumps in the ceiling, and, besides the principal window giving on the ladder of stones, a purblind little window of a single pane of glass, peeping out of an abutting corner at the sun-lighted ocean, and winking at its brightness.

"How do you do, ma'am?" said the captain. "I am very glad to see you. I have come a long way to see you."

"Have you, sir? Then I am sure I am very glad to see you, though I don't know you from Adam."

Thus a comely elderly woman, short of stature, plump of form, sparkling and dark of eye, who, perfectly clean and neat herself, stood in the midst of her perfectly clean and neat arrangements, and surveyed Captain Jorgan with smiling curiosity. "Ah! but you are a sailor, sir," she added,

almost immediately, and with a slight movement of her
hands, that was not very unlike wringing them; "then you
are heartily welcome."

"Thank'ee, ma'am," said the captain, "I don't know what
it is, I am sure, that brings out the salt in me, but everybody
seems to see it on the crown of my hat and the collar of my
coat. Yes, ma'am, I am in that way of life."

"And the other gentleman, too," said Mrs. Raybrock.

"Well now, ma'am," said the captain, glancing shrewdly
at the other gentleman, "you are that nigh right, that he
goes to sea,—if that makes him a sailor. This is my steward,
ma'am, Tom Pettifer; he's been a'most all trades you could
name, in the course of his life,—would have bought all your
chairs and tables once, if you had wished to sell 'em,—but
now he's my steward. My name's Jorgan, and I'm a ship-
owner, and I sail my own and my partners' ships, and have
done so this five-and-twenty year. According to custom I
am called Captain Jorgan, but I am no more a captain, bless
your heart! than you are."

"Perhaps you'll come into my parlour, sir, and take a
chair?" said Mrs. Raybrock.

"Ex-actly what I was going to propose myself, ma'am.
After you."

Thus replying, and enjoining Tom to give an eye to the
shop, Captain Jorgan followed Mrs. Raybrock into the little,
low back-room,—decorated with divers plants in pots, tea-
trays, old china teapots, and punch-bowls,—which was at
once the private sitting-room of the Raybrock family and
the inner cabinet of the post-office of the village of Steepways.

"Now, ma'am," said the captain, "it don't signify a cent
to you where I was born, except——" But here the shadow
of some one entering fell upon the captain's figure, and he
broke off to double himself up, slap both his legs, and
ejaculate, "Never knew such a thing in all my life! Here
he is again! How are you?"

These words referred to the young fellow who had so taken

Captain Jorgan's fancy down at the pier. To make it all quite complete he came in accompanied by the sweetheart whom the captain had detected looking over the wall. A prettier sweetheart the sun could not have shone upon that shining day. As she stood before the captain, with her rosy lips just parted in surprise, her brown eyes a little wider open than was usual from the same cause, and her breathing a little quickened by the ascent (and possibly by some mysterious hurry and flurry at the parlour door, in which the captain had observed her face to be for a moment totally eclipsed by the Sou'wester hat), she looked so charming, that the captain felt himself under a moral obligation to slap both his legs again. She was very simply dressed, with no other ornament than an autumnal flower in her bosom. She wore neither hat nor bonnet, but merely a scarf or kerchief, folded squarely back over the head, to keep the sun off,—according to a fashion that may be sometimes seen in the more genial parts of England as well as of Italy, and which is probably the first fashion of head-dress that came into the world when grasses and leaves went out.

"In my country," said the captain, rising to give her his chair, and dexterously sliding it close to another chair on which the young fisherman must necessarily establish himself, —"in my country we should call Devonshire beauty first-rate!"

Whenever a frank manner is offensive, it is because it is strained or feigned; for there may be quite as much intolerable affectation in plainness as in mincing nicety. All that the captain said and did was honestly according to his nature; and his nature was open nature and good nature; therefore, when he paid this little compliment, and expressed with a sparkle or two of his knowing eye, "I see how it is, and nothing could be better," he had established a delicate confidence on that subject with the family.

"I was saying to your worthy mother," said the captain to the young man, after again introducing himself by name and occupation,—"I was saying to your mother (and you're very like her) that it didn't signify where I was born, except that I was raised on question-asking ground, where the babies as soon as ever they come into the world, inquire of their mothers, 'Neow, how old may *you* be, and wa'at air you a goin' to name me?'—which is a fact." Here he slapped his leg. "Such being the case, I may be excused for asking you if your name's Alfred?"

"Yes, sir, my name is Alfred," returned the young man.

"I am not a conjurer," pursued the captain, "and don't think me so, or I shall right soon undeceive you. Likewise don't think, if you please, though I *do* come from that country of the babies, that I am asking questions for question-asking's sake, for I am not. Somebody belonging to you went to sea?"

"My elder brother, Hugh," returned the young man. He said it in an altered and lower voice, and glanced at his mother, who raised her hands hurriedly, and put them together across her black gown, and looked eagerly at the visitor.

"No! For God's sake, don't think that!" said the captain, in a solemn way; "I bring no good tidings of him."

There was a silence, and the mother turned her face to the fire and put her hand between it and her eyes. The young fisherman slightly motioned toward the window, and the captain, looking in that direction, saw a young widow, sitting at a neighbouring window across a little garden, engaged in needlework, with a young child sleeping on her bosom. The silence continued until the captain asked of Alfred,—

"How long is it since it happened?"

"He shipped for his last voyage better than three years ago."

"Ship struck upon some reef or rock, as I take it," said the captain, "and all hands lost?"

"Yes."

"Wa'al!" said the captain, after a shorter silence, "Here

I sit who may come to the same end, like enough. He holds
the seas in the hollow of His hand. We must all strike
somewhere and go down. Our comfort, then, for ourselves
and one another is to have done our duty. I'd wager your
brother did his!"

"He did!" answered the young fisherman. "If ever man
strove faithfully on all occasions to do his duty, my brother
did. My brother was not a quick man (anything but that),
but he was a faithful, true, and just man. We were the
sons of only a small tradesman in this county, sir; yet our
father was as watchful of his good name as if he had been a
king."

"A precious sight more so, I hope,—bearing in mind the
general run of that class of crittur," said the captain. "But
I interrupt."

"My brother considered that our father left the good
name to us, to keep clear and true."

"Your brother considered right," said the captain; "and
you couldn't take care of a better legacy. But again I
interrupt."

"No; for I have nothing more to say. We know that
Hugh lived well for the good name, and we feel certain that
he died well for the good name. And now it has come into
my keeping. And that's all."

"Well spoken!" cried the captain. "Well spoken, young
man! Concerning the manner of your brother's death,"—by
this time the captain had released the hand he had shaken,
and sat with his own broad, brown hands spread out on his
knees, and spoke aside,—"concerning the manner of your
brother's death, it may be that I have some information to
give you; though it may not be, for I am far from sure.
Can we have a little talk alone?"

The young man rose; but not before the captain's quick
eye had noticed that, on the pretty sweetheart's turning to
the window to greet the young widow with a nod and a
wave of the hand, the young widow had held up to her the

needlework on which she was engaged, with a patient and pleasant smile. So the captain said, being on his legs,—

"What might she be making now?"

"What is Margaret making, Kitty?" asked the young fisherman,—with one of his arms apparently mislaid somewhere.

As Kitty only blushed in reply, the captain doubled himself up as far as he could, standing, and said, with a slap of his leg,—

"In my country we should call it wedding-clothes. Fact! We should, I do assure you."

But it seemed to strike the captain in another light too; for his laugh was not a long one, and he added, in quite a gentle tone,—

"And it's very pretty, my dear, to see her—poor young thing, with her fatherless child upon her bosom—giving up her thoughts to your home and your happiness. It's very pretty, my dear, and it's very good. May your marriage be more prosperous than hers, and be a comfort to her too. May the blessed sun see you all happy together, in possession of the good name, long after I have done ploughing the great salt field that is never sown!"

Kitty answered very earnestly, "O! Thank you, sir, with all my heart!" And, in her loving little way, kissed her hand to him, and possibly by implication to the young fisherman, too, as the latter held the parlour-door open for the captain to pass out.

CHAPTER II.

"THE stairs are very narrow, sir," said Alfred Raybrock to Captain Jorgan.

"Like my cabin-stairs," returned the captain, "on many a voyage."

"And they are rather inconvenient for the head."

"If my head can't take care of itself by this time, after all the knocking about the world it has had," replied the captain, as unconcernedly as if he had no connection with it, "it's not worth looking after."

Thus they came into the young fisherman's bedroom, which was as perfectly neat and clean as the shop and parlour below; though it was but a little place, with a sliding window, and a phrenological ceiling expressive of all the peculiarities of the house-roof. Here the captain sat down on the foot of the bed, and glancing at a dreadful libel on Kitty which ornamented the wall,—the production of some wandering limner, whom the captain secretly admired as having studied portraiture from the figure-heads of ships, —motioned to the young man to take the rush-chair on the other side of the small, round table. That done, the captain put his hand in the deep breast-pocket of his long-skirted blue coat, and took out of it a strong square case-bottle,— not a large bottle, but such as may be seen in any ordinary ship's medicine-chest. Setting this bottle on the table without removing his hand from it, Captain Jorgan then spake as follows:—

"In my last voyage homeward-bound," said the captain, "and that's the voyage off of which I now come straight, I encountered such weather off the Horn as is not very often met with, even there. I have rounded that stormy Cape pretty often, and I believe I first beat about there in the identical storms that blew the Devil's horns and tail off, and led to the horns being worked up into tooth-picks for the plantation overseers in my country, who may be seen (if you travel down South, or away West, fur enough) picking their teeth with 'em, while the whips, made of the tail, flog hard. In this last voyage, homeward-bound for Liverpool from South America, I say to you, my young friend, it blew. Whole measures! No half measures, nor making believe to blow; it blew! Now I warn't blown clean out of the water into the sky,—though I expected to be even that,—but I was blown clean out of my course; and when at last it fell calm, it fell dead calm, and a strong current set one way, day and night, night and day, and I drifted—drifted—drifted —out of all the ordinary tracks and courses of ships, and drifted yet, and yet drifted. It behooves a man who takes charge of fellow-critturs' lives, never to rest from making himself master of his calling. I never did rest, and consequently I knew pretty well ('specially looking over the side in the dead calm of that strong current) what dangers to expect, and what precautions to take against 'em. In short, we were driving head on to an island. There was no island in the chart, and, therefore, you may say it was ill-manners in the island to be there; I don't dispute its bad breeding, but there it was. Thanks be to Heaven, I was as ready for the island as the island was ready for me. I made it out myself from the masthead, and I got enough way upon her in good time to keep her off. I ordered a boat to be lowered and manned, and went in that boat myself to explore the island. There was a reef outside it, and, floating in a corner

of the smooth water within the reef, was a heap of sea-weed,
and entangled in that sea-weed was this bottle."

Here the captain took his hand from the bottle for a
moment, that the young fisherman might direct a wondering
glance at it; and then replaced his hand and went on :—

"If ever you come—or even if ever you don't come—to a
desert place, use you your eyes and your spy-glass well; for
the smallest thing you see may prove of use to you, and may
have some information or some warning in it. That's the
principle on which I came to see this bottle. I picked up
the bottle and ran the boat alongside the island, and made
fast and went ashore armed, with a part of my boat's crew.
We found that every scrap of vegetation on the island (I give
it you as my opinion, but scant and scrubby at the best of
times) had been consumed by fire. As we were making our
way, cautiously and toilsomely, over the pulverised embers,
one of my people sank into the earth breast-high. He
turned pale, and "Haul me out smart, shipmates," says he,
"for my feet are among bones." We soon got him on his
legs again, and then we dug up the spot, and we found that
the man was right, and that his feet had been among bones.
More than that, they were human bones ; though whether
the remains of one man, or of two or three men, what with
calcination and ashes, and what with a poor practical knowledge of anatomy, I can't undertake to say. We examined
the whole island and made out nothing else, save and except
that, from its opposite side, I sighted a considerable tract
of land, which land I was able to identify, and according
to the bearings of which (not to trouble you with my log)
I took a fresh departure. When I got aboard again I
opened the bottle, which was oilskin-covered as you see,
and glass-stoppered as you see. Inside of it," pursued the
captain, suiting his action to his words, "I found this little
crumpled, folded paper, just as you see. Outside of it was
written, as you see, these words: ' *Whoever finds this, is
solemnly entreated by the dead to convey it unread to Alfred*

Raybrock, Steepways, North Devon, England.' A sacred charge," said the captain, concluding his narrative, "and, Alfred Raybrock, there it is!"

"This is my poor brother's writing!"

"I suppose so," said Captain Jorgan. "I'll take a look out of this little window while you read it."

"Pray no, sir! I should be hurt. My brother couldn't know it would fall into such hands as yours."

The captain sat down again on the foot of the bed, and the young man opened the folded paper with a trembling hand, and spread it on the table. The ragged paper, evidently creased and torn both before and after being written on, was much blotted and stained, and the ink had faded and run, and many words were wanting. What the captain and the young fisherman made out together, after much re-reading and much humouring of the folds of the paper, is given on the next page.

The young fisherman had become more and more agitated, as the writing had become clearer to him. He now left it lying before the captain, over whose shoulder he had been reading it, and dropping into his former seat, leaned forward on the table and laid his face in his hands.

"What, man," urged the captain, "don't give in! Be up and doing *like* a man!"

"It is selfish, I know,—but doing what, doing what?" cried the young fisherman, in complete despair, and stamping his sea-boot on the ground.

"Doing what?" returned the captain. "Something! I'd go down to the little breakwater below yonder, and take a wrench at one of the salt-rusted iron rings there, and either wrench it up by the roots or wrench my teeth out of my head, sooner than I'd do nothing. Nothing!" ejaculated the captain. "Any fool or fainting heart can do *that*, and nothing can come of nothing,—which was pretended to be found out, I believe, by one of them Latin critters," said the captain with the deepest disdain; "as if

Adam hadn't found it out, afore ever he so much as named the beasts!"

Yet the captain saw, in spite of his bold words, that there was some greater reason than he yet understood for the young man's distress. And he eyed him with a sympathising curiosity.

"Come, come!" continued the captain. "Speak out. What is it, boy!"

"You have seen how beautiful she is, sir," said the young man, looking up for the moment, with a flushed face and rumpled hair.

"Did any man ever say she warn't beautiful?" retorted the captain. "If so, go and lick him."

The young man laughed fretfully in spite of himself, and said,

"It's not that, it's not that."

"Wa'al, then, what is it?" said the captain in a more soothing tone.

The young fisherman mournfully composed himself to tell the captain what it was, and began: "We were to have been married next Monday week——"

"Were to have been!" interrupted Captain Jorgan. "And are to be? Hey?"

Young Raybrock shook his head, and traced out with his forefinger the words, "*poor father's five hundred pounds*," in the written paper.

"Go along," said the captain. "Five hundred pounds? Yes?"

"That sum of money," pursued the young fisherman, entering with the greatest earnestness on his demonstration, while the captain eyed him with equal earnestness, "was all my late father possessed. When he died, he owed no man more than he left means to pay, but he had been able to lay by only five hundred pounds."

"Five hundred pounds," repeated the captain. "Yes?"

"In his lifetime, years before, he had expressly laid the money aside to leave to my mother,—like to settle upon her, if I make myself understood."

"Yes?"

"He had risked it once—my father put down in writing at that time, respecting the money—and was resolved never to risk it again."

"Not a spec'lator," said the captain. "My country wouldn't have suited him. Yes?"

"My mother has never touched the money till now. And now it was to have been laid out, this very next week, in buying me a handsome share in our neighbouring fishery here, to settle me in life with Kitty."

The captain's face fell, and he passed and repassed his sun-browned right hand over his thin hair, in a discomfited manner.

"Kitty's father has no more than enough to live on, even

In the sparing way in which we live about here.   He is a kind
of bailiff or steward of manor rights here, and they are not
much, and it is but a poor little office.   He was better off
once, and Kitty must never marry to mere drudgery and
hard living."

The captain still sat stroking his thin hair, and looking at
the young fisherman.

"I am as certain that my father had no knowledge that
any one was wronged as to this money, or that any restitution ought to be made, as I am certain that the sun now
shines.   But, after this solemn warning from my brother's
grave in the sea, that the money is Stolen Money," said
Young Raybrock, forcing himself to the utterance of the
words, "can I doubt it?   Can I touch it?"

"About not doubting, I ain't so sure," observed the captain;
"but about not touching—no—I don't think you can."

"See then," said Young Raybrock, "why I am so grieved.
Think of Kitty.   Think what I have got to tell her!"

His heart quite failed him again when he had come round
to that, and he once more beat his sea-boot softly on the
floor.   But not for long; he soon began again, in a quietly
resolute tone.

"However!   Enough of that!   You spoke some brave
words to me just now, Captain Jorgan, and they shall not
be spoken in vain.   I have got to do something.   What I
have got to do, before all other things, is to trace out the
meaning of this paper, for the sake of the Good Name that
has no one else to put it right.   And still for the sake of
the Good Name, and my father's memory, not a word of this
writing must be breathed to my mother, or to Kitty, or to
any human creature.   You agree in this?"

"I don't know what they'll think of us below," said the
captain, "but for certain I can't oppose it.   Now, as to
tracing.   How will you do?"

They both, as by consent, bent over the paper again, and
again carefully puzzled out the whole of the writing.

"I make out that this would stand, if all the writing was here, 'Inquire among the old men living there, for'—some one. Most like, you'll go to this village named here?" said the captain, musing, with his finger on the name.

"Yes! And Mr. Tregarthen is a Cornishman, and—to be sure!—comes from Lanrean."

"Does he?" said the captain quietly. "As I ain't acquainted with him, who may *he* be?"

"Mr. Tregarthen is Kitty's father."

"Ay, ay!" cried the captain. "Now you speak! Tregarthen knows this village of Lanrean, then?"

"Beyond all doubt he does. I have often heard him mention it, as being his native place. He knows it well."

"Stop half a moment," said the captain. "We want a name here. You could ask Tregarthen (or if you couldn't I could) what names of old men he remembers in his time in those diggings? Hey?"

"I can go straight to his cottage, and ask him now."

"Take me with you," said the captain, rising in a solid way that had a most comfortable reliability in it, "and just a word more first. I have knocked about harder than you, and have got along further than you. I have had, all my sea-going life long, to keep my wits polished bright with acid and friction, like the brass cases of the ship's instruments. I'll keep you company on this expedition. Now you don't live by talking any more than I do. Clench that hand of yours in this hand of mine, and that's a speech on both sides."

Captain Jorgan took command of the expedition with that hearty shake. He at once refolded the paper exactly as before, replaced it in the bottle, put the stopper in, put the oilskin over the stopper, confided the whole to Young Raybrock's keeping, and led the way down-stairs.

But it was harder navigation below-stairs than above. The instant they set foot in the parlour the quick, womanly eye detected that there was something wrong. Kitty exclaimed, frightened, as she ran to her lover's side, "Alfred! What's the matter?" Mrs. Raybrock cried out to the captain, "Gracious! what have you done to my son to change him like this all in a minute?" And the young widow—who was there with her work upon her arm—was at first so agitated that she frightened the little girl she held in her hand, who hid her face in her mother's skirts and screamed. The captain, conscious of being held responsible for this domestic change, contemplated it with quite a guilty expression of countenance, and looked to the young fisherman to come to his rescue.

"Kitty, darling," said Young Raybrock, "Kitty, dearest love, I must go away to Lanrean, and I don't know where else or how much further, this very day. Worse than that —our marriage, Kitty, must be put off, and I don't know for how long."

Kitty stared at him, in doubt and wonder and in anger, and pushed him from her with her hand.

"Put off?" cried Mrs. Raybrock. "The marriage put off? And you going to Lanrean! Why, in the name of the dear Lord?"

"Mother dear, I can't say why; I must not say why. It would be dishonourable and undutiful to say why."

"Dishonourable and undutiful?" returned the dame. "And is there nothing dishonourable or undutiful in the boy's breaking the heart of his own plighted love, and his mother's heart too, for the sake of the dark secrets and counsels of a wicked stranger? Why did you ever come here?" she apostrophised the innocent captain. "Who wanted you? Where did you come from? Why couldn't you rest in your own bad place, wherever it is, instead of disturbing the peace of quiet unoffending folk like us?"

"And what," sobbed the poor little Kitty, "have I ever done to you, you hard and cruel captain, that you should come and serve me so?"

And then they both began to weep most pitifully, while

the captain could only look from the one to the other, and
lay hold of himself by the coat collar.

"Margaret," said the poor young fisherman, on his knees
at Kitty's feet, while Kitty kept both her hands before her
tearful face, to shut out the traitor from her view,—but kept
her fingers wide asunder and looked at him all the time,—
"Margaret, you have suffered so much, so uncomplainingly,
and are always so careful and considerate! Do take my part,
for poor Hugh's sake!"

The quiet Margaret was not appealed to in vain. "I will,
Alfred," she returned, "and I do. I wish this gentleman
had never come near us;" whereupon the captain laid hold
of himself the tighter: "but I take your part for all that.
I am sure you have some strong reason and some sufficient
reason for what you do, strange as it is, and even for not
saying why you do it, strange as that is. And, Kitty darling,
you are bound to think so more than any one, for true love
believes everything, and bears everything, and trusts everything. And, mother dear, you are bound to think so too,
for you know you have been blest with good sons, whose word
was always as good as their oath, and who were brought up
in as true a sense of honour as any gentleman in this land.
And I am sure you have no more call, mother, to doubt
your living son than to doubt your dead son; and for the
sake of the dear dead, I stand up for the dear living."

"Wa'al now," the captain struck in, with enthusiasm, "this
I say, That whether your opinions flatter me or not, you are
a young woman of sense, and spirit, and feeling; and I'd
sooner have you by my side, in the hour of danger, than
a good half of the men I've ever fallen in with—or fallen
out with, ayther."

Margaret did not return the captain's compliment, or
appear fully to reciprocate his good opinion, but she applied
herself to the consolation of Kitty, and of Kitty's mother-
in-law that was to have been next Monday week, and soon
restored the parlour to a quiet condition.

"Kitty, my darling," said the young fisherman, "I must go to your father to entreat him still to trust me in spite of this wretched change and mystery, and to ask him for some directions concerning Lanrean. Will you come home? Will you come with me, Kitty?"

Kitty answered not a word, but rose sobbing, with the end of her simple head-dress at her eyes. Captain Jorgan followed the lovers out, quite sheepishly, pausing in the shop to give an instruction to Mr. Pettifer.

"Here, Tom!" said the captain, in a low voice.. "Here's something in your line. Here's an old lady poorly and low in her spirits. Cheer her up a bit, Tom. Cheer 'em all up."

Mr. Pettifer, with a brisk nod of intelligence, immediately assumed his steward face, and went with his quiet, helpful, steward step into the parlour, where the captain had the great satisfaction of seeing him, through the glass door, take the child in his arms (who offered no objection), and bend over Mrs. Raybrock, administering soft words of consolation.

"Though what he finds to say, unless he's telling her that 't'll soon be over, or that most people is so at first, or that it'll do her good afterward, I cannot imaginate!" was the captain's reflection as he followed the lovers.

He had not far to follow them, since it was but a short descent down the stony ways to the cottage of Kitty's father. But short as the distance was, it was long enough to enable the captain to observe that he was fast becoming the village Ogre; for there was not a woman standing working at her door, or a fisherman coming up or going down, who saw Young Raybrock unhappy and little Kitty in tears, but he or she instantly darted a suspicious and indignant glance at the captain, as the foreigner who must somehow be responsible for this unusual spectacle. Consequently, when they came into Tregarthen's little garden,—which formed the platform from which the captain had seen Kitty peeping over the wall, —the captain brought to, and stood off and on at the gate, while Kitty hurried to hide her tears in her own room, and

Alfred spoke with her father, who was working in the garden. He was a rather infirm man, but could scarcely be called old yet, with an agreeable face and a promising air of making the best of things. The conversation began on his side with great cheerfulness and good humour, but soon became distrustful, and soon angry. That was the captain's cue for striking both into the conversation and the garden.

"Morning, sir!" said Captain Jorgan. "How do you do?"

"The gentleman I am going away with," said the young fisherman to Tregarthen.

"O!" returned Kitty's father, surveying the unfortunate captain with a look of extreme disfavour. "I confess that I can't say I am glad to see you."

"No," said the captain, "and, to admit the truth, that seems to be the general opinion in these parts. But don't be hasty; you may think better of me by-and-by."

"I hope so," observed Tregarthen.

"Wa'al, I hope so," observed the captain, quite at his ease; "more than that, I believe so,—though you don't. Now, Mr. Tregarthen, you don't want to exchange words of mistrust with me; and if you did, you couldn't, because I wouldn't. You and I are old enough to know better than to judge against experience from surfaces and appearances; and if you haven't lived to find out the evil and injustice of such judgments, you are a lucky man."

The other seemed to shrink under this remark, and replied, "Sir, I *have* lived to feel it deeply."

"Wa'al," said the captain, mollified, "then I've made a good cast without knowing it. Now, Tregarthen, there stands the lover of your only child, and here stand I who know his secret. I warrant it a righteous secret, and none of his making, though bound to be of his keeping. I want to help him out with it, and tewwards that end we ask you to favour us with the names of two or three old residents in the village of Lanrean. As I am taking out my pocket-

book and pencil to put the names down, I may as well observe
to you that this, wrote atop of the first page here, is my
name and address : ' Silas Jonas Jorgan, Salem, Massachusetts,
United States.' If ever you take it in your head to run over
any morning, I shall be glad to welcome you. Now, what
may be the spelling of these said names ? "

"There was an elderly man," said Tregarthen, "named
David Polreath. He may be dead."

" Wa'al," said the captain, cheerfully, " if Polreath's dead
and buried, and can be made of any service to us, Polreath
won't object to our digging of him up. Polreath's down,
anyhow."

" There was another named Penrewen. I don't know his
Christian name."

"Never mind his Chris'en name," said the captain.
" Penrewen, for short."

" There was another named John Tredgear."

" And a pleasant-sounding name, too," said the captain :
John Tredgear's booked."

" I can recall no other except old Parvis."

"One of old Parvis's fam'ly I reckon," said the captain,
"kept a dry-goods store in New York city, and realised a
handsome competency by burning his house to ashes. Same
name, anyhow. David Polreath, Unchris'en Penrewen, John
Tredgear, and old Arson Parvis."

" I cannot recall any others at the moment."

"Thank'ee," said the captain. "And so, Tregarthen,
hoping for your good opinion yet, and likewise for the fair
Devonshire Flower's, your daughter's, I give you my hand,
sir, and wish you good day."

Young Raybrock accompanied him disconsolately ; for there
was no Kitty at the window when he looked up, no Kitty in
the garden when he shut the gate, no Kitty gazing after them
along the stony ways when they began to climb back.

" Now I tell you what," said the captain. " Not being at
present calc'lated to promote harmony in your family, I won't

come in. You go and get your dinner at home, and I'll get
mine at the little hotel. Let our hour of meeting be two
o'clock, and you'll find me smoking a cigar in the sun afore
the hotel door. Tell Tom Pettifer, my steward, to consider
himself on duty, and to look after your people till we come
back ; you'll find he'll have made himself useful to 'em already,
and will be quite acceptable."

All was done as Captain Jorgan directed. Punctually at
two o'clock the young fisherman appeared with his knapsack
at his back ; and punctually at two o'clock the captain jerked
away the last feather-end of his cigar.

"Let me carry your baggage, Captain Jorgan ; I can easily
take it with mine."

"Thank'ee," said the captain. "I'll carry it myself. It's
only a comb."

They climbed out of the village, and paused among the
trees and fern on the summit of the hill above, to take breath,
and to look down at the beautiful sea. Suddenly the captain
gave his leg a resounding slap, and cried, " Never knew such
a right thing in all my life!"—and ran away.

The cause of this abrupt retirement on the part of the
captain was little Kitty among the trees. The captain went
out of sight and waited, and kept out of sight and waited,
until it occurred to him to beguile the time with another
cigar. He lighted it, and smoked it out, and still he was
out of sight and waiting. He stole within sight at last, and
saw the lovers, with their arms entwined and their bent
heads touching, moving slowly among the trees. It was the
golden time of the afternoon then, and the captain said
to himself, " Golden sun, golden sea, golden sails, golden
leaves, golden love, golden youth,—a golden state of things
altogether ! "

Nevertheless the captain found it necessary to hail his
young companion before going out of sight again. In a few
moments more he came up and they began their journey.

"That still young woman with the fatherless child," said

Captain Jorgan, as they fell into step, "didn't throw her words away; but good honest words are never thrown away. And now that I am conveying you off from that tender little thing that loves, and relics, and hopes, I feel just as if I was the snarling crittur in the picters, with the tight legs, the long nose, and the feather in his cap, the tips of whose moustaches get up nearer to his eyes the wickeder he gets."

The young fisherman knew nothing of Mephistopheles; but he smiled when the captain stopped to double himself up and slap his leg, and they went along in right good-fellowship.

NOTE.—The third and fourth chapters of this Christmas number were not by Mr. Dickens. After the first and second he did not resume the pen until the chapter entitled the "Restitution," here numbered as the fifth. For the two intervening chapters the reader is referred to the number as republished in the volume of the *Nine Christmas numbers of All the Year Round.*

CHAPTER V.

CAPTAIN JORGAN, up and out betimes, had put the whole village of Lanrean under an amicable cross-examination, and was returning to the King Arthur's Arms to breakfast, none the wiser for his trouble, when he beheld the young fisherman advancing to meet him, accompanied by a stranger. A glance at this stranger assured the captain that he could be no other than the Seafaring Man; and the captain was about to hail him as a fellow-craftsman, when the two stood still and silent before the captain, and the captain stood still, silent, and wondering before them.

"Why, what's this?" cried the captain, when at last he broke the silence. "You two are alike. You two are much alike! What's this?"

Not a word was answered on the other side, until after the seafaring brother had got hold of the captain's right hand, and the fisherman brother had got hold of the captain's left hand; and if ever the captain had had his fill of handshaking, from his birth to that hour, he had it then. And presently up and spoke the two brothers, one at a time, two at a time, two dozen at a time for the bewilderment into which they plunged the captain, until he gradually had Hugh Raybrock's deliverance made clear to him, and also unravelled the fact that the person referred to in the half-obliterated paper was Tregarthen himself.

"Formerly, dear Captain Jorgan," said Alfred, "of

Lanrean, you recollect? Kitty and her father came to live at Steepways after Hugh shipped on his last voyage."

"Ay, ay!" cried the captain, fetching a breath. "*Now* you have me in tow. Then your brother here don't know his sister-in-law that is to be so much as by name?"

"Never saw her; never heard of her!"

"Ay, ay, ay!" cried the captain. "Why then we every one go back together—paper, writer, and all—and take Tregarthen into the secret we kept from him?"

"Surely," said Alfred, "we can't help it now. We must go through with our duty."

"Not a doubt," returned the captain. "Give me an arm apiece, and let us set this ship-shape."

So walking up and down in the shrill wind on the wild moor, while the neglected breakfast cooled within, the captain and the brothers settled their course of action.

It was that they should all proceed by the quickest means they could secure to Barnstaple, and there look over the father's books and papers in the lawyer's keeping; as Hugh had proposed to himself to do if ever he reached home. That, enlightened or unenlightened, they should then return to Steepways and go straight to Mr. Tregarthen, and tell him all they knew, and see what came of it, and act accordingly. Lastly, that when they got there they should enter the village with all precautions against Hugh's being recognised by any chance; and that to the captain should be consigned the task of preparing his wife and mother for his restoration to this life.

"For you see," quoth Captain Jorgan, touching the last head, "it requires caution any way, great joys being as dangerous as great griefs, if not more dangerous, as being more uncommon (and therefore less provided against) in this round world of ours. And besides, I should like to free my name with the ladies, and take you home again at your brightest and luckiest; so don't let's throw away a chance of success."

The captain was highly lauded by the brothers for his kind interest and foresight.

"And now stop!" said the captain, coming to a standstill, and looking from one brother to the other, with quite a new rigging of wrinkles about each eye; "you are of opinion," to the elder, "that you are ra'ather slow?"

"I assure you I am very slow," said the honest Hugh.

"Wa'al," replied the captain, "I assure *you* that to the best of my belief I am ra'ather smart. Now a slow man ain't good at quick business, is he?"

That was clear to both.

"You," said the captain, turning to the younger brother, "are a little in love; ain't you?"

"Not a little, Captain Jorgan."

"Much or little, you're sort preoccupied; ain't you?"

It was impossible to be denied.

"And a sort preoccupied man ain't good at quick business, is he?" said the captain.

Equally clear on all sides.

"Now," said the captain, "I ain't in love myself, and I've made many a smart run across the ocean, and I should like to carry on and go ahead with this affair of yours and make a run slick through it. Shall I try? Will you hand it over to me?"

They were both delighted to do so, and thanked him heartily.

"Good," said the captain, taking out his watch. "This is half-past eight A.M., Friday morning. I'll jot that down, and we'll compute how many hours we've been out when we run into your mother's post-office. There! The entry's made, and now we go ahead."

They went ahead so well that before the Barnstaple lawyer's office was open next morning, the captain was sitting whistling on the step of the door, waiting for the clerk to come down the street with his key and open it. But instead of the clerk there came the master, with whom the captain fraternised on the spot to an extent that utterly confounded him.

As he personally knew both Hugh and Alfred, there was no difficulty in obtaining immediate access to such of the father's papers as were in his keeping. These were chiefly old letters and cash accounts; from which the captain, with a shrewdness and despatch that left the lawyer far behind, established with perfect clearness, by noon, the following particulars :—

That one Lawrence Clissold had borrowed of the deceased, at a time when he was a thriving young tradesman in the town of Barnstaple, the sum of five hundred pounds. That he had borrowed it on the written statement that it was to be laid out in furtherance of a speculation which he expected would raise him to independence; he being, at the time of writing that letter, no more than a clerk in the house of Dringworth Brothers, America-square, London. That the money was borrowed for a stipulated period; but that, when the term was out, the aforesaid speculation failed, and Clissold was without means of repayment. That, hereupon, he had written to his creditor, in no very persuasive terms, vaguely requesting further time. That the creditor had refused this concession, declaring that he could not afford delay. That Clissold then paid the debt, accompanying the remittance of the money with an angry letter describing it as having been advanced by a relative to save him from ruin. That, in acknowledging the receipt, Raybrock had cautioned Clissold to seek to borrow money of him no more, as he would never so risk money again.

Before the lawyer the captain said never a word in reference to these discoveries. But when the papers had been put back in their box, and he and his two companions were well out of the office, his right leg suffered for it, and he said,—

"So far this run's begun with a fair wind and a prosperous; for don't you see that all this agrees with that dutiful trust

in his father maintained by the slow member of the Raybrock
family?"

Whether the brothers had seen it before or no, they saw
it now. Not that the captain gave them much time to
contemplate the state of things at their ease, for he instantly
whipped them into a chaise again, and bore them off to
Steepways. Although the afternoon was but just beginning
to decline when they reached it, and it was broad daylight,
still they had no difficulty, by dint of muffling the returned
sailor up, and ascending the village rather than descending
it, in reaching Tregarthen's cottage unobserved. Kitty was
not visible, and they surprised Tregarthen sitting writing in
the small bay-window of his little room.

"Sir," said the captain, instantly shaking hands with him,
pen and all, "I'm glad to see you, sir. How do you do,
sir? I told you you'd think better of me by-and-by, and I
congratulate you on going to do it."

Here the captain's eye fell on Tom Pettifer Ho, engaged
in preparing some cookery at the fire.

"That critter," said the captain, smiting his leg, "is
a born steward, and never ought to have been in any
other way of life. Stop where you are, Tom, and make
yourself useful. Now, Tregarthen, I'm going to try a
chair."

Accordingly the captain drew one close to him, and went
on :—

"This loving member of the Raybrock family you know,
sir. This slow member of the same family you don't know,
sir. Wa'al, these two are brothers,—fact! Hugh's come
to life again, and here he stands. Now see here, my friend!
You don't want to be told that he was cast away, but you
do want to be told (for there's a purpose in it) that he was
cast away with another man. That man by name was
Lawrence Clissold."

At the mention of this name Tregarthen started and
changed colour. "What's the matter?" said the captain.

"He was a fellow-clerk of mine thirty—five-and-thirty—years ago."

"True," said the captain, immediately catching at the clew: "Dringworth Brothers, America-square, London City."

The other started again, nodded, and said, "That was the house."

"Now," pursued the captain, "between those two men cast away there arose a mystery concerning the round sum of five hundred pound."

Again Tregarthen started, changing colour. Again the captain said, "What's the matter?"

As Tregarthen only answered, "Please to go on," the captain recounted, very tersely and plainly, the nature of Clissold's wanderings on the barren island, as he had condensed them in his mind from the seafaring man. Tregarthen became greatly agitated during this recital, and at length exclaimed,—

"Clissold was the man who ruined me! I have suspected it for many a long year, and now I know it."

"And how," said the captain, drawing his chair still closer to Tregarthen, and clapping his hand upon his shoulder,— "how may you know it?"

"When we were fellow-clerks," replied Tregarthen, "in that London house, it was one of my duties to enter daily in a certain book an account of the sums received that day by the firm, and afterward paid into the bankers'. One memorable day,—a Wednesday, the black day of my life,— among the sums I so entered was one of five hundred pounds."

"I begin to make it out," said the captain. "Yes?"

"It was one of Clissold's duties to copy from this entry a memorandum of the sums which the clerk employed to go to the bankers' paid in there. It was my duty to hand the money to Clissold; it was Clissold's to hand it to the clerk, with that memorandum of his writing. On that Wednesday I entered a sum of five hundred pounds received. I handed that sum, as I handed the other sums in the day's entry,

to Clissold. I was absolutely certain of it at the time; I
have been absolutely certain of it ever since. A sum of
five hundred pounds was afterward found by the house to
have been that day wanting from the bag, from Clissold's
memorandum, and from the entries in my book. Clissold,
being questioned, stood upon his perfect clearness in the
matter, and emphatically declared that he asked no better
than to be tested by 'Tregarthen's book.' My book was examined, and the entry of five hundred pounds was not there."

"How not there," said the captain, "when you made it
yourself?"

Tregarthen continued:—

"I was then questioned. Had I made the entry? Certainly
I had. The house produced my book, and it was not there.
I could not deny my book; I could not deny my writing. I
knew there must be forgery by some one; but the writing
was wonderfully like mine, and I could impeach no one if
the house could not. I was required to pay the money back.
I did so; and I left the house, almost broken-hearted, rather
than remain there,—even if I could have done so,—with a
dark shadow of suspicion always on me. I returned to my
native place, Lanrean, and remained there, clerk to a mine,
until I was appointed to my little post here."

"I well remember," said the captain, "that I told you
that if you had no experience of ill judgments on deceiving
appearances, you were a lucky man. You went hurt at that,
and I see why. I'm sorry."

"'Thus it is," said Tregarthen. "Of my own innocence I
have of course been sure; it has been at once my comfort
and my trial. Of Clissold I have always had suspicions
almost amounting to certainty; but they have never been
confirmed until now. For my daughter's sake and for my
own I have carried this subject in my own heart, as the only
secret of my life, and have long believed that it would die
with me."

"Wa'al, my good sir," said the captain cordially, "the

present question is, and will be long, I hope, concerning living, and not dying. Now, here are our two honest friends, the loving Raybrock and the slow. Here they stand, agreed on one point, on which I'd back 'em round the world, and right across it from north to south, and then again from east to west, and through it, from your deepest Cornish mine to China. It is, that they will never use this same so-often-mentioned sum of money, and that restitution of it must be made to you. These two, the loving member and the slow, for the sake of the right and of their father's memory, will have it ready for you to-morrow. Take it, and ease their minds and mine, and end a most unfort'nate transaction."

Tregarthen took the captain by the hand, and gave his hand to each of the young men, but positively and finally answered No. He said, they trusted to his word, and he was glad of it, and at rest in his mind; but there was no proof, and the money must remain as it was. All were very earnest over this; and earnestness in men, when they are right and true, is so impressive, that Mr. Pettifer deserted his cookery and looked on quite moved.

"And so," said the captain, "so we come—as that lawyer-crittur over yonder where we were this morning might—to mere proof; do we? We must have it; must we? How? From this Clissold's wanderings, and from what you say, it ain't hard to make out that there was a neat forgery of your writing committed by the too smart rowdy that was grease and ashes when I made his acquaintance, and a substitution of a forged leaf in your book for a real and true leaf torn out. Now was that real and true leaf then and there destroyed? No,—for says he, in his drunken way, he slipped it into a crack in his own desk, because you came into the office before there was time to burn it, and could never get back to it afterwards. Wait a bit. Where is that desk now? Do you consider it likely to be in America-square, London City?"

Tregarthen shook his head.

"The house has not, for years, transacted business in that place. I have heard of it, and read of it, as removed, enlarged, every way altered. Things alter so fast in these times."

"You think so," returned the captain, with compassion; "but you should come over and see *me* afore you talk about *that*. Wa'al, now. This desk, this paper,—this paper, this desk," said the captain, ruminating and walking about, and looking, in his uneasy abstraction, into Mr. Pettifer's hat on a table, among other things. "This desk, this paper,— this paper, this desk," the captain continued, musing and roaming about the room, "I'd give—— "

However, he gave nothing, but took up his steward's hat instead, and stood looking into it, as if he had just come into church. After that he roamed again, and again said, "This desk, belonging to this house of Dringworth Brothers, America-square, London City—— "

Mr. Pettifer, still strangely moved, and now more moved than before, cut the captain off as he backed across the room, and bespake him thus:—

"Captain Jorgan, I have been wishful to engage your attention, but I couldn't do it. I am unwilling to interrupt Captain Jorgan, but I must do it. *I* know something about that house."

The captain stood stock-still and looked at him,—with his (Mr. Pettifer's) hat under his arm.

"You're aware," pursued his steward, "that I was once in the broking business, Captain Jorgan?"

"I was aware," said the captain, "that you had failed in that calling, and in half the businesses going, Tom."

"Not quite so, Captain Jorgan; but I failed in the broking business. I was partners with my brother, sir. There was a sale of old office furniture at Dringworth Brothers' when the house was moved from America-square, and me and my brother made what we call in the trade a Deal there, sir. And I'll make bold to say, sir, that the only thing I ever had from my brother, or from any relation,—for my relations have mostly taken property from me instead of giving me any,—was an old desk we bought at that same sale, with a crack in it. My brother wouldn't have given me even that, when we broke partnership, if it had been worth anything."

" Where is that desk now?" said the captain.

" Well, Captain Jorgan," replied the steward, "I couldn't say for certain where it is now; but when I saw it last,— which was last time we were outward bound,—it was at a very nice lady's at Wapping, along with a little chest of mine which was detained for a small matter of a bill owing."

The captain, instead of paying that rapt attention to his steward which was rendered by the other three persons present, went to Church again, in respect of the steward's hat. And a most especially agitated and memorable face the captain produced from it, after a short pause.

"Now, Tom," said the captain, "I spoke to you, when we first came here, respecting your constitutional weakness on the subject of sunstroke."

" You did, sir."

" Will my slow friend," said the captain, " lend me his arm, or I shall sink right back'ards into this blessed steward's cookery? Now, Tom," pursued the captain, when the required assistance was given, " on your oath as a steward, didn't you take that desk to pieces to make a better one of it, and put it together fresh,—or something of the kind?"

" On my oath I did, sir," replied the steward.

" And by the blessing of Heaven, my friends, one and all," cried the captain, radiant with joy,—" of the Heaven that put it into this Tom Pettifer's head to take so much care of his head against the bright sun,—he lined his hat with the original leaf in Tregarthen's writing,—and here it is!"

With that the captain, to the utter destruction of Mr. Pettifer's favourite hat, produced the book-leaf, very much worn, but still legible, and gave both his legs such tremendous slaps that they were heard far off in the bay, and never accounted for.

"A quarter past five P.M.," said the captain, pulling out his watch, "and that's thirty-three hours and a quarter in all, and a pritty run!"

How they were all overpowered with delight and triumph; how the money was restored, then and there, to Tregarthen; how Tregarthen, then and there, gave it all to his daughter; how the captain undertook to go to Dringworth Brothers and reëstablish the reputation of their forgotten old clerk; how Kitty came in, and was nearly torn to pieces, and the marriage was reappointed, needs not to be told. Nor how she and the young fisherman went home to the post-office to prepare the way for the captain's coming, by declaring him to be the mightiest of men, who had made all their fortunes, —and then dutifully withdrew together, in order that he might have the domestic coast entirely to himself. How he availed himself of it is all that remains to tell.

Deeply delighted with his trust, and putting his heart into it, he raised the latch of the post-office parlour where Mrs. Raybrock and the young widow sat, and said,—

"May I come in?"

"Sure you may, Captain Jorgan!" replied the old lady. "And good reason you have to be free of the house, though you have not been too well used in it by some who ought to have known better. I ask your pardon."

"No you don't, ma'am," said the captain, "for I won't let you. Wa'al, to be sure!"

By this time he had taken a chair on the hearth between them.

"Never felt such an evil spirit in the whole course of my life! There! I tell you! I could a'most have cut my own connection. Like the dealer in my country, away West, who when he had let himself be outdone in a bargain, said to himself, 'Now I tell you what! I'll never speak to you again.' And he never did, but joined a settlement of oysters, and translated the multiplication table into their language,— which is a fact that can be proved. If you doubt it, mention it to any oyster you come across, and see if he'll have the face to contradict it."

He took the child from her mother's lap and set it on his knee.

"Not a bit afraid of me now, you see. Knows I am fond of small people. I have a child, and she's a girl, and I sing to her sometimes."

"What do you sing?" asked Margaret.

"Not a long song, my dear.

> Silas Jorgan
> Played the organ.

That's about all. And sometimes I tell her stories,—stories of sailors supposed to be lost, and recovered after all hope was abandoned." Here the captain musingly went back to his song,—

> Silas Jorgan
> Played the organ;

repeating it with his eyes on the fire, as he softly danced the child on his knee. For he felt that Margaret had stopped working.

"Yes," said the captain, still looking at the fire, "I make up stories and tell 'em to that child. Stories of shipwreck on desert islands, and long delay in getting back to civilised lands. It is to stories the like of that, mostly, that

> Silas Jorgan
> Plays the organ."

There was no light in the room but the light of the fire; for the shades of night were on the village, and the stars had begun to peep out of the sky one by one, as the houses of the village peeped out from among the foliage when the night departed. The captain felt that Margaret's eyes were upon him, and thought it discreetest to keep his own eyes on the fire.

"Yes; I make 'em up," said the captain. "I make up stories of brothers brought together by the good providence of God,—of sons brought back to mothers, husbands brought back to wives, fathers raised from the deep, for little children like herself."

Margaret's touch was on his arm, and he could not choose but look round now. Next moment her hand moved imploringly to his breast, and she was on her knees before him,—supporting the mother, who was also kneeling.

"What's the matter?" said the captain. "What's the matter?

Silas Jorgan
Played the——"

Their looks and tears were too much for him, and he could not finish the song, short as it was.

"Mistress Margaret, you have borne ill fortune well. Could you bear good fortune equally well, if it was to come?"

"I hope so. I thankfully and humbly and earnestly hope so!"

"Wa'al, my dear," said the captain, "p'r'haps it has come. He's—don't be frightened—shall I say the word——"

"Alive?"

"Yes!"

The thanks they fervently addressed to Heaven were again too much for the captain, who openly took out his handkerchief and dried his eyes.

"He's no further off," resumed the captain, "than my country. Indeed, he's no further off than his own native country. To tell you the truth, he's no further off than Falmouth. Indeed, I doubt if he's quite so fur. Indeed, if you was sure you could bear it nicely, and I was to do no more than whistle for him——"

The captain's trust was discharged. A rush came, and they were all together again.

This was a fine opportunity for Tom Pettifer to appear with a tumbler of cold water, and he presently appeared

with it, and administered it to the ladies; at the same time
soothing them, and composing their dresses, exactly as if
they had been passengers crossing the Channel. The extent
to which the captain slapped his legs, when Mr. Pettifer
acquitted himself of this act of stewardship, could have been
thoroughly appreciated by no one but himself; inasmuch as
he must have slapped them black and blue, and they must
have smarted tremendously.

He couldn't stay for the wedding, having a few appoint-
ments to keep at the irreconcilable distance of about four
thousand miles. So next morning all the village cheered him
up to the level ground above, and there he shook hands with
a complete Census of its population, and invited the whole,
without exception, to come and stay several months with him
at Salem, Mass., U.S. And there as he stood on the spot
where he had seen that little golden picture of love and
parting, and from which he could that morning contemplate
another golden picture with a vista of golden years in it,
little Kitty put her arms around his neck, and kissed him on
both his bronzed cheeks, and laid her pretty face upon his
storm-beaten breast, in sight of all,—ashamed to have called
such a noble captain names. And there the captain waved
his hat over his head three final times; and there he was
last seen, going away accompanied by Tom Pettifer Ho, and
carrying his hands in his pockets. And there, before that
ground was softened with the fallen leaves of three more
summers, a rosy little boy took his first unsteady run to a
fair young mother's breast, and the name of that infant
fisherman was Jorgan Raybrock.

TOM TIDDLER'S GROUND

[1861]

TOM TIDDLER'S GROUND.

In Three Chapters.*

I.

PICKING UP SOOT AND CINDERS.

"And why Tom Tiddler's ground?" asked the Traveller.

"Because he scatters halfpence to Tramps and such-like," returned the Landlord, "and of course they pick 'em up. And this being done on his own land (which it *is* his own land, you observe, and were his family's before him), why it is but regarding the halfpence as gold and silver, and turning the ownership of the property a bit round your finger, and there you have the name of the children's game complete. And it's appropriate too," said the Landlord, with his favourite action of stooping a little, to look across the table out of window at vacancy, under the window-blind which was half drawn down. "Leastwise it has been so considered by many gentlemen which have partook of chops and tea in the present humble parlour."

The Traveller was partaking of chops and tea in the present humble parlour, and the Landlord's shot was fired obliquely at him.

"And you call him a Hermit?" said the Traveller.

* The original has seven chapters; but those not printed here were not written by Mr. Dickens.

"They call him such," returned the Landlord, evading personal responsibility; "he is in general so considered."

"What *is* a Hermit?" asked the Traveller.

"What is it?" repeated the Landlord, drawing his hand across his chin.

"Yes, what is it?"

The Landlord stooped again, to get a more comprehensive view of vacancy under the window-blind, and—with an asphyxiated appearance on him as one unaccustomed to definition—made no answer.

"I'll tell you what I suppose it to be," said the Traveller. "An abominably dirty thing."

"Mr. Mopes is dirty, it cannot be denied," said the Landlord.

"Intolerably conceited."

"Mr. Mopes is vain of the life he leads, some do say," replied the Landlord, as another concession.

"A slothful, unsavoury, nasty reversal of the laws of human nature," said the Traveller; "and for the sake of God's working world and its wholesomeness, both moral and physical, I would put the thing on the treadmill (if I had my way) wherever I found it; whether on a pillar, or in a hole; whether on Tom Tiddler's ground, or the Pope of Rome's ground, or a Hindoo fakeer's ground, or any other ground."

"I don't know about putting Mr. Mopes on the treadmill," said the Landlord, shaking his head very seriously. "There ain't a doubt but what he has got landed property."

"How far may it be to this said Tom Tiddler's ground?" asked the Traveller.

"Put it at five mile," returned the Landlord.

"Well! When I have done my breakfast," said the Traveller, "I'll go there. I came over here this morning, to find it out and see it."

"Many does," observed the Landlord.

The conversation passed, in the Midsummer weather of no

remote year of grace, down among the pleasant dales and
trout-streams of a green English county. No matter what
county. Enough that you may hunt there, shoot there, fish
there, traverse long grass-grown Roman roads there, open
ancient barrows there, see many a square mile of richly
cultivated land there, and hold Arcadian talk with a bold
peasantry, their country's pride, who will tell you (if you
want to know) how pastoral housekeeping is done on nine
shillings a week.

Mr. Traveller sat at his breakfast in the little sanded parlour
of the Peal of Bells village alehouse, with the dew and dust
of an early walk upon his shoes—an early walk by road and
meadow and coppice, that had sprinkled him bountifully with
little blades of grass, and scraps of new hay, and with leaves
both young and old, and with other such fragrant tokens of
the freshness and wealth of summer. The window through
which the landlord had concentrated his gaze upon vacancy
was shaded, because the morning sun was hot and bright on
the village street. The village street was like most other
village streets: wide for its height, silent for its size, and
drowsy in the dullest degree. The quietest little dwellings
with the largest of window-shutters (to shut up Nothing as
carefully as if it were the Mint, or the Bank of England)
had called in the Doctor's house so suddenly, that his brass
door-plate and three stories stood among them as conspicuous
and different as the Doctor himself in his broadcloth, among
the smock-frocks of his patients. The village residences
seemed to have gone to law with a similar absence of consideration, for a score of weak little lath-and-plaster cabins
clung in confusion about the Attorney's red-brick house,
which, with glaring door-steps and a most terrific scraper,
seemed to serve all manner of ejectments upon them. They
were as various as labourers—high-shouldered, wry-necked,
one-eyed, goggle-eyed, squinting, bow-legged, knock-knee'd,
rheumatic, crazy. Some of the small tradesmen's houses,
such as the crockery-shop and the harness-makers, had a

Cyclops window in the middle of the gable, within an inch
or two of its apex, suggesting that some forlorn rural Pren-
tice must wriggle himself into that apartment horizontally,
when he retired to rest, after the manner of the worm. So
bountiful in its abundance was the surrounding country, and
so lean and scant the village, that one might have thought
the village had sown and planted everything it once possessed,
to convert the same into crops. This would account for the
bareness of the little shops, the bareness of the few boards
and trestles designed for market purposes in a corner of the
street, the bareness of the obsolete Inn and Inn Yard, with
the ominous inscription " Excise Office" not yet faded out
from the gateway, as indicating the very last thing that
poverty could get rid of. This would also account for the
determined abandonment of the village by one stray dog, fast
lessening in the perspective where the white posts and the
pond were, and would explain his conduct on the hypothesis
that he was going (through the act of suicide) to convert
himself into manure, and become a part proprietor in turnips
or mangold-wurzel.

Mr. Traveller having finished his breakfast and paid his
moderate score, walked out to the threshold of the Peal of
Bells, and, thence directed by the pointing finger of his host,
betook himself towards the ruined hermitage of Mr. Mopes
the hermit.

For, Mr. Mopes, by suffering everything about him to go
to ruin, and by dressing himself in a blanket and skewer,
and by steeping himself in soot and grease and other nasti-
ness, had acquired great renown in all that country-side—far
greater renown than he could ever have won for himself, if
his career had been than of any ordinary Christian, or decent
Hottentot. He had even blanketed and skewered and sooted
and greased himself, into the London papers. And it was
curious to find, as Mr. Traveller found by stopping for a
new direction at this farm-house or at that cottage as he
went along, with how much accuracy the morbid Mopes had

counted on the weakness of his neighbours to embellish him. A mist of home-brewed marvel and romance surrounded Mopes, in which (as in all fogs) the real proportions of the real object were extravagantly heightened. He had murdered his beautiful beloved in a fit of jealousy and was doing penance; he had made a vow under the influence of grief; he had made a vow under the influence of a fatal accident; he had made a vow under the influence of religion; he had made a vow under the influence of drink; he had made a vow under the influence of disappointment; he had never made any vow, but "had got led into it" by the possession of a mighty and most awful secret; he was enormously rich, he was stupendously charitable, he was profoundly learned, he saw spectres, he knew and could do all kinds of wonders. Some said he went out every night, and was met by terrified wayfarers stalking along dark roads, others said he never went out, some knew his penance to be nearly expired, others had positive information that his seclusion was not a penance at all, and would never expire but with himself. Even, as to the easy facts of how old he was, or how long he had held verminous occupation of his blanket and skewer, no consistent information was to be got, from those who must know if they would. He was represented as being all the ages between five-and-twenty and sixty, and as having been a hermit seven years, twelve, twenty, thirty,—though twenty, on the whole, appeared the favourite term.

"Well, well!" said Mr. Traveller. "At any rate, let us see what a real live Hermit looks like."

So, Mr. Traveller went on, and on, and on, until he came to Tom Tiddler's ground.

It was a nook in a rustic by-road, which the genius of Mopes had laid waste as completely, as if he had been born an Emperor and a Conqueror. Its centre object was a dwelling-house, sufficiently substantial, all the window-glass of which had been long ago abolished by the surprising genius of Mopes, and all the windows of which were barred across with rough-split logs of trees nailed over them on the outside. A rickyard, hip-high in vegetable rankness and ruin, contained outbuildings, from which the thatch had lightly fluttered away, on all the winds of all the seasons of the year, and from which the planks and beams had heavily dropped and rotted. The frosts and damps of winter, and the heats of summer, had warped what wreck remained, so that not a post or a board retained the position it was meant to hold, but everything was twisted from its purpose, like its owner, and degraded and debased. In this homestead of the sluggard, behind the ruined hedge, and sinking away among the ruined grass and the nettles, were the last perishing fragments of certain ricks: which had gradually mildewed and collapsed, until they looked like mounds of rotten honeycomb, or dirty sponge. Tom Tiddler's ground could even show its ruined water; for, there was a slimy pond into which a tree or two had fallen—one soppy trunk and branches lay across it then —which in its accumulation of stagnant weed, and in its black decomposition, and in all its foulness and filth, was almost comforting, regarded as the only water that could have reflected the shameful place without seeming polluted by that low office.

Mr. Traveller looked all around him on Tom Tiddler's ground, and his glance at last encountered a dusky Tinker lying among the weeds and rank grass, in the shade of the dwelling-house. A rough walking-staff lay on the ground by his side, and his head rested on a small wallet. He met Mr. Traveller's eye without lifting up his head, merely depressing his chin a little (for he was lying on his back) to get a better view of him.

"Good day!" said Mr. Traveller.

"Same to you, if you like it," returned the Tinker.

"Don't *you* like it? It's a very fine day."

"I ain't partickler in weather," returned the Tinker, with a yawn.

Mr. Traveller had walked up to where he lay, and was

looking down at him. "This is a curious place," said Mr. Traveller.

"Ay, I suppose so!" returned the Tinker. "Tom Tiddler's ground, they call this."

"Are you well acquainted with it?"

"Never saw it afore to-day," said the Tinker, with another yawn, "and don't care if I never see it again. There was a man here just now, told me what it was called. If you want to see Tom himself, you must go in at that gate." He faintly indicated with his chin a little mean ruin of a wooden gate at the side of the house.

"Have you seen Tom?"

"No, and I ain't partickler to see him. I can see a dirty man anywhere."

"He does not live in the house, then?" said Mr. Traveller, casting his eyes upon the house anew.

"The man said," returned the Tinker, rather irritably,— "him as was here just now,—'this what you're a lying on, mate, is Tom Tiddler's ground. And if you want to see Tom,' he says, 'you must go in at that gate.' The man come out at that gate himself, and he ought to know."

"Certainly," said Mr. Traveller.

"'Though, perhaps," exclaimed the Tinker, so struck by the brightness of his own idea, that it had the electric effect upon him of causing him to lift up his head an inch or so, "perhaps he was a liar! He told some rum'uns—him as was here just now, did about this place of Tom's. He says —him as was here just now—'When Tom shut up the house, mate, to go to rack, the beds was left, all made, like as if somebody was a-going to sleep in every bed. And if you was to walk through the bedrooms now, you'd see the ragged mouldy bedclothes a heaving and a heaving like seas. And a heaving and a heaving with what?' he says. 'Why, with the rats under 'em.'"

"I wish I had seen that man," Mr. Traveller remarked.

"You'd have been welcome to see him instead of me

seeing him," growled the Tinker; "for he was a long-winded one."

Not without a sense of injury in the remembrance, the Tinker gloomily closed his eyes. Mr. Traveller, deeming the Tinker a short-winded one, from whom no further breath of information was to be derived, betook himself to the gate.

Swung upon its rusty hinges, it admitted him into a yard in which there was nothing to be seen but an outhouse attached to the ruined building, with a barred window in it. As there were traces of many recent footsteps under this window, and as it was a low window, and unglazed, Mr. Traveller made bold to peep within the bars. And there to be sure he had a real live Hermit before him, and could judge how the real dead Hermits used to look.

He was lying on a bank of soot and cinders, on the floor, in front of a rusty fireplace. There was nothing else in the dark little kitchen, or scullery, or whatever his den had been originally used as, but a table with a litter of old bottles on it. A rat made a clatter among these bottles, jumped down, and ran over the real live Hermit on his way to his hole, or the man in *his* hole would not have been so easily discernible. Tickled in the face by the rat's tail, the owner of Tom Tiddler's ground opened his eyes, saw Mr. Traveller, started up, and sprang to the window.

"Humph!" thought Mr. Traveller, retiring a pace or two from the bars. "A compound of Newgate, Bedlam, a Debtors' Prison in the worst time, a chimney-sweep, a mudlark, and the Noble Savage! A nice old family, the Hermit family. Hah!"

Mr. Traveller thought this, as he silently confronted the sooty object in the blanket and skewer (in sober truth it wore nothing else), with the matted hair and the staring eyes. Further, Mr. Traveller thought, as the eye surveyed him with a very obvious curiosity in ascertaining the effect they produced, "Vanity, vanity, vanity! Verily, all is vanity!"

"What is your name, sir, and where do you come from?"

asked Mr. Mopes the Hermit—with an air of authority, but
in the ordinary human speech of one who has been to school.

Mr. Traveller answered the inquiries.

"Did you come here, sir, to see *me?*"

"I did. I heard of you, and I came to see you.—I know
you like to be seen." Mr. Traveller coolly threw the last
words in, as a matter of course, to forestall an affectation
of resentment or objection that he saw rising beneath the
grease and grime of the face. They had their effect.

"So," said the Hermit, after a momentary silence, un-
clasping the bars by which he had previously held, and
seating himself behind them on the ledge of the window,
with his bare legs and feet crouched up, "you know I like
to be seen?"

Mr. Traveller looked about him for something to sit on,
and, observing a billet of wood in a corner, brought it
near the window. Deliberately seating himself upon it, he
answered, "Just so."

Each looked at the other, and each appeared to take some
pains to get the measure of the other.

"Then you have come to ask me why I lead this life,"
said the Hermit, frowning in a stormy manner. "I never
tell that to any human being. I will not be asked that."

"Certainly you will not be asked that by me," said Mr.
Traveller, "for I have not the slightest desire to know."

"You are an uncouth man," said Mr. Mopes the Hermit.

"You are another," said Mr. Traveller.

The Hermit, who was plainly in the habit of overawing
his visitors with the novelty of his filth and his blanket and
skewer, glared at his present visitor in some discomfiture and
surprise: as if he had taken aim at him with a sure gun,
and his piece had missed fire.

"Why do you come here at all?" he asked, after a pause.

"Upon my life," said Mr. Traveller, "I was made to ask
myself that very question only a few minutes ago—by a
Tinker too."

As he glanced towards the gate in saying it, the Hermit glanced in that direction likewise.

"Yes. He is lying on his back in the sunlight outside," said Mr. Traveller, as if he had been asked concerning the man, "and he won't come in; for he says—and really very reasonably—'What should I come in for? I can see a dirty man anywhere.'"

"You are an insolent person. Go away from my premises. Go!" said the Hermit, in an imperious and angry tone.

"Come, come!" returned Mr. Traveller, quite undisturbed. "This is a little too much. You are not going to call yourself clean? Look at your legs. And as to these being your premises:—they are in far too disgraceful a condition to claim any privilege of ownership, or anything else."

The Hermit bounced down from his window-ledge, and cast himself on his bed of soot and cinders.

"I am not going," said Mr. Traveller, glancing in after him; "you won't get rid of me in that way. You had better come and talk."

"I won't talk," said the Hermit, flouncing round to get his back towards the window.

"Then I will," said Mr. Traveller. "Why should you take it ill that I have no curiosity to know why you live this highly absurd and highly indecent life? When I contemplate a man in a state of disease, surely there is no moral obligation on me to be anxious to know how he took it."

After a short silence, the Hermit bounced up again, and came back to the barred window.

"What? You are not gone?" he said, affecting to have supposed that he was.

"Nor going," Mr. Traveller replied; "I design to pass this summer day here."

"How dare you come, sir, upon my premises——" the Hermit was returning, when his visitor interrupted him.

"Really, you know, you must *not* talk about your premises.

I cannot allow such a place as this to be dignified with the name of premises."

"How dare you," said the Hermit, shaking his bars, "come in at my gate, to taunt me with being in a diseased state?"

"Why, Lord bless my soul," returned the other, very composedly, "you have not the face to say that you are in a wholesome state? Do allow me again to call your attention to your legs. Scrape yourself anywhere—with anything—and then tell me you are in a wholesome state. The fact is, Mr. Mopes, that you are not only a Nuisance—"

"A Nuisance?" repeated the Hermit, fiercely.

"What is a place in this obscene state of dilapidation but a Nuisance? What is a man in your obscene state of dilapidation but a Nuisance? Then, as you very well know, you cannot do without an audience, and your audience is a Nuisance. You attract all the disreputable vagabonds and prowlers within ten miles around, by exhibiting yourself to them in that objectionable blanket, and by throwing copper money among them, and giving them drink out of those very dirty jars and bottles that I see in there (their stomachs need be strong!); and in short," said Mr. Traveller, summing up in a quietly and comfortably settled manner, "you are a Nuisance, and this kennel is a Nuisance, and the audience that you cannot possibly dispense with is a Nuisance, and the Nuisance is not merely a local Nuisance, because it is a general Nuisance to know that there *can be* such a Nuisance left in civilisation so very long after its time."

"Will you go away? I have a gun in here," said the Hermit.

"Pooh!"

"I *have*!"

"Now, I put it to you. Did I say you had not? And as to going away, didn't I say I am not going away? You have made me forget where I was. I now remember that I was remarking on your conduct being a Nuisance. Moreover, it is in the last and lowest degree inconsequent foolishness and weakness."

" Weakness?" echoed the Hermit.

" Weakness," said Mr. Traveller, with his former comfortably settled final air.

" I weak, you fool?" cried the Hermit, "I, who have held to my purpose, and my diet, and my only bed there, all these years?"

" The more the years, the weaker you," returned Mr. Traveller. " Though the years are not so many as folks say, and as you willingly take credit for. The crust upon your face is thick and dark, Mr. Mopes, but I can see enough of you through it, to see that you are still a young man."

" Inconsequent foolishness is lunacy, I suppose?" said the Hermit.

" I suppose it is very like it," answered Mr. Traveller.

" Do I converse like a lunatic?"

" One of us two must have a strong presumption against him of being one, whether or no. Either the clean and decorously clad man, or the dirty and indecorously clad man. I don't say which."

" Why, you self-sufficient bear," said the Hermit, " not a day passes but I am justified in my purpose by the conversations I hold here; not a day passes but I am shown, by everything I hear and see here, how right and strong I am in holding my purpose."

Mr. Traveller, lounging easily on his billet of wood, took out a pocket pipe and began to fill it. " Now, that a man," he said, appealing to the summer sky as he did so, " that a man—even behind bars, in a blanket and skewer—should tell me that he can see, from day to day, any orders or conditions of men, women, or children, who can by any possibility teach him that it is anything but the miserablest drivelling for a human creature to quarrel with his social nature—not to go so far as to say, to renounce his common human decency, for that is an extreme case; or who can teach him

that he can in any wise separate himself from his kind and
the habits of his kind, without becoming a deteriorated
spectacle calculated to give the Devil (and perhaps the
monkeys) pleasure,—is something wonderful! I repeat,
said Mr. Traveller, beginning to smoke, "the unreasoning
hardihood of it is something wonderful—even in a man with
the dirt upon him an inch or two thick—behind bars—in
a blanket and skewer!"

The Hermit looked at him irresolutely, and retired to his
soot and cinders and lay down, and got up again and came
to the bars, and again looked at him irresolutely, and finally
said with sharpness: "I don't like tobacco."

"I don't like dirt," rejoined Mr. Traveller; "tobacco is
an excellent disinfectant. We shall both be the better for
my pipe. It is my intention to sit here through this summer
day, until that blessed summer sun sinks low in the west,
and to show you what a poor creature you are, through the
lips of every chance wayfarer who may come in at your gate."

"What do you mean?" inquired the Hermit, with a
furious air.

"I mean that yonder is your gate, and there are you,
and here am I; I mean that I know it to be a moral impossibility that any person can stray in at that gate from any
point of the compass, with any sort of experience, gained at
first hand, or derived from another, that can confute me and
justify you."

"You are an arrogant and boastful hero," said the Hermit.
"You think yourself profoundly wise."

"Bah!" returned Mr. Traveller, quietly smoking. "There
is little wisdom in knowing that every man must be up and
doing, and that all mankind are made dependent on one
another."

"You have companions outside," said the Hermit. "I
am not to be imposed upon by your assumed confidence in
the people who may enter."

"A depraved distrust," returned the visitor, compassionately raising his eyebrows, "of course belongs to your state. I can't help that."

"Do you mean to tell me you have no confederates?"

"I mean to tell you nothing but what I have told you. What I have told you is, that it is a moral impossibility that any son or daughter of Adam can stand on this ground that I put my foot on, or on any ground that mortal treads, and gainsay the healthy tenure on which we hold our existence."

"Which is," sneered the Hermit, "according to you——"

"Which is," returned the other, "according to Eternal Providence, that we must arise and wash our faces and do our gregarious work and act and re-act on one another, leaving only the idiot and the palsied to sit blinking in the corner. "Come!" apostrophising the gate. "Open Sesame! Show his eyes and grieve his heart! I don't care who comes, for I know what must come of it!"

With that, he faced round a little on his billet of wood towards the gate; and Mr. Mopes, the Hermit, after two or three ridiculous bounces of indecision at his bed and back again, submitted to what he could not help himself against, and coiled himself on his window-ledge, holding to his bars and looking out rather anxiously.

VI.

THE day was by this time waning, when the gate again opened, and, with the brilliant golden light that streamed from the declining sun and touched the very bars of the sooty creature's den, there passed in a little child; a little · girl with beautiful bright hair. She wore a plain straw hat, had a door-key in her hand, and tripped towards Mr. Traveller as if she were pleased to see him and were going to repose some childish confidence in him, when she caught sight of the figure behind the bars, and started back in terror.

"Don't be alarmed, darling!" said Mr. Traveller, taking her by the hand.

"Oh, but I don't like it!" urged the shrinking child; "it's dreadful."

"Well! I don't like it either," said Mr. Traveller.

"Who has put it there?" asked the little girl. "Does it bite?"

"No,—only barks. But can't you make up your mind to see it, my dear?" For she was covering her eyes.

"O no no no!" returned the child. "I cannot bear to look at it!"

Mr. Traveller turned his head towards his friend in there, as much as to ask him how he liked that instance of his success, and then took the child out at the still open gate,

and stood talking to her for some half an hour in the
mellow sunlight. At length he returned, encouraging her
as she held his arm with both her hands; and laying his
protecting hand upon her head and smoothing her pretty
hair, he addressed his friend behind the bars as follows:

Miss Pupford's establishment for six young ladies of tender
years, is an establishment of a compact nature, an establishment in miniature, quite a pocket establishment. Miss
Pupford, Miss Pupford's assistant with the Parisian accent,
Miss Pupford's cook, and Miss Pupford's housemaid, complete
what Miss Pupford calls the educational and domestic staff
of her Lilliputian College.

Miss Pupford is one of the most amiable of her sex; it
necessarily follows that she possesses a sweet temper, and
would own to the possession of a great deal of sentiment
if she considered it quite reconcilable with her duty to
parents. Deeming it not in the bond, Miss Pupford keeps
it as far out of sight as she can—which (God bless her!) is
not very far.

Miss Pupford's assistant with the Parisian accent, may be
regarded as in some sort an inspired lady, for she never
conversed with a Parisian, and was never out of England—
except once in the pleasure-boat Lively, in the foreign waters
that ebb and flow two miles off Margate at high water.
Even under those geographically favourable circumstances
for the acquisition of the French language in its utmost
politeness and purity, Miss Pupford's assistant did not fully
profit by the opportunity; for the pleasure-boat, Lively, so
strongly asserted its title to its name on that occasion, that
she was reduced to the condition of lying in the bottom
of the boat pickling in brine—as if she were being salted
down for the use of the Navy—undergoing at the same time
great mental alarm, corporeal distress, and clear-starching
derangement.

When Miss Pupford and her assistant first foregathered,

is not known to men, or pupils. But, it was long ago. A
belief would have established itself among pupils that the
two once went to school together, were it not for the
difficulty and audacity of imagining Miss Pupford born
without mittens, and without a front, and without a bit of
gold wire among her front teeth, and without little dabs of
powder on her neat little face and nose. Indeed, whenever
Miss Pupford gives a little lecture on the mythology of the
misguided heathens (always carefully excluding Cupid from
recognition), and tells how Minerva sprang, perfectly equipped,
from the brain of Jupiter, she is half supposed to hint, " So
I myself came into the world, completely up in Pinnock,
Mangnall, Tables, and the use of the Globes."

Howbeit, Miss Pupford and Miss Pupford's assistant are
old old friends. And it is thought by pupils that, after
pupils are gone to bed, they even call one another by their
christian names in the quiet little parlour. For, once upon
a time on a thunderous afternoon, when Miss Pupford fainted
away without notice, Miss Pupford's assistant (never heard,
before or since, to address her otherwise than as Miss
Pupford) ran to her, crying out "My dearest Euphemia!"
And Euphemia is Miss Pupford's christian name on the
sampler (date picked out) hanging up in the College-hall,
where the two peacocks, terrified to death by some German
text that is waddling down hill after them out of a cottage,
are scuttling away to hide their profiles in two immense
bean-stalks growing out of flower-pots.

Also, there is a notion latent among pupils, that Miss
Pupford was once in love, and that the beloved object still
moves upon this ball. Also, that he is a public character,
and a personage of vast consequence. Also, that Miss
Pupford's assistant knows all about it. For, sometimes of
an afternoon when Miss Pupford has been reading the paper
through her little gold eye-glass (it is necessary to read it
on the spot, as the boy calls for it, with ill-conditioned
punctuality, in an hour), she has become agitated, and has

said to her assistant "G!" Then Miss Pupford's assistant
has gone to Miss Pupford, and Miss Pupford has pointed
out, with her eye-glass, G in the paper, and then Miss Pupford's assistant has read about G, and has shown sympathy.
So stimulated has the pupil-mind been in its time to curiosity
on the subject of G, that once, under temporary circumstances
favourable to the bold sally, one fearless pupil did actually
obtain possession of the paper, and range all over it in search
of G, who had been discovered therein by Miss Pupford not
ten minutes before. But no G could be identified, except
one capital offender who had been executed in a state of
great hardihood, and it was not to be supposed that Miss
Pupford could ever have loved *him*. Besides, he couldn't be
always being executed. Besides, he got into the paper again,
alive, within a month.

On the whole, it is suspected by the pupil-mind that G is
a short chubby old gentleman, with little black sealing-wax
boots up to his knees, whom a sharply observant pupil, Miss
Linx, when she once went to Tunbridge Wells with Miss
Pupford for the holidays, reported on her return (privately
and confidentially) to have seen come capering up to Miss
Pupford on the Promenade, and to have detected in the act
of squeezing Miss Pupford's hand, and to have heard
pronounce the words, "Cruel Euphemia, ever thine!"—or
something like that. Miss Linx hazarded a guess that he
might be House of Commons, or Money Market, or Court
Circular, or Fashionable Movements; which would account
for his getting into the paper so often. But, it was fatally
objected by the pupil-mind, that none of those notabilities
could possibly be spelt with a G.

There are other occasions, closely watched and perfectly
comprehended by the pupil-mind, when Miss Pupford imparts
with mystery to her assistant that there is special excitement
in the morning paper. These occasions are, when Miss
Pupford finds an old pupil coming out under the head of
Births, or Marriages. Affectionate tears are invariably seen

In Miss Pupford's meek little eyes when this is the case; and
the pupil-mind, perceiving that its order has distinguished
itself—though the fact is never mentioned by Miss Pupford
—becomes elevated, and feels that it likewise is reserved for
greatness.

Miss Pupford's assistant with the Parisian accent has a
little more bone than Miss Pupford, but is of the same trim
orderly diminutive cast, and, from long contemplation, admiration, and imitation of Miss Pupford, has grown like her.
Being entirely devoted to Miss Pupford, and having a pretty
talent for pencil-drawing, she once made a portrait of that
lady: which was so instantly identified and hailed by the
pupils, that it was done on stone at five shillings.   Surely
the softest and milkiest stone that ever was quarried, received
that likeness of Miss Pupford!   The lines of her placid little
nose are so undecided in it that strangers to the work of
art are observed to be exceedingly perplexed as to where the
nose goes to, and involuntarily feel their own noses in a
disconcerted manner.   Miss Pupford being represented in a
state of dejection at an open window, ruminating over a bowl
of gold fish, the pupil-mind has settled that the bowl was
presented by G, and that he wreathed the bowl with flowers
of soul, and that Miss Pupford is depicted as waiting for
him on a memorable occasion when he was behind his time.

The approach of the last Midsummer holidays had a
particular interest for the pupil-mind, by reason of its
knowing that Miss Pupford was bidden, on the second day
of those holidays, to the nuptials of a former pupil.   As it
was impossible to conceal the fact—so extensive were the
dress-making preparations—Miss Pupford openly announced
it.   But, she held it due to parents to make the announcement with an air of gentle melancholy, as if marriage were
(as indeed it exceptionally has been) rather a calamity.
With an air of softened resignation and pity, therefore, Miss
Pupford went on with her preparations: and meanwhile no
pupil ever went up-stairs, or came down, without peeping in

at the door of Miss Pupford's bedroom (when Miss Pupford wasn't there), and bringing back some surprising intelligence concerning the bonnet.

The extensive preparations being completed on the day before the holidays, an unanimous entreaty was preferred to Miss Pupford by the pupil-mind—finding expression through Miss Pupford's assistant—that she would deign to appear in all her splendour. Miss Pupford consenting, presented a lovely spectacle. And although the oldest pupil was barely thirteen, every one of the six became in two minutes perfect in the shape, cut, colour, price, and quality, of every article Miss Pupford wore.

Thus delightfully ushered in, the holidays began. Five of the six pupils kissed little Kitty Kimmeens twenty times over (round total, one hundred times, for she was very popular), and so went home. Miss Kitty Kimmeens remained behind, for her relations and friends were all in India, far away. A self-helpful steady little child is Miss Kitty Kimmeens: a dimpled child too, and a loving.

So, the great marriage-day came, and Miss Pupford, quite as much fluttered as any bride could be (G! thought Miss Kitty Kimmeens), went away, splendid to behold, in the carriage that was sent for her. But not Miss Pupford only went away; for Miss Pupford's assistant went away with her, on a dutiful visit to an aged uncle—though surely the venerable gentleman couldn't live in the gallery of the church where the marriage was to be, thought Miss Kitty Kimmeens—and yet Miss Pupford's assistant had let out that she was going there. Where the cook was going, didn't appear, but she generally conveyed to Miss Kimmeens that she was bound, rather against her will, on a pilgrimage to perform some pious office that rendered new ribbons necessary to her best bonnet, and also sandals to her shoes.

"So you see," said the housemaid, when they were all gone, "there's nobody left in the house but you and me, Miss Kimmeens."

"Nobody else," said Miss Kitty Kimmeens, shaking her curls a little sadly. "Nobody!"

"And you wouldn't like your Bella to go too; would you, Miss Kimmeens?" said the housemaid. (She being Bella.)

"N—no," answered little Miss Kimmeens.

"Your poor Bella is forced to stay with you, whether she likes it or not; ain't she, Miss Kimmeens?"

"*Don't* you like it?" inquired Kitty.

"Why, you're such a darling, Miss, that it would be unkind of your Bella to make objections. Yet my brother-in-law has been took unexpected bad by this morning's post. And your poor Bella is much attached to him, letting alone her favourite sister, Miss Kimmeens."

"Is he very ill?" asked little Kitty.

"Your poor Bella has her fears so, Miss Kimmeens," returned the housemaid, with her apron at her eyes. "It was but his inside, it is true, but it might mount, and the doctor said that if it mounted he wouldn't answer." Here the housemaid was so overcome that Kitty administered the only comfort she had ready: which was a kiss.

"If it hadn't been for disappointing Cook, dear Miss Kimmeens," said the housemaid, "your Bella would have asked her to stay with you. For Cook is sweet company, Miss Kimmeens, much more so than your own poor Bella."

"But you are very nice, Bella."

"Your Bella could wish to be so, Miss Kimmeens," returned the housemaid, "but she knows full well that it do not lay in her power this day."

With which despondent conviction, the housemaid drew a heavy sigh, and shook her head, and dropped it on one side.

"If it had been anyways right to disappoint Cook," she pursued, in a contemplative and abstracted manner, "it might have been so easy done! I could have got to my brother-in-law's, and had the best part of the day there, and got back, long before our ladies come home at night, and neither the one nor the other of them need never have known

it. Not that Miss Pupford would at all object, but that it
might put her out, being tender-hearted. Hows'ever, your
own poor Bella, Miss Kimmeens," said the housemaid, rousing
herself, "is forced to stay with you, and you're a precious
love, if not a liberty."

"Bella," said little Kitty, after a short silence.

"Call your own poor Bella, *your* Bella, dear," the housemaid besought her.

"My Bella, then."

"Bless your considerate heart!" said the housemaid.

"If you would not mind leaving me, I should not mind
being left. I am not afraid to stay in the house alone. And
you need not be uneasy on my account, for I would be very
careful to do no harm."

"O! As to harm, you more than sweetest, if not a
liberty," exclaimed the housemaid, in a rapture, "your Bella
could trust you anywhere, being so steady, and so answerable.
The oldest head in this house (me and Cook says), but for
its bright hair, is Miss Kimmeens. But no, I will not leave
you; for you would think your Bella unkind."

"But if you are my Bella, you *must* go," returned the
child.

"Must I?" said the housemaid, rising, on the whole with
alacrity. "What must be, must be, Miss Kimmeens. Your
own poor Bella acts according, though unwilling. But go
or stay, your own poor Bella loves you, Miss Kimmeens."

It was certainly go, and not stay, for within five minutes
Miss Kimmeens's own poor Bella—so much improved in point
of spirits as to have grown almost sanguine on the subject
of her brother-in-law—went her way, in apparel that seemed
to have been expressly prepared for some festive occasion.
Such are the changes of this fleeting world, and so short-
sighted are we poor mortals!

When the house door closed with a bang and a shake, it
seemed to Miss Kimmeens to be a very heavy house door,
shutting her up in a wilderness of a house. But, Miss

Kimmeens being, as before stated, of a self-reliant and methodical character, presently began to parcel out the long summer-day before her.

And first she thought she would go all over the house, to make quite sure that nobody with a great-coat on and a carving-knife in it, had got under one of the beds or into one of the cupboards. Not that she had ever before been troubled by the image of anybody armed with a great-coat and a carving-knife, but that it seemed to have been shaken into existence by the shake and the bang of the great street door, reverberating through the solitary house. So, little Miss Kimmeens looked under the five empty beds of the five departed pupils, and looked under her own bed, and looked under Miss Pupford's bed, and looked under Miss Pupford's assistant's bed. And when she had done this, and was making the tour of the cupboards, the disagreeable thought came into her young head, What a very alarming thing it would be to find somebody with a mask on, like Guy Fawkes, hiding bolt upright in a corner and pretending not to be alive! However, Miss Kimmeens having finished her inspection without making any such uncomfortable discovery, sat down in her tidy little manner to needlework, and began stitching away at a great rate.

The silence all about her soon grew very oppressive, and the more so because of the odd inconsistency that the more silent it was, the more noises there were. The noise of her own needle and thread as she stitched, was infinitely louder in her ears than the stitching of all the six pupils, and of Miss Pupford, and of Miss Pupford's assistant, all stitching away at once on a highly emulative afternoon. Then, the school-room clock conducted itself in a way in which it had never conducted itself before—fell lame, somehow, and yet persisted in running on as hard and as loud as it could: the consequence of which behaviour was, that it staggered among the minutes in a state of the greatest confusion, and knocked them about in all directions without appearing to get on with its regular work. Perhaps this alarmed the stairs: but be that as it might, they began to creak in a most unusual manner, and then the furniture began to crack, and then poor little Miss Kimmeens, not liking the furtive aspect of things in general, began to sing as she stitched. But, it was not her own voice that she heard—it was somebody else making believe to be Kitty, and singing excessively flat, without any heart—so as that would never mend matters, she left off again.

By and by, the stitching became so palpable a failure that Miss Kitty Kimmeens folded her work neatly, and put it away in its box, and gave it up. Then the question arose about reading. But no; the book that was so delightful when there was somebody she loved for her eyes to fall on when they rose from the page, had not more heart in it than her own singing now. The book went to its shelf as the needlework had gone to its box, and, since something *must* be done—thought the child, "I'll go put my room to rights."

She shared her room with her dearest little friend among the other five pupils, and why then should she now conceive a lurking dread of the little friend's bedstead? But she did. There was a stealthy air about its innocent white curtains, and there were even dark hints of a dead girl lying under the coverlet. The great want of human company, the great need of a human face, began now to express itself in the facility with which the furniture put on strange exaggerated resemblances to human looks. A chair with a menacing frown was horribly out of temper in a corner; a most vicious chest of drawers snarled at her from between the windows. It was no relief to escape from those monsters to the looking-glass, for the reflection said, "What? Is that you all alone there? How you stare!" And the background was all a great void stare as well.

The day dragged on, dragging Kitty with it very slowly by the hair of her head, until it was time to eat. There were good provisions in the pantry, but their right flavour and relish had evaporated with the five pupils, and Miss Pupford, and Miss Pupford's assistant, and the cook and housemaid. Where was the use of laying the cloth symmetrically for one small guest, who had gone on ever since the morning growing smaller and smaller, while the empty house had gone on swelling larger and larger? The very Grace came out wrong, for who were "we" who were going to receive and be thankful? So, Miss Kimmeens was *not* thankful, and found herself taking her dinner in very slovenly style— gobbling it up, in short, rather after the manner of the lower animals, not to particularise the pigs.

But, this was by no means the worst of the change wrought out in the naturally loving and cheery little creature as the solitary day wore on. She began to brood and be suspicious. She discovered that she was full of wrongs and injuries. All the people she knew, got tainted by her lonely thoughts and turned bad.

It was all very well for Papa, a widower in India, to send her home to be educated, and to pay a handsome round sum every year for her to Miss Pupford, and to write charming letters to his darling little daughter; but what did he care for her being left by herself, when he was (as no doubt he always was) enjoying himself in company from morning till night? Perhaps he only sent her here, after all, to get her out of the way. It looked like it—looked like it to-day, that is, for she had never dreamed of such a thing before.

And this old pupil who was being married. It was insupportably conceited and selfish in the old pupil to be married. She was very vain, and very glad to show off; but it was highly probable that she wasn't pretty; and even if she were pretty (which Miss Kimmeens now totally denied), she had no business to be married; and, even if marriage were conceded, she had no business to ask Miss Pupford to her wedding. As to Miss Pupford, she was too old to go to any wedding. She ought to know that. She had much better attend to her business. She had thought she looked nice in the morning, but she didn't look nice. She was a stupid old thing. G was another stupid old thing. Miss Pupford's assistant was another. They were all stupid old things together.

More than that: it began to be obvious that this was a plot. They had said to one another, "Never mind Kitty; you get off, and I'll get off; and we'll leave Kitty to look after herself. Who cares for *her?*" To be sure they were right in that question; for who *did* care for her, a poor little lonely thing against whom they all planned and plotted? Nobody, nobody! Here Kitty sobbed.

At all other times she was the pet of the whole house, and loved her five companions in return with a child's tenderest and most ingenuous attachment; but now, the five companions put on ugly colours, and appeared for the first time under a sullen cloud. There they were, all at their homes that day, being made much of, being taken out, being spoilt and made disagreeable, and caring nothing for her. It was like their artful selfishness always to tell her when they came back, under pretence of confidence and friendship, all those details about where they had been, and what they had done and seen, and how often they had said, "O! If we had only darling little Kitty here!" Here indeed! I dare say! When they came back after the holidays, they were used to being received by Kitty, and to saying that coming to Kitty was like coming to another home. Very well then, why did they go away? If they meant it, why did they go away? Let them answer that. But they didn't mean it, and couldn't answer that, and they didn't tell the truth, and people who didn't tell the truth were hateful. When they came back next time, they should be received in a new manner; they should be avoided and shunned.

And there, the while she sat all alone revolving how ill she was used, and how much better she was than the people who were not alone, the wedding breakfast was going on: no question of it! With a nasty great bride-cake, and with those ridiculous orange-flowers, and with that conceited bride, and that hideous bridegroom, and those heartless bridesmaids, and Miss Pupford stuck up at the table! They thought they were enjoying themselves, but it would come home to them one day to have thought so. They would all be dead in a few years, let them enjoy themselves ever so much. It was a religious comfort to know that.

It was such a comfort to know it, that little Miss Kitty Kimmeens suddenly sprang from the chair in which she had been musing in a corner, and cried out, "O those envious thoughts are not mine, O this wicked creature isn't me! Help me, somebody! I go wrong, alone by my weak self! Help me, anybody!"

"—Miss Kimmeens is not a professed philosopher, sir," said Mr. Traveller, presenting her at the barred window, and smoothing her shining hair, "but I apprehend there was some tincture of philosophy in her words, and in the prompt action with which she followed them. That action was, to emerge from her unnatural solitude, and look abroad for wholesome sympathy, to bestow and to receive. Her footsteps strayed to this gate, bringing her here by chance, as an apposite contrast to you. The child came out, sir. If you have the wisdom to learn from a child (but I doubt it, for that requires more wisdom than one in your condition would seem to possess), you cannot do better than imitate the child, and come out too—from that very demoralising hutch of yours."

PICKING UP THE TINKER.

It was now sunset. The Hermit had betaken himself to his
bed of cinders half an hour ago, and lying on it in his
blanket and skewer with his back to the window, took not
the smallest heed of the appeal addressed to him.

All that had been said for the last two hours, had been
said to a tinkling accompaniment performed by the Tinker,
who had got to work upon some villager's pot or kettle, and
was working briskly outside. This music still continuing,
seemed to put it into Mr. Traveller's mind to have another
word or two with the Tinker. So, holding Miss Kimmeens
(with whom he was now on the most friendly terms) by the
hand, he went out at the gate to where the Tinker was
seated at his work on the patch of grass on the opposite
side of the road, with his wallet of tools open before him,
and his little fire smoking.

"I am glad to see you employed," said Mr. Traveller.

"I am glad to *be* employed," returned the Tinker, looking
up as he put the finishing touches to his job. "But why
are you glad?"

"I thought you were a lazy fellow when I saw you this
morning."

"I was only disgusted," said the Tinker.

"Do you mean with the fine weather?"

"With the fine weather?" repeated the Tinker, staring.

"You told me you were not particular as to weather, and I thought——"

"Ha, ha! How should such as me get on, if we *was* particular as to weather? We must take it as it comes, and make the best of it. There's something good in all weathers. If it don't happen to be good for my work to-day, it's good for some other man's to-day, and will come round to me to-morrow. We must all live."

"Pray shake hands," said Mr. Traveller.

"Take care, sir," was the Tinker's caution, as he reached up his hand in surprise; "the black comes off."

"I am glad of it," said Mr. Traveller. "I have been for several hours among other black that does not come off."

"You are speaking of Tom in there?"

"Yes."

"Well now," said the Tinker, blowing the dust off his job: which was finished. "Ain't it enough to disgust a pig, if he could give his mind to it?"

"If he could give his mind to it," returned the other, smiling, "the probability is that he wouldn't be a pig."

"There you clench the nail," returned the Tinker. "Then what's to be said for Tom?"

"Truly, very little."

"Truly nothing you mean, sir," said the Tinker, as he put away his tools.

"A better answer, and (I freely acknowledge) my meaning. I infer that he was the cause of your disgust?"

"Why, look'ee here, sir," said the Tinker, rising to his feet, and wiping his face on the corner of his black apron energetically; "I leave you to judge!—I ask you!—Last night I has a job that needs to be done in the night, and I works all night. Well, there's nothing in that. But this morning I comes along this road here, looking for a sunny and soft spot to sleep in, and I sees this desolation and ruination. I've lived myself in desolation and ruination; I knows many a fellow-creetur that's forced to live life long in

desolation and ruination; and I sits me down and takes pity
on it, as I casts my eyes about. Then comes up the long-
winded one as I told you of, from that gate, and spins
himself out like a silkworm concerning the Donkey (if my
Donkey at home will excuse me) as has made it all—made
it of his own choice! And tells me, if you please, of his
likewise choosing to go ragged and naked, and grimy—
maskerading, mountebanking, in what is the real hard lot of
thousands and thousands! Why, then I say it's a unbearable
and nonsensical piece of inconsistency, and I'm disgusted. I'm
ashamed and disgusted!"

"I wish you would come and look at him," said Mr.
Traveller, clapping the Tinker on the shoulder.

"Not I, sir," he rejoined. "*I* ain't a going to flatter him
up by looking at him!"

"But he is asleep."

"Are you sure he is asleep?" asked the Tinker, with an
unwilling air, as he shouldered his wallet.

"Sure."

"Then I'll look at him for a quarter of a minute," said
the Tinker, "since you so much wish it; but not a moment
longer."

They all three went back across the road; and, through
the barred window, by the dying glow of the sunset coming in
at the gate—which the child held open for its admission—he
could be pretty clearly discerned lying on his bed.

"You see him?" asked Mr. Traveller.

"Yes," returned the Tinker, "and he's worse than I
thought him."

Mr. Traveller then whispered in few words what he had
done since morning; and asked the Tinker what he thought
of that?

"I think," returned the Tinker, as he turned from the
window, "that you've wasted a day on him."

"I think so too; though not, I hope, upon myself. Do
you happen to be going anywhere near the Peal of Bells?"

"'That's my direct way, sir," said the Tinker.

"I invite you to supper there. And as I learn from this young lady that she goes some three-quarters of a mile in the same direction, we will drop her on the road, and we will spare time to keep her company at her garden gate until her own Bella comes home."

So, Mr. Traveller, and the child, and the Tinker, went along very amicably in the sweet-scented evening; and the moral with which the Tinker dismissed the subject was, that he said in his trade that metal that rotted for want of use, had better be left to rot, and couldn't rot too soon, considering how much true metal rotted from over-use and hard service.

SOMEBODY'S LUGGAGE

[1862]

SOMEBODY'S LUGGAGE.

In four Chapters.

CHAPTER I.

HIS LEAVING IT TILL CALLED FOR.

THE writer of these humble lines being a Waiter, and having come of a family of Waiters, and owning at the present time five brothers who are all Waiters, and likewise an only sister who is a Waitress, would wish to offer a few words respecting his calling; first having the pleasure of hereby in a friendly manner offering the Dedication of the same unto JOSEPH, much respected Head Waiter at the Slamjam Coffee-house, London, E.C., than which a individual more eminently deserving of the name of man, or a more amenable honour to his own head and heart, whether considered in the light of a Waiter or regarded as a human being, do not exist.

In case confusion should arise in the public mind (which it is open to confusion on many subjects) respecting what is meant or implied by the term Waiter, the present humble lines would wish to offer an explanation. It may not be generally known that the person as goes out to wait is *not* a Waiter. It may not be generally known that the hand as is called in extra, at the Freemasons' Tavern, or the London, or the Albion, or otherwise, is *not* a Waiter. Such hands may be took on for Public Dinners by the bushel (and you may know them by their breathing with difficulty when in attendance, and taking away the bottle ere yet it is half out); but such are *not* Waiters. For you cannot lay down the tailoring, or the shoemaking, or the brokering, or the green-grocering, or the pictorial-periodicalling, or the second-hand wardrobe, or the small fancy businesses,—you cannot lay down those lines of life at your will and pleasure by the half-day or evening, and take up Waitering. You may suppose you can, but you cannot; or you may go so far as to say you do, but you do not. Nor yet can you lay down the gentleman's-service when stimulated by prolonged incompatibility on the part of Cooks (and here it may be remarked that Cooking and Incompatibility will be mostly found united), and take up Waitering. It has been ascertained that what a gentleman will sit meek under, at home, he will not bear out of doors, at the Slamjam or any similar establishment. Then, what is the inference to be drawn respecting true Waitering? You must be bred to it. You must be born to it.

Would you know how born to it, Fair Reader,—if of the adorable female sex? Then learn from the biographical experience of one that is a Waiter in the sixty-first year of his age.

You were conveyed,—ere yet your dawning powers were otherwise developed than to harbour vacancy in your inside, —you were conveyed, by surreptitious means, into a pantry adjoining the Admiral Nelson, Civic and General Dining-Rooms, there to receive by stealth that healthful sustenance which is the pride and boast of the British female constitution. Your mother was married to your father (himself a distant Waiter) in the profoundest secrecy; for a Waitress known to be married would ruin the best of businesses,—it is the same as on the stage. Hence your being smuggled into the pantry, and that—to add to the infliction—by an unwilling grandmother. Under the combined influence of the smells of roast and boiled, and soup, and gas, and malt liquors, you partook of your earliest nourishment; your unwilling grandmother sitting prepared to catch you when your mother was called and dropped you; your grandmother's shawl ever ready to stifle your natural complainings; your innocent mind surrounded by uncongenial cruets, dirty plates, dish-covers, and cold gravy; your mother calling down the pipe for veals and porks, instead of soothing you with nursery rhymes. Under these untoward circumstances you were early weaned. Your unwilling grandmother, ever growing more unwilling as your food assimilated less, then contracted habits of shaking you till your system curdled, and your food would not assimilate at all. At length she was no longer spared, and could have been thankfully spared much sooner. When your brothers began to appear in succession, your mother retired, left off her smart dressing (she had previously been a smart dresser), and her dark ringlets (which had previously been flowing), and haunted your father late of nights, lying in wait for him, through all weathers, up the shabby court which led to the back door of the Royal Old Dust-Bin (said to have been so named by George the Fourth), where your father was Head. But the Dust-Bin was going down then, and your father took but little,—excepting from a liquid point of view. Your mother's object in those visits was of a housekeeping character, and you was set on to whistle your father out. Sometimes he came out, but generally not. Come or not come, however, all that part of his existence which was unconnected with open Waitering was kept a close secret, and was acknowledged by your mother to be a close secret, and you and your mother flitted about the court, close secrets both of you, and would scarcely have confessed under torture that you knew your father, or that your father had any name than Dick (which wasn't his name, though he was never known by any other), or that he had kith or kin or chick or child. Perhaps the attraction of this mystery, combined with your father's having a damp compartment to himself, behind a leaky cistern, at the Dust-Bin,—a sort of a cellar compartment, with a sink in it, and a smell, and a

plate-rack, and a bottle-rack, and three windows that didn't
match each other or anything else, and no daylight,—caused
your young mind to feel convinced that you must grow up
to be a Waiter too; but you did feel convinced of it, and
so did all your brothers, down to your sister. Every one of
you felt convinced that you was born to the Waitering. At
this stage of your career, what was your feelings one day
when your father came home to your mother in open broad
daylight,—of itself an act of Madness on the part of a Waiter,
—and took to his bed (leastwise, your mother and family's
bed), with the statement that his eyes were devilled kidneys.
Physicians being in vain, your father expired, after repeating
at intervals for a day and a night, when gleams of reason
and old business fitfully illuminated his being, "Two and
two is five.   And three is sixpence." Interred in the parochial
department of the neighbouring churchyard, and accompanied
to the grave by as many Waiters of long standing as could
spare the morning time from their soiled glasses (namely,
one), your bereaved form was attired in a white neckankecher,
and you was took on from motives of benevolence at The
George and Gridiron, theatrical and supper.   Here, supporting
nature on what you found in the plates (which was as it
happened, and but too often thoughtlessly, immersed in
mustard), and on what you found in the glasses (which rarely
went beyond driblets and lemon), by night you dropped asleep
standing, till you was cuffed awake, and by day was set to
polishing every individual article in the coffee-room.   Your
couch being sawdust; your counterpane being ashes of cigars.
Here, frequently hiding a heavy heart under the smart tie
of your white neckankecher (or correctly speaking lower
down and more to the left), you picked up the rudiments of
knowledge from an extra, by the name of Bishops, and by
calling plate-washer, and gradually elevating your mind with
chalk on the back of the corner-box partition, until such time
as you used the inkstand when it was out of hand, attained
to manhood, and to be the Waiter that you find yourself.

I could wish here to offer a few respectful words on behalf
of the calling so long the calling of myself and family, and
the public interest in which is but too often very limited.
We are not generally understood. No, we are not. Allowance
enough is not made for us. For, say that we ever show a
little drooping listlessness of spirits, or what might be termed
indifference or apathy. Put it to yourself what would your
own state of mind be, if you was one of an enormous family
every member of which except you was always greedy, and
in a hurry. Put it to yourself that you was regularly replete
with animal food at the slack hours of one in the day and
again at nine P.M., and that the repleter you was, the more
voracious all your fellow-creatures came in. Put it to
yourself that it was your business, when your digestion was
well on, to take a personal interest and sympathy in a
hundred gentlemen fresh and fresh (say, for the sake of
argument, only a hundred), whose imaginations was given
up to grease and fat and gravy and melted butter, and
abandoned to questioning you about cuts of this, and dishes
of that,—each of 'em going on as if him and you and the
bill of fare was alone in the world. Then look what you
are expected to know. You are never out, but they seem
to think you regularly attend everywhere. "What's this,
Christopher, that I hear about the smashed Excursion Train?"
—"How are they doing at the Italian Opera, Christopher?"
—"Christopher, what are the real particulars of this business
at the Yorkshire Bank?" Similarly a ministry gives me
more trouble than it gives the Queen. As to Lord Palmerston,
the constant and wearing connection into which I have been
brought with his lordship during the last few years is deserving of a pension. Then look at the Hypocrites we are made,
and the lies (white, I hope) that are forced upon us! Why
must a sedentary-pursuited Waiter be considered to be a
judge of horseflesh, and to have a most tremenjous interest
in horse-training and racing? Yet it would be half our
little incomes out of our pockets if we didn't take on to

have those sporting tastes. It is the same (inconceivable why!) with Farming. Shooting, equally so. I am sure that so regular as the months of August, September, and October come round, I am ashamed of myself in my own private bosom for the way in which I make believe to care whether or not the grouse is strong on the wing (much their wings, or drumsticks either, signifies to me, uncooked!), and whether the partridges is plentiful among the turnips, and whether the pheasants is shy or bold, or anything else you please to mention. Yet you may see me, or any other Waiter of my standing, holding on by the back of the box, and leaning over a gentleman with his purse out and his bill before him, discussing these points in a confidential tone of voice, as if my happiness in life entirely depended on 'em.

I have mentioned our little incomes. Look at the most unreasonable point of all, and the point on which the greatest injustice is done us! Whether it is owing to our always carrying so much change in our right-hand trousers-pocket, and so many halfpence in our coat-tails, or whether it is human nature (which I were loth to believe), what is meant by the everlasting fable that Head Waiters is rich? How did that fable get into circulation? Who first put it about, and what are the facts to establish the unblushing statement? Come forth, thou slanderer, and refer the public to the Waiter's will in Doctors' Commons supporting thy malignant hiss! Yet this is so commonly dwelt upon—especially by the screws who give Waiters the least—that denial is vain; and we are obliged, for our credit's sake, to carry our heads as if we were going into a business, when of the two we are much more likely to go into a union. There was formerly a screw as frequented the Slamjam ere yet the present writer had quitted that establishment on a question of tea-ing his assistant staff out of his own pocket, which screw carried the taunt to its bitterest height. Never soaring above threepence, and as often as not grovelling on the earth a penny lower, he yet represented the present writer as a large holder of

Consols, a lender of money on mortgage, a Capitalist. He has been overheard to dilate to other customers on the allegation that the present writer put out thousands of pounds at interest in Distilleries and Breweries. " Well, Christopher," he would say (having grovelled his lowest on the earth, half a moment before), " looking out for a House to open, eh? Can't find a business to be disposed of on a scale as is up to your resources, humph?" To such a dizzy precipice of falsehood has this misrepresentation taken wing, that the well-known and highly-respected OLD CHARLES, long eminent at the West Country Hotel, and by some considered the Father of the Waitering, found himself under the obligation to fall into it through so many years that his own wife (for he had an unbeknown old lady in that capacity towards himself) believed it! And what was the consequence? When he was borne to his grave on the shoulders of six picked Waiters, with six more for change, six more acting as pall-bearers, all keeping step in a pouring shower without a dry eye visible, and a concourse only inferior to Royalty, his pantry and lodgings was equally ransacked high and low for property, and none was found! How could it be found, when, beyond his last monthly collection of walking-sticks, umbrellas, and pocket-handkerchiefs (which happened to have been not yet disposed of, though he had ever been through life punctual in clearing off his collections by the month), there was no property existing? Such, however, is the force of this universal libel, that the widow of Old Charles, at the present hour an inmate of the Almshouses of the Cork-Cutters' Company, in Blue Anchor-road (identified sitting at the door of one of 'em, in a clean cap and a Windsor arm-chair, only last Monday), expects John's hoarded wealth to be found hourly! Nay, ere yet he had succumbed to the grisly dart, and when his portrait was painted in oils life-size, by subscription of the frequenters of the West Country, to hang over the coffee-room chimney-piece, there were not wanting those who contended that what is termed the accessories of such a portrait ought to be the Bank of England out of window, and a strong-box on the table. And but for better-regulated minds contending for a bottle and screw and the attitude of drawing,—and carrying their point,—it would have been so handed down to posterity.

I am now brought to the title of the present remarks. Having, I hope without offence to any quarter, offered such observations as I felt it my duty to offer, in a free country which has ever dominated the seas, on the general subject, I will now proceed to wait on the particular question.

At a momentous period of my life, when I was off, so far as concerned notice given, with a House that shall be nameless,—for the question on which I took my departing stand was a fixed charge for waiters, and no House as commits itself to that eminently Un-English act of more than foolishness and baseness shall be advertised by me,—I repeat, at a momentous crisis, when I was off with a House too mean for mention, and not yet on with that to which I have ever since had the honour of being attached in the capacity of Head,* I was casting about what to do next. Then it were that proposals were made to me on behalf of my present establishment. Stipulations were necessary on my part, emendations were necessary on my part: in the end, ratifications ensued on both sides, and I entered on a new career.

We are a bed business, and a coffee-room business. We are not a general dining business, nor do we wish it. In consequence, when diners drop in, we know what to give 'em as will keep 'em away another time. We are a Private Room or Family business also; but Coffee-room principal. Me and the Directory and the Writing Materials and cetrer occupy a place to ourselves—a place fended off up a step or two at the end of the Coffee-room, in what I call the good old-fashioned style. The good old-fashioned style is, that whatever you want, down to a wafer, you must be olely and solely dependent

* Its name and address at length, with other full particulars, all editorially struck out.

on the Head Waiter for. You must put yourself a new-born Child into his hands. There is no other way in which a business untinged with Continental Vice can be conducted. (It were bootless to add, that if languages is required to be jabbered and English is not good enough, both families and gentlemen had better go somewhere else.)

When I began to settle down in this right-principled and well-conducted House, I noticed, under the bed in No. 24 B (which it is up a anglo off the staircase, and usually put off upon the lowly-minded), a heap of things in a corner. I asked our Head Chambermaid in the course of the day,

" What are them things in 24 B ? "

To which she answered with a careless air,

" Somebody's Luggage.",.

Regarding her with a eye not free from severity, I says,

" Whose Luggage ? "

Evading my eye, she replied,

" Lor! How should *I* know ! "

—Being, it' may be right to mention, a female of some pertness, though acquainted with her business.

A Head Waiter must be either Head or Tail. He must be at one extremity or the other of the social scale. He cannot be at the waist of it, or anywhere else but the extremities. It is for him to decide which of the extremities.

On the eventful occasion under consideration, I give Mrs. Pratchett so distinctly to understand my decision, that I broke her spirit as towards myself, then and there, and for good. Let not inconsistency be suspected on account of my mentioning Mrs. Pratchett as " Mrs.," and having formerly remarked that a waitress must not be married. Readers are respectfully requested to notice that Mrs. Pratchett was not a waitress, but a chambermaid. Now a chambermaid *may* be married; if Head, generally is married,—or says so. It comes to the same thing as expressing what is customary. (N.B. Mr. Pratchett is in Australia, and his address there is " the Bush.")

Having took Mrs. Pratchett down as many pegs as was

essential to the future happiness of all parties, I requested
her to explain herself.

" For instance," I says, to give her a little encouragement,
" who is Somebody ? "

" I give you my sacred honour, Mr. Christopher," answers
Pratchett, " that I haven't the faintest notion."

But for the manner in which she settled her cap-strings,
I should have doubted this; but in respect of positiveness it
was hardly to be discriminated from an affidavit.

" Then you never saw him?" I followed her up with.

" Nor yet," said Mrs. Pratchett, shutting her eyes and
making as if she had just took a pill of unusual circumference,
—which gave a remarkable force to her denial,—" nor yet
any servant in this house. All have been changed, Mr.
Christopher, within five year, and Somebody left his Luggage
here before then."

Inquiry of Miss Martin yielded (in the language of the
Bard of A. 1.) "confirmation strong." So it had really and
truly happened. Miss Martin is the young lady at the bar
as makes out our bills; and though higher than I could wish
considering her station, is perfectly well-behaved.

Farther investigations led to the disclosure that there was
a bill against this Luggage to the amount of two sixteen six.
The luggage had been lying under the bedstead of 24 B over
six year. The bedstead is a four-poster, with a deal of old
hanging and valance, and is, as I once said, probably connected with more than 24 Bs,—which I remember my hearers
was pleased to laugh at, at the time.

I don't know why,—when DO we know why?—but this
Luggage laid heavy on my mind. I fell a wondering about
Somebody, and what he had got and been up to. I couldn't
satisfy my thoughts why he should leave so much Luggage
against so small a bill. For I had the Luggage out within
a day or two and turned it over, and the following were the
items :—A black portmanteau, a black bag, a desk, a dressing-case, a brown-paper parcel, a hat-box, and an umbrella

strapped to a walking-stick. It was all very dusty and fluey.
I had our porter up to get under the bed and fetch it out;
and though he habitually wallows in dust,—swims in it from
morning to night, and wears a close-fitting waistcoat with
black calimanco sleeves for the purpose,—it made him sneeze
again, and his throat was that hot with it that it was
obliged to be cooled with a drink of Allsopp's draft.

The Luggage so got the better of me, that instead of
having it put back when it was well dusted and washed with
a wet cloth,—previous to which it was so covered with
feathers that you might have thought it was turning into
poultry, and would by and by begin to Lay,—I say, instead
of having it put back, I had it carried into one of my places
down-stairs. There from time to time I stared at it and
stared at it, till it seemed to grow big and grow little, and
come forward at me and retreat again, and go through all
manner of performances resembling intoxication. When this
had lasted weeks,—I may say months, and not be far out,—
I one day thought of asking Miss Martin for the particulars
of the Two sixteen six total. She was so obliging as to
extract it from the books,—it dating before her time,—and
here follows a true copy:

Coffee-Room.

						£	s.	d.
1856.		No. 4.						
Feb. 2d, Pen and Paper		.	.	.	.	0	0	6
	Port Negus	.	.	.	.	0	2	0
	Ditto	.	.	.	.	0	2	0
	Pen and Paper	.	.	.	.	0	0	6
	Tumbler broken	.	.	.	.	0	2	6
	Brandy	.	.	.	.	0	2	0
	Pen and paper	.	.	.	.	0	0	6
	Anchovy toast	.	.	.	.	0	2	6
	Pen and paper	.	.	.	.	0	0	6
	Bed	.	.	.	.	0	3	0
	Carried forward		.	.	0	16	0

		£	s	d
Brought forward	.	0	16	0
Feb. 3d, Pen and paper . . .	.	0	0	6
Breakfast . . .	.	0	2	6
„ Broiled ham . .	.	0	2	0
„ Eggs . . .	.	0	1	0
„ Watercresses . .	.	0	1	0
Breakfast—Shrimps . . .	.	0	1	0
Pen and paper . . .	.	0	0	6
Blotting-paper . . .	.	0	0	6
Messenger to Paternoster-row and back	.	0	1	6
Again, when No Answer . . .		0	1	6
Brandy 2s., Devilled Pork chop 2s.		0	4	0
Pens and paper . . .	.	0	1	0
Messenger to Albemarle-street and back	.	0	1	0
Again (detained), when No Answer .		0	1	6
Salt-cellar broken . . .	.	0	3	6
Large Liqueur-glass Orange Brandy		0	1	6
Dinner, Soup, Fish, Joint, and bird .		0	7	6
Bottle old East India Brown .	.	0	8	0
Pen and paper . . .	.	0	0	6
		£2	16	6

Mem. : January 1st, 1857. He went out after dinner, directing Luggage to be ready when he called for it. Never called.

So far from throwing a light upon the subject, this bill appeared to me, if I may so express my doubts, to involve it in a yet more lurid halo. Speculating it over with the Mistress, she informed me that the luggage had been advertised in the Master's time as being to be sold after such and such a day to pay expenses, but no farther steps had been taken. (I may here remark, that the Mistress is a widow in her fourth year. The Master was possessed of one of those unfortunate

constitutions in which Spirits turns to Water, and rises in
the ill-starred Victim.)

My speculating it over, not then only, but repeatedly,
sometimes with the Mistress, sometimes with one, sometimes
with another, led up to the Mistress's saying to me,—whether
at first in joke or in earnest, or half joke and half earnest, it
matters not:

"Christopher, I am going to make you a handsome offer."

(If this should meet her eye—a lovely blue,—may she not
take it ill my mentioning that if I had been eight or ten
year younger, I would have done as much by her! That is,
I would have made her a offer. It is for others than me
to denominate it a handsome one.)

"Christopher, I am going to make you a handsome offer."

"Put a name to it, ma'am."

"Look here, Christopher. Run over the articles of Somebody's Luggage. You've got it all by heart, I know."

"A black portmanteau, ma'am, a black bag, a desk, a
dressing-case, a brown-paper parcel, a hat-box, and an
umbrella strapped to a walking-stick."

"All just as they were left. Nothing opened, nothing
tampered with."

"You are right, ma'am. All locked but the brown-paper
parcel, and that sealed."

The Mistress was leaning on Miss Martin's desk at the
bar-window, and she taps the open book that lays upon the
desk,—she has a pretty-made hand to be sure,—and bobs her
head over it and laughs.

"Come," says she, "Christopher. Pay me Somebody's bill,
and you shall have Somebody's Luggage."

I rather took to the idea from the first moment; but,

"It mayn't be worth the money," I objected, seeming to
hold back.

"That's a Lottery," says the Mistress, folding her arms
upon the book,—it ain't her hands alone that's pretty made,
the observation extends right up her arms. "Won't you

venture two pound sixteen shillings and sixpence in the
Lottery? Why, there's no blanks!" says the Mistress, laughing and bobbing her head again, "you *must* win. If you
lose, you must win! All prizes in this Lottery! Draw a
blank, and remember, Gentlemen-Sportsmen, you'll still be
entitled to a black portmanteau, a black bag, a desk, a dressing-case, a sheet of brown paper, a hat-box, and an umbrella
strapped to a walking-stick!"

To make short of it, Miss Martin come round me, and
Mrs. Pratchett come round me, and the Mistress she was
completely round me already, and all the women in the
house come round me, and if it had been Sixteen two instead
of Two sixteen, I should have thought myself well out of it.
For what can you do when they do come round you?

So I paid the money—down—and such a laughing as there
was among 'em! But I turned the tables on 'em regularly,
when I said:

"My family-name is Blue-Beard. I'm going to open Somebody's Luggage all alone in the Secret Chamber, and not a
female eye catches sight of the contents!"

Whether I thought proper to have the firmness to keep to
this, don't signify, or whether any female eye, and if any,
how many, was really present when the opening of the
Luggage came off. Somebody's Luggage is the question at
present: Nobody's eyes, nor yet noses.

What I still look at most, in connection with that Luggage, is the extraordinary quantity of writing-paper, and
all written on! And not our paper neither,—not the paper
charged in the bill, for we know our paper,—so he must
have been always at it. And he had crumpled up this
writing of his, everywhere, in every part and parcel of his
luggage. There was writing in his dressing-case, writing in
his boots, writing among his shaving-tackle, writing in his
hat-box, writing folded away down among the very whalebones
of his umbrella.

His clothes wasn't bad, what there was of 'em. His

dressing-case was poor,—not a particle of silver stopper,—bottle apertures with nothing in 'em, like empty little dog-kennels,—and a most searching description of tooth-powder diffusing itself around, as under a deluded mistake that all the chinks in the fittings was divisions in teeth. His clothes I parted with, well enough, to a second-hand dealer not far from St. Clement's Danes, in the Strand,—him as the officers in the Army mostly dispose of their uniforms to, when hard pressed with debts of honour, if I may judge from their coats and epaulets diversifying the window with their backs towards the public. The same party bought in one lot the port-manteau, the bag, the desk, the dressing-case, the hat-box, the umbrella, strap, and walking-stick. On my remarking that I should have thought those articles not quite in his line, he said : "No more ith a man'th grandmother, Mithter Chrith-topher; but if any man will bring hith grandmother here, and offer her at a fair trifle below what the'll feth with good luck when the'th thcoured and turned—I'll buy her!"

These transactions brought me home, and, indeed, more than home, for they left a goodish profit on the original investment. And now there remained the writings ; and the writings I particular wish to bring under the candid attention of the reader.

I wish to do so without postponement, for this reason. This is to say, namely, viz. i.e., as follows, thus:—Before I proceed to recount the mental sufferings of which I became the prey in consequence of the writings, and before following up that harrowing tale with a statement of the wonderful and impressive catastrophe, as thrilling in its nature as unlooked for in any other capacity, which crowned the ole and filled the cup of unexpectedness to overflowing, the writings themselves ought to stand forth to view. Therefore it is that they now come next. One word to introduce them, and I lay down my pen (I hope, my unassuming pen) until I take it up to trace the gloomy sequel of a mind with something on it.

He was a smeary writer, and wrote a dreadful bad hand. Utterly regardless of ink, he lavished it on every undeserving object,—on his clothes, his desk, his hat, the handle of his tooth-brush, his umbrella. Ink was found freely on the coffee-room carpet by No 4 table, and two blots was on his restless couch. A reference to the document I have given entire will show that on the morning of the third of February, eighteen fifty-six, he procured his no less than fifth pen and paper. To whatever deplorable act of ungovernable composition he immolated those materials obtained from the bar, there is no doubt that the fatal deed was committed in bed, and that it left its evidences but too plainly, long afterwards, upon the pillow-case.

He had put no Heading to any of his writings. Alas! Was he likely to have a Heading without a Head, and where was *his* Head when he took such things into it? In some cases, such as his Boots, he would appear to have hid the writings; thereby involving his style in greater obscurity. But his boots was at least pairs,—and no two of his writings can put in any claim to be so regarded. Here follows (not to give more specimens) what was found in—

CHAPTER II.

"Eh! well then, Monsieur Mutuel! What do I know, what can I say? I assure you that he calls himself Monsieur The Englishman."

"Pardon. But I think it is impossible," said Monsieur Mutuel,—a spectacled, snuffy, stooping old gentleman in carpet shoes and a cloth cap with a peaked shade, a loose blue frock-coat reaching to his heels, a large limp white shirt-frill, and cravat to correspond,—that is to say, white was the natural colour of his linen on Sundays, but it toned down with the week.

"It is," repeated Monsieur Mutuel, his amiable old walnut-shell countenance very walnut-shelly indeed as he smiled and blinked in the bright morning sunlight,—"it is, my cherished Madame Bouclet, I think, impossible!"

"Hey!" (with a little vexed cry and a great many tosses of her head.) "But it is not impossible that you are a Pig!" retorted Madame Bouclet, a compact little woman of thirty-five or so. "See then,—look there,—read! 'On the second floor Monsieur L'Anglais.' Is it not so?"

"It is so," said Monsieur Mutuel.

"Good. Continue your morning walk. Get out!" Madame Bouclet dismissed him with a lively snap of her fingers.

The morning walk of Monsieur Mutuel was in the brightest patch that the sun made in the Grande Place of a dull old fortified French town. The manner of his morning walk was

with his hands crossed behind him; an umbrella, in figure
the express image of himself, always in one hand ; a snuff-box
in the other. Thus, with the shuffling gait of the Elephant
(who really does deal with the very worst trousers-maker
employed by the Zoological world, and who appeared to
have recommend him to Monsieur Mutuel), the old gentleman
sunned himself daily when sun was to be had—of course, at
the same time sunning a red ribbon at his button-hole ; for
was he not an ancient Frenchman?

Being told by one of the angelic sex to continue his morning walk and get out, Monsieur Mutuel laughed a walnut-
shell laugh, pulled off his cap at arm's length with the hand
that contained his snuff-box, kept it off for a considerable
period after he had parted from Madame Bouclet, and continued his morning walk and got out, like a man of gallantry
as he was.

The documentary evidence to which Madame Bouclet had
referred Monsieur Mutuel was the list of her lodgers, sweetly
written forth by her own Nephew and Bookkeeper, who held
the pen of an Angel, and posted up at the side of her gateway, for the information of the Police: "Au second, M.
L'Anglais, Propriétaire." On the second floor, Mr. The
Englishman, man of property. So it stood ; nothing could
be plainer.

Madame Bouclet now traced the line with her forefinger, as
it were to confirm and settle herself in her parting snap at
Monsieur Mutuel, and so placing her right hand on her hip
with a defiant air, as if nothing should ever tempt her to
unsnap that snap, strolled out into the Place to glance up
at the windows of Mr. The Englishman. That worthy
happening to be looking out of window at the moment,
Madame Bouclet gave him a graceful salutation with her
head, looked to the right and looked to the left to account
to him for her being there, considered for a moment, like
one who accounted to herself for somebody she had expected
not being there, and reëntered her own gateway. Madame

Bouclet let all her house giving on the Place in furnished flats or floors, and lived up the yard behind in company with Monsieur Bouclet her husband (great at billiards), an inherited brewing business, several fowls, two carts, a nephew, a little dog in a big kennel, a grape-vine, a counting-house, four horses, a married sister (with a share in the brewing business), the husband and two children of the married sister, a parrot, a drum (performed on by the little boy of the married sister), two billeted soldiers, a quantity of pigeons, a fife (played by the nephew in a ravishing manner), several domestics and supernumeraries, a perpetual flavour of coffee and soup, a terrific range of artificial rocks and wooden precipices at least four feet high, a small fountain, and half-a-dozen large sunflowers.

Now the Englishman, in taking his Appartement,—or, as one might say on our side of the Channel, his set of chambers, —had given his name, correct to the letter, LANGLEY. But as he had a British way of not opening his mouth very wide on foreign soil, except at meals, the Brewery had been able to make nothing of it but L'Anglais. So Mr. The Englishman he had become and he remained.

"Never saw such a people!" muttered Mr. The Englishman, as he now looked out of window. "Never did, in my life!"

This was true enough, for he had never before been out of his own country,—a right little island, a tight little island, a bright little island, a show-fight little island, and full of merit of all sorts; but not the whole round world.

"These chaps," said Mr. The Englishman to himself, as his eye rolled over the Place, sprinkled with military here and there, "are no more like soldiers—" Nothing being sufficiently strong for the end of his sentence, he left it unended.

This again (from the point of view of his experience) was strictly correct; for though there was a great agglomeration of soldiers in the town and neighbouring country, you might have held a grand Review and Field-day of them every one, and looked in vain among them all for a soldier choking behind his foolish stock, or a soldier lamed by his ill-fitting shoes, or a soldier deprived of the use of his limbs by straps and buttons, or a soldier elaborately forced to be self-helpless in all the small affairs of life. A swarm of brisk, bright, active, bustling, handy, odd, skirmishing fellows, able to turn cleverly at anything, from a siege to soup, from great guns to needles and thread, from the broadsword exercise to slicing an onion, from making war to making omelets, was all you would have found.

What a swarm! From the Great Place under the eye of Mr. The Englishman, where a few awkward squads from the last conscription were doing the goose-step—some members of those squads still as to their bodies, in the chrysalis peasant-state of Blouse, and only military butterflies as to their regimentally-clothed legs—from the Great Place, away outside the fortifications, and away for miles along the dusty roads, soldiers swarmed. All day long, upon the grass-grown ramparts of the town, practising soldiers trumpeted and bugled; all day long, down in angles of dry trenches, practising soldiers drummed and drummed. Every forenoon, soldiers burst out of the great barracks into the sandy gymnasium-ground hard by, and flew over the wooden horse, and hung on to flying ropes, and dangled upside-down between parallel bars, and shot themselves off wooden platforms,—splashes, sparks, coruscations, showers of soldiers. At every corner of the town-wall, every guard-house, every gateway, every sentry-box, every drawbridge, every reedy ditch, and rushy dike, soldiers, soldiers, soldiers. And the town being pretty well all wall, guard-house, gateway, sentry-box, drawbridge, reedy ditch, and rushy dike, the town was pretty well all soldiers.

What would the sleepy old town have been without the soldiers, seeing that even with them it had so overslept itself as to have slept its echoes hoarse, its defensive bars and locks and bolts and chains all rusty, and its ditches stagnant! From the days when VAUBAN engineered it to that perplex-ing extent that to look at it was like being knocked on the

head with it, the stranger becoming stunned and stertorous
under the shock of its incomprehensibility,—from the days
when VAUBAN made it the express incorporation of every
substantive and adjective in the art of military engineering,
and not only twisted you into it and twisted you out of it,
to the right, to the left, opposite, under here, over there, in
the dark, in the dirt, by the gateway, archway, covered way,
dry way, wet way, fosse, portcullis, drawbridge, sluice, squat
tower, pierced wall, and heavy battery, but likewise took a
fortifying dive under the neighbouring country, and came to
the surface three or four miles off, blowing out incomprehen-
sible mounds and batteries among the quiet crops of chicory
and beet-root,—from those days to these the town had been
asleep, and dust and rust and must had settled on its drowsy
Arsenals and Magazines, and grass, had grown up in its
silent streets.

On market-days alone, its Great Place suddenly leaped out
of bed. On market-days, some friendly enchanter struck his
staff upon the stones of the Great Place, and instantly arose
the liveliest booths and stalls, and sittings and standings,
and a pleasant hum of chaffering and huckstering from
many hundreds of tongues, and a pleasant, though peculiar,
blending of colours,—white caps, blue blouses, and green
vegetables,—and at last the Knight destined for the adventure
seemed to have come in earnest, and all the Vaubanois
sprang up awake. And now, by long, low-lying avenues of
trees, jolting in white-hooded donkey-cart, and on donkey-
back, and in tumbril and wagon, and cart and cabriolet, and
afoot with barrow and burden,—and along the dikes and
ditches and canals, in little peak-prowed country boats,—
came peasant-men and women in flocks and crowds, bringing
articles for sale. And here you had boots and shoes, and
sweetmeats and stuffs to wear, and here (in the cool shade
of the Town-hall) you had milk and cream and butter and
cheese, and here you had fruits and onions and carrots, and
all things needful for your soup, and here you had poultry

and flowers and protesting pigs, and here new shovels, axes, spades, and bill-hooks for your farming work, and here huge mounds of bread, and here your unground grain in sacks, and here your children's dolls, and here the cake-seller, announcing his wares by beat and roll of drum. And hark! fanfaronade of trumpets, and here into the Great Place, resplendent in an open carriage, with four gorgeously-attired servitors up behind, playing horns, drums, and cymbals, rolled "the Daughter of a Physician" in massive golden chains and ear-rings, and blue-feathered hat, shaded from the admiring sun by two immense umbrellas of artificial roses, to dispense (from motives of philanthropy) that small and pleasant dose which had cured so many thousands! Tooth-ache, earache, headache, heartache, stomachache, debility, nervousness, fits, fainting, fever, ague, all equally cured by the small and pleasant dose of the great Physician's great daughter! The process was this,—she, the Daughter of a Physician, proprietress of the superb equipage you now admired with its confirmatory blasts of trumpet, drum, and cymbal, told you so: On the first day after taking the small and pleasant dose, you would feel no particular influence beyond a most harmonious sensation of indescribable and irresistible joy; on the second day you would be so astonish-ingly better that you would think yourself changed into somebody else; on the third day you would be entirely free from your disorder, whatever its nature and however long you had had it, and would seek out the Physician's Daughter to throw yourself at her feet, kiss the hem of her garment, and buy as many more of the small and pleasant doses as by the sale of all your few effects you could obtain; but she would be inaccessible,—gone for herbs to the Pyramids of Egypt,—and you would be (though cured) reduced to despair! Thus would the Physician's Daughter drive her trade (and briskly too), and thus would the buying and selling and mingling of tongues and colours continue, until the changing sunlight, leaving the Physician's Daughter in

the shadow of high roofs, admonished her to jolt out west-
ward, with a departing effect of gleam and glitter on the
splendid equipage and brazen blast. And now the enchanter
struck his staff upon the stones of the Great Place once
more, and down went the booths, the sittings and standings,
and vanished the merchandise, and with it the barrows,
donkeys, donkey-carts, and tumbrils, and all other things on
wheels and feet, except the slow scavengers with unwieldy
carts and meagre horses clearing up the rubbish, assisted by
the sleek town pigeons, better plumped out than on non-
market days. While there was yet an hour or two to wane
before the autumn sunset, the loiterer outside town-gate and
drawbridge, and postern and double-ditch, would see the last
white-hooded cart lessening in the avenue of lengthening
shadows of trees, or the last country boat, paddled by the
last market-woman on her way home, showing black upon
the reddening, long, low, narrow dike between him and
the mill; and as the paddle-parted scum and weed closed
over the boat's track, he might be comfortably sure that
its sluggish rest would be troubled no more until next
market-day.

As it was not one of the Great Place's days for getting
out of bed, when Mr. The Englishman looked down at the
young soldiers practising the goose-step there, his mind was
left at liberty to take a military turn.

"These fellows are billeted everywhere about," said he;
"and to see them lighting the people's fires, boiling the
people's pots, minding the people's babies, rocking the
people's cradles, washing the people's greens, and making
themselves generally useful, in every sort of unmilitary way,
is most ridiculous! Never saw such a set of fellows,—never
did in my life!"

All perfectly true again. Was there not Private Valentine
in that very house, acting as sole housemaid, valet, cook,
steward, and nurse, in the family of his captain, Monsieur
le Capitaine de la Cour,—cleaning the floors, making the

beds, doing the marketing, dressing the captain, dressing the
dinners, dressing the salads, and dressing the baby, all with
equal readiness? Or, to put him aside, he being in loyal
attendance on his Chief, was there not Private Hyppolite,
billeted at the Perfumer's two hundred yards off, who, when
not on duty, volunteered to keep shop while the fair
Perfumeress stepped out to speak to a neighbour or so, and
laughingly sold soap with his war-sword girded on him?
Was there not Emile, billeted at the Clock-maker's, perpetually turning to of an evening, with his coat off, winding
up the stock? Was there not Eugène, billeted at the Tinman's, cultivating, pipe in mouth, a garden four feet square,
for the Tinman, in the little court, behind the shop, and
extorting the fruits of the earth from the same, on his
knees, with the sweat of his brow? Not to multiply
examples, was there not Baptiste, billeted on the poor
Water-carrier, at that very instant sitting on the pavement
in the sunlight, with his martial legs asunder, and one of
the Water-carrier's spare pails between them, which (to the
delight and glory of the heart of the Water-carrier coming
across the Place from the fountain, yoked and burdened) he
was painting bright-green outside and bright-red within?
Or, to go no farther than the Barber's at the very next
door, was there not Corporal Théophile——

"No," said Mr. The Englishman, glancing down at the
Barber's, "he is not there at present. There's the child,
though."

A mere mite of a girl stood on the steps of the Barber's
shop, looking across the Place. A mere baby, one might call
her, dressed in the close white linen cap which small French
country children wear (like the children in Dutch pictures),
and in a frock of homespun blue, that had no shape except
where it was tied round her little fat throat. So that, being
naturally short and round all over, she looked, behind, as if
she had been cut off at her natural waist, and had had her
head neatly fitted on it.

"There's the child, though."

To judge from the way in which the dimpled hand was rubbing the eyes, the eyes had been closed in a nap, and were newly opened. But they seemed to be looking so intently across the Place, that the Englishman looked in the same direction.

"O!" said he presently. "I thought as much. The Corporal's there."

The Corporal, a smart figure of a man of thirty, perhaps a thought under the middle size, but very neatly made,—a sun-burnt Corporal with a brown peaked beard,—faced about at the moment, addressing voluble words of instruction to the squad in hand. Nothing was amiss or awry about the Corporal. A lithe and nimble Corporal, quite complete, from the sparkling dark eyes under his knowing uniform cap to his sparkling white gaiters. The very image and present-ment of a Corporal of his country's army, in the line of his shoulders, the line of his waist, the broadest line of his Bloomer trousers, and their narrowest line at the calf of his leg.

Mr. The Englishman looked on, and the child looked on, and the Corporal looked on (but the last-named at his men), until the drill ended a few minutes afterwards, and the military sprinkling dried up directly, and was gone. Then said Mr. The Englishman to himself, "Look here! By George!" And the Corporal, dancing towards the Barber's with his arms wide open, caught up the child, held her over his head in a flying attitude, caught her down again, kissed her, and made off with her into the Barber's house.

Now Mr. The Englishman had had a quarrel with his erring and disobedient and disowned daughter, and there was a child in that case too. Had not his daughter been a child, and had she not taken angel-flights above his head as this child had flown above the Corporal's?

"He's a"—National Participled—"fool!" said the Eng-lishman, and shut his window.

But the windows of the house of Memory, and the windows of the house of Mercy, are not so easily closed as windows of glass and wood. They fly open unexpectedly; they rattle in the night; they must be nailed up. Mr. The Englishman had tried nailing them, but had not driven the nails quite home. So he passed but a disturbed evening and a worse night.

By nature a good-tempered man? No; very little gentleness, confounding the quality with weakness. Fierce and wrathful when crossed? Very, and stupendously unreasonable. Moody? Exceedingly so. Vindictive? Well; he *had* had scowling thoughts that he would formally curse his daughter, as he had seen it done on the stage. But remembering that the real Heaven is some paces removed from the mock one in the great chandelier of the Theatre, he had given that up.

And he had come abroad to be rid of his repudiated daughter for the rest of his life. And here he was.

At bottom, it was for this reason, more than for any other, that Mr. The Englishman took it extremely ill that Corporal Théophile should be so devoted to little Bebelle, the child at the Barber's shop. In an unlucky moment he had chanced to say to himself, "Why, confound the fellow, he is not her father!" There was a sharp sting in the speech which ran into him suddenly, and put him in a worse mood. So he had National Participled the unconscious Corporal with most hearty emphasis, and had made up his mind to think no more about such a mountebank.

But it came to pass that the Corporal was not to be dismissed. If he had known the most delicate fibres of the Englishman's mind, instead of knowing nothing on earth about him, and if he had been the most obstinate Corporal in the Grand Army of France, instead of being the most obliging, he could not have planted himself with more determined immovability plump in the midst of all the Englishman's thoughts. Not only so, but he seemed to be always in his view. Mr. The Englishman had but to look out of window, to look upon the Corporal with little Bebelle. He

had but to go for a walk, and there was the Corporal walking with Bebelle. He had but to come home again, disgusted,
and the Corporal and Bebelle were at home before him. If
he looked out at his back windows early in the morning, the
Corporal was in the Barber's back yard, washing and dressing
and brushing Bebelle. If he took refuge at his front windows,
the Corporal brought his breakfast out into the Place, and
shared it there with Bebelle. Always Corporal and always
Bebelle. Never Corporal without Bebelle. Never Bebelle
without Corporal.

Mr. The Englishman was not particularly strong in the
French language as a means of oral communication, though
he read it very well. It is with languages as with people,—
when you only know them by sight, you are apt to mistake
them; you must be on speaking terms before you can be said
to have established an acquaintance.

For this reason, Mr. The Englishman had to gird up his
loins considerably before he could bring himself to the point
of exchanging ideas with Madame Bouclet on the subject of
this Corporal and this Bebelle. But Madame Bouclet looking in apologetically one morning to remark, that, O Heaven !
she was in a state of desolation because the lamp-maker had
not sent home that lamp confided to him to repair, but that
truly he was a lamp-maker against whom the whole world
shrieked out, Mr. The Englishman seized the occasion.

" Madame, that baby—— "

" Pardon, monsieur. That lamp."

" No, no, that little girl."

" But, pardon !" said Madame Bouclet, angling for a clew,·
" one cannot light a little girl, or send her to be repaired ? "

" The little girl—at the house of the barber."

" Ah-h-h !" cried Madame Bouclet, suddenly catching the
idea with her delicate little line and rod. " Little Bebelle ?
Yes, yes, yes ! And her friend the Corporal ? Yes, yes, yes,
yes ! So genteel of him,—is it not ? "

" He is not—— ? "

"Not at all; not at all! He is not one of her relations. Not at all!"

"Why, then, he——"

"Perfectly!" cried Madame Bouclet, "you are right, monsieur. It is so genteel of him. The less relation, the more genteel. As you say."

"Is she——?"

"The child of the barber?" Madame Bouclet whisked up her skilful little line and rod again. "Not at all, not at all! She is the child of—in a word, of no one."

"The wife of the barber, then——?"

"Indubitably. As you say. The wife of the barber receives a small stipend to take care of her. So much by the month. Eh, then! It is without doubt very little, for we are all poor here."

"You are not poor, madame."

"As to my lodgers," replied Madame Bouclet, with a smiling and a gracious bend of her head, "no. As to all things else, so-so."

"You flatter me, madame."

"Monsieur, it is you who flatter me in living here."

Certain fishy gasps on Mr. The Englishman's part, denoting that he was about to resume his subject under difficulties, Madame Bouclet observed him closely, and whisked up her delicate line and rod again with triumphant success.

"O no, monsieur, certainly not. The wife of the barber is not cruel to the poor child, but she is careless. Her health is delicate, and she sits all day, looking out at window. Consequently, when the Corporal first came, the poor little Bebelle was much neglected."

"It is a curious——" began Mr. The Englishman.

"Name? That Bebelle? Again you are right, monsieur. But it is a playful name for Gabrielle."

"And so the child is a mere fancy of the Corporal's?" said Mr. The Englishman, in a gruffly disparaging tone of voice.

"Eh, well!" returned Madame Bouclet, with a pleading shrug: "one must love something. Human nature is weak."

("Devilish weak," muttered the Englishman, in his own language.)

"And the Corporal," pursued Madame Bouclet, "being billeted at the barber's,—where he will probably remain a long time, for he is attached to the General,—and finding the poor unowned child in need of being loved, and finding himself in need of loving,—why, there you have it all, you see!"

Mr. The Englishman accepted this interpretation of the matter with an indifferent grace, and observed to himself, in an injured manner, when he was again alone: "I shouldn't mind it so much, if these people were not such a"—National Participled—"sentimental people!"

There was a Cemetery outside the town, and it happened ill for the reputation of the Vaubanois, in this sentimental connection, that he took a walk there that same afternoon. To be sure there were some wonderful things in it (from the Englishman's point of view), and of a certainty in all Britain you would have found nothing like it. Not to mention the fanciful flourishes of hearts and crosses in wood and iron, that were planted all over the place, making it look very like a Firework-ground, where a most splendid pyro-technic display might be expected after dark, there were so many wreaths upon the graves, embroidered, as it might be, "To my mother," "To my daughter," "To my father," "To my brother," "To my sister," "To my friend," and those many wreaths were in so many stages of elaboration and decay, from the wreath of yesterday, all fresh colour and bright beads, to the wreath of last year, a poor mouldering wisp of straw! There were so many little gardens and grottoes made upon graves, in so many tastes, with plants and shells and plaster figures and porcelain pitchers, and so many odds and ends! There were so many tributes of remembrance

hanging up, not to be discriminated by the closest inspection
from little round waiters, whereon were depicted in glowing
hues either a lady or a gentleman with a white pocket-handkerchief out of all proportion, leaning, in a state of the most
faultless mourning and most profound affliction, on the most
architectural and gorgeous urn! There were so many surviving wives who had put their names on the tombs of their
deceased husbands, with a blank for the date of their own
departure from this weary world; and there were so many
surviving husbands who had rendered the same homage to
their deceased wives; and out of the number there must have
been so many who had long ago married again! In fine,
there was so much in the place that would have seemed
mere frippery to a stranger, save for the consideration that
the lightest paper flower that lay upon the poorest heap of
earth was never touched by a rude hand, but perished there,
a sacred thing!

"Nothing of the solemnity of Death here," Mr. The
Englishman had been going to say, when this last consideration touched him with a mild appeal, and on the whole he
walked out without saying it. "But these people are," he
insisted, by way of compensation, when he was well outside
the gate, "they are so"—Participled—"sentimental!"

His way back lay by the military gymnasium-ground.
And there he passed the Corporal glibly instructing young
soldiers how to swing themselves over rapid and deep water-
courses on their way to Glory, by means of a rope, and
himself deftly plunging off a platform, and flying a hundred
feet or two, as an encouragement to them to begin. And
there he also passed, perched on a crowning eminence (probably by the Corporal's careful hands), the small Bebelle,
with her round eyes wide open, surveying the proceeding like
a wondering sort of blue and white bird.

"If that child was to die," this was his reflection as he
turned his back and went his way,—"and it would almost
serve the fellow right for making such a fool of himself,—I

suppose we should have *him* sticking up a wreath and a waiter in that fantastic burying-ground."

Nevertheless, after another early morning or two of looking out of window, he strolled down into the Place, when the Corporal and Bebelle were walking there, and touching his hat to the Corporal (an immense achievement), wished him Good-day.

"Good-day, monsieur."

"This is a rather pretty child you have here," said Mr. The Englishman, taking her chin in his hand, and looking down into her astonished blue eyes.

"Monsieur, she is a very pretty child," returned the Corporal, with a stress on his polite correction of the phrase.

"And good?" said the Englishman.

"And very good. Poor little thing!"

"Hah!" The Englishman stooped down and patted her cheek, not without awkwardness, as if he were going too far in his conciliation. "And what is this medal round your neck, my little one?"

Bebelle having no other reply on her lips than her chubby right fist, the Corporal offered his services as interpreter.

"Monsieur demands, what is this, Bebelle?"

"It is the Holy Virgin," said Bebelle.

"And who gave it you?" asked the Englishman.

"Théophile."

"And who is Théophile?"

Bebelle broke into a laugh, laughed merrily and heartily, clapped her chubby hands, and beat her little feet on the stone pavement of the Place.

"He doesn't know Théophile! Why, he doesn't know any one! He doesn't know anything!" Then, sensible of a small solecism in her manners, Bebelle twisted her right hand in a leg of the Corporal's Bloomer trousers, and, laying her check against the place, kissed it.

"Monsieur Théophile, I believe?" said the Englishman to the Corporal.

"It is I, monsieur."

"Permit me." Mr. The Englishman shook him heartily
by the hand and turned away. But he took it mighty ill
that old Monsieur Mutuel in his patch of sunlight, upon
whom he came as he turned, should pull off his cap to him
with a look of pleased approval. And he muttered, in his
own tongue, as he returned the salutation, "Well, walnut-
shell! And what business is it of *yours?*"

Mr. The Englishman went on for many weeks passing
but disturbed evenings and worse nights, and constantly
experiencing that those aforesaid windows in the houses of
Memory and Mercy rattled after dark, and that he had very
imperfectly nailed them up. Likewise, he went on for many
weeks daily improving the acquaintance of the Corporal and
Bebelle. That is to say, he took Bebelle by the chin, and the
Corporal by the hand, and offered Bebelle sous and the
Corporal cigars, and even got the length of changing pipes
with the Corporal and kissing Bebelle. But he did it all
in a shamefaced way, and always took it extremely ill that
Monsieur Mutuel in his patch of sunlight should note what
he did. Whenever that seemed to be the case, he always
growled in his own tongue, "There you are again, walnut-
shell! What business is it of *yours?*"

In a word, it had become the occupation of Mr. The
Englishman's life to look after the Corporal and little Bebelle,
and to resent old Monsieur Mutuel's looking after *him*. An
occupation only varied by a fire in the town one windy night,
and much passing of water-buckets from hand to hand (in
which the Englishman rendered good service), and much
beating of drums,—when all of a sudden the Corporal
disappeared.

Next, all of a sudden, Bebelle disappeared.

She had been visible a few days later than the Corporal,
—sadly deteriorated as to washing and brushing,—but she
had not spoken when addressed by Mr. The Englishman,
and had looked scared and had run away. And now it would

seem that she had run away for good. And there lay the Great Place under the windows, bare and barren.

In his shamefaced and constrained way, Mr. The Englishman asked no question of any one, but watched from his front windows and watched from his back windows, and lingered about the Place, and peeped in at the Barber's shop, and did all this and much more with a whistling and tune-humming pretence of not missing anything, until one afternoon when Monsieur Mutuel's patch of sunlight was in shadow, and when, according to all rule and precedent, he had no right whatever to bring his red ribbon out of doors, behold here he was, advancing with his cap already in his hand twelve paces off!

Mr. The Englishman had got as far into his usual objurgation as, "What bu—si—" when he checked himself.

"Ah, it is sad, it is sad! Hélas, it is unhappy, it is sad!" Thus old Monsieur Mutuel, shaking his gray head.

"What busin—at least, I would say, what do you mean, Monsieur Mutuel?"

"Our Corporal. Hélas, our dear Corporal!"

"What has happened to him?"

"You have not heard?"

"No."

"At the fire. But he was so brave, so ready. Ah, too brave, too ready!"

"May the Devil carry you away!" the Englishman broke in impatiently; "I beg your pardon,—I mean me,—I am not accustomed to speak French,—go on, will you?"

"And a falling beam——"

"Good God!" exclaimed the Englishman. "It was a private soldier who was killed?"

"No. A Corporal, the same Corporal, our dear Corporal. Beloved by all his comrades. The funeral ceremony was touching,— penetrating. Monsieur The Englishman, your eyes fill with tears."

"What bu—si——"

"Monsieur The Englishman, I honour those emotions. I salute you with profound respect. I will not obtrude myself upon your noble heart."

Monsieur Mutuel,—a gentleman in every thread of his cloudy linen, under whose wrinkled hand every grain in the quarter of an ounce of poor snuff in his poor little tin box became a gentleman's property,—Monsieur Mutuel passed on, with his cap in his hand.

"I little thought," said the Englishman, after walking for several minutes, and more than once blowing his nose, "when I was looking round that cemetery—I'll go there!"

Straight he went there, and when he came within the gate he paused, considering whether he should ask at the lodge for some direction to the grave. But he was less than ever in a mood for asking questions, and he thought, "I shall see something on it to know it by."

In search of the Corporal's grave he went softly on, up this walk and down that, peering in, among the crosses and hearts and columns and obelisks and tombstones, for a recently disturbed spot. It troubled him now to think how many dead there were in the cemetery,—he had not thought them a tenth part so numerous before,—and after he had walked and sought for some time, he said to himself, as he struck down a new vista of tombs, "I might suppose that every one was dead but I."

Not every one. A live child was lying on the ground asleep. Truly he had found something on the Corporal's grave to know it by, and the something was Bebelle.

With such a loving will had the dead soldier's comrades worked at his resting-place, that it was already a neat garden. On the green turf of the garden Bebelle lay sleeping, with her cheek touching it. A plain, unpainted little wooden Cross was planted in the turf, and her short arm embraced this little Cross, as it had many a time embraced the Corporal's neck. They had put a tiny flag (the flag of France) at his head, and a laurel garland.

Mr. The Englishman took off his hat, and stood for a while silent. Then, covering his head again, he bent down on one knee, and softly roused the child.

"Bebelle! My little one!"

Opening her eyes, on which the tears were still wet, Bebelle was at first frightened; but seeing who it was, she suffered him to take her in his arms, looking steadfastly at him.

"You must not lie here, my little one. You must come with me."

"No, no. I can't leave Théophile. I want the good dear Théophile."

"We will go and seek him, Bebelle. We will go and look for him in England. We will go and look for him at my daughter's, Bebelle."

"Shall we find him there?"

"We shall find the best part of him there. Come with me, poor forlorn little one. Heaven is my witness," said the Englishman, in a low voice, as, before he rose, he touched the turf above the gentle Corporal's breast, "that I thankfully accept this trust!"

It was a long way for the child to have come unaided. She was soon asleep again, with her embrace transferred to the Englishman's neck. He looked at her worn shoes, and her galled feet, and her tired face, and believed that she had come there every day.

He was leaving the grave with the slumbering Bebelle in his arms, when he stopped, looked wistfully down at it, and looked wistfully at the other graves around. "It is the innocent custom of the people," said Mr. The Englishman, with hesitation. "I think I should like to do it. No one sees."

Careful not to wake Bebelle as he went, he repaired to the lodge where such little tokens of remembrance were sold, and bought two wreaths. One, blue and white and glistening silver, "To my friend;" one of a soberer red and black and yellow, "To my friend." With these he went back to the grave, and so down on one knee again. Touching the child's lips with the brighter wreath, he guided her hand to hang it on the Cross; then hung his own wreath there. After all, the wreaths were not far out of keeping with the little garden. To my friend. To my friend.

Mr. The Englishman took it very ill when he looked round a street corner into the Great Place, carrying Bebelle in his arms, that old Mutuel should be there airing his red ribbon. He took a world of pains to dodge the worthy Mutuel, and devoted a surprising amount of time and trouble to skulking into his own lodging like a man pursued by Justice. Safely arrived there at last, he made Bebelle's toilet with as accurate a remembrance as he could bring to bear upon that work of the way in which he had often seen the poor Corporal make it, and having given her to eat and drink, laid her down on his own bed. Then he slipped out into the barber's shop, and after a brief interview with the barber's wife, and a brief recourse to his purse and card-case, came back again with the whole of Bebelle's personal property in such a very little bundle that it was quite lost under his arm.

As it was irreconcilable with his whole course and character that he should carry Bebelle off in state, or receive any compliments or congratulations on that feat, he devoted the next day to getting his two portmanteaus out of the house by artfulness and stealth, and to comporting himself in every particular as if he were going to run away,—except, indeed, that he paid his few debts in the town, and prepared a letter to leave for Madame Bouclet, enclosing a sufficient sum of money in lieu of notice. A railway train would come through at midnight, and by that train he would take away Bebelle to look for Théophile in England and at his forgiven daughter's.

At midnight, on a moonlight night, Mr. The Englishman came creeping forth like a harmless assassin, with Bebelle on his breast instead of a dagger. Quiet the Great Place, and quiet the never-stirring streets; closed the cafés; huddled together motionless their billiard-balls; drowsy the guard or sentinel on duty here and there; lulled for the time, by sleep, even the insatiate appetite of the Office of Town-dues.

Mr. The Englishman left the Place behind, and left the streets behind, and left the civilian-inhabited town behind, and descended down among the military works of Vauban, hemming all in. As the shadow of the first heavy arch and postern fell upon him and was left behind, as the shadow of the second heavy arch and postern fell upon him and was left behind, as his hollow tramp over the first drawbridge was succeeded by a gentler sound, as his hollow tramp over the second drawbridge was succeeded by a gentler sound, as he overcame the stagnant ditches one by one, and passed out where the flowing waters were and where the moonlight, so the dark shades and the hollow sounds and the unwholesomely locked currents of his soul were vanquished and set free. See to it, Vaubans of your own hearts, who gird them in with triple walls and ditches, and with bolt and chain and bar and lifted bridge,—raze those fortifications, and lay them level with the all-absorbing dust, before the night cometh when no hand can work!

All went prosperously, and he got into an empty carriage in the train, where he could lay Bebelle on the seat over against him, as on a couch, and cover her from head to foot with his mantle. He had just drawn himself up from perfecting this arrangement, and had just leaned back in his own seat contemplating it with great satisfaction, when he became aware of a curious appearance at the open carriage window, —a ghostly little tin box floating up in the moonlight, and hovering there.

He leaned forward, and put out his head. Down among the rails and wheels and ashes, Monsieur Mutuel, red ribbon and all!

"Excuse me, Monsieur The Englishman," said Monsieur Mutuel, holding up his box at arm's length, the carriage being so high and he so low; "but I shall reverence the little box for ever, if your so generous hand will take a pinch from it at parting."

Mr. The Englishman reached out of the window before complying, and—without asking the old fellow what business it was of his—shook hands and said, "Adieu! God bless you!"

"And, Mr. The Englishman, God bless *you!*" cried Madame Bouclet, who was also there among the rails and wheels and ashes. "And God will bless you in the happiness of the protected child now with you. And God will bless you in your own child at home. And God will bless you in your own remembrances. And this from me!"

He had barely time to catch a bouquet from her hand, when the train was flying through the night. Round the paper that enfolded it was bravely written (doubtless by the nephew who held the pen of an Angel), "Homage to the friend of the friendless."

"Not bad people, Bebelle!" said Mr. The Englishman, softly drawing the mantle a little from her sleeping face, that he might kiss it, "though they are so——"

Too "sentimental" himself at the moment to be able to get out that word, he added nothing but a sob, and travelled for some miles, through the moonlight, with his hand before his eyes.

CHAPTER III.

My works are well known. I am a young man in the Art
line. You have seen my works many a time, though it's
fifty thousand to one if you have seen me. You say you
don't want to see me? You say your interest is in my works,
and not in me? Don't be too sure about that. Stop a bit.

Let us have it down in black and white at the first go off,
so that there may be no unpleasantness or wrangling afterwards. And this is looked over by a friend of mine, a ticket
writer, that is up to literature. I am a young man in the Art
line—in the Fine-Art line. You have seen my works over
and over again, and you have been curious about me, and
you think you have seen me. Now, as a safe rule, you never
have seen me, and you never do see me, and you never will
see me. I think that's plainly put—and it's what knocks
me over.

If there's a blighted public character going, I am the party.

It has been remarked by a certain (or an uncertain)
philosopher, that the world knows nothing of its greatest
men. He might have put it plainer if he had thrown his
eye in my direction. He might have put it, that while the
world knows something of them that apparently go in and
win, it knows nothing of them that really go in and don't
win. There it is again in another form—and that's what
knocks me over.

Not that it's only myself that suffers from injustice, but that I am more alive to my own injuries than to any other man's. Being, as I have mentioned, in the Fine-Art line, and not the Philanthropic line, I openly admit it. As to company in injury, I have company enough. Who are you passing every day at your Competitive Excruciations? The fortunate candidates whose heads and livers you have turned upside down for life? Not you. You are really passing the Crammers and Coaches. If your principle is right, why don't you turn out to-morrow morning with the keys of your cities on velvet cushions, your musicians playing, and your flags flying, and read addresses to the Crammers and Coaches on your bended knees, beseeching them to come out and govern you? Then, again, as to your public business of all sorts, your Financial statements and your Budgets; the Public knows much, truly, about the real doers of all that! Your Nobles and Right Honourables are first-rate men? Yes, and so is a goose a first-rate bird. But I'll tell you this about the goose;—you'll find his natural flavour disappointing, without stuffing.

Perhaps I am soured by not being popular? But suppose I AM popular. Suppose my works never fail to attract. Suppose that, whether they are exhibited by natural light or by artificial, they inevitably draw the public. Then no doubt they are preserved in some Collection? No, they are not; they are not preserved in any Collection. Copyright? No, nor yet copyright. Anyhow they must be somewhere? Wrong again, for they are often nowhere.

Says you, "At all events, you are in a moody state of mind, my friend." My answer is, I have described myself as a public character with a blight upon him—which fully accounts for the curdling of the milk in *that* cocoa-nut.

Those that are acquainted with London are aware of a locality on the Surrey side of the river Thames, called the Obelisk, or, more generally, the Obstacle. Those that are not acquainted with London will also be aware of it, now that

I have named it. My lodging is not far from that locality.
I am a young man of that easy disposition, that I lie abed
till it's absolutely necessary to get up and earn something,
and then I lie abed again till I have spent it.

It was on an occasion when I had had to turn to with
a view to victuals, that I found myself walking along the
Waterloo Road, one evening after dark, accompanied by an
acquaintance and fellow-lodger in the gas-fitting way of life.
He is very good company, having worked at the theatres,
and, indeed, he has a theatrical turn himself, and wishes to
be brought out in the character of Othello; but whether on
account of his regular work always blacking his face and
hands more or less, I cannot say.

"Tom," he says, "what a mystery hangs over you!"

"Yes, Mr. Click"—the rest of the house generally give
him his name, as being first, front, carpeted all over, his
own furniture, and if not mahogany, an out-and-out imitation
—"yes, Mr. Click, a mystery does hang over me."

"Makes you low, you see, don't it?" says he, eyeing me
sideways.

"Why, yes, Mr. Click, there are circumstances connected
with it that have," I yielded to a sigh, "a lowering effect."

"Gives you a touch of the misanthrope too, don't it?"
says he. "Well, I'll tell you what. If I was you, I'd shake
it off."

"If I was you, I would, Mr. Click; but, if you was me,
you wouldn't.

"Ah!" says he, "there's something in that."

When we had walked a little further, he took it up again
by touching me on the chest.

"You see, Tom, it seems to me as if, in the words of the
poet who wrote the domestic drama of The Stranger, you
had a silent sorrow there."

"I have, Mr. Click."

"I hope, Tom," lowering his voice in a friendly way, "it
isn't coining, or smashing?"

"No, Mr. Click. Don't be uneasy."

"Nor yet forg——" Mr. Click checked himself, and added, "counterfeiting anything, for instance?"

"No, Mr. Click. I am lawfully in the Art line—Fine-Art line—but I can say no more."

"Ah! Under a species of star? A kind of malignant spell? A sort of a gloomy destiny? A cankerworm pegging away at your vitals in secret, as well as I make it out?" said Mr. Click, eyeing me with some admiration.

I told Mr. Click that was about it, if we came to particulars; and I thought he appeared rather proud of me.

Our conversation had brought us to a crowd of people, the greater part struggling for a front place from which to see something on the pavement, which proved to be various designs executed in coloured chalks on the pavement stones, lighted by two candles stuck in mud sconces. The subjects consisted of a fine fresh salmon's head and shoulders, supposed to have been recently sent home from the fishmonger's; a moonlight night at sea (in a circle); dead game; scroll-work; the head of a hoary hermit engaged in devout contemplation; the head of a pointer smoking a pipe; and a cherubim, his flesh creased as in infancy, going on a horizontal errand against the wind. All these subjects appeared to me to be exquisitely done.

On his knees on one side of this gallery, a shabby person of modest appearance who shivered dreadfully (though it wasn't at all cold), was engaged in blowing the chalk-dust off the moon, toning the outline of the back of the hermit's head with a bit of leather, and fattening the down-stroke of a letter or two in the writing. I have forgotten to mention that writing formed a part of the composition, and that it also—as it appeared to me—was exquisitely done. It ran as follows, in fine round characters: "An honest man is the noblest work of God. 1 2 3 4 5 6 7 8 9 0. £ s. d. Employment in an office is humbly requested. Honour the Queen. Hunger is a 0 9 8 7 6 5 4 3 2 1 sharp thorn.

Chip chop, cherry chop, fol de rol de ri do. Astronomy and mathematics. I do this to support my family."

Murmurs of admiration at the exceeding beauty of this performance went about among the crowd. The artist, having finished his touching (and having spoilt those places), took his seat on the pavement, with his knees crouched up very nigh his chin; and halfpence began to rattle in.

"A pity to see a man of that talent brought so low; ain't it?" said one of the crowd to me.

"What he might have done in the coach-painting, or house-decorating!" said another man, who took up the first speaker because I did not.

"Why, he writes—alone—like the Lord Chancellor!" said another man.

"Better," said another. "I know *his* writing. *He* couldn't support his family this way."

Then, a woman noticed the natural fluffiness of the hermit's hair, and another woman, her friend, mentioned of the salmon's gills that you could almost see him gasp. Then, an elderly country gentleman stepped forward and asked the modest man how he executed his work? And the modest man took some scraps of brown paper with colours in 'em out of his pockets, and showed them. Then a fair-complexioned donkey, with sandy hair and spectacles, asked if the hermit was a portrait? To which the modest man, casting a sorrowful glance upon it, replied that it was, to a certain extent, a recollection of his father. This caused a boy to yelp out, "Is the Pinter a smoking the pipe your mother?" who was immediately shoved out of view by a sympathetic carpenter with his basket of tools at his back.

At every fresh question or remark the crowd leaned forward more eagerly, and dropped the halfpence more freely, and the modest man gathered them up more meekly. At last, another elderly gentleman came to the front, and gave the artist his card, to come to his office to-morrow, and get some copying to do. The card was accompanied by sixpence, and

the artist was profoundly grateful, and, before he put the
card in his hat, read it several times by the light of his candles
to fix the address well in his mind, in case he should lose it.
The crowd was deeply interested by this last incident, and
a man in the second row with a gruff voice growled to the
artist, " You've got a chance in life now, ain't you?" The
artist answered (sniffing in a very low-spirited way, however),
" I'm thankful to hope so." Upon which there was a
general chorus of ' You are all right,' and the halfpence
slackened very decidedly.

I felt myself pulled away by the arm, and Mr. Click and
I stood alone at the corner of the next crossing.

" Why, Tom," said Mr. Click, " what a horrid expression
of face you've got ! "

" Have I ?" says I.

" Have you?" says Mr. Click. " Why, you looked as if
you would have his blood."

" Whose blood ? "

" The artist's."

" The artist's ?" I repeated. And I laughed, frantically,
wildly, gloomily, incoherently, disagreeably. I am sensible
that I did. I know I did.

Mr. Click stared at me in a scared sort of a way, but said
nothing until we had walked a street's length. He then
stopped short, and said, with excitement on the part of his
forefinger :

" Thomas, I find it necessary to be plain with you. I
don't like the envious man. I have identified the cankerworm
that's pegging away at *your* vitals, and it's envy, Thomas."

" Is it ?" says I.

" Yes, it is," says he. " Thomas, beware of envy. It is the
green-eyed monster which never did and never will improve
each shining hour, but quite the reverse. I dread the envious
man, Thomas. I confess that I am afraid of the envious
man, when he is so envious as you are. Whilst you contemplated the works of a gifted rival, and whilst you heard that

rival's praises, and especially whilst you met his humble glance
as he put that card away, your countenance was so malevolent
as to be terrific. Thomas, I have heard of the envy of them
that follows the Fine-Art line, but I never believed it could
be what yours is. I wish you well, but I take my leave of
you. And if you should ever get into trouble through
knifeing—or say, garotting—a brother artist, as I believe
you will, don't call me to character, Thomas, or I shall be
forced to injure your case."

Mr. Click parted from me with those words, and we broke
off our acquaintance.

I became enamoured. Her name was Henrietta. Contending
with my easy disposition, I frequently got up to go after
her. She also dwelt in the neighbourhood of the Obstacle,
and I did fondly hope that no other would interpose in the
way of our union.

To say that Henrietta was volatile is but to say that she
was woman. To say that she was in the bonnet-trimming
is feebly to express the taste which reigned predominant in
her own.

She consented to walk with me. Let me do her the justice
to say that she did so upon trial. "I am not," said Henrietta,
"as yet prepared to regard you, Thomas, in any other light
than as a friend; but as a friend I am willing to walk with
you, on the understanding that softer sentiments may flow."

We walked.

Under the influence of Henrietta's beguilements, I now
got out of bed daily. I pursued my calling with an industry
before unknown, and it cannot fail to have been observed
at that period, by those most familiar with the streets of
London, that there was a larger supply. But hold! The
time is not yet come!

One evening in October I was walking with Henrietta,
enjoying the cool breezes wafted over Vauxhall Bridge.
After several slow turns, Henrietta gaped frequently (so
inseparable from woman is the love of excitement), and said,

"Let's go home by Grosvenor Place, Piccadilly, and Waterloo" —localities, I may state for the information of the stranger and the foreigner, well known in London, and the last a Bridge.

"No. Not by Piccadilly, Henrietta," said I.

"And why not Piccadilly, for goodness' sake?" said Henrietta.

Could I tell her? Could I confess to the gloomy presentiment that overshadowed me? Could I make myself intelligible to her? No.

"I don't like Piccadilly, Henrietta."

"But I do," said she. "It's dark now, and the long rows of lamps in Piccadilly after dark are beautiful. I *will* go to Piccadilly!"

Of course we went. It was a pleasant night, and there were numbers of people in the streets. It was a brisk night, but not too cold, and not damp. Let me darkly observe, it was the best of all nights—FOR THE PURPOSE.

As we passed the garden wall of the Royal Palace, going up Grosvenor Place, Henrietta murmured:

"I wish I was a Queen!"

"Why so, Henrietta?"

"I would make *you* Something," said she, and crossed her two hands on my arm, and turned away her head.

Judging from this that the softer sentiments alluded to above had begun to flow, I adapted my conduct to that belief. Thus happily we passed on into the detested thoroughfare of Piccadilly. On the right of that thoroughfare is a row of trees, the railing of the Green Park, and a fine broad eligible piece of pavement.

"Oh my!" cried Henrietta presently. "There's been an accident!"

I looked to the left, and said, "Where, Henrietta?"

"Not there, stupid!" said she. "Over by the Park railings. Where the crowd is. Oh no, it's not an accident, it's something else to look at! What's them lights?"

She referred to two lights twinkling low amongst the legs of the assemblage: two candles on the pavement.

"Oh, do come along!" cried Henrietta, skipping across the road with me. I hung back, but in vain. "Do let's look!"

Again, designs upon the pavement. Centre compartment, Mount Vesuvius going it (in a circle), supported by four oval compartments, severally representing a ship in heavy weather, a shoulder of mutton attended by two cucumbers, a golden harvest with distant cottage of proprietor, and a knife and fork after nature; above the centre compartment a bunch of grapes, and over the whole a rainbow. The whole, as it appeared to me, exquisitely done.

The person in attendance on these works of art was in all respects, shabbiness excepted, unlike the former personage. His whole appearance and manner denoted briskness. Though threadbare, he expressed to the crowd that poverty had not subdued his spirit, or tinged with any sense of shame this honest effort to turn his talents to some account. The writing which formed a part of his composition was conceived in a similarly cheerful tone. It breathed the following sentiments: "The writer is poor, but not despondent. To a British 1 2 3 4 5 6 7 8 9 0 Public he £ s. d. appeals. Honour to our brave Army! And also 0 9 8 7 6 5 4 3 2 1 to our gallant Navy. Barrows Strike the A B C D E F G writer in common chalks would be grateful for any suitable employment Home! Hurrah!" The whole of this writing appeared to me to be exquisitely done.

But this man, in one respect like the last, though seemingly hard at it with a great show of brown paper and rubbers, was only really fattening the down-stroke of a letter here and there, or blowing the loose chalk off the rainbow, or toning the outside edge of the shoulder of mutton. Though he did this with the greatest confidence, he did it (as it struck me) in so ignorant a manner, and so spoilt everything he touched, that when he began upon the purple

smoke from the chimney of the distant cottage of the proprietor of the golden harvest (which smoke was beautifully
soft), I found myself saying aloud, without considering of it:
"Let that alone, will you?"

"Halloa!" said the man next me in the crowd, jerking me
roughly from him with his elbow, "why didn't you send a
telegram? If we had known you was coming, we'd have
provided something better for you. You understand the
man's work better than he does himself, don't you? Have
you made your will? You're too clever to live long."

"Don't be hard upon the gentleman, sir," said the person
in attendance on the works of art, with a twinkle in his eye
as he looked at me; "he may chance to be an artist himself.
If so, sir, he will have a fellow-feeling with me, sir, when I"
—he adapted his action to his words as he went on, and
gave a smart slap of his hands between each touch, working
himself all the time about and about the composition—
"when I lighten the bloom of my grapes—shade off the
orange in my rainbow—dot the i of my Britons—throw a
yellow light into my cow-cum-*ber*—insinuate another morsel
of fat into my shoulder of mutton—dart another zigzag flash
of lightning at my ship in distress!"

He seemed to do this so neatly, and was so nimble about
it, that the halfpence came flying in.

"Thanks, generous public, thanks!" said the professor.
"You will stimulate me to further exertions. My name will
be found in the list of British Painters yet. I shall do
better than this, with encouragement. I shall indeed."

"You never can do better than that bunch of grapes,"
said Henrietta. "Oh, Thomas, them grapes!"

"Not better than *that*, lady? I hope for the time when I
shall paint anything but your own bright eyes and lips equal
to life."

"(Thomas, did you ever?) But it must take a long time,
sir," said Henrietta, blushing, "to paint equal to that."

"I was prenticed to it, miss," said the young man, smartly

touching up the composition—"prenticed to it in the caves of Spain and Portingale, ever so long and two year over."

There was a laugh from the crowd; and a new man who had worked himself in next me, said, "He's a smart chap, too; ain't he?"

"And what a eye!" exclaimed Henrietta softly.

"Ah! He need have a eye," said the man.

"Ah! He just need," was murmured among the crowd.

"He couldn't come that 'ere burning mountain without a eye," said the man. He had got himself accepted as an authority, somehow, and everybody looked at his finger as it pointed out Vesuvius. "To come that effect in a general illumination would require a eye; but to come it with two dips—why, it's enough to blind him!"

That impostor, pretending not to have heard what was said, now winked to any extent with both eyes at once, as if the strain upon his sight was too much, and threw back his long hair—it was very long—as if to cool his fevered brow. I was watching him doing it, when Henrietta suddenly whispered, "Oh, Thomas, how horrid you look!" and pulled me out by the arm.

Remembering Mr. Click's words, I was confused when I retorted, "What do you mean by horrid?"

"Oh gracious! Why, you looked," said Henrietta, "as if you would have his blood."

I was going to answer, "So I would, for twopence——from his nose," when I checked myself and remained silent.

We returned home in silence. Every step of the way, the softer sentiments that had flowed, ebbed twenty mile an hour. Adapting my conduct to the ebbing, as I had done to the flowing, I let my arm drop limp, so as she could scarcely keep hold of it, and I wished her such a cold good night at parting, that I keep within the bounds of truth when I characterise it as a Rasper.

In the course of the next day I received the following document:

" Henrietta informs Thomas that my eyes are open to you.
I must ever wish you well, but walking and us is separated
by an unfarmable abyss.   One so malignant to superiority—
Oh that look at him!—can never never conduct

                                             HENRIETTA

P.S.—To the altar."

Yielding to the easiness of my disposition, I went to bed
for a week, after receiving this letter.   During the whole of
such time, London was bereft of the usual fruits of my labour.
When I resumed it, I found that Henrietta was married to
the artist of Piccadilly.
    Did I say to the artist?   What fell words were those,
expressive of what a galling hollowness, of what a bitter
mockery!   I—I—I—am the artist.   I was the real artist of
Piccadilly, I was the real artist of the Waterloo Road, I am
the only artist of all those pavement-subjects which daily and
nightly arouse your admiration.   I do 'em, and I let 'em out.
The man you behold with the papers of chalks and the
rubbers, touching up the down-strokes of the writing and
shading off the salmon, the man you give the credit to, the
man you give the money to, hires—yes! and I live to tell it!
—hires those works of art of me, and brings nothing to 'em
but the candles.
    Such is genius in a commercial country.   I am not up to the
shivering, I am not up to the liveliness, I am not up to the
wanting-employment-in-an-office move; I am only up to
originating and executing the work.   In consequence of which
you never see me; you think you see me when you see somebody else, and that somebody else is a mere Commercial
character.   The one seen by self and Mr. Click in the Waterloo
Road can only write a single word, and that I taught him,
and it's MULTIPLICATION—which you may see him execute
upside down, because he can't do it the natural way.   The
one seen by self and Henrietta by the Green Park railings
can just smear into existence the two ends of a rainbow,

with his cuff and a rubber—if very hard put upon making a
show—but he could no more come the arch of the rainbow,
to save his life, than he could come the moonlight, fish,
volcano, shipwreck, mutton, hermit, or any of my most
celebrated effects.

To conclude as I began: if there's a blighted public
character going, I am the party.   And often as you have
seen, do see, and will see, my Works, it's fifty thousand to
one if you'll ever see me, unless, when the candles are burnt
down and the Commercial character is gone, you should
happen to notice a neglected young man perseveringly rubbing
out the last traces of the pictures, so that nobody can renew
the same.   That's me.

CHAPTER IV.

HIS WONDERFUL END.

It will have been, ere now, perceived that I sold the foregoing writings. From the fact of their being printed in these pages, the inference will, ere now, have been drawn by the reader (may I add, the gentle reader?) that I sold them to One who never yet——*

Having parted with the writings on most satisfactory terms,—for, in opening negotiations with the present Journal, was I not placing myself in the hands of One of whom it may be said, in the words of Another,*—I resumed my usual functions. But I too soon discovered that peace of mind had fled from a brow which, up to that time, Time had merely took the hair off, leaving an unruffled expanse within.

It were superfluous to veil it,—the brow to which I allude is my own.

Yes, over that brow uneasiness gathered like the sable wing of the fabled bird, as—as no doubt will be easily identified by all right-minded individuals. If not, I am unable, on the spur of the moment, to enter into particulars of him. The reflection that the writings must now inevitably get into print, and that He might yet live and meet with them, sat like the Hag of Night upon my jaded form. The elasticity of my spirits departed. Fruitless was the Bottle, whether Wine or Medicine. I had recourse to both, and the effect of both upon my system was witheringly lowering.

* The remainder of this complimentary sentence editorially struck out.

In this state of depression, into which I subsided when I first began to revolve what could I ever say if He—the unknown—was to appear in the Coffee-room and demand reparation, I one forenoon in this last November received a turn that appeared to be given me by the finger of Fate and Conscience, hand in hand. I was alone in the Coffee-room, and had just poked the fire into a blaze, and was standing with my back to it, trying whether heat would penetrate with soothing influence to the Voice within, when a young man in a cap, of an intelligent countenance, though requiring his hair cut, stood before me.

"Mr. Christopher, the Head Waiter?"

"The same."

The young man shook his hair out of his vision,—which it impeded,—took a packet from his breast, and handing it over to me, said, with his eye (or did I dream?) fixed with a lambent meaning on me, "THE PROOFS."

Although I smelt my coat-tails singeing at the fire, I had not the power to withdraw them. The young man put the packet in my faltering grasp, and repeated,—let me do him the justice to add, with civility:

"THE PROOFS. A. Y. R."

With those words he departed.

A. Y. R.? And You Remember. Was that his meaning? At Your Risk. Were the letters short for *that* reminder? Anticipate Your Retribution. Did they stand for *that* warning? Out-dacious Youth Repent? But no: for that, a O was happily wanting, and the vowel here was a A.

I opened the packet, and found that its contents were the foregoing writings printed just as the reader (may I add the discerning reader?) peruses them. In vain was the reassuring whisper,—A. Y. R., All the Year Round,—it could not cancel the Proofs. Too appropriate name. The Proofs of my having sold the Writings.

My wretchedness daily increased. I had not thought of

the risk I ran, and the defying publicity I put my head into, until all was done, and all was in print. Give up the money to be off the bargain and prevent the publication, I could not. My family was down in the world, Christmas was coming on, a brother in the hospital and a sister in the rheumatics could not be entirely neglected. And it was not only ins in the family that had told on the resources of one unaided Waitering; outs were not wanting. A brother out of a situation, and another brother out of money to meet an acceptance, and another brother out of his mind, and another brother out at New York (not the same, though it might appear so), had really and truly brought me to a stand till I could turn myself round. I got worse and worse in my meditations, constantly reflecting "The Proofs," and reflecting that when Christmas drew nearer, and the Proofs were published, there could be no safety from hour to hour but that He might confront me in the Coffee-room, and in the face of day and his country demand his rights.

The impressive and unlooked-for catastrophe towards which I dimly pointed the reader (shall I add, the highly intellectual reader?) in my first remarks now rapidly approaches.

It was November still, but the last echoes of the Guy Foxes had long ceased to reverberate. We was slack,—several joints under our average mark, and wine, of course, proportionate. So slack had we become at last, that Beds Nos. 26, 27, 28, and 31, having took their six o'clock dinners, and dozed over their respective pints, had drove away in their respective Hansoms for their respective Night Mail-trains and left us empty.

I had took the evening paper to No. 6 table,—which is warm and most to be preferred,—and, lost in the all-absorbing topics of the day, had dropped into a slumber. I was recalled to consciousness by the well-known intimation, "Waiter!" and replying, "Sir!" found a gentleman standing at No. 4 table. The reader (shall I add, the observant

reader?) will please to notice the locality of the gentleman,
—at No. 4 table.

He had one of the new-fangled uncollapsable bags in his
hand (which I am against, for I don't see why you shouldn't
collapse, while you are about it, as your fathers collapsed
before you), and he said:

"I want to dine, waiter.   I shall sleep here to-night."

"Very good, sir.   What will you take for dinner, sir?"

"Soup, bit of codfish, oyster sauce, and the joint."

"Thank you, sir."

I rang the chambermaid's bell; and Mrs. Pratchett
marched in, according to custom, demurely carrying a
lighted flat candle before her, as if she was one of a long
public procession, all the other members of which was
invisible.

In the meanwhile the gentleman had gone up to the mantel-
piece, right in front of the fire, and had laid his forehead
against the mantelpiece (which it is a low one, and brought
him into the attitude of leap-frog), and had heaved a
tremenjous sigh.   His hair was long and lightish; and when
he laid his forehead against the mantelpiece, his hair all fell
in a dusty fluff together over his eyes; and when he now
turned round and lifted up his head again, it all fell in a
dusty fluff together over his ears.   This give him a wild
appearance, similar to a blasted heath.

"O! The chambermaid.   Ah!"   He was turning something in his mind.   "To be sure.   Yes.   I won't go up-stairs
now, if you will take my bag.   It will be enough for the
present to know my number.—Can you give me 24 B?"

(O Conscience, what a Adder art thou!)

Mrs. Pratchett allotted him the room, and took his bag
to it.   He then went back before the fire, and fell a biting
his nails.

"Waiter!" biting between the words, "give me," bite,
"pen and paper; and in five minutes," bite, "let me have, if
you please," bite, "a," bite, "Messenger."

Unmindful of his waning soup, he wrote and sent off six
notes before he touched his dinner. Three were City; three
West-End. The City letters were to Cornhill, Ludgate-hill,
and Farringdon-street. The West-End letters were to Great
Marlborough-street, New Burlington-street, and Piccadilly.
Everybody was systematically denied at every one of the six
places, and there was not a vestige of any answer. Our light
porter whispered to me, when he came back with that report,
" All Booksellers."

But before then he had cleared off his dinner, and his
bottle of wine. He now—mark the concurrence with the
document formerly given in full!—knocked a plate of biscuits
off the table with his agitated elber (but without breakage),
and demanded boiling brandy-and-water.

Now fully convinced that it was Himself, I perspired with
the utmost freedom. When he become flushed with the
heated stimulant referred to, he again demanded pen and
paper, and passed the succeeding two hours in producing a
manuscript which he put in the fire when completed. He
then went up to bed, attended by Mrs. Pratchett. Mrs.
Pratchett (who was aware of my emotions) told me, on
coming down, that she had noticed his eye rolling into every
corner of the passages and staircase, as if in search of his
Luggage, and that, looking back as she shut the door of
24 B, she perceived him with his coat already thrown off
immersing himself bodily under the bedstead, like a chimley-
sweep before the application of machinery.

The next day—I forbear the horrors of that night—was a
very foggy day in our part of London, insomuch that it was
necessary to light the Coffee-room gas. We was still alone,
and no feverish words of mine can do justice to the fitfulness
of his appearance as he sat at No. 4 table, increased by there
being something wrong with the meter.

Having again ordered his dinner, he went out, and was
out for the best part of two hours. Inquiring on his return
whether any of the answers had arrived, and receiving an

unqualified negative, his instant call was for mulligatawny, the cayenne pepper, and orange brandy.

Feeling that the mortal struggle was now at hand, I also felt that I must be equal to him, and with that view resolved that whatever he took I would take. Behind my partition, but keeping my eye on him over the curtain, I therefore operated on Mulligatawny, Cayenne Pepper, and Orange Brandy. And at a later period of the day, when he again said, "Orange Brandy," I said so too, in a lower tone, to George, my Second Lieutenant (my First was absent on leave), who acts between me and the bar.

Throughout that awful day he walked about the Coffee-room continually. Often he came close up to my partition, and then his eye rolled within, too evidently in search of any signs of his Luggage. Half-past six came, and I laid his cloth. He ordered a bottle of Old Brown. I likewise ordered a bottle of Old Brown. He drank his. I drank mine (as nearly as my duties would permit) glass for glass against his. He topped with coffee and a small glass. I topped with coffee and a small glass. He dozed. I dozed. At last, "Waiter!"—and he ordered his bill. The moment was now at hand when we two must be locked in the deadly grapple.

Swift as the arrow from the bow, I had formed my resolution; in other words, I had hammered it out between nine and nine. It was, that I would be the first to open up the subject with a full acknowledgment, and would offer any gradual settlement within my power. He paid his bill (doing what was right by attendance) with his eye rolling about him to the last for any tokens of his Luggage. One only time our gaze then met, with the lustrous fixedness (I believe I am correct in imputing that character to it?) of the well-known Basilisk. The decisive moment had arrived.

With a tolerable steady hand, though with humility, I laid The Proofs before him.

"Gracious Heavens!" he cries out, leaping up, and catching hold of his hair. "What's this? Print!"

"Sir," I replied, in a calming voice, and bending forward, "I humbly acknowledge to being the unfortunate cause of it. But I hope, sir, that when you have heard the circumstances explained, and the innocence of my intentions——"

To my amazement, I was stopped short by his catching me in both his arms, and pressing me to his breast-bone; where I must confess to my face (and particular, nose) having undergone some temporary vexation from his wearing his coat buttoned high up, and his buttons being uncommon hard.

"Ha, ha, ha!" he cries, releasing me with a wild laugh, and grasping my hand. "What is your name, my Benefactor?"

"My name, sir" (I was crumpled, and puzzled to make him out), "is Christopher; and I hope, sir, that, as such, when you've heard my ex——"

"In print!" he exclaims again, dashing the proofs over and over as if he was bathing in them. "In print!! O Christopher! Philanthropist! Nothing can recompense you, —but what sum of money would be acceptable to you?"

I had drawn a step back from him, or I should have suffered from his buttons again.

"Sir, I assure you, I have been already well paid, and——"

"No, no, Christopher! Don't talk like that! What sum of money would be acceptable to you, Christopher? Would you find twenty pounds acceptable, Christopher?"

However great my surprise, I naturally found words to say, "Sir, I am not aware that the man was ever yet born without more than the average amount of water on the brain as would *not* find twenty pounds acceptable. But— extremely obliged to you, sir, I'm sure;" for he had tumbled it out of his purse and crammed it in my hand in two bank-notes; "but I could wish to know, sir, if not intruding, how I have merited this liberality?"

"Know then, my Christopher," he says, "that from boy-hood's hour I have unremittingly and unavailingly endeavoured to get into print. Know, Christopher, that all the Booksellers alive—and several dead—have refused to put me into print. Know, Christopher, that I have written unprinted Reams. But they shall be read to you, my friend and brother. You sometimes have a holiday?"

Seeing the great danger I was in, I had the presence of mind to answer, "Never!" To make it more final, I added, "Never! Not from the cradle to the grave."

"Well," says he, thinking no more about that, and chuckling at his proofs again. "But I am in print! The first flight of ambition emanating from my father's lowly cot is realised at length! The golden bow,"—he was getting on, —"struck by the magic hand, has emitted a complete and perfect sound! When did this happen, my Christopher?"

"Which happen, sir?"

"This," he held it out at arm's length to admire it,—"this Per-rint."

When I had given him my detailed account of it, he grasped me by the hand again, and said:

"Dear Christopher, it should be gratifying to you to know that you are an instrument in the hands of Destiny. Because you are."

A passing Something of a melancholy cast put it into my head to shake it, and to say, "Perhaps we all are."

"I don't mean that," he answered; "I don't take that wide range; I confine myself to the special case. Observe me well, my Christopher! Hopeless of getting rid, through any effort of my own, of any of the manuscripts among my Luggage,—all of which, send them where I would, were always coming back to me,—it is now some seven years since I left that Luggage here, on the desperate chance, either that the too, too faithful manuscripts would come back to me no more, or that some one less accursed than I might give them to the world. You follow me, my Christopher?"

"Pretty well, sir." I followed him so far as to judge that he had a weak head, and that the Orange, the Boiling, and

Old Brown combined was beginning to tell. (The Old Brown, being heady, is best adapted to seasoned cases.)

"Years elapsed, and those compositions slumbered in dust. At length, Destiny, choosing her agent from all mankind, sent You here, Christopher, and lo! the Casket was burst asunder, and the Giant was free!"

He made hay of his hair after he said this, and he stood a-tiptoe.

"But," he reminded himself in a state of excitement, "we must sit up all night, my Christopher. I must correct these Proofs for the press. Fill all the inkstands, and bring me several new pens."

He smeared himself and he smeared the Proofs, the night through, to that degree that when Sol gave him warning to depart (in a four-wheeler), few could have said which was them, and which was him, and which was blots. His last instructions was, that I should instantly run and take his corrections to the office of the present Journal. I did so. They most likely will not appear in print, for I noticed a message being brought round from Beauford Printing House, while I was a throwing this concluding statement on paper, that the ole resources of that establishment was unable to make out what they meant. Upon which a certain gentleman in company, as I will not more particularly name,—but of whom it will be sufficient to remark, standing on the broad basis of a wave-girt isle, that whether we regard him in the light of,—* laughed, and put the corrections in the fire.

* The remainder of this complimentary parenthesis editorially struck out.

Note.—Mr. Dickens partly contributed to another of the chapters, entitled "His Umbrella;" but for this the reader is referred to the number as republished in a collected volume—the *Nine Christmas numbers of All the Year Round*.

NOTES ON CHRISTMAS STORIES.

THE SEVEN POOR TRAVELLERS.

"The shrieking of horses, which, newly taken from the peaceful pursuits of life, could not endure the sight of the stragglers lying by the wayside."

In the tenth book of the *Iliad*, Homer describes the terror of the horses of Rhesus, newly come to the war, at the sight of dead bodies. But Homer does not say that the horses shrieked—a thing very unusual on their part, and caused only, it is believed, by sudden and extreme pain.

THE HOLLY-TREE.

"Stage-coaches . . . which I occasionally find myself . . . affecting to lament."

This can scarcely have been affectation in Dickens. His best and most congenial work is of the old coaching days; the romance and humour of the road.

"A secret door behind the head of the bed."

An antiquarian friend informs me that he found such a secret door, in the panelling behind the bed, in an old house, at one time used as a kind of inn for poor travellers. This was in St. Andrew's, and a kind of passage down to the door from a room above, left little doubt as to the purpose of the arrangement. The ringing of a mysterious nocturnal bell every night lent confirmation to the most extreme theory !

"Brave and lovely servant-maid."

This was Mercy, who had none on him—Dickens's nurse of the fearsome tales, described in *The Uncommercial Traveller*.

" Every night since . . . I had dreamed of that friend."

This was Dickens's sister-in-law, Miss Mary Hogarth. If Mr. Forster is right, the dream of her never entirely ceased to occur, as in the text. That it should pass away with the communication of the secret is in accordance with the Highland superstition of the second sight. A seer will lose the faculty if he reveals his first vision.

Cornwall.

Dickens visited Cornwall, with Forster, Maclise, and Stanfield, and in festive circumstances, in 1843. The anecdote here is probably autobiographical, but it does not seem possible to trace the Swiss experiences, and the story of the Welsh haunting, or "strange influence." There are many such anecdotes, vaguely suggesting that the stress of passion in the past " photographs itself, we know not how, on we know not what," and occasionally becomes sensible to sensitive minds.

"Athol brose."

This is a mixture of cream, honey, and whiskey.   "This is the true balm of Gilead, John," said a sportsman to a Highlander. "I rather think, sir," answered the Gael, "that that is a figure of sanctifying grace."

THE HAUNTED HOUSE.

A school "where everybody, large and small, was cruel."

Not much is known of Dickens's school-days, but nobody suggests that cruelty prevailed at Wellington House Academy, in Mornington Place, where he was only a day-boy.   Yet, except at David Copperfield's last school, cruelty pervades Dickens's descriptions of school-life.   It seems as if certain early experiences of flogging masters and of bullies, as well as of Chadbands and Stigginses, had slipped out of his biography.

END OF VOL. I.

www.ingramcontent.com/pod-product-compliance
Lightning Source LLC
Chambersburg PA
CBHW030950110726
47900CB00004B/1201